Three particularly entertaining novels from Harlequin's famed Romance Library by worldwide-favorite author Violet Winspear

The Silver Slave...Rosary Bell was young, confident and completely opposed to the governor's views on bringing up the daughter she was to tutor. She soon discovered, however, that the totally different way of life on the Portuguese island, Vozes do Mar, had a magic of its own! (#1637)

Dear Puritan...Travel, Romy's grandmother had urged, so Romy did. It was in Mexico she met the lordly Don Delgado. To save their honor in a compromising situation he insisted on taking her home as his future wife. But Romy's idea of marriage just happened to include love! (#1658)

Rapture of the Desert...Chrys Devrel, at the pinnacle of her ballet career, had kept her life clear of distractions—particularly men. Now, when an accident freed her from demands for a year, she discovered how little she really knew of life and love. (#1680)

**Another collection
of Romance favorites...
by a best-selling Harlequin author!**

In the pages of this specially selected
anthology are three delightfully
absorbing Romances—all by an
author whose vast readership all over
the world has shown her to be an
outstanding favorite.

For those of you who are missing
these love stories from your
Harlequin library shelf, or who wish
to collect great romance fiction by
favorite authors, these Harlequin
Romance anthologies are for you.

We're sure you'll enjoy each of the
engrossing and heartwarming stories
contained within. They're treasures
from our library...and we know
they'll become treasured additions
to yours!

The sixth anthology of 3 Harlequin Romances by

Violet Winspear

Harlequin Books

TORONTO • NEW YORK • LOS ANGELES • LONDON
AMSTERDAM • PARIS • SYDNEY • HAMBURG
STOCKHOLM • ATHENS • TOKYO • MILAN

Harlequin Romance anthology 69

Copyright ©1977 by Harlequin Enterprises Limited. Philippine copyright 1983. Australian copyright 1983. All rights reserved. Except for use in any review, the reproduction or utilization of this work in whole or in part in any form by any electronic, mechanical or other means, now known or hereafter invented, including xerography, photocopying and recording, or in any information storage or retrieval system, is forbidden without the permission of the publisher, Harlequin Enterprises Limited, 225 Duncan Mill Road, Don Mills, Ontario, Canada M3B 3K9.

These books by Violet Winspear were originally published as follows:

THE SILVER SLAVE
Copyright © 1972 by Violet Winspear
First published in 1972 by Mills & Boon Limited
Harlequin edition (#1637) published November 1972

DEAR PURITAN
Copyright © 1971 by Violet Winspear
First published in 1971 by Mills & Boon Limited
Harlequin edition (#1658) published February 1973

RAPTURE OF THE DESERT
Copyright © 1972 by Violet Winspear
First published in 1972 by Mills & Boon Limited
Harlequin edition (#1680) published April 1973

Cover photograph ©, Bob Gelberg/The Image Bank of Canada

ISBN 0-373-20069-2

First edition published as Harlequin Omnibus in May 1977
Second printing February 1983

Printed in Canada

Contents

The
Silver
Slave

Rosary Bell, fair-haired and English, was conspicuous among the Portuguese islanders of Vozes do Mar. But the difference was more than physical.

Dom Duarte de Montqueiro Ardo, whose daughter Rosary was to tutor, warned her to restrain her independent behavior. He was a man of considerable power and charm, and as Rosary quickly discovered, he was not to be ignored!

CHAPTER ONE

THE road was uphill and rather uneven, and only the deep upholstery of the car saved Rosary from being tossed against her companion each time the driver swept them around a precarious bend or through a cobble-paved village. The country through which they drove was scenic and eye-catching, and many of the houses had a Moorish look, while others were set within gardens ablaze with tropical flowers, amid great arching trees and vines that tumbled over old and tawny walls. There was a sense of history, a tinge of magic, a rampant charm to Vozes do Mar.

To imagine the island was not the same as seeing it, and even the vivid descriptions of Lola Cortez, who was a resident, had not prepared Rosary for the excitement she felt as she gazed from the windows of the car and came fully alive to the fact that she was here and actually breathing the fabulous air of this Portuguese island.

Lola, a friend of the Governor, had travelled from Lisbon with the English girl, who was on her way right now to become tutor to his young daughter, who was fifteen years old and an only child. Lola talked on gaily about the *palacete*, the official residence of Dom Duarte de Montqueiro Ardo. She and her brother, who was an artist, lived in a villa close to the small palace and they were received by the Dom, and the Latin girl obviously admired him.

'Often we are invited to dine, and sometimes there is a reception and very smart and titled guests come by private plane from Lisbon and it is all very exciting.'

Lola paused and played a moment with a soft black glove. 'Sometimes Duarte seems a little distant, but that is expected.'

Rosary gazed enquiringly at the Portuguese girl, whose lively dark eyes flashed over her, taking in her simple suit of pearl-grey, and the rather tense way her hands were clenching her soft handbag.

'You seem suddenly much fairer here on the island ... almost alien, and not much older than Gisela herself.'

'I'm exactly five years older than my prospective pupil,' Rosary smiled, albeit a little tensely. Never before had she been described as alien, but here on Vozes do Mar she was the stranger whose looks the islanders would find a little strange. The brilliant sun, she knew, would make her hair seem ashen.

'That makes you twenty!' Lola exclaimed, her eyes looking denser than ever in the deep cream of her skin. 'I know the Dom told Dacio, my brother, that he hoped to acquire a *sensible* woman for the tutelage of Gisela. Sensible!' Lola broke into a laugh. 'At the age of twenty it is not possible, unless one is a wife. You know, of course, that Portuguese men expect sense and sensibility in their wives?'

'Most men probably expect it,' Rosary said drily, 'but I wonder if they always have their hopes realized? What sort of a person is the Dom's wife? I imagine she is beautiful?'

'She was beautiful.' The laughter faded from Lola's eyes. 'Did you not know ... did he not explain in his letter to you that Gisela is motherless?'

Rosary caught her breath in surprise. Somehow she had not connected the Governor of Vozes do Mar with widowerhood. She had pictured a gracious hostess for the *palacete*: a woman so busy with her duties that she could not teach Gisela herself the attributes of being entertaining and well-read. The Dom in his letter had merely said that Gisela had been away at school in a convent but had become so homesick for the island that he had decided to employ a tutor for her ... and being so very Portuguese, Rosary had added in her own mind, he had not fancied placing his daughter in the hands of a male tutor!

'One takes these things for granted,' she murmured. 'How sad for him, and the young girl. Has it been ... long?'

'Since Gisela was nine.'

'And I imagine he couldn't help but give in to her homesick plea to leave her school in Portugal.'

'He can be thoughtful,' Lola fingered one of her pearl earrings, 'but he can also be very much the autocrat. I suppose you are feeling nervous of meeting him?'

'Rather more so than before,' Rosary admitted. 'I expected to deal with ... has the palace no woman in charge of things?'

'Yes, his Aunt Azenha is the holder of the household keys and she sees to the smooth running of the domain, but she is without the authority to choose a teacher for Gisela. I believe she would not have chosen you.'

'And why not?' Rosary looked a trifle indignant. 'I have been trained in music and language by Courland Bell, and it was this fact alone which qualified me in the opinion of Dom Duarte.'

'Your surname is Bell!' Lola looked inquisitive.

'Exactly!' Rosary broke into the smile that slowly revealed a deep, sweet dent at the left side of her softly curved mouth. 'That great old man is my grandfather, and there are few good singers today who have not been taught their art by Cibby, as I call him. I men-

11

tioned this fact in my application for this post——'

'But did you also mention your age?' Lola asked, a trifle wickedly.

'No ... but does it matter?'

'It might. Portuguese people are very circumspect and it might be thought a little more than daring for so young a foreign girl to be living under the same roof as our eminent Governor.'

'You mean ...?'

Lola inclined her dark, pretty head, with the glistening curls caught back at her nape by a tortoiseshell clip. 'You are not young enough to be thought a schoolgirl, and not old enough to be thought a *duena*. You are not plain enough, either, to be thought harmless.'

'Whatever harm could I do?' Rosary laughed scornfully. 'I'm not a man-chaser, and my only intent is to do a good job and make Gisela like me. I have no designs on the ... father.'

'You may change your mind when you see him. From his head to his heels he is a man to notice. When one calls him Your Excellency the words have meaning!'

Rosary gripped the soft bag in her lap even harder, for not at any time had she thought of her future employer as a man unfettered by a wife, and she knew enough of the world to know that even in England a single girl under the roof of an attractive widower stood in danger of being gossiped about. It was the way of life, and she hoped to goodness that she had not come all this way only to be found unsuitable because she was young. Oh, why had she not mentioned in her letter that she was twenty? Because Cibby was now eighty the Dom must have concluded that his granddaughter was a spinster lady!

'Look, we are turning in through the boundary gates!' said Lola.

At once Rosary was on the alert for her first glimpse of the stately home in which, she hoped, she would be living for a while. Her initial excitement was now replaced by a certain apprehension, and Lola did not alleviate it when she tapped on the glass partition separating them from the driver and asked him to drop her off at a turn in the drive, a tree-shaded one leading through the gardens and lawns of the *palacete*.

'Come all the way with me,' Rosary pleaded.

Lola shook her head. 'No, it is better that you arrive formally. Dom Duarte merely asked me to meet you in Lisbon. He did not suggest that I present you to him.'

Rosary bit her lip and studied the face of the other girl. 'I begin to think that Portuguese people are a little ... ruthless,' she said.

Lola smiled, even as she opened the door beside her. 'You may be right, Rosary Bell. You may indeed find that our charm has running through it a fine thread of steel. Perhaps that is why we have some things in common with the British, eh?'

'Perhaps.' Rosary watched as Lola stepped from the car with grace and took from the driver the overnight case which he had stowed in the boot for her. 'We will meet again, I hope?'

'Of course,' said Lola. 'Unless the Dom decides to be ruled by convention instead of innovation. All the Portuguese I have ever known have preferred that nannies and companions for their children be on the mature side. But good luck! I shall hear soon enough whether or not he sends you packing.'

'From whom?' Rosary looked enquiring. 'Who will tell you?'

'Dacio, of course. He is working at the palace, restoring the paintings and portraits in the picture gallery.' With a wave of her hand Lola departed along the path that led, presumably, to the villa in which she and her artistic brother lived. Rosary sank back in her seat as the sumptuous car proceeded on its way, and she felt beneath the shell-pink of her blouse the fast beating of her heart. Taking this job had seemed like an adventure, now all at once she realized the setbacks and complications involved in dealing with people of Latin blood.

They might in some ways be like the British ... as they had been during the reign of the Victorians!

Amused by her own thought, she gazed at the back of the driver, smartly uniformed, with his peaked cap squarely on his dark head. He was formal and polite, and not by the flicker of an eyelash had he betrayed surprise at conveying to his master a fair stranger who looked as if she needed a *duena* herself.

Cibby, the old dear, would have been a little amused. He had taught her not only to love music but to be independent and proud and ready for all that life could offer. From a child she had been with him, for her parents had been in Hungary on a concert tour when there had been an uprising and their hotel had been shelled. From a child she had learned so many things from him and behind her slender façade, her look of youth, there lay a warm, responsive heart and a quick mind.

'Yes, by all means go to Vozes do Mar,' Cibby had said. 'Everyone should live on a tropic isle at some time in their lives.'

And here she was, and when she glanced from the car window she saw that high walls had taken the place of the shade trees, and over the walls hung tangles of flower, cloaking the stone in colour and giving off scent as they passed a tumbling sleeve of lemon-blossom, a veil of jessamine and then a cascade of frangipani, that starry flower of love and legend.

It was as if in the dim past a woman of imagination had asked that exotic blooms be planted here so that whoever came to the small palace was welcomed by untamed beauty before the walls divided widely to reveal the building itself.

Rosary leaned forward, the breath catching in her throat as the residence of the Governor came into view. It stood as if painted against the swell of the land and the arch of the sky, its stone towers and terraces as if sculptured, the iron of its curving balconies as finely filigreed as a lady's lacework. It was mellowed and perfect, as if growing from the ground itself, and there were white peacocks on its lawns, spreading their snowy fans in the golden sunlight.

She had expected Manoeline flamboyance, or a facing of *azulejos* so dear to the Portuguese heart, and instead she found grace and unforgettable charm. And as the car drew to a standstill in front of the terrace she saw the armorial crest of the family carved in the stonework above the great door. She emerged eagerly from the car, her gaze flashing from the baroque fountains to the curve of the steps leading gracefully to the columned portico.

She released her breath in a sigh of wonderment. It was a wonderful house, and she would surely be sent away as a nonentity who had no place in such an establishment!

As she stood at the foot of the steps, both entranced and struck to shyness, the front door opened and a man in neat livery came down the steps to take her suitcases and to escort her into the residence. Taking a deep breath, she preceded him, and cool upon the sunlit air was the calling of birds and the sound of water falling into the wide basins of the fountains. The peacocks strutted, certain of their place here, and their snowy beauty that enhanced the wide green lawns.

Rosary entered the hall, with a gleaming marble floor that made her feel like skimming across it. Tall smooth pillars supported an arcade in which stood marble figures and great pots of flowers. Overhead glowed a ceiling teeming with the gods and nymphs of mythology, twining and romping among suspended lamps like enormous jewels set in wrought-iron.

The coolness of purring fans made the atmosphere inviting after the warmth of the car. The manservant stood in polite silence while she studied the hall, and when she glanced at him she saw only a polite face that revealed nothing, though she knew he had been studying her. 'I will show you to your room, *senhorita*. Please to come this way.'

There were three galleries reached by a graceful wrought-iron staircase, which formed a trio of delicate iron bridges above the hall. Rosary was conducted to the upper gallery and along a corridor that was lit by sunlight through a great rose window, which sparkled as if its facets were those of a diamond. The manservant paused in front of a door and opened it, and Rosary stepped upon the firm softness of an emerald green carpet, a striking contrast to the golden wood of the furniture, and the paler gold of the long silken curtains at the balconied windows.

She had seen photographs of such rooms in stylish magazines, but never had she been ushered into one and informed it was hers; through an archway she glimpsed a smaller room and guessed it to be her private sitting-room.

Rosary just stood there, feeling as unreal as a figure in a dream. The man in livery carried her suitcases to a long stool at the foot of the big bed, draped in creamy net and covered by a green silk spread that rippled to the carpet.

A little shiver of delight ran all the way through Rosary, from the tips of her ears to her toes. This was really happening, and she was here because Cibby had insisted that she learn several languages, and Portuguese and Italian had appealed to her. When the manservant spoke to her, she understood him perfectly.

'The Senhora de Ardo will wish to speak with you.' he said. 'A message will be sent to you in a short while, when the *senhora* is free of her duties and can see you.'

'Thank you.' Rosary half-smiled at him, but with a politely blank face he withdrew from the room and quietly closed the door behind him, leaving her alone in a silence that was softly broken by the ceiling fan, which cast a wing-like shadow as it revolved. The silk curtains hung without movement at the windows, and tall flowers in a vase gave off a rather sensuous perfume.

Rosary wondered if Gisela had been lurking about to watch for her arrival, and she gazed at the door, half-hopeful that the girl would come bursting in, ready at once to be friends with her. Despite Lola's flashes of friendship during the journey, she had not at the end of it been very encouraging. Rosary troubled her lip with her teeth. She had a feeling the Senhora de Ardo was going to be rather stiff-necked and disinclined to welcome a young, modern-minded English Miss into the Governor's palace.

Restlessly she walked to a window and on impulse

she went out on the balcony and peered over the edge of it. The afternoon sun dazzled her eyes and her nostrils were filled with the tropical island air. It went to her head like wine and a sudden feeling of excitement raced through her blood.

Her balcony hung like a plant-basket high above a garden patio, where amid low, plant-covered walls was a large pond covered in a mass of water-lotus and their big leaves of metallic green. Further back there were willow trees, making a veil of green through which she glimpsed a lurking figure in white. She felt sure whoever it was had eyes fixed upon her balcony, seeing her there and curious. Then the veil was impenetrably green again and the white-clad figure was gone.

Someone gave a polite cough inside her room and Rosary turned and stood framed between the windows. A uniformed maid stood looking at her, and for the first time since entering the palace she was treated to an uncertain smile. She smiled back. 'Am I wanted?' she asked.

The girl nodded, and her eyes were large with surprise as they dwelt on Rosary. 'Please to come to the *sala, senhorita*. The *dona de casa* wishes to see you.'

Rosary straightened the jacket of her suit and glanced swiftly in the dressing-table mirror to make sure her hair was tidy and her nose not shiny. She saw a tense figure, chin tilted for battle. She saw that the pearl-grey suit looked good and was glad she had let Cibby buy it for her. The dusty-pink suede shoes and bag were nice, and she never wore a lot of make-up. She surely looked discreet, and if she wore a serious expression she would convince the Senhora de Ardo that she was capable.

Down the stairs they went, she and the young maid, and along a corridor lined with dark and formal portraits in carved frames. The eyes in the portraits seemed to watch her as she passed, and she thought of what Lola had said about her alien appearance. Wafted here by jet plane and car, she felt suddenly uprooted ... a daisy in a jam-jar in a place filled with porcelain pots of exotic jessamine and geranium!

The thought made her smile nervously, but was quickly suppressed as they paused in front of one of the tall doors. The maid tapped upon it, opened it, and then left Rosary to face alone the lady of the house.

'Good afternoon, Miss Bell.' The woman stood beside a window that opened on to the terrace, and there was about her an air of cool courtesy but not a hint of warmth. Her eyes saw Rosary in one swift glance, and then she came forward and indicated with a ringed hand that Rosary be seated in one of the high-backed, silk-upholstered chairs.

'Good afternoon, *senhora*.' Rosary sat down and assumed an air of composure. She was determined not to let this imperious woman undermine her confidence in her abilities. Given a fair chance she would prove that she had not wasted her own or anyone else's time in coming here. 'How delightful to see so many flowers,' she said.

'You are fond of flowers?' Senhora de Ardo bent to a table on which stood delicate teacups, a silver teapot and a cake stand on which were arranged pastries that looked almost too good to eat.

'Yes, I am a lover of gardens.' Rosary ventured a smile. 'That was one of the reasons why I wanted to come to Vozes do Mar. I had heard that it was an island of flowers.'

Rosary's smile was answered by a skimming of dark eyes that held not a glimmer of response. 'You will

19

take tea and cakes, Miss Bell?'

'I should love a cup of tea, thank you.' Rosary tried to suppress a cold little shiver; the tea, at least, would warm her chilled feelings.

'Sugar and cream?'

'Both, please.'

While the *senhora* poured the tea Rosary studied her as casually as she could. When younger her hair must have been raven dark to match her eyes, but now it was silvery and worn in a severe chignon style. There were jet pearls at her earlobes, and her dress was of dark purple silk, severely tailored, with a pattern of jet beads on the bodice. Upon both her hands were heavy-stoned rings, and one of them was a wide band of gold. A certain sternness and dignity were mingled in her features, and Rosary had the feeling that she was a widow. One of those high-born Portuguese women who were trained from girlhood to run smoothly and perfectly a household for a man, and to place romantic dreams on a lower plane to correct and rather unsmiling behaviour.

She handed Rosary her tea, and placed on the table beside her a plate, a lace-paper napkin and a silver pastry fork. 'Please to help yourself to a pastry, Miss Bell.'

'I will, *senhora*. They look delicious.'

The *senhora* nodded and sat down, as if to say that everything here at the palace had the perfect touch. Her eyes studied Rosary as she stirred her tea. 'It was understood,' she said, 'that Gisela's tutor be a person of expert knowledge. You are . . . young!'

'Yes, *senhora*. But I am well trained in all that Gisela's father applied for in a tutor. My age is surely immaterial?'

'When dealing with a girl of Gisela's age and temperament discipline must be maintained. Can you be sure of doing so when you are so young yourself?'

'I can't pretend that I am a martinet,' Rosary admitted, with a slight smile. 'I happen to believe that more can be done with kindness than with severity.'

'Have you had other private pupils, Miss Bell?'

'Not private pupils, *senhora*. But as I explained in my letter to Dom Duarte I have worked as a teacher for the past year at Courland Bell's school of music in Surrey. I wished to travel, however, and when my grandfather was told by a business associate of his that the Governor of Vozes do Mar was anxious to acquire a music teacher for his daughter, I decided to apply for the post. I was trained in all I know by my grandfather, and you will, *senhora*, have heard of Irena Marcos, the Portuguese singer who is now famous in opera? She was a pupil of his, and surely there could be no better recommendation for me, that I learned at his knee and now possess knowledge I know I can pass on to Gisela.'

'You certainly sound very confident, Miss Bell.' The jetty eyes flashed over Rosary, as if assessing her clothes and her deportment. 'When my nephew decided to allow Gisela to be educated here instead of at the convent, he had in mind a post for a teacher who would stay several years on the island. I repeat that you are young, and you are attractive. You may wish to leave after a while in order to . . . marry.'

'But I have no such plans,' Rosary argued. 'There is no one I have the remotest intention of marrying!'

'Really?' Senhora de Ardo arched a thin black eyebrow. 'Are British girls so different from our Latin girls? The main aim of our girls is to marry as soon as possible.'

'Aren't they married to men who are chosen for

them?' Rosary retaliated. 'If parents direct, then daughters will obey, but in my country we often choose a career in preference to domesticity, and my own grandfather would never dream of picking out a certain man for me to marry. He has taught me to think and act for myself.'

'Which may be all very well, for an English girl.' Senhora de Ardo looked all the way down her Latin nose as she said this. 'But I hope you don't intend to implant in Gisela your own rebellious ideas. Her father is a true Portuguese and naturally he has made plans for his daughter.'

Rosary didn't doubt it, but as it happened she had no intention of inciting the girl to rebel against the old and tried methods of the Portuguese of finding marital stability for their sons as well as their daughters. 'I am only interested in being a good tutor,' she replied, and she looked the *senhora* straight in the eye, letting her know that she had no intention of being cowed by her manner. 'I would not dream of imposing my personal views on Gisela. No more than I intend to have Latin views imposed on me.'

'You are outspoken, Miss Bell.'

'Yes,' said Rosary, for she didn't intend to apologize for being so. She had been hired as a tutor, not as a backstairs maid! 'I work for my living, *senhora*, but that doesn't make me a menial. If that type of person was required, then it might have been better had Dom Duarte applied outside of England. Very few of my countrywomen would tolerate these days being treated like Victorian women who had to work for a wage. I am afraid I am no Jane Eyre!'

'No.' For the briefest of moments a hint of amusement seemed to gleam in the *senhora's* eyes, then it was quickly veiled as she turned her gaze to the sunlit terrace. 'What are your views on the *palacete*? A small palace but none the less imposing, eh?'

'Quite overpowering at first glance,' Rosary agreed, a hint of humour in her own eyes. She knew what the woman meant. A girl like herself could never have lived or worked in such surroundings in her life before.

'It is a place of grace and history, Miss Bell. And many times over have the Montqueiros been in charge of the island and its people. Were my nephew a less obstinate and democratic a man he would use the title bestowed on the family many years ago.' Senhora de Ardo again met Rosary's eyes, gazing straight into them, as if to impress on her the honour it was to be in the service of her nephew. 'He is the Duque de Montqueiro, you understand, but he insists upon the lesser title of Dom Duarte.'

Despite herself Rosary was impressed ... not by the ducal title, but by the fact that this man she was yet to meet should discard what many another man would have given his eye teeth and half he owned to possess. He sounded ... intriguing.

'I hope most sincerely that Dom Duarte won't feel that my youth disqualifies me from the task which I feel mentally qualified to tackle,' she said, dabbing cream from her lips with her napkin. 'I think I should enjoy working in such superb surroundings, and not being a city girl I shan't pine for smart distractions. Gisela is allowed to swim?'

The *senhora* hesitated. 'The child, Miss Bell, is not one of your robust, hockey-playing English girls. At the age of nine she had a bad illness ...'

'At the time her mother died?' Rosary murmured.

'Exactly so. It was a great shock to the child and as there were no brothers or sisters to alleviate the loss,

23

Gisela took it very much to heart and she ran away...'

'Ran away?' Rosary echoed.

'Yes, in a storm. It was all terribly worrying, and when she was found she developed rheumatic fever and for several weeks we feared the worst.' The ringed hands spread themselves in a very Latin gesture. 'You will therefore understand that my nephew is extra protective of the child, and I do warn you that he will not be too pleased to find you so youthful. He will undoubtedly feel that you might not be careful enough of Gisela's health.'

'Really!' A flash of anger winged its way through Rosary. 'If she is delicate and must take care, then I shall certainly not overtax her strength in any way. I am not thoughtless, and I am certainly not flighty. If Gisela's father has laid down rules regarding his daughter, then I shall not disregard them.'

'Perhaps not,' said the *senhora*. 'But you do appear to have a lot of spirit, and it might be better if someone more placid were in charge of Gisela. Anyway, we must leave it to Duarte to decide. He is the one in authority here, and I am only in charge of the household. He will interview you. I have merely given you tea and a little advice.'

Senhora de Ardo rose to her feet, and Rosary followed her example. 'Thank you for tea and the delicious cakes,' she said. 'When will Dom Duarte wish to see me?'

'When he is free of his duties to do so,' was the dismissive reply.

'In the meantime ... could I not meet Gisela?'

'It would not be correct, Miss Bell. As I have told you, you may not be suitable and it is best that neither your hopes nor Gisela's be raised too high.'

'Then you think Gisela might like me?' Rosary

24

dared to say.

The woman shrugged her thin shoulders and escorted Rosary to the door of the *sala*. 'Because you are young she would immediately assume that you would let her off lessons and make of every day a holiday.' The door was opened and Rosary walked out into the hall. She felt rather like a schoolgirl, herself, being dismissed after a lecture. Lola had been right to warn her about the *dona de casa*. She wanted not a tutor of spirit about the palace, but some older and placid woman whom she could keep in her place. She wanted no sort of changes brought into these hallowed precincts by a foreign outsider, and Rosary smiled slightly as she glanced about the large hall, where everything gleamed and stood exactly in its place.

Rosary noticed a half-open door that seemed to lead out to one of the side patios, and impulsively she made for the door and stepped out into the sunlight and the scent of the flowers that softened the outlines of the enclosing walls and the scrolled iron seats.

She walked about the patio and found that one wall was covered in pomegranates, rusty-gold with their fruit. As she stood there in delight, for never before had she seen the fruits actually growing, she heard a step behind her and swung round hoping to see Gisela and to have at last a glimpse of a friendly face. Instead she was confronted by a lean young man in a dark blue shirt and brown slacks. His hair was black and rumpled, and when he slowly smiled attractive lines came into his face and his eyes admired instead of criticizing her slender figure, ashen-haired, there by the wall flamy with colourful fruit.

'Don't tell me,' he said. 'You are Persephone of the pomegranate!'

She smiled herself, and wished he might be the Dom. Instinctively she knew him to be far too human to be a member of the Montqueiro family.

'As a matter of fact,' she said, 'I am the tutor.'

'Really?' His eyes swept over her and dwelt on her hair, which the sunshine stroked to a white-gold fairness, its thick soft curves framing her amused face. 'In my day tutors were far less attractive, all straight lines and bombazine, not to mention the silver-rimmed spectacles, and the silver in the hair. You make a most welcome addition to the palace.'

'You are kind to say so, *senhor*. But I have been warned——'

'Not about me, I hope?' He strolled closer to where she stood and with a lean hand he stroked his hair into place. He was good-looking, but not in a flaunting way, and when he stood near to her she caught a whiff of turpentine. When he introduced himself as Dacio Cortez she was not a bit surprised.

'Did you enjoy your journey here with my sister?' he asked, reaching up a hand to fondle one of the pomegranates. 'Lola likes the occasional trip to Lisbon and I expect she showed you some of the fine old buildings?'

'We did visit a couple of smart shops and a very chic restaurant,' Rosary told him drily.

He laughed, and his teeth gleamed against the dark olive of his skin. 'She is pretty, no? A lively young thing who would really like to live all the time in Lisbon, but I am her guardian and so she must live where I choose to live ... until she marries, of course.'

'Of course,' said Rosary. 'You Portuguese men seem hell-bent on believing that young women are helpless without a male shoulder to lean upon. Would you not permit Lola to take a job?'

'She has one.' He continued to smile, but a note of arrogance had crept into his voice. 'She looks after the villa and sees that I have my meals on time. Apart from that she has no need to do anything but look pretty. The nicest function in life for a girl.'

'Then you must disapprove heartily of anyone like me, who goes out to work?' Rosary gazed up at him, feeling more than ever like a girl who had stepped through a door into Victorian times. Good heavens, if this young Latin was old-fashioned with regard to women, whatever sort of man was the master of the house?

'I should be most ungallant to disapprove of someone like you.' He gave her a gallant bow to endorse his words. 'I am only sad that you have to go out alone into the world——'

'But I wanted to,' she broke in. 'I longed beyond anything else to travel and to meet people. I'd stifle tied down in a house looking after a man!'

Her words rang out, freely and defiantly, in her clear English voice, and at the same time something made her glance across the patio to where that cloistered section of it led to and from the palace. A man was standing there and he must have heard her every word. He wore an impeccable white suit with a dark tie, and there was in his bearing that indefinable air of authority that marked out each thing about him for immediate notice.

Even before he moved and came out into the sunlight, Rosary knew that he was Dom Duarte de Montqueiro Ardo.

CHAPTER TWO

THE room in which Rosary was interviewed by Dom Duarte was a panelled study lined with books and prints. There were deep leather chairs and a large desk on lion-claw feet, its leather top much used. In a high-backed swivel chair sat the man in whose power she strangely felt now she was alone with him.

He sat there studying her in the chair facing his. His left hand toyed with a brass paperweight, and she couldn't help but notice the hands that in an earlier century would have been richly jewelled. Like their owner they had a strength and grace of movement. His hair was sable dark, growing thickly against a finely shaped head. He had the taut lines and bones of good breeding, a proud flare to his nostrils, and a rather deep groove between the blackness of his brows. She had noticed when he stood beside Dacio that he was well above the average height of the Latin male, and his eyes held a glint of steel under the oblique slant of his brows.

He was a man to notice ... a man to obey ... yet as Rosary met his eyes she was determined not to be browbeaten.

'So you are Rosary Bell, eh?' There were startling depths to his voice, and he spoke in English, the first person to address her in her own language since she had arrived here. 'You will already have spoken with the Senhora de Ardo?'

'Yes, Your Excellency.'

'There is no need to address me so formally, Miss Bell.' The glint in his eyes seemed to burn dangerously, as if he had caught the note of defiance in her voice. 'Whatever impression you made upon my aunt will not sway me one way or the other. I imagine she found you more youthful than the person we expected?'

'Yes, *senhor*. But in my opinion it might be better for Gisela to have a tutor who is not years removed from her own ideas and dreams. Your aunt told me she was a lonely child——'

'Are you lonely also, Miss Bell?' His voice seemed to have an extra resonant ring when he spoke her name, and his gaze impaled her as if upon a steel pin.

'I know what it feels like to be an only child,' she rejoined. 'I know how it can hurt never to see your mother's face again. I believe that semi-orphaned children are lonelier than other children. They are deprived of the maternal security for which material things can't compensate.'

'That is very true,' he agreed. 'But I am not in need of a mother for Gisela, merely a competent person who will stimulate her interest in music and make of her an interesting young woman.'

Rosary flushed, for it seemed to her heightened senses that he implied that she was here in order to interest *him*. She felt like telling him that in the first place she had not known of his eligibility; and in the second place he was not in any way the type of man she could fall in love with. He was imperious beyond belief, and certainly he had no need to use his ducal title when his entire manner was so cool and haughty.

'By letter you approved my qualifications for this post,' she said, in her coolest voice. 'And it would be unfair to send me away before I have proved or disproved my competency as a tutor.'

'I quite agree,' he said. 'Despite your youth, I am

going to allow you to stay a while on approval.'

'Approval!' she exclaimed. 'Like a washing machine? No, thank you!' She rose to her feet and her eyes were stormy. Not only was she the granddaughter of Courland Bell, she was one of his star graduates, and she'd be darned if this Portuguese duke would speak to her as if he were taking on trial a gauche parlourmaid. 'I think, *senhor*, that it would be better if you found someone more staid and therefore, in your opinion, more suitable——'

'Sit down,' he ordered. 'Instantly.'

She stared at him, and then once again she flushed. He made her feel as if she had behaved like a school-girl.

'You are not in the least like a washing machine,' he crisped. 'You are more like a young cat on edge in a strange house. Sit down, Miss Bell, and stop glaring at me.'

She hesitated, hating herself for being a little afraid of him. She sat down, stiffly, a slim and offended figure in the high-backed chair of dark carving that pressed against her bones. It was an inquisitorial chair, like the eyes that studied her, taking in with a cool object-ivity her fair English looks in this sombre panelled room ... the only room she had so far seen which was not fragrant with vases of island flowers.

'Have you ever worked privately before, *senhorita*?'

'No,' she admitted. 'I have been a teacher at the school, but if I work here, it will be my first private tutorial.'

'You have seen something of the *palacete*. Do you think it would suit you to work here?'

'Without a doubt, *senhor*. I—I sense its history, its appeal to the imagination. As I explained to your aunt, it appealed greatly to me to journey abroad to work.'

'Your grandfather made no objection?'

'On the contrary. He thought it would broaden my mind, and my appreciation of music, to meet people of a culture so different from my own. Even as I teach Gisela, I shall be studying your Portuguese folk music and melodies.'

'Have you no ambition to be a concert pianist, Miss Bell?'

She thought over his words, and for the first time in his presence she gave a slight smile. 'It would be marvellous to follow into the concert world my parents, who were a dual team. My mother played as my father's accompanist. He was a superb violinist. I can't remember him so well as I remember my mother, for he was always practising and shut away from a child's noise. But I have albums of his recordings and I know how fine a musician he was. I believe my mother could have been a soloist had she chosen to be, but I am told by Courland Bell that she sacrificed her solo triumphs for the sake of . . . love.'

The steely Latin eyes dwelt thoughtfully on Rosary's uplifted face, then he arose to his feet and approached a smoking table on which stood a carved box and a swan-shaped lighter. He opened the box and took from it a small cigar. He clipped the end and placed it in the flame, then he carried the cigar to his lips. Rosary's eyes followed the movement, and for the first time she noticed that his mouth was more sensuous than the rest of his firmly chiselled features.

It was faintly disturbing and made her wonder why he had never remarried. Had he loved his wife too well ever to bother again with marriage?

'So you desired to travel?' he said. 'You are not the

31

type for being tied to domesticity?'

She knew he had caught the words which she had flung at Dacio, and through the cigar smoke she saw a gleam of amusement in his eyes, as if he thought her young and impetuous.

'What is wrong, *senhor*, in wanting a career? The women of your own country are beginning to clamour for more freedom, and I don't blame them.'

'I am sure you don't. However, most women find it temperamentally more suitable, and perhaps even more exciting, to let themselves be loved and married.'

'Men certainly find it more suitable,' she retorted, 'to have someone always on hand to wait on them, flatter them and be blamed if anything upsets them.'

He was silent when she finished speaking and he just stood looking at her, his cigar smoke wreathing about his lips, his high cheekbones, and his rather imperious nose. It was a look that said she was foolish and untouched by the emotions that drove a woman into the arms of a man; it was a look which reminded her that he no longer had a wife for his consolation, or his martyr.

'From a moralistic point of view you will be perfect for Gisela,' he said, smoothly drawling the words. 'There seems no doubt that you have spent most of your time in study. But all the same I am going to insist that you are engaged as tutor for a trial run of six weeks. My aunt no doubt told you that I wish Gisela to be tutored for several years, but I must be certain that she is in the charge of the best possible teacher. As a parent I am not being unreasonable, and you accept my terms, Miss Bell, or you leave tomorrow. It is for you to decide.'

'The decision seems to be yours, *senhor*,' she replied. 'It seems I must agree to your terms or return home like—like an expelled schoolgirl.'

'Then you agree to remain on approval?' His lip twitched as he spoke.

'I have no choice but to agree, *senhor*. The island appeals to me, and I am obstinate. I like to prove myself.'

'Six weeks should give you ample time in which to prove your worth, *senhorita*. As my daughter's tutor and companion you will take your meals at my table. You will set aside the cooler hours for walking, riding and playing games. In the heat of the afternoon I shall require Gisela to take *siesta*. She is not entirely robust, though I am assured by our doctor that sensible exercise can do her no harm. Sometimes I may wish myself and certain of my guests to be entertained by your musical ability as a pianist, Miss Bell. I hope you will agree to play for us. There is a fine grand piano in the music *sala*, and another smaller instrument has been provided for the use of Gisela. Now, have you any questions?'

'I shall be free to make a few friends of my own, *senhor*?'

'But of course, so long as you confine your friendships to people known to me. While you are here you will be my responsibility, and even on a Portuguese island it is not unknown for a young girl to go astray.'

'You mean in the company of a young man?' she said drily.

'Exactly so.'

'But I am the studious, not the flirtatious type, Dom Duarte.'

'As a Portuguese I know my countrymen, *senhorita*. Quite frankly I did wish for a sober-looking, more mature woman to be in charge of Gisela. You are neither of those things, and therefore you will be a source of interest to the young men of Vozes do Mar. Surely I am not incorrect in saying that Dacio Cortez has already flattered you?'

For a fighting instant Rosary felt inclined to tell this dominant male creature that in her free time she would please herself, and make her own friends, and be flattered by them if she wished, but upon meeting his eyes she decided that discretion was the better part of valour. He wouldn't hesitate to send her packing if she defied the rules laid down for her correct behaviour. Not only was he Portuguese but he was of the ancient, ruling order who would not release too readily their hold on the restrictive chains attached to the females in their care. It was a protective attitude, but it also ensured that the man remained the master.

'You were about to say?' He quirked an eyebrow in mocking politeness.

'That I must not be too exuberant in my—attachments, is that correct, *senhor*?'

'I should not advise it.'

'But as you requested Senhorita Cortez to meet me in Lisbon, you can surely have no objection to a friendship between myself and the Cortez couple?'

'They live within the precincts of the *palacete*, therefore you are bound to have contact with them. I merely ask you not to be seen alone with strangers.'

'*I* am a stranger, *senhor*. I am English and I have ways different from your own women.'

'Naturally. And that is why I suggest that you moderate them to match the discretion expected by the Portuguese of young women. This is a Portuguese island and your looks will seem alien enough to those who have not travelled in other parts of the world. You comprehend?'

'I am to behave demurely,' she replied. 'To stand by

the rules, and to be available as an entertainer when you have guests.'

An instant and dangerous silence followed her words, and she almost felt those steely fingers hustling her off the hallowed soil of Vozes do Mar. Then he gave a shrug and seemed to dismiss her remark as the sort he would soon tame on her tongue.

'Then it is agreed that you stay,' he said. 'I shall write to explain the terms to your grandfather, and to assure him that I shall see you come to no harm.'

'Very well, *senhor*.' She suppressed a quick smile, picturing Cibby's amusement when he realized that she would be working for the type of man her independence would strike against like flint against steel. He would chuckle, that grand old man of humour and forbearance. He would know that Dom Duarte de Montqueiro Ardo had admitted a spirited young cat into his dovecote, and that a few feathers were bound to fly in the coming weeks.

She stood up, for instinct told her that the interview was at an end. She followed him as he strode to the door and opened it. For a moment as she stood quite near to him she realized his height, his authority and a certain iron charm to the smile he slanted down at her. 'I am sure we shall come to an understanding of each other before too long, Miss Bell. In the meantime avail yourself of the music room, the library and the gardens. You are sure to find Gisela in one of them and the two of you must make friends. If at any time you wish to discuss a problem with me, then you have only to seek me out. I am not entirely the stern and hidebound tyrant, you know.'

She accepted this remark in silence and wondered if she was expected to give him a curtsey on making her departure from his ducal presence. As she looked at him a subtle change came over his face and he seemed to read her mind with alarming speed.

'I see that you have formed an opinion of me, Miss Bell. You have decided that I am still at the turn of the century in my ideas, and that I rule my daughter, my household and this island with the inflexible hand in the velvet gauntlet. *Por Deus*, you English have a cool arrogance of your own which would be hard to match! You make your way through the world believing that everything should be as the English think best. Well, *senhorita*, my daughter is a Portuguese girl and you have not been hired to fill her head with some of your own foolish notions ... those regarding men and women in particular. I happen still to believe that women are ruled by their emotions, and if we placed this world in their hands it would soon become a crazy Disneyland filled with gingerbread castles and fashion parlours!'

'And what is wrong with that, *senhor*?' Rosary asked demurely. 'Surely it would be better than making war?'

'You imagine that women make no sort of war?' His eyes and his voice took on a dangerous, velvety smoothness.

'Of course they don't! Women hate war!'

'Then how young you really are!' He smiled and showed the gleaming edge of his teeth. 'They make a battlefield of each meeting with a man. They arm themselves for battle in silk and perfume, and they use the most deadly of weapons ... seduction.'

And so saying he clicked his heels, bowed and withdrew into his study. The door closed, leaving her alone in the wide marbled hall, where the fans purred and wafted to her the scent of flowers. Go to the library or the music room, he had said, but he had given her no directions, and there seemed no one around whom she could ask. She glanced at her wristwatch and saw that the afternoon was waning. She would go to her room instead and unpack her belongings, and take another look at the quarters she would occupy for the next few weeks.

As she walked up the marble stairs with the scrolled iron balustrade she tried to remember the exact location of her apartment. Although called a small palace, it seemed immense to her, with the columns rearing high to hold the three galleries with their various rooms and arcades; their corridors and odd little flights of steps leading, she imagined, to belvederes.

She paused on the second gallery and glanced about for the gemmed lighting of the rose window. Ah, there it was! And the tall door of her apartment was on the left. She turned the wrought-brass handle and entered, and after closing the door behind her she kicked off her shoes and walked about in her nyloned feet on the thick velvet carpet while she unpacked her cases and hung in the deep closet her dresses and skirts, her tailored trouser-suit and her two evening gowns. She had wondered if she should pack them, and as she stroked the chiffon and the silk, she thought of her employer's remark that he would wish her upon occasion to play for himself or his guests.

She placed her lingerie in the long drawer at the foot of the dress closet, and she smiled, ruefully, at her own image of him during the air journey from London and the boat trip from Lisbon. Portuguese men had seemed to her more stocky than tall, and good-looking in the usual dark-haired, olive-skinned fashion of the Latin male. She had thought of him with a wife to whom he was devoted. She had believed he would be benevolent, and not entirely interested in the pursuits of his girl child.

How different was the reality from that Dom Duarte she had imagined!

She opened a door leading out of her sitting-room, and caught her breath first in amazement, and then in delight. It was a bathroom and the walls were tiled with *azulejos*, some in patterns and others to represent mermaids, sea-horses, boats and giant shells. It was a mad and wonderful bathroom, with a tub sunk into the floor, a shower fixed overhead and a pale blue lavatory and bidet set side by side. It was foreign, and luxurious, and irresistibly inviting to Rosary who had been travelling since the early hours and craved a soak in bubbly, scented water.

She set about filling the deep tub with water, and added her own bubble-bath lotion, though there were glass shelves of various bath aids with expensive labels on them. She placed fresh lingerie on the padded stool, and then she stood indecisive and wondered if the family dressed formally for dinner. She tried to imagine Dom Duarte looking informal and found that her imagination wouldn't stretch that far. He was the type of autocrat who only bent his straight backbone in a brief courteous bow, and was never anything but impeccable in appearance and aloof in behaviour. She couldn't picture him with a hair out of place ... nor with the wild urges of passion storming through his veins. She couldn't help but wonder if Gisela was the result of an arranged marriage.

Then, with a shrug, Rosary took from her bedroom closet a dress of pale shantung, simply cut, but with wrist-length sleeves of nude silk, the wristbands embroidered with silver roses. She studied it with a wicked little gleam in her eyes and decided to wear it. It might not be as formal as his lordship would wish, but it had a long skirt and he obviously wished that women were still hampered by the bustle and the train!

She laid the dress across the foot of her bed and went to have her bath. The water was warm and delicious and she lay in a veil of bubbles and drowsed with her head against the rubber headrest. Never in her wildest dreams had she ever imagined herself as a tutor in a palace of all places! Yet here she was, luxuriating in a scented bath and lulled by the low, persistent chorus of the cicadas as evening began to fall and the sun's strength died in the hot-cold flame of sunset.

There was beauty here on this island called Voices of the Sea. The name itself was like music . . . and there her thoughts broke off as the door of the bathroom was suddenly pushed open and a figure appeared in the doorway. Rosary's eyes flew open in alarm, and she seemed half-mermaid herself as she lay there half concealed by bubbles, her fair hair pinned to the crown of her head, with wet tendrils clinging to her neck.

She and the invader of her privacy stared at each other. 'You are Gisela!' she exclaimed, even as the girl said: 'You are Miss Bell!'

They laughed together, and then gravity masked the young face once again. It was a thin face, with high cheekbones, an oval chin and very dark eyebrows. It might have been a plain face but for the oblique dark eyes set round with dense short lashes. It was, in fact, a rather oriental face, Rosary thought, and as this girl grew older and developed poise, those eyes would make of her quite an enchantress.

'I hoped we would meet today,' smiled Rosary, 'but I hoped with a little more dignity on my part.'

'It was Dacio who suggested I introduce myself. He

said I should be surprised by you.'

'I know! Like your father you expected a martinet with a rule book in her hand and a bun on her head. Instead you find me without a stitch on my person.'

'I had better go into the other room while you dress——'

'Don't run away,' said Rosary. 'Stay there and we will have a little talk.'

'*Sim, senhorita.*' Gisela withdrew into the bedroom and closed the mirrored door behind her. Rosary released the bath water and stood up to let the cool shower water rinse the soap bubbles from her body. In the mirrored panels she could see herself, slender and pale-skinned, with long, slim and rather pretty legs. Although it was true that she had been wrapped up in her musical and linguistic studies for the past few years, there had been young students at the school who had wished to become closer acquainted with her. In particular there had been Erick Stornheim, an Austrian composer rather older than the students; a friend of Cibby's, who had sent her several expensive gifts, Swiss chocolates, French gloves and web-fine stockings.

As she swathed her body in a large soft towel, she remembered that last time she had seen him, in the drawing-room of Cibby's house. The lazy, smouldering look in his penetrating blue eyes, when she had walked in from her classes, books under her arm, her fair hair swinging and her skirt a short one. Without asking permission he had reached out a hand to touch her hair, blown in the wind as she crossed the lawns of the adjacent school building. His hand had slipped to the soft wool of her sweater.

'You grow lovely, *liebchen*,' he had said. 'It seems but yesterday when first I saw you as a *real* schoolgirl.'

Rosary turned away from her reflection as she

slipped into her lingerie, and she wondered briefly about men and their passions. The secret side of male hunger was still unknown to her, and at times it half scared her. As the brief silky garments covered her slim and untouched body, and she felt the smoothness of her own skin, the firm delicacy of her structure, she knew with certainty that she would have to be madly in love with a man before she ever gave herself.

She wasn't old-fashioned, but she felt rather sad for girls who thought it fun to experiment with all that secret side of life ... which could surely only offer the ultimate with a man adored?

She tied the belt of her robe and entered the bedroom, where Gisela stood by the balcony doors and watched the darkening of the sky. The girl turned as she heard Rosary, and her smile was hesitant. 'Is my father going to permit you to stay?' she asked.

'Don't you wish me to stay?' Rosary countered, taking the pins from her hair and brushing it into a long, almost straight swathe about her shoulders. She looked young, and she felt far more unsure than she liked to admit. It was essential that she and Gisela like each other, for it seemed certain that the Senhora de Ardo was not going to unbend very easily, and Rosary didn't even try to imagine Dom Duarte on amicable terms with her. That man was a creature of steel sheathed in dark velvet! No doubt he had charm, of a remote kind, which he rationed out to those of whom he approved.

Rosary had answered him back and defended her right to have a mind and a will of her own.

'The only wishes that count are my father's,' said Gisela.

'But he allowed you home from the convent, he said you might have a private tutor. Are you disappointed

41

in me, Gisela?'

'It is too early to say.' The girl stared at Rosary's fair hair, which seemed unreal in contrast to her eyes. Rosary had always thought of them as brown until the evening Cibby had poured brandy for himself and Erick Stornheim. The Austrian had raised his glass and said deliberately that her eyes were the colour of cognac ... and indeed they were. A deep golden brown, not only the colour of cognac, but with a warmth, a slumbering fire and tiny sparks of gaiety.

'Is your hair really that colour?' Gisela asked, with the frankness of youth. 'One of our teachers at the convent used to dye her hair black.'

'I can assure you mine doesn't come out of a bottle.' Rosary walked out on to the balcony and breathed the air, which seemed even more intoxicating now that darkness lay over the island and the glimmer of golden star-points could be seen. 'Jessamine,' she murmured. 'Perfume of the Arabian Nights. No wonder you couldn't stay away, Gisela. You must love this island.'

'I was born here, and so was my mother, and her mother. I am a true islander, Miss Bell. Way back in my mother's family there is Arabian blood, for there was a time when the island was occupied by them. Some of the girls were put into *harems*, and then they were rescued when the Portuguese took the island back again.' Gisela breathed an excited little sigh as she stood upon the curved balcony with Rosary. 'I do think everything was terribly exciting in those olden days. There were armoured knights and pirates. Arabian lords and girls who were veiled all the way down from their eyes!'

Rosary smiled. 'When we start our lessons we will read all the old operas and ballets together. I am sure you will love them.'

42

'Then my father has asked you to stay?'

'He has given me a trial term of six weeks. I am to prove in that time that I am a good teacher, and if I don't satisfy his requirements I shall be dismissed.'

Gisela stood quiet a moment, stroking a pale blossom that sprouted through the ironwork of the balcony enclosure. It was almost a *miradoura* from the days when women had watched in terror the approach of pirate galleons. Rosary half-closed her eyes as a soft and sensuous breeze stirred her loosened hair and the wide sleeves of her robe. How almost easy to imagine this island as untouched by the modern world, governed as it was by a feudal aristocrat who even in a tailored white suit gave the impression of being clad in armour.

'Did my father make you feel nervous?' Gisela asked, a knowing note in her voice.

'Of course not,' said Rosary, a little too quickly. 'We merely discussed your lessons, the recreations we shall enjoy together, and the time when you take siesta. I am sure that if we get along smoothly there will be no need for your father to disapprove. The root of all learning is that the student and the tutor should be compatible. The parent should not interfere, even if the teacher is not to his personal liking.'

'Did my father seem not to like you, Miss Bell?'

'The feeling was mutual——' Rosary bit her lip, for this was hardly a remark to make to his teenage daughter. 'Perhaps, Gisela, you would like to call me by my first name? It would be more friendly, and less likely to make me feel the Victorian governess.'

'I don't know your first name——'

'It's Rosary.'

'You mean like prayer beads?' Gisela gave a small excited gasp.

43

'If you like, Gisela. But the name also means a rose arbour.'

'How romantic to have so unusual a name!'

'I think Gisela is rather fable-like. There is a ballet called *Giselle*, and what could be more romantic than that?'

Gisela shrugged and wandered back into the bedroom, where she stood by the fourposter and stroked the long skirt of the dress that lay across the bed. 'Aunt Azinha will expect you to be drab and retiring,' she said. 'She won't like it if you look too glamorous. She will think you are setting your cap at my father.'

'What an idea!' Rosary frowned at the dress and wondered after all if it would be better if she wore something more subdued.

'It isn't that Aunt Azinha would object to him marrying again,' Gisela continued, 'but she would naturally expect him to marry a Portuguese woman of his own class.'

Rosary gave the girl an amused look. 'Even if I were a duchess, my dear, I would still not be your father's type, or he mine. I was not brought up to treat any man like a god, but I am aware that the Latin attitude to marriage is different from ours. Here the man is the master, but in my country the partners are equal, and the woman speaks her mind when it pleases her.'

Rosary picked up the silk dress and with a pang of regret she hung it away in the closet and took out instead a simple brown dress with a white, appliquéd collar. She saw ahead of her some inevitable clashes with Dom Duarte, but she wished to stay on the right side of Senhora de Ardo. In any household it was more comfortable all round if the mistress was a friend and not an enemy.

'Do you think this dress is more suitable?' she asked

Gisela, with a slight smile. 'This is my first post in a Portuguese household and I don't wish to do the wrong thing.'

'Such a dress will make you look more subdued,' Gisela agreed. 'Does it feel very strange to be living here—Rosary?'

'Strange, but interesting, and I'm looking forward to exploring the island with your help. I'm sure it's very lovely, and I want to soak up all the sunshine I can, as well as the history and legends, and the folk music. I want to know the island and its people, and not feel too much the stranger.' Rosary stood thoughtful a moment, holding the brown dress that would make her seem more like a governess in the eyes of her employer and his aunt. 'I suppose I want to feel—accepted.'

'Which means you will have to conform.' Gisela's rather serious young face took on an impish look. 'Portuguese people make a lot of rules for young women to obey.'

'Such as?' Rosary sat down in a cane chair and prepared to listen; her eyes were amused, but she knew that up to a point she must conform if she was to become part of the island community. She would remain alien to these people if she shrugged off their rules of etiquette as old-fashioned.

'The foremost rule for girls is that male friends are taboo, and only the young man selected for one's future husband is permitted to call, or to take one for a car ride, or to the theatre. And even when alone the couple are on their honour to behave discreetly. Often a father insists that they be chaperoned by an aunt or a cousin, in case their feelings for each other should become too warm. Then,' Gisela added, 'when they are married, the husband is dominant, and the wife is often obliged to live in the household of her mother-in-law.'

'How delightful,' Rosary murmured. 'Your men may be handsome, Gisela, but I shall make an effort not to fall in love with one of them.'

'But love happens, whether we want it or not,' Gisela said, with the reasonable, and surprising precociousness of the Latin schoolgirl.

'Falling in love could prove awkward for a Portuguese couple, when marriages are arranged by the parents,' said Rosary. 'How do you convent girls skate around that little problem?'

Gisela gave a little laugh. 'Many Portuguese girls fall in love with the young man chosen for them.'

'The wish being father to the thought, eh? If you must marry the man, then you might as well love him?'

'Portuguese girls are practical,' Gisela agreed. 'It is often the men who are idealistic. They have a saying: Illusion is a great enchantress—she attracts and seduces.'

'Illusion, mother of romance,' Rosary murmured, thoughtful eyes upon the girl who lounged against a carved post of the enormous bed, young in body and yet old in the head, with deep in her blood the sophistication of the east. 'Exactly how old are you, Gisela?'

'I am almost fifteen. Sometimes on this island girls are married at the age of fifteen.'

Rosary was not shocked. She knew that all things tropical came to an early blooming, that for a few years they were lovely as tropical flowers, and then as that ripe bloom faded they grew plump and languid and were immersed in raising several children. To an English girl it was a little sad rather than shocking, but it was the custom, the way of life, and no doubt practical for a hot-natured people.

'I don't think, Gisela, that your father plans to marry you off so young,' she said. 'And now I had better get dressed for dinner! Do you join us at late table?'

'Yes. And then I am allowed half an hour in the *sala* before going to bed.' Gisela smiled. 'I am already treated as quite grown up. My father is a worldly man.'

'You will be company for me!' Rosary had been anticipating with reluctance the evening that lay ahead in the company of Dom Duarte and his rather severe aunt. 'I am pleased!'

Gisela gazed at her, and her cheekbones flushed. 'You are different from Lola,' she said. 'Lola likes to be alone with my father.'

Rosary was not surprised. She had somehow formed the opinion herself that the vivacious Portuguese girl had a crush on the Governor of the island. She had spoken hopefully of hearing that Rosary was unsuitable for the post of tutor ... by now her brother Dacio would have told her that the English girl was staying.

CHAPTER THREE

THIS was the second week Rosary had spent at the *palacete*, and each morning she never failed to feel wonderment when she awoke to find sunlight bright against the walls of her room, and sprawled like a golden cloak across her bed. Breakfast would be brought to her by a young maid, and because she couldn't get enough of the sunshine, so rationed at home by the English climate, she would eat on her balcony and feel the touch of the sun on her white skin. She wanted so much to become tanned. She felt so conspicuous when she took walks with Gisela and people stared at her hair and her pallor in contrast to their sun-browned vigour.

She loved the fact that her balcony overlooked that old part of the garden, where the lotus flowers spun on the dark green skirts of their leaves, and where in the night a thousand frogs made it their park. In the distance, the far blue distance, lay the mountains of colder lands, but here on Vozes do Mar it seemed eternal summer, and she knew with each new day that she had wanted all her life to find a place where the beauty of nature was unspoiled by noise and smoke of traffic; great tall buildings, and people always in a hurry.

Here the life had a slower beat, a warm and sensuous quality, with the island gone to a golden stillness in the afternoon hours, when shutters were closed against the blaze of the sun and the wives and workers took their siesta.

Clad in a brown shirt and a crisp white blouse,

Rosary ate rolls with quince jam, and drank a second cup of tea. It seemed that the *senhora* was fond of tea and it was an available blessing for someone English, like Rosary, who preferred coffee at lunchtime. A slim silver bracelet shone on her wrist, and her hair was clipped back softly at the nape of her neck. She knew that she was expected to look efficient and she did her best to look the part. It was during the siesta, when Gisela rested, that Rosary let loose her hair and her feelings on the beach that shelved from the terraced gardens of the palace. There she swam and explored the rocky coves and groynes. There she made sketches and notes, and ran about in bare feet.

If the Dom knew that she spent the siesta in this way, he never spoke of it. If he disapproved, it was just too bad. She needed during the day a break from routine, and after a morning of lessons Gisela was always ready for a rest in her cool, shuttered room.

Her breakfast completed, Rosary left her apartment and walked along the quiet corridor to the stairs. A study at the far end of the hall had been provided for the lessons; a small rotunda in which the piano stood between the windows, with a wide padded bench, and a table piled with folios of music. Gisela's mother had been a friend of Irena Marcos, the singer, so there had always been music available for her whenever she came on a visit.

She still came, Gisela said, and she was every bit as lovely as her rich soprano voice. Rosary half remembered her, for Cibby had been her teacher. She had seemed a dark-haired goddess, who smiled distantly at young things in gym-slips. Now, if they met again, it would be as women assessing each other's attraction with regard to the opposite sex.

Rosary opened the door of the study, but Gisela was

not yet down. It was still quite early, and a stroll outdoors would be pleasant while she awaited her pupil.

She wandered along the crazy-paved paths where gardeners were already at work among the lawns and the bright beds of flowers. Gay green birds flew about, and the silvery stalks of asphodel brushed her legs as she walked around a curving wall of the palace and smelled the white lavender massed beneath a window. Suddenly she halted and drew back into the shadow of a ferny tree as a figure in light grey suiting came out upon the front steps. He stood a moment, there between the marble columns, then he turned his dark head and looked directly at Rosary.

'Good morning, Miss Bell.' He inclined his head, and his gaze was so insistent that it drew her out from among the fronds of greenery. 'I see you are up early as usual. Your energy is confounding, but don't overdo things until you are more used to our climate.'

She knew at once that he was referring to the fact that she never took a siesta, and as always with this man she felt the urge to offer a little defiance. 'I'm so interested in everything, *senhor*, that I don't get tired.'

'Excellent. I am pleased that we don't bore you.' He stood there with great assurance, and he carried his shoulders as if they wore a cloak, the full and sweeping *cambiada*. Somehow he had the features and the attributes of a man of bygone days, and even the modern tailoring of his suit, the narrow cut of the lapels and the trousers, and the hip vents of the jacket could not dispel that air he had of ancient nobility and proud instincts.

Rosary felt the flick of his eyes over her slim sedateness, and for a startled moment she wondered if he had seen her in her bathing suit on the beach, with her hair in damp disorder. He was always so impeccable himself that an untidy woman would seem, she felt sure, distasteful to him.

'I hope you find my daughter a good pupil?' he said. 'I must say that she seems of a less serious countenance these days. My aunt informs me that she often hears the two of you laughing together.'

'Yes, *senhor*. But we don't waste time. We are reading the plays of Molière, and you will admit——'

'Quite.' He held up a lean, restraining hand, and a glint of amusement came and went in his eyes. 'Molière is amusing, and very worldly. I must get used to the idea that I have acquired for my daughter a tutor of exceptional intelligence.'

'Thank you, *senhor*.' She spoke stiffly, for she felt sure he was being a little mocking. He was a Latin and such men did not admire intellectual qualities in a woman. 'It isn't that I am trying to impose my tastes upon Gisela, but I am pleased to say that she enjoys reading the plays. She is very grown up for her years——'

'So I am aware, Miss Bell. Ah, here is my car, and I will bid you *adeus*.'

He went down the steps with a lithe ease of body, and took the wheel of the streamlined Porsche, a car which somehow suited the *grande* elegance of the man. It did, she thought, in place of a mettlesome horse with a high saddle. It suited today the way he was dressed, but she had not yet seen him on horseback and had an idea she would like to ... for the sake of artistic appeal.

He drove off, swiftly and with assurance, and Rosary entered the palace and as the coolness of the purring fans struck at her face and neck, she realized that her cheeks were hot. She stood there in the hall, hands to her cheeks, and was unaware for several seconds that a male figure was lounging against the balustrade of the stairs and was regarding her with amused interest.

'You look, *senhorita*, less serene than usual,' drawled Dacio. 'Has our eminent Governor been rebuking you ... or paying you a compliment?'

Rosary glanced up and her eyes were startled because her thoughts had been so occupied by the man who had just driven away; her eyes against the pale frame of her hair were a deep gold-brown, an illusion of velvet flowers, which Dacio seemed to reach forward to pluck as she looked at him.

'Dom Duarte has an unpredictable quality,' she said. 'Without moving a muscle he gives one the feeling that he might pounce.'

'To kiss, or strike?'

'No—to the first!' she said hastily. 'I shouldn't care to make an enemy of the *duque*. Even as a friend he might prove uncome-atable.'

'As opposed to uncomfortable?'

'Yes. I can see he has charm, of an aloof sort. But I don't envy those women who—love him.'

'Frightening, eh?'

'Terribly fastidious! Dacio, did you know Gisela's mother?'

The artist shook his black hair, which grew rather long and was attractively untidy. He took the three steps that brought him to her side. 'Come with me and I will show you her portrait.'

Rosary hesitated, and Dacio took her by the hand and drew her to the stairs. 'It won't take but a few minutes, and curiosity will buzz in your brain until it is satisfied.'

'Was she beautiful?' Rosary walked with him up the curving staircase and she felt a mounting sense of excitement. It would surely give her a clue to the inner man to see the face of the woman who had actually shared his life. 'You as an artist must know beauty when you see it?'

'There are varying kinds, *senhorita*. Many lines and curves and fleeting moments that create beauty. It can't always be captured, that look, that turn of the head, that fleeting smile, and only the sun is the perfect artist, and sometimes the sun is cruel and reveals what a little dusk might turn to loveliness.'

'You speak like a poet, Dacio.'

'A touch of poety is not out of place in a painter.' He flashed a smile at her, and an answering smile lit her eyes. When they paused on the bend of the second gallery she waited for him to lead her to the portrait of the woman who had once been the mistress of this marvellous house ... someone who must have been reared for such a position, such a man as Dom Duarte.

Dacio beckoned her through an archway, and at last she was seeing the picture gallery, a panorama of small, large and enormous paintings, stretching along the walls to the turn of the room, created by artists of varying degrees of talent, and most of them in fine old frames of gilt or carved wood. Some of them were landscapes, a captured gem of a house set among trees, or a baroque church among quaint cottages. The walls were alive with their movement and their colour, but here and there were blank spaces and upon a large table at the centre of the gallery were paintings which had been removed from their frames and were undergoing removal of stain and bloom, and the restoration of rich or pastel colouring.

'Oh—it would take hours, days to enjoy all these!' Rosary gazed about her with delight. 'How many, many years it must have taken for so large a collection to crowd these walls!'

She glanced upwards and saw a ceiling of turquoise
glass, a long arching dome that poured a sort of sea-
light down into the gallery.

'Some of the paintings are not so good,' said Dacio,
'but there are others worth a lot of money. Dom
Duarte has an eye for real art, so I am here to restore
part of the collection, and the remainder will be
crated and stored away in the vaults. He has decided
that the gallery will be much improved as a show place
if the more worthwhile pictures are better arranged
so as ot reveal their individual beauty or distinction.'

'Yes,' she agreed, and then she gave a little laugh.
'But some of the fun of hunting for a treasure will be
lost. Now, Dacio, do show me the wife he loved!'

Dacio raised a slow and taunting eyebrow as he
stood there looking at her, with the sea-blue light
sheening her hair, mystifying her eyes, softening the
crisp whiteness of her blouse and blue-shading her slim
white neck.

'How romantic you sound, *senhorita*. Do you believe
that a man and a woman marry only from love?'

'As an English person I like to believe it,' she said,
her gazed fixed upon a flower study that had the
charm of a bygone, more romantic age. 'I do know, of
course, that the arranged marriage is still a part of
Portuguese life. Are you saying, Dacio, that the *senhor's* marriage was one of expediency rather than
love?'

'Come and judge for yourself.' He took her lightly
by the wrist and led her to the table where he had
some canvases at rest against a chair. He cleared a
space on the table and lifted one of the canvases to the
flat surface. The light caught the brushwork, the texture of the deep red velvet of the dress, with a full skirt

just showing the velvet slippers decorated by silk pearl-coloured roses. Rosary's gaze moved slowly upwards, taking in the plump hands clasped in the rich velvet and weighted with rings. Her gaze followed the swan-like neck as it arose from the V of the dress and she stared at the vivid, oval face with that touch of the orient in the dark slanting eyes and the glossy pile of dark hair.

'Isabela de Montquiero Ardo.' Dacio spoke the name with a sort of reluctant admiration. 'She was beautiful, of course, but too – too exotic for my taste.'

'Superb,' Rosary murmured, but with a sense of shock she was thinking to herself. 'Isabela was stunning, but like an orchid that might hate to be handled!'

'Look at that ruby necklace,' Dacio murmured. 'She knew how well that rich colour suited the rich texture of her skin. Strange. She should strike a man as sensuous, and yet I merely have the feeling that she was really as cool as marble.'

'Then,' said Rosary, 'they must have been a well-suited couple.'

'Does *he* strike you that way?' Dacio slanted a look at Rosary. 'He's self-contained, but even a volcano has been known to bear ice.'

'You know him better than I.' Rosary smiled with a touch of devilry, and leaned forward to study the beauty of Isabela's face. That marriage had been no mating of a demure dove and an arrogant duke ... each had wanted something from the other. A desire, brilliant in the eyes of the woman, for jewels and splendid gowns. A wish on the part of the man for a son, perhaps. But instead Gisela had been born and after her birth there had been no more children.

'How did she die?' Rosary couldn't help but think it

cruel that so beautiful a woman should have died so comparatively young.

'Her death was a dramatic one.' Dacio glanced along the gallery to the entrance and his voice sank down, as if he didn't wish to be overheard. 'Gisela may not know the full facts ... one cannot tell, for she's an oddly adult young creature, with a touch of secretiveness. It was an accident, you see, which killed Isabela. Dom Duarte liked to ride and sometimes she would go with him, clad in one of those dashing, full-skirted riding-habits which make it necessary for a woman to ride side-saddle. They had gone off together in an amicable mood, but when they returned Isabela was riding like a fury and whipping her horse until the poor creature leapt and bounded in an attempt to escape the lash. It was a thoroughbred, sable-black, and unused to being treated like a mule. As he came bounding into the stableyard, he suddenly reared up where the stone arches and Isabela struck her head, lost control of the animal and was dragged beneath the stamping hooves. Dom Duarte threw himself out of his own saddle and ran to catch the reins of the black horse ... his wife in her purple habit was there under the hooves, and there was blood all over her face. She had been kicked above the left temple and half her cheek had been laid open. She breathed for ten minutes, but by the time the doctor arrived she was dead.'

In the silence which followed Dacio's account of the tragic accident, Rosary could almost hear her heart beating. How terrible! And how Dom Duarte must blame himself for having quarrelled with her! And how shocking must have been the quarrel to have roused her to such a temper, which she had taken out on the poor brute of a horse.

A slow, cold shudder ran through Rosary, for Dacio,

with his eye for dramatic detail, had painted a too vivid picture of the tragedy.

'I hope Gisela doesn't know the full facts,' she said quietly. 'But the Senhora de Ardo did say that she ran away from home after her mother died, and was ill after they found her.'

'She probably knew the details of the accident,' said Dacio, with equal quietness. 'But she may not have known that her parents had words and that Isabela was in a raging temper a few moments before she fell from her horse.'

Rosary stared at the portrait and thought to herself that it must haunt Dom Duarte, for he had been the first person to reach Isabela, the first to see her beauty ravaged by that awful fall to the cobbles of the stable-yard, where she had been trampled to death.

'Are you cleaning the portrait?' she asked Dacio.

'Yes. It used to hang in the main *sala*, but after the tragedy Dom Duarte had it transferred to the far end of the galley. Perhaps to be unreminded himself of her broken beauty, or perhaps to keep the child from being reminded that her mother was no longer a living presence in the palace. Last year, when she seemed stronger, he sent her to a convent school in Portugal, but as she pined to come home, he decided it would be for the best.' Dacio gave Rosary a long, deliberate look. 'I am glad. It has brought you to the island, and already your fair hair seems to light up these formal old rooms filled with their grand old furniture.'

'The *palacete* is a lovely place,' she objected. 'You with your artistic eye must see that.'

'My artistic eye, *senhorita*, prefers what is living and warm with emotion. For me there is nothing lovelier than a lovely woman.' He slowly smiled and thrust a

57

truant lock of hair from his eyes. 'I never dreamed that a tutor could be so nice ... or are you a modern young woman who objects to being called nice?'

'I am modern-minded up to a point,' she said. 'But I certainly don't object to being thought nice. I was brought up by my grandfather and he could be strict about certain things.'

'For instance?' His gaze dwelt on her lips as he spoke, at the full, soft curves of her mouth, lightly outlined by rose-coloured lipstick. 'He would not allow you to have friends of the opposite sex?'

'They were allowed ... as friends,' she said demurely, and meaningly.

'Are you warning me to keep my distance?' He moved his hand along the table top as he spoke, until his fingertips were touching hers. 'I am flattered rather than downcast; for I should hate to be thought harmless by a woman.'

'You Latin men are far from modest.' She transferred her fingers to the belt of her skirt. 'You have, in fact, an outrageous amount of self-esteem.'

'Perhaps this esteem arises from the fact that the Latin knows he is a man.'

'I don't doubt for a moment that you are a man, Dacio.' She began to walk away from him, along the gallery that had such a peculiar, sea-lit charm. Her lips held a smile, for it would be impossible not to find him a charmer. One would have to be very stiff-necked and frigid, and Rosary was neither of those things.

He fell into step beside her and he glanced down at her with a taunting, half-questioning look in his eyes. 'Are you an iceberg? I have heard it said of English women, and if it is so, and I must warn you that our island sun will soon start to melt you. Not to mention our music and our wine. May I invite you to a *festa*? I have some friends who are soon to marry and there is to be a celebration, with music and dancing, and good food and wine? Will you come if I ask you?'

'I live under the roof of Dom Duarte,' she said. 'He informs me that he is my guardian, so you will have to ask him.'

'Then you will come?' Dacio spoke eagerly, and thrust again at that truant lock of hair that was so dark against the tanned olive of his skin. 'He cannot do anything else but agree. I am no stranger to him, and Lola will be at the wedding *festa*.'

'It sounds fun!' They reached the archway that led out of the gallery and Rosary stood there a moment, before bidding Dacio *adeus*. 'I will come if you'd like me to. When is it to be?'

'Next week! On the Saturday. Ah, how I shall be envied by the other young men!' Dacio gave a laugh that rang out boldly, wending its way along the corridor and bringing from one of the rooms a woman in a dark dress with high-swathed silvery hair who lifted her lorgnette on a silver chain and stared through the eyeglasses at Rosary and the young painter.

'I had better be on my way to the study.' Rosary walked away from Dacio, and murmured, '*Bom dias, senhora*,' as she passed her employer's disapproving aunt.

'*Senhorita*, you will wait a moment!'

Rosary paused and gave the *senhora* a polite look of enquiry.

The woman came up to her and studied the way she was dressed, the way she had her hair styled, and the light colouring on her lips. 'In this establishment, Miss Bell, the staff do not laugh loudly together, nor do I approve of paint on the face. You will remember in future to leave Senhor Cortez to his work, and you will at this moment go and remove the paint from your lips.'

Rosary stared at the woman as if she had not heard her correctly. 'I beg your pardon, *senhora*?'

'You will go and wash your face, Miss Bell. Neither my nephew nor I wish Gisela to pick up decadent habits from foreign women. Indeed, if I had my way——'

'I am fully aware of what you would do if you had your way, *senhora*.' Rosary was fuming with sudden anger. 'I don't know whether it's considered polite in a Portuguese household to insult people, but you have just insulted me. I have known for the past week that you have been awaiting the opportunity to find fault with me, and I am quite sure that when Dom Duarte returns you will lose no time in telling him that I have behaved like a loose woman with Senhor Cortez. You wish Gisela to be placed in the hands of an unintelligent martinet who will teach her to be as narrow in outlook and as joyless as yourself. Who will punish her for laughing when she shouldn't, and implant in her the idea that women are made for keeping house and being subservient to the man who has graciously agreed to take charge of her dowry, her person and her entire freedom!'

There Rosary broke off, and knew that by speaking out in this way she had lost her post at the palace. But she wasn't sorry. She had tried to be friends with this rigid woman, but it had been only a matter of time before they aired their mutual antagonism.

'Yes,' said the *senhora*, 'I shall indeed speak to my nephew about you. You should not have been allowed to stay here. I told him from the very start that you were unsuitable, and obviously insubordinate.'

'Senhora de Ardo,' Rosary's look became frankly

incredulous, 'I am not an unruly child to be scolded and rapped over the knuckles. I am a woman with a life of my own when I am not actually tutoring my pupil. Senhor Cortez was showing me the pictures in the gallery, not seducing me.'

'*Silenzio!*' The *senhora* lifted a hand as if to shield herself from such a downright expression. 'How dare you speak to me in such a way! You are insolent, and no lady——'

'I am a tutor, and even if I say it myself a darn good one. But obviously my ideas on how to teach a young girl to face life are a bit advanced for this household.' So saying, Rosary tilted her chin and proceeded on her way downstairs. She would carry on with her duties until summoned by His Excellency, and then she would tell him that if he wished his daughter to grow up to be a narrow replica of her aunt, then he must by all means allow the *senhora* to poison his judgement.

Yes, she would be perfectly frank with him before she packed her bags and said *adeus* to Vozes do Mar.

She caught her breath on a sigh ... it would be a shame to miss the wedding *festa*. She would have liked seeing a real island wedding, for she was sure not all Portuguese people were like the woman she had just quarrelled with.

She thought the study empty when she entered, and then Gisela slid out from behind the long curtains at the windows. She looked rather pale, and her eyes held a hectic brightness. Rosary knew at once that she had overheard that recent quarrel; Gisela knew also that her father would not keep a tutor who had upset his aunt.

'We had better start work,' she said briskly. 'I said yesterday that we would study the works of the romantic composers, starting with Chopin and going on to

Chaminade——'

'What is the use?' Gisela broke in. 'My father will send you away and whoever comes in your place will teach me dull things, and never laugh with me as you do.'

'I tried to hold my peace with the *senhora*, but she—well, you heard what she said, Gisela. I am not a painted flirt, but she implied that I was, and I'm afraid I had to defend myself.'

'Were you flirting with Dacio?' Gisela asked, and a look of jealousy flickered in her eyes. 'He is very good-looking and gay, and I have thought to myself that he would soon notice you and wish to charm you.'

'He was showing me the work he is doing in the gallery, and I found it most interesting. I can't ignore him just to please your aunt——'

'Did he show you the painting of my mother?' Gisela demanded.

'Yes—she was very beautiful.' Rosary spoke softly. 'You must always remember her like that, looking like a vision in her gorgeous red gown and her rubies.'

'I loved her,' Gisela said, 'but she never loved me.'

'My dear . . . !'

'She would never let me kiss her. She said children were a nuisance when they were young, and when they grew up they made a woman seem old. Now,' Gisela bit her lip, 'now she will never grow old, will she? My father and I can always remember her as proud and beautiful.'

'Yes,' said Rosary, but she was thinking of what Dacio had told her. Dom Duarte had knelt on the cobbles beside the dying figure of his wife, he had held her and seen her savaged face. That was the image he would always carry in his mind. 'Come, Gisela, let us settle down to our studies. There may be a chance that your father will consider I was justified in standing up to your aunt.'

'Yes,' said Gisela, 'if you speak with him before he sees Aunt Azinha. If you tell him how it happened that you had words with her.'

Rosary considered this and looked doubtful. 'I don't think he'd accept my word in preference to hers. I am still quite a stranger to him, and I believe he thinks my ways a little odd, as it is. You must remember that he put me on trial as your tutor, and now I have gone and called his aunt a narrow-minded and joyless woman!'

'All the same,' Gisela said eagerly, 'it can be arranged that you see him before Aunt Azinha has a chance to paint you a scarlet woman. Today he goes to the Courthouse, and he will be there all the morning. At noon he will lunch with Judge Lorenzo, and afterwards he will drive to Bahia de Roches——'

'The Bay of Rocks?' Rosary exclaimed. 'But why?'

'Because he likes to go there.'

'You mean the bay is a sort of getaway place for him?'

'Yes, that is how to describe it.' Gisela smiled. 'He is like other people and needs sometimes to be alone. Are you surprised?'

'I suppose,' Rosary shrugged, and gestured beyond the study windows to where the lawns lay like velvet, and where the white peacocks preened their plumage, lovely and strangely more exotic than their 'painted' kin. 'Your father is the overlord of the island, so aloof and certain of himself that I can't imagine him tramping a beach alone.'

'He may not be alone,' said Gisela. 'Sometimes I have known him to meet Lola there. I think he likes her and finds her attractive. But of course . . .'

'Yes?' Rosary coaxed. 'Tell it all.'

'If he married again he would have to choose a woman of position and good birth. That is the way of it with a man who has much property, and if he dies without a son to inherit, then a cousin in Portugal will be declared the heir, both to the title and my father's property in the south of Portugal. He has a castle there, and great vineyards, but it is the family tradition to govern Vozes do Mar for a number of years before the Duque feels free to return home.'

'I see,' said Rosary, and found it all very intriguing. 'So you believe your father would rather like to make Lola ... ah, but I shouldn't be gossiping about him in this way. It isn't ethical, and by this time tomorrow I may be on my way home! Dismissed for behaviour unfitting a tutor.'

Although Rosary smiled, she was inwardly upset. It seemed so absurd that the *senhora* should rebuke her for being friendly with Dacio when Dom Duarte himself was more than friendly with the sister of the young artist. Of course, Lola was Portuguese, and the *senhora* was of the class that allowed its men to have their little distractions, so long as they were kept quiet and did not upset the traditions of the family. Rosary couldn't help but wonder how that unbending woman would react if her nephew decided to flaunt tradition and marry the vivacious Lola. Gisela had just said that he must have a son, and Lola Cortez did not look cool and passionless, unlike that lovely woman named Isabela.

'I—I don't want you to go away.' Gisela leaned against the piano and ran her fingers along the keys, producing a discordant sound. 'You understand me better than the teachers at the convent ... they said I was moody, but I am not so with you. Am I?'

'No, because I treat you like an adult, or almost. But what can I do, Gisela? If I beard your father at Bahia de Roches he may have Senhorita Cortez with him, and a man hardly likes an importunate tutor to butt in ... it would be disastrous, worse than being scolded by your Aunt Azinha! You are accustomed to your father. You can't imagine how he strikes a stranger.'

'He would not strike you!' Gisela turned her head and gave Rosary a startled look. 'Do you think he would?'

'No ... what I mean is that he is not like ... not like Dacio, for example. There are some people whom one accepts quite naturally. There are others who seem bounded by high walls of conventions, so that it seems hazardous to approach them.'

'Are you afraid of him?' Gisela asked.

'Not exactly afraid.' Rosary scorned the idea. 'Nor am I overawed by his title, it is just a feeling I have that a barrier exists between us, and it would be painful for me to—to plead with him.'

'Because your pride would be battling with his pride,' said Gisela. 'But if you really wanted to stay here you would not be afraid——'

'I'm not afraid!' Rosary insisted. 'I have never felt fear of anyone in my life, and the Duque is but a man!'

'There you are! He is but a man, and I dare you to go and confront him before he returns home and Aunt Azinha whispers like the serpent in his ear.'

'Gisela, you really mustn't say such things. Your aunt has her codes of honour, her bred-in-the-bone ideas, and I am alien to her. And I also think to some of the old women of the island. The other day as I walked in the village one of the old lace-makers crossed herself as I passed by her doorway. I wasn't

65

wearing a scarf over my hair, and she looked at me as if—as if I were Eve!'

The young pupil looked at her young tutor, and they burst together into a sort of guilty laughter. 'Gisela, perhaps it would be best if you had a Portuguese teacher. Someone more attuned to the ways and the prejudices of your father's people——'

'No.' Gisela shook her head, and her eyes gave warning of temper and tears. 'I don't want to know only Portuguese things! To be told that I must grow up like my mother ... I want to be *myself*.'

'Of course you do.' Rosary put her arms around the girl and stroked her hair. 'And you shall. I'll talk to Dom Duarte——'

'Away from the *palacete*, Rosary, so Aunt Azenha won't know. If she knows, then she will find some other way to have you sent away.'

Rosary gazed with troubled eyes over the dark head bowed on her shoulder. She hadn't dreamed of becoming so personally involved when she had applied for this tutorial. She had merely thought it would be fun to work on an island ... fun! She was ashamed by her own flippancy. Cibby had insisted that she study human relationships if she meant to teach, so she would know in advance that each human being, young and old, had a problem. That it was part of humanity to be troubled by life, by the hope and expectation of love, and by the conflict that was a natural part of being in contact with other human beings.

It struck Rosary that she had almost looked upon this teaching post as a sort of holiday in the sun. It was the distress and tension which she felt in Gisela that made her realize the girl's innate loneliness; her need for companionship ... that little more than a teacher was asked to give ... that little less than a mother should give.

Rosary cupped the oval young face in her hands and raised it so her eyes were looking down into Gisela's. 'I promise you that I shan't be sent away, not if eloquence can help me to stay. How on earth do I find the Bay of Rocks?'

She learned that Amadeu the boatman would take her, if she paid him. He couldn't go out with the fishing crews because he had only one arm, but he made a living off the shellfish out on the reefs, and he also hired out his boat to young couples who wanted to be alone as they were allowed to be. He was considered chaperon enough, seated at the tiller, with his awesome empty sleeve and his patriarchal beard.

Gisela would not come, for it would be breaking her father's rule that she rest during the heat of the sun. So after lunch, and wearing white slacks and a sleeveless blouse of anchusa blue, Rosary set out for the weathered cabin on the beach where Amadeu lived. She found him idle and thought he looked more of a pirate than a patriarch as he argued about the price she should pay him for taking her to Bahia de Roches during his siesta.

'All right, here's the money!' She took some folded notes from the pocket of her slacks, and felt the flick of his eyes over her person as she handed him the money. She didn't like to admit to herself that he gave her a slightly creepy feeling, but she told herself he couldn't do much harm with that single arm of his busy on the tiller of his boat. It was tied by the little stepped jetty, its paintwork weathered but still as sturdy as Amadeu himself. Rosary took the seat facing the tiller, and as he cast off and sat facing her, she was glad she had worn slacks and didn't have to tolerate those wicked old eyes upon her legs ... she had not been all that

aware of her own physical attraction until Erick Stornheim had made her aware. Strange that youthful
students did not possess the ability to make a girl
aware of masculine danger; that mixture of indulgence and desire in the experienced male. She had
mixed daily with students without ever feeling
alarmed or curious ... and then one day Erick had
looked at her legs and touched her hair, and she had
suddenly come alive to the fact that men and women
lived in different physical worlds, and that a girl was
an object of desire to a man whether she liked it or
not.

'So the *senhorita* wishes me to take her to the Bay of
Rocks, eh?' Amadeu steered the boat with a brown
and tensile hand which was probably as strong as two
hands. 'It is a lonely place, not much visited by the
people of the island. Long, long ago it was a wreckers'
bay, and the bird cries sound like people lost in the
water. Why would the English Miss wish to go there?'

'Just to see it,' she replied, in a cool voice. 'It sounds
a most interesting place, and as you can see I have my
sketch book with me. I should like to sketch you,
Amadeu, if I may?'

He was flattered, and she had found to her secret
relief a way to keep him quiet. Her charcoal pencil
moved swiftly over the thick paper and as always it
amused her to be able to capture the likeness of a face.
It was one of those odd little gifts that did not inspire
her to be an artist like Dacio. She knew her limita-
tions, and her aspirations. One day she hoped to com-
pose a lovely piece of music, but for now it was enough
to be alive and young, and eager for the challenge of
living.

'Why should such an educated woman come to our
island?' Amadeu asked.

'Don't wiggle your beard,' she said, sketching swiftly that long black and silver badge of his seafaring years, forked and curling like a demon's. He must have been a devil as a younger man, she thought. Unruly-haired and black-eyed, making her wonder if he had lost that arm after a seashore fight over a wench, perhaps. He was a character, and still a rakish one.

'I am the tutor of the Governor's daughter,' she said.

'We all know it,' he said, 'and we all wonder why His Excellency chose someone so *d'ouro.*'

She felt his knowing gaze upon her hair, flaxen as the sunlight burning on the water, pale and shining looped back from her smoothly curving cheeks. 'You have my assurance that I came as a complete stranger to Dom Duarte. I applied for the post, but was not asked for a photograph. I could have been a stick in blue stockings for all he knew.'

Amadeu chuckled, 'The *senhorita* is quick with the reply, and men like it so. Better a wild heron than a tame goose!'

She had to laugh herself. 'Would you like to have this sketch when I finish it?'

'I hoped you would give it to me.' He was steering the boat towards a shoreline where the water beat in frills against large, strange-looking rocks. 'Is the *senhorita* meeting His Excellency at the Bay of Rocks?' Amadeu asked, in a sly voice.

'No——' She fought to look composed, for she might have guessed that the old sea-rover knew the comings and goings of everyone on the island. 'I am merely exploring the place, though I imagine Dom Duarte is always here or there, ensuring that all goes well with the island and its habitants.'

Amadeu looked at her with quizzical eyes, but he said no more as he gave his full attention to steering the boat to the shore, along a pathway of the sun that made the sea shimmer as if diamonds lay in thousands just below the surface. As they neared the rocks, they rode on the waves at the edge of the bay, a scimitar of rather dark sand studded with the green and gold rocks.

They passed skilfully between the barrier of high sea rocks, and the place was evocative of the savage past, and as the seabirds cried overhead they did sound strangely human.

The boat nosed the sands, and Rosary swept her gaze along that lonely stretch of beach, curving up and away into a tangle of tropical growth.

'I'd like you to wait for me,' she said to Amadeu, and she stood up and prepared to step on shore. 'You might as well take your siesta while I walk about.'

'It would be the discreet thing to do, eh?' He gave her an openly wicked look, and she thrust into his hand the sketch which she had made of him. She left him studying it as she jumped down on to the sands and began to make her way among the rocks to the incline. There seemed not to be a soul about, and she hoped that old reprobate wouldn't take it into his head to follow her. She quickened her pace, eager to see what lay beyond that boundary of tropic trees and veils of greenery. The air was warm, and heavy with the scent of creepers as she reached them and went in among them.

What was it that brought Dom Duarte here? A clandestine meeting with Lola Cortez . . . or that touch of *saudade* in the soul of the Portuguese? That search for something beyond everyday living . . . and everyday loving.

Rosary felt apprehensive, of seeing him with Lola, and seeing him alone. In both instances it would be an intrusion. He would be annoyed, and she didn't much fancy the annoyance of this man who, when he looked at her, and made her feel she had many things yet to learn about life.

She stood still as the cry of a bird touched her nerves. Perhaps she should turn back and not look for him ... but that would be the coward's way, and she had promised Gisela to do this thing, to find him and dare his temper, and insist on her right to be a human being in his employ, without the constant threat of dismissal because she spoke to Dacio, or laughed with Gisela and tried to make their studies a pleasure instead of a chore.

Sprays of orchids grew wild on the trees that formed this small belt of jungle and she was surrounded by the low-pitched shrilling of the invisible cicadas, folded in among the trees like living leaves. It was so cool and green, and then suddenly the sun struck down and opened a golden path out of the foliage, the bushes and ferns entangled in red and gold cane flowers.

She stood staring at a lonely sea-tower, with worn steps leading upwards in a spiral around that mossy relic of the past. Her gaze travelled upwards and her pulse beats quickened as she caught a slight movement on the stone shelf that encircled the tower, open to the elements and insecure-looking from the safety of the ground.

She knew instinctively that she had found the Dom's hideaway, where he came to enjoy the solitude of his own company ... or that of the attractive Lola. Rosary shaded her eyes with her hand, but she caught no glimpse of a bright skirt, and obeying instinct she made for the steps and started to climb them. It wasn't the tower she feared so much as the man who stood up there, but she was determined to speak to him about the situation which had developed at the palace. If she bearded him in this his lonely eyrie, then he would have to listen to her.

As she climbed higher and higher the wind off the sea caught at her hair and blew it about her face. The stone was hot from the sun, and so was the iron balustrade to which she clung as she climbed the last few steps. Gazing upwards to see if he had yet seen her, her foot caught against a broken step and she stumbled, and with a pounding heart she clung to the iron railing like a fly to a strand of dark webbing. She must have given a startled cry, for suddenly a shadow fell over her and Dom Duarte was standing there, looking down at her, but his face was as inscrutable as a mask of gold.

The wind tossed her hair, and she heard him say: 'What are you trying to do, break your neck?'

'Why, *senhor*, you!' She managed to sound breathlessly surprised. 'Fancy seeing you here of all places!'

CHAPTER FOUR

'FANCY!' he drawled, and the next moment he had gripped her by the wrists and she found herself standing beside him on the sea-tower, with only the wheeling sea-birds in attendance. Her eyes dwelt on his face and they were filled with the eternal question asked by a girl when she finds herself alone with a man whom her instincts know to be more subtle than other men.

A girl could take a teasing line with some men and flatter them into being nice, but this man was different. He could not be easily charmed or cajoled ... his features were those of an autocrat; his touch was cool and steely.

He made Rosary feel unsure of herself, and aware that she knew more about music than men. That aspect of life had never really infringed. Romance had not yet entered her life, though she had been conscious when listening to a moving piece of music of something poignant as well as exciting in the prospect of love. Love should be like music, she had thought.

But having seen today a portrait of this man's wife she could not believe that love between him and Isabela had been like music ... unless one thought of Wagner and the high clash of temperament. Knowing about Isabela added to the tension of this moment, as if he would hate above all to have a stranger know that he came to this solitary place to pay penance to the memory of his wife.

Rosary felt the grip of his hands, the warning that he could hurt her if he chose to do so. 'What are you doing here?' he demanded, holding her with his eyes as well as his hands. 'Did you find this place by chance, or did you know that I would be here?'

'I—I knew you would be here,' she admitted. 'I had a reason for wanting to find you alone.'

'I see.' He studied her upraised face and still held her by the wrists, so she was unable to brush the wind-blown hair from her eyes. 'And how did you get here, Miss Bell? The Bay of Rocks is a long way from the *palacete*, so I presume someone brought you, either by road or across the water?'

'I came in Amadeu's boat——'

'Unescorted?'

'Of course, *senhor*. I'm not a child.'

'Exactly so.' His eyes swept over her and his fingers hurt the bones of her wrists, holding her firmly in the grip of shock as he went on relentlessly: 'You are no child but an extremely attractive young woman, with hair so beautiful that it should be covered, and yet if it were covered by the black lace which our women wear it would shine through as the sun does through shadow and shutter. I think you made a big mistake in coming here——'

'Here—to the tower?' she blurted.

For a long moment his face was sardonic and for the first time, here where the light was almost pure, she saw the tawny flecks in his eyes, tiny stabs of fire that might blaze with temper ... or smoulder with the passions of his Latin blood.

'I meant the island itself, Miss Bell. Why did you come looking for me?'

She flushed, for he made it sound as if she wished to be alone with him in order to flirt with him. The very thought of being caressed and kissed by him made her heart flutter with such panic that she attempted to pull her hands free of his touch. This instinctive

74

action made her pull towards the edge of the platform, and at once he swung her back against the wall so that his tallness confronted her in almost a threatening way. 'You are too impetuous for high places,' he grated. 'It would not be much to my liking to have to write and tell your grandparent that you had a fall and broke your charming but impulsive neck. Now be still and tell me why you took this risk in seeing me alone.'

'I—I had to talk to you, Dom Duarte—before your aunt did so.'

'Ah, this sounds like an appeal! What have you been doing to upset the *senhora*?'

'It wouldn't occur to you, would it, *senhor*, that she might have upset me?' Rosary looked him in the eye and would not be intimidated by his superior strength, or by his position as Governor of the island. Only that morning he had been at the Courthouse listening to appeals of innocence ... now he could listen to hers.

'What have you done, Miss Bell, outraged my aunt's rather rigid sense of decorum? For instance,' his eyes agleam with sardonic humour flicked the white slacks she was wearing, 'have you been wearing trousers around the *palacete*?'

'I only wish it were only that, but she has near enough accused me of being loose and immoral because I wear a little make-up, and don't behave with monstrous false modesty in the presence of a man.'

'Which man?' snapped the Dom.

'Why, Dacio Cortez. We are both working at the palace and naturally we speak to each other. This morning your aunt chose to consider that I was behaving like a scarlet woman, and she told me to wash the paint off my face and to expect a summary dismissal from my job.'

'And what did you say, *senhorita*? I am sure you didn't retire from the fray without a retort or two.'

'I—well, I told her she was narrow-minded and joyless.'

'That was hardly the diplomatic thing to do.'

'My temper was up *senhor*. I wear less make-up than some of the Portuguese girls I have seen during the evening promenade——'

'In my aunt's eyes they are village girls and have no connection with the etiquette of the *palacete*. She merely expects you to be discreet, Miss Bell, and to be an example for Gisela to follow.'

'I realize that, but do you think I overdo the lipstick? I have seen Lola——'

'We are not discussing the Senhorita Cortez.' Suddenly his voice was rather cutting. 'You are employed as a tutor and my aunt expects you to behave like one.'

'You mean I am expected to wear my hair in a bun, and to stare at the ground each time I happen to see Dacio?'

'What was he doing that induced my aunt to leap to the conclusion that you were not behaving with decorum? Were his arms around you? Was he kissing you?'

Rosary met the eyes that seemed to hold a certain scorn, and suddenly her temper was afire again, and despite Gisela she was strongly tempted to tell this man to take his job and give it to some straitlaced woman who would obey his rules without thinking herself a human being.

'If I wished to be kissed, *senhor*, I should want it to happen in a more secluded place than a gallery of your house! No, Senhor Cortez was not making love to me!

We were discussing his work in the picture gallery and your aunt merely needed an excuse to be disagreeable. She wishes Gisela to have a keeper rather than a friend, and that was why I risked seeing you in this unorthodox way. I promised your daughter that I would state my case to you before your aunt had a chance to distort the whole thing.'

'And do you imagine I would listen to a distortion of facts without consulting you or Cortez?' The question had the cool smoothness of ice, but the eyes that penetrated Rosary were flickering with tiny points of flame. 'I am aware, Miss Bell, that your personality is a little too vital for the approval of my aunt, therefore I shall make up my own mind about your continuing suitability as a tutor for Gisela. Tell me, has the child any real feeling for the piano? Her mother used to play.'

Feeling somewhat startled that he should mention his wife, Rosary took a moment or two before answering him. Then she said quite honestly, 'Gisela has a light and pretty touch and I can help her to improve as a musician, but the depth of true talent isn't there. Is that what you hoped for, *senhor*?'

'Quite frankly, no. I have made plans already for Gisela's future and I don't wish for a career daughter. It is enough that her talent can be made socially pleasing. We Portuguese have not yet succumbed to the pop music of your country and we still enjoy a Chopin *étude*, or a Latin lament.'

'I enjoy those things as well, *senhor*.' A smile came and went on Rosary's lips. 'I am far from being a pop music fan, and I do assure you there are still people in my country who enjoy real music. We have not all gone crazy.'

'I am relieved to hear it.' Amusement played over

his features, softening for a moment the stern lines of his mouth. Rosary felt, then, the attraction of the man, for there was something in herself that couldn't help but respond to that proudly held black head, that high-arched nose, those bold satanic eyebrows. He was born to command and she was too feminine not to feel it.

'So you came to the Bay of Rocks in the boat of Amadeu, eh? You are not easily intimidated, are you, Miss Bell? I wonder, in fact, what it would take to make you nervous. What do you think of my sea-tower?'

'It's solitary, rather dangerous and evocative. A place to which a person would come to meditate.' And to dwell on the past, she thought. 'I should apologize, *senhor*, for disturbing you, but you do understand my motive? I don't wish to be sent away merely because your aunt has taken a dislike to me. It is far more important that Gisela likes me.'

'Do you feel you are good for my daughter, Miss Bell?'

'Yes. I have awoken her interest in several things since I came to Vozes do Mar. After all, you just intimated that you don't want a vegetable for a daughter. You want one who will glow in Portuguese society, and these days it isn't enough for a girl to be merely pretty.'

'You think Gisela a pretty person?' And he seemed to dwell on the words with the same deliberation that his eyes dwelt on Rosary's silk blouse of anchusa blue, and her hair that held the hot sunlight. He studied rather than looked into her eyes that were deep and warm as cognac.

'She promises to be a beauty, *senhor*, and she should

have personality to match her looks as she grows into a woman.'

'The cask should hold wine and not soda water, eh?'

'Exactly, for when the cask begins to wear what is left?'

'That is rather a quaint philosophy for such a young woman. At your age you should be thinking of only the romance in life.'

'But, *senhor*,' she said demurely, 'as your daughter's tutor I am not allowed to be romantic.'

'But, *senhorita*,' he mocked, 'you assured me that you were only talking of work with the good-looking Dacio.'

'Yes, in working hours,' she agreed. 'But as your employee would I be allowed in my free time to think of romance?'

'I see no harm in thinking of it, but as I have said before it would be advisable, while you are here on the island, to conduct yourself more like a Latin young woman than a free-thinking British girl.'

'I notice that you make a subtle distinction, *senhor*. Do you consider Latin girls are more sensible than I am?'

'Let us say they are less impulsive than you are.' He gestured at the breakneck view from the sea tower. 'I have never known a girl of this island to climb those precarious steps to this high and windy place.'

'Not even Lola——?' The words were spoken and could not be recalled, and Rosary felt her pulses leap as he looked at her between narrowed eyelids. She had come here with the intention of conciliating him, and yet she seemed driven by some wayward reaction to his personality to make him annoyed. It was a foolish and dangerous thing to do, for they were very much alone and he seemed a man who wouldn't hesitate to punish an offence to his dignity.

'For a second time, Miss Bell, you seem to imply that I arrange secret meetings with Senhorita Cortez. Are you merely young and curious, or are you deliberately provoking me by prying into something which has nothing to do with you?'

'I—I have never supposed for a moment, Dom Duarte, that your affairs are anything to do with me.' Her cheekbones seemed to burn and she felt like a small, impudent girl under his gaze. 'I only wondered if Lola had ever wanted to see the view from this height. I should imagine that it takes in most of the island.'

'From the other side one can see the countryside. Come, let me show you, and be careful of that iron railing. The stonework of the tower is old and in places the railing is not as secure as it should be.' As they made their way to the other side of the tower Rosary could feel, like a fine steel manacle, the grip of his fingers about her left wrist. He was treating her as if she were little older than his daughter, and far less tractable.

They stood side by side gazing over the land that undulated far below them. Rosary saw the flutter of snowy egret wings above the green rice fields. The revolving sails of the windmills, full-bodied and catching the sunlight upon their shafts. Field workers could be seen, the women with the lower part of the face covered in the oriental way. There were clusters of small white houses, with chimneys that flared into turrets, almost like miniature castles, castles and minarets. The palm trees and tropical vegetation, the hot sunlight on shimmering water, completed a picture that Rosary couldn't help but fall in love with.

'Vozes do Mar is a lovely island,' she murmured. 'I don't want to leave it, just yet. That was why I put my pride in my pocket and came to find you alone, *senhor*. I am not the flirt your aunt would like to make me seem. I am a good tutor and given half a chance I can do a good job.'

'You hope to soften my heart of stone, eh?'

'If you had such a heart, Dom Duarte, you wouldn't care if your daughter had music or not. You may have a stern heart, but that is a different thing.'

'How different, *senhorita*?' Though he had warned her about the iron railing he leaned an elbow on it himself and regarded her as she stood there beside him, her pale hair blown to one side of her face by the wind, leaving exposed her left ear, the fine curve of her neck and her youthful, flawless skin.

'Stone cannot be softened, it can only be broken, or it can break.'

'But you believe that a stern heart can be softened, eh?'

'I like to think so.' She gazed straight ahead of her and tried not to be so overpoweringly conscious of his eyes, knowing they had slipped from her profile to her shoulder, bared by the softly curving blue of her blouse. It was strange that a man so aloof should make her so aware of herself.

'You are optimistic as well as impulsive, Miss Bell. What if I said that I don't believe for one moment that the intentions of Cortez are impersonal with regard to yourself? What if I thought it wise at this stage to send you home before that young man becomes too *simpatico*?'

'Really, *senhor*, do you think I am so unused to young men that I shall lose my head over Dacio? I studied alongside male students at my grandfather's

81

school, and I learned to keep a level head, and not to take flattery as a declaration of love.'

'Cortez is Portuguese, and the tongue of the young Latin is smooth and varied as the *azulejo*.'

'Does it grow less smooth as a Latin male matures?' she asked, with a wicked demureness.

'The Latin becomes more skilful, more practised, *senhorita*, just as a musician does if he has at the start a gift for playing on the senses.'

'Are you trying to make me feel afraid, *senhor*?' She gave a laugh, for he mustn't know that it was he, not Dacio, who could make her feel unsure of herself. Power and charm ran together in his very bones, and combined with his fatal marriage they made of him a man no woman could possibly ignore, or take lightly. He had depths to him upon which a young man like Dacio bobbed like a buoyant cork. Rosary knew that for a girl there was danger in being drawn into those depths ... dark, fascinating and painful.

'Life can be tragic, Miss Bell. Men can be cruel ... women can be hurt. None of this has yet touched you, therefore you are vulnerable, a term you might repudiate being a modern-minded English Miss, but all the same a valid one. What would you do right now, for instance, if I felt the impulse to kiss you?'

'But you wouldn't!' She turned intensely shocked eyes to his face. 'It would be against your principles as the man in command! You are bound to set a good example——'

'But we are here alone, Miss Bell, and did you not say that you would choose to be kissed in solitude?'

'Yes—I said that, but I didn't mean that I would submit to any man, regardless of my feelings. I'm not a girl who kisses lightly, even if you are a man who does so!'

'Be careful, Miss Bell.' Suddenly his hands were spinning her to face him and he held her by the waist, like something he could snap in two with the living steel of his fingers. 'You might be speaking to a man who makes the tears of women his wine.'

'Y-you shouldn't threaten me,' she gasped. 'Why are you doing it, to test my morals? To see if I am the sort of girl to lose her head over the Governor of Vozes do Mar? Or over any man ... as your aunt suggests?'

'I am naturally curious about a young woman with hair like a blaze of pale silk, and eyes that hold the dark-gold fires of the topaz. It seems unusual that a girl so attractive should choose to be a tutor on a remote and foreign island. Can it be that you have come here to escape from a man?'

In that instant Rosary could have told the exact truth, that there was no romantic love in her life, but the physical closeness of this dark and compelling man acted like a spur to her frightened senses. She thought of Erick and the way he had looked at her the last time they had met. She reached out in panic to Erick because she had known him since she was a schoolgirl.

'I'm not running away from a man,' she said. 'We thought it would be a good idea to be apart for a while, so he could concentrate on his career as a conductor of music. I am sure you realize that while a man is making his name as a musical conductor there should be no other distractions.'

'And Vozes do Mar is many miles from London, eh? The young man cannot be tempted away from his career by the topaz eyes?'

'No, *senhor*.' She felt a terrible fraud, and yet she felt secure in the knowledge that he would never be likely to meet Erick. She could now pretend to be 'spoken for' and being a rigid Portuguese he would respect that invisible barrier. There had to be a barrier between them, for when he came close to a girl he was much too devastating. Now when she looked at him the mockery was gone and his face was once again a cool bronze mask, with above it the windblown sable hair. She didn't dare to look at his lips, for she dared not be curious about his kiss.

'Soon the afternoon will be over and we must return to the *palacete*.' His hands slipped away from her waist and she almost shivered at the coldness that encircled her body in place of his touch.' You will come with me, of course. I can't allow you to be alone with Amadeu as twilight falls. He is an old pirate and not to be trusted.'

Rosary didn't make the obvious answer, that for several tense minutes she had not trusted Dom Duarte himself. '*Senhor*, your aunt will know when she sees us together that I have pleaded my cause before she has had time to condemn me.'

'Then I will let you leave the car at a side entrance and you can slip in through the back way. There is no harm in being discreet, eh?'

'I would prefer it, *senhor*. Until she decides to accept me.'

'Be as discreet with the young artist, Miss Bell.' There was a sudden note of hardness in the deep voice. 'And now shall we leave our friends the birds and go to the car?'

'What of Amadeu?' she asked. 'I told him to wait for me.'

'He will not wait all night. Come, Miss Bell, and be careful of these steps as we descend. I notice that you wear the sensible sandals, at least, and not those high heels which seem to make a woman walk as if upon unbroken eggs.'

'I always understood, *senhor*, that men preferred women to be uncomfortable and helpless.'

'Even men, *senhorita*, are becoming less barbaric in their taste.'

She wondered about that as she walked ahead of him down the winding steps and heard the cries of the birds with less distinction. He had a silent way of walking, as if his every muscle was controlled and supple as that of a tiger. The skin seemed to tighten at the nape of her neck and she could feel his eyes upon her, alive with those tiny tawny lights. Today she had learned how his wife had died ... and she had learned also that she was capable of a fabrication in order to keep him at arm's length.

As she reached the security of the ground she gave him a look from wild-fawn eyes and felt the impulse of the fawn to flee into the underbrush. It was crazy! Never in her life had she felt so potently this sense of danger ... of seduction. It was as if the island air from way up there had gone to her head like wine, and now with her feet on the earth her legs felt trembly. Because of it, because he was the heart and cause of this awareness that made her silly and weak, she turned on him. 'But you don't like to see a woman in trousers, do you, Dom Duarte? That is too much a sign of female emancipation.'

'Or dissipation,' he drawled, and he stood over her, tall, sheathed in his perfectly fitting suit like a rapier in its scabbard. 'Untidy hair and trousers make me think of a slut.'

Her head shook, as if he had slapped her. Her eyes blazed ... and then she hated him and the intoxication was gone. Your cruelty is really highly refined, isn't it, Dom Duarte?' she said, and knew exactly what she was going to say next. 'I wonder if you will ever forgive yourself for the words which killed your wife?'

'No,' he said coldly, 'I shall never forgive myself. Nor shall I forgive your audacity in raking over the ashes of memories private and painful to me.' And as he spoke, and the island light was caught and held in his eyes, she saw the flare of pain as he remembered as only he could that shocking moment when Isabela had been thrown from her sable mount, the beauty kicked from her face. Rosary could have cried out, then, that she was sorry ... achingly sorry for what she had said, but he walked past her, among the trees, and she followed him in silence, and knew that now he must send her away, for how could she stay and be unforgiven by him?

He reached ahead of her the strip of road where the Porsche stood waiting, its bodywork agleam under the rays of the slanting sun, which now held a gleam of red as the afternoon began to die.

Dom Duarte opened the passenger door and Rosary slid inside the car without looking at him. She was beyond understanding herself, and she sat withdrawn in her seat, staring ahead of her as he took the wheel and the car shot away from the roadside with speed and elegance, and flashed through the reddening sunlight along the undulating road that cut through the centre of the island, dividing the countryside from the sea. Rosary turned aching eyes to the sea and it shimmered and seemed to be running with the life-blood of the dying sun. It was so painfully beautiful that she gasped, and only then did she realize that she was pressing a hand to her throat as if to hold back her stricken apology which he would treat with all the scorn it deserved.

How long they drove in silence she never knew, but dusk was painting the palace with shadows when the car came to a halt at a side entrance and Dom Duarte told her, curtly, to get out. She obeyed him and was about to close the door behind her when he said:

'What has been between us this afternoon had best be forgotten, but I would ask you not to discuss with Gisela the way her mother died.'

'I—I wouldn't dream of doing so.' Rosary clenched the handle of the car door so hard that a fingernail broke. 'I will pack my things tonight—I expect you would like me to leave in the morning?'

'Don't be so childish!' he snapped. 'I am not so cruel that I would deprive you of your living in order to punish you for having an opinion of me. You may continue to work with Gisela, and I will tell the *senhora* that she must show more understanding of your ways, which are naturally different from our own. *Ate a vista*, Miss Bell!'

It was so cool, so indifferent, till we meet again, and Rosary felt a chastised child as she slipped through the side entrance and heard the Porsche speed on towards the front of the palace, where it would make a smart turn in against the steps...

There her breath caught in her throat as she heard a sudden scream of brakes, a crashing of glass and a tearing of metal. In an instant she was running in the wake of the car and as she entered through the forecourt gates she gave an involuntary cry of horror. The Porsche was overturned against the steps and the entire front of it was a mass of spinning wheels and shattered glass from the wide front windows. Even as she ran she saw oil and petrol snaking like dark blood along the tiles of the forecourt ... she knew that Dom Duarte was trapped inside the overturned car and at any moment the tank was going to explode. She heard the crunch of the glass as she stepped on it and her hands reached blindly for the shoulders that jutted from the door which had been forced open by the crash. She tugged and pulled, and was vaguely aware of someone running down the front steps of the house. She felt the *senhor* stir, and then another pair of hands were helping her and they had pulled him free, and they kept on pulling, with desperate urgency, as a tongue of flame leapt and the next moment engulfed the car in a hot sheet of fire that lit up the front of the palace

Dom Duarte gave a groan and stirred again where they laid him. Blood was running down his face, and in that nightmare moment it seemed to Rosary that tragic history was repeating itself ... and then his eyes opened and he was staring up at her and she saw the tips of the flames reflected in his eyes.

'You will be all right.' It was Dacio who spoke. 'You braked too late and crashed into the steps.'

'M-my head is humming.' He stared a moment more at Rosary's shocked white face in the blazing illumination of the burning car, and then he fainted away.

When the doctor came hastily to the *palacete* it was found that Dom Duarte had concussion, several badly bruised ribs and a badly wrenched left ankle. That his injuries were not worse was a miracle, and everyone drew a shaky breath of relief when Doctor Rivas reported that the *senhor* had been made comfortable in the master bedroom. Gisela broke down and cried after her ordeal of waiting for the doctor to descend from her father's bedside. She shook with sobs, and when the *senhora* told her to control herself, for after all her father had not been killed, the girl turned on her and said stormily that she was stony-hearted and thought of nothing but correct behaviour and never giving way to human feelings.

As the hot, broken words struck at her, twin flushes appeared on the rather gaunt cheekbones of the *senhora* and her eyes bored into Rosary like daggers of accusation. *She* was being blamed for Gisela's very natural display of emotion, and hastily, before anything more could be said, Rosary led the distressed girl from the *sala* and upstairs to her room.

'C-can't we peep in at him?' she begged. 'Just to make sure he is all right?'

Rosary hesitated, and then decided that it couldn't harm Dom Duarte, who was sleeping now, and would put Gisela's mind at rest. Together they made their way along the gallery upon which his master suite was situated and very quietly she turned the handle of the tall door and glanced inside. His valet was seated on a chair near the bedroom door and he rose at once when he saw Rosary and came quietly across the carpeted floor to where she stood with Gisela.

'May we see him, Manoel?' Gisela caught at the valet's arm. 'We shall be as quiet as mice and won't make a murmur to disturb him.'

Rosary didn't speak, for suddenly she couldn't. She felt as though her heart were in her mouth, and she dreaded even as she desired to see the man whom she had helped to drag from the wreckage of his car. It had seemed like a bad omen that he should crash like that ... driving in a temper.

When Manoel beckoned them to the bedroom door, Rosary hung back. Gisela immediately caught at her arm and she had to go with her, into that big, silent, darkly furnished room where Dom Duarte lay sleeping, his black hair ruffled and damp and showing the edge of a dressing over his brow. His features looked more chiselled than ever, and distant as a rather beautiful mask.

Those moments beside his bed were so strange, so unreal, and as Rosary saw the breath stir his lips, she thought how angry he would be to be seen in this helpless state by her, who had reminded him only a short while before the car crash of his wife's painful death.

As Rosary backed quietly away from his bed, she knew that his mind had been upon Isabela when he had failed to apply those brakes in time. She turned and walked swiftly from his suite, stricken by the guilt of knowing that she had helped to cause the accident which could so easily have killed him.

CHAPTER FIVE

FOR several days the atmosphere at the *palacete* was subdued and anxious. There was no way of keeping Gisela's mind on her lessons, so Rosary gave up the struggle. She knew the girl was haunted by the loss of her mother, and she hung about near her father's rooms, and even Dacio could find no way of amusing her.

The only relief was that the accident had taken the *senhora's* mind off her feud with Rosary, and for the time being she seemed to become more human. Her nephew was one of the few people she was fond of, and she took upon herself the task of nursing him. She carried trays to his room, soothed his brow with iced water and made sure no one disturbed him.

As soon as possible he was up and about again, but his ankle was still painful and he used a walking stick with a polished knob to assist him in getting about the small palace, and his large study where the letters were piled up and the telephone kept ringing to ask his progress, and when would he be fit enough to attend to this matter or that. Dr. Rivas insisted that he remain at home for at least a week, and during that time Lola came often to the *palacete* to keep him company.

After seeing them together, strolling the sunlit lawns or sitting in cane chairs, Rosary was convinced that the Latin girl was in love with him, but as usual it was impossible to fathom the true state of his feelings. But always with Lola he seemed charmed and amused; a smile clung about his lips, and he wore informal shirt and slacks, and the stick that aided his limp gave him a subtle attraction. It also gave Lola the excuse to prop a stool under his ankle whenever he sat down, and she obviously enjoyed waiting on him.

In the evenings Lola and her brother were invited to dinner, and in the salon afterwards the *senhor*, with an air of laziness, would request that Rosary play the piano for them. Immediately she would turn to Gisela and suggest a duet, and she would feel the mockery in his eyes as they played together. He knew, with all his devilish shrewdness, that she was shy of playing alone for him. The others didn't matter; they were not so demanding as he.

Then one evening it came, the quietly spoken yet definite demand for a solo performance from her.

'I am sure you are acquainted with the Chopin *études*,' he said, leaning back in a comfortable chair, with a glass of cognac in his hand and a glint of the diabolical in his eye. 'They are too complicated for Gisela at present, and I feel in the mood for the E Major Etude. Do you know it, Miss Bell, and can you play it?'

Rosary had refused cognac and held instead a small cup of the rich dark Portuguese coffee. There was a long-tailed bird painted in lovely colours on the cup and she gave it her attention as she replied that she knew the music but she was sure she could not do it the justice the *senhor* would expect.

'I shall make allowances for any mistakes,' he drawled. 'I realize that the *études* are complex under their veil of beauty, but the mood is set for such music, with the lamps glimmering and the scents of the night stealing in from the gardens. Come, *senhorita*, you owe the invalid his whim.'

She looked at him, then, and wondered if his words held a double meaning. She owed him more than a

whim, for they both knew that she was partly responsible for that dark bruise concealed by the sweep of his
hair, for the strapping across his ribs and the pain he
still felt in his ankle. He smiled slightly as she looked
at him, and she glimpsed the tantalizing challenge in
his eyes.

'Do play for us,' urged Lola, with the assured gaiety
of a girl who could do no wrong in the eyes of the man
who sat near to her, so that the dark formality of his
evening suit was a foil to set off the rose brocade of her
long dress. Her glossy hair was looped back smoothly
from her brow, and she looked a madonna by lamplight, softly glowing and desirable.

'Yes, do give us a treat,' Dacio encouraged. 'I have
heard you teaching Gisela her scales and arpeggios,
but you have never yet played seriously for us. Are you
shy?' he added wickedly.

'No,' she said, but she was nervous in the presence of
Dom Duarte when he chose to play the spotlight of his
attention upon her. He did it mockingly (she could see
that) but to everyone else he appeared the quintes-
sence of courtesy. The master of the house, flattering
the tutor by requesting that she play for him a favourite piece of music. Rosary could feel everyone looking
at her. The hands of the *senhora* paused beneath the
lamp where she worked the silver hook into the
strands of crochet silk. Gisela stopped stroking the
tabby kitten which had been given to her by the lean
young gardener with the face of a boyish Byron.

Everyone seemed motionless, and then Dom Duarte
asked Dacio to open the piano for Miss Bell. With
resignation she arose from her chair and walked across
the salon, with its sheen of long curtains framing the
terrace, the dark gloss of the antique furniture, and
the carpet woven with gigantic flowers. Against the

93

panelled walls glowed watercolours as fine as silk, and baroque carved cabinets held books, and things of porcelain and silver. She arrived at the piano, an Empire grand of ivory white and gilding, with reclining ivory figures holding the candelabra. The top was opened and the candles had been lit by Dacio, and she felt his breath stir warm against the nape of her neck as he arranged the padded seat for her and she sat down.

'Don't be nervous,' he murmured. 'Even *he* cannot eat you.'

She cast a side-glance at the artist and suddenly she smiled. It was true. Dom Duarte was only a man, and she had played for Erick who was a conductor of music, and he had applauded her.

Dacio melted into the shadows and she was alone, isolated at the superb piano, with the candlelight sheening her hair, and etching in soft silver and shadow the slim lines of her figure, and the curve of her wrists as she laid her touch upon the keys and willed herself to forget the man who watched her with eyes that flickered with points of gold ... hawk's eyes, waiting narrowly to swoop on her faults and punish her for daring to be the only female on the island who didn't fall over her own feet in a rush to please him.

The *étude* he had asked for drifted from the tips of her fingers with all its haunting magic, and in the midst of it a nightingale awoke in the garden and began to sing. She was so thrilled that she forgot her audience and she played on and on, rippling into a scherzo, joining the iridescent notes of the bird with those of a nocturne, wandering without thought into the soul of a waltz. What brought her back to earth was the realization that she was playing a melody of her own. She broke off in the middle of it, and as if by magic the nightingale stopped singing, and someone laughed, breathlessly. Gisela came running to the piano, where she bent to hug Rosary. 'You were marvellous! Do go on—please!'

'No——' She was suddenly all nerves and her wrists were pounding with her pulse beats; she couldn't have played one more note tonight. 'I've done my party piece!'

She jumped to her feet and faced the others almost with defiance. 'I hope I didn't make too much of a fool of myself,' she said.

'A fool?' It was Dacio who stirred in the shadows, who almost groaned the words. 'That was beautiful.'

'It was delightful,' Lola broke in, but even as she smiled there seemed a flash of resentment in her eyes, as if she had been secretly hoping that the English girl would spoil the music and reveal herself as inept.

'It was spellbinding,' said Dacio, determined to have his say.

'Obrigado, Miss Bell,' said the man who had challenged her to play. 'I did not recognize that final piece, which you ended so abruptly. May I know the composer of it?'

'I—I forget, senhor.' She couldn't tell him that it was something of her own, half realized in the last few days, singing through her blood and flashing from her fingertips during that sweet-wild duet with the nightingale. 'It's probably a sentimental tune I picked up from a film, or a radio serial. A piece of airy nonsense that sticks in a girl's mind.'

'Perhaps,' he murmured, and his eyes flicked the wisps of hair that clung to her temples, and the soft heat of her skin. 'Take a seat and cool down, Miss Bell. We have enjoyed your music and you must be rewarded. Would you like a glass of wine?'

'No—thank you.' She shook her head and the swing of her hair fanned a light breeze against her flushed skin. 'I think I'll go out on the terrace, if you don't mind? Just to catch my breath.' She caught at the skirt of her blue-grey striped silk dress and brushed past his chair, hastening into the cool night air, out of sight of the room with its soft lamplight making a halo around that dark polished head. Was it possible that she was the faintest bit disappointed because he had not been the one to praise her playing; to say it was spellbinding ... that it had beauty? She rested against the stone parapet and she could smell the roses that clambered against the latticework of iron that scrolled the terrace. The nostalgic scent of the roses reminded her of home, so many miles away from this Portuguese palace on an island, with its people whose ways were so subtle they seemed to heighten one's sense of the dramatic.

The men here were not given to that robust laughter of the Englishman, and they smiled with a charming gravity that hinted of the mysterious. There shimmered under all exchange with a woman a hint of passion, and that *saudade* of theirs, that longing for the perfect romance.

Or the perfect woman!

She stood where the terrace branched away from the salon, and the darkness was softly broken by the glimmer of the stars. The air she breathed was an intoxicant, like wine, and it wasn't chill but softly warm, and her thoughts turned to the sea and swimming in the starlight. Her breath quickened and the longing to swim ran in sudden tumult along her veins.

Why not? If she went quietly, while the *senhor* and his guests still talked in the salon, there would be no one to see her, no one to ask questions, or to suggest that it was improper and the sort of thing a Portuguese girl wouldn't do. But first she must collect her swimsuit and her wrap, and to do so she must slip past the salon windows and enter the house through the drawing-room windows. She turned and was about to hasten back along the terrace when she was brought to a standstill by the lean figure of a man, his white tuxedo glimmering in the soft darkness.

'Dacio—what do you want?' She was impatient with him because she wanted to get away, to play truant in the sea all by herself.

'Aren't you pleased to see me?' He sounded rather hurt. 'I wanted to say again how much I enjoyed your music. It was a revelation.'

'A revelation of what?' she asked. 'Surely the grand-daughter of a famous music master should be able to play a few tunes on the piano?'

'Don't belittle your gift.' He advanced towards her and made her retreat to the parapet. 'Modesty can go too far, and though it might suit His Excellency to have you the self-effacing tutor, it doesn't suit your personality, or please my sense of beauty and art. You must know, Rosary, that you have a disturbing qual-ity. Even your name hints of a secret place where roses might grow, and where bells might softly ring.'

'You're kind to say so, Dacio, but if you were to see me in England you would think me quite ordinary. I seem unusual because I am the only English girl on this island, among so many raven-haired, dark-eyed *senhoritas*.'

'Rare would be a better word.' He stretched an arm and enclosed her within a niche of the terrace, among the roses and their night-drawn scent that was more sensuous than the scent of other flowers. It wasn't the beauty of the rose alone that inspired men to send them to the woman desired. The velvet petals held within them the magic power to stir the senses, and Rosary was aware of this as she looked into Dacio's dark eyes and saw their admiration.

'I—I was about to go to my room,' she said, then panic quickened in her as he came a littler nearer. 'Dacio, we can't be alone like this! The *senhora* doesn't approve, and she has threatened already to have me dismissed if I am seen flirting——'

'Are we flirting?' he murmured, and his eyes sparkled darkly in his handsome face. 'Are you enjoying it?'

'Dacio, do you want me to lose my job?' she tried to push away his arm, but it was solid, well-muscled, the arm of an artist who was accustomed to holding a brush and palette for hours at a stretch. He had the diabolical patience of the artist, as well, and she knew herself trapped by him. There was only one way to get him and herself off this terrace before they were seen and their position was misconstrued as a lover-like one.

'To tell you the truth,' she said, 'I was going to fetch my bathing things. The night is so warm that I want to go swimming.'

'Are you inviting me to go with you?' he asked, a note of pleasure running in his voice. 'I should be delighted! As a Latin male I have never enjoyed swimming at night with a girl.'

'What about swimming trunks?' She was committed now, and besides he looked so boyishly pleased, and she could well believe that he had never indulged in the adventure of a late night swim with a Portuguese girl; too many family restrictions were imposed to allow of it. Also, the very idea of defying Dom Duarte appealed to Rosary ... so long as it was done in secret and he didn't find out.

98

'We must be quiet about it, Dacio,' she said. 'I have to slip into the house for my swimming things, and you must fetch yours. I suggest that we meet in about fifteen minutes on that narrow path that leads down to the *palacete* beach.'

'I shall be waiting!' He quickly took her hand and brushed it with his lips, and for a moment she wondered if she was being altogether wise in going with him to the beach, where they would be alone.

'You will behave yourself?' she demanded. 'I mean to swim, not to indulge in a—a flirtation.'

'You are afraid I shall make love to you?' he said, half smiling.

'I'm not afraid, but I shall be annoyed. It will spoil our friendship, Dacio, for I shan't speak to you again.'

'I believe,' he murmured, 'that the British are more prim than the Portuguese.'

'We have our codes,' she agreed. 'A friendship and a love affair are very different things.'

'And you want my friendship, eh?'

'Yes, I need a friend. See you in a while, *amigo*.'

'*Até a vista, amiga*.'

She hoped he meant it when he called her *amiga*, and she smiled as she sped swiftly and silently along the terrace.

She made it from the palace without being detected and they met on the path that was narrow and steep in the darkness. Hand in hand, and stifling their laughter, they made it to the beach, where the bathing *caseta* was situated, fitted out with a couple of changing cubicles, a lounger of cane with a matching table, and a cabinet in which there were glasses and bottles of orange and lemon squash to quench the thirst after a swim in the sea.

Dacio must have had his trunks on under his slacks, for he was ready and waiting when Rosary came out of the *caseta*.

'Such a night!' he said, and his head was thrown back in a sort of pagan worship of the stars that were so brilliant above the sea that the beach was lit to a soft shimmer by their light. There were clusters of palm trees near the water, their fronds spread gracefully to catch the starlight. The air was tangy with island spices and foliage which had been sun-drenched all day.

'Race you!' she said, and she sped past him down the beach to the creaming surf, gasping with delight as the water splashed high about her legs. She struck out with a laugh as he dived in behind her, and she heard him call out to her that she had forgotten to wear a cap.

'I never do,' she said, for the water streaming through her hair gave her a lovely free feeling.

'You are a naiad.' He was alongside her and they swam in unison through the dark sapphire sea. 'You are glad I am with you?'

'Yes—it's lovely swimming at night, isn't it? More primeval than in daylight.'

'Have you ever said a thing like that to any other man?' he asked, and she saw the glint of his teeth as he turned his head to her, and she felt all around them the illimitable loneliness of the sea. They were two specks in that ocean, and yet they were far more. They were a girl and a man, and she had not yet been awakened to all it meant to be a part of the plan that made life as eternal as the sea. Curiosity stirred and she wondered about desire. She knew the facts, but the feelings had so far eluded her.

Exhausted at last, they turned and swam back to the

shore, and she felt the sea ripples curling about her toes, and the water streaming from her hair as they walked across the velvety sand and flung themselves down with their backs to the palm trees. She knew he was watching her as she wrung the water from her hair and tossed the long damp tail over her shoulder. She knew that her minutest action was of interest to him because he had known only Portuguese girls and they didn't behave with such a lack of modesty in front of a man. They were always superbly groomed, almost sedate, and their conversation was aimed to flatter rather than to provoke.

Shades of the harem lingered in the Latin girl, and more than a hint of the Moor lingered in the men!

'Do you suppose your sister will guess that we're together?' she asked. 'You are usually there to take her home.'

'His Excellency will perform that duty, and I am certain he will enjoy it. You must have noticed that when he looks at Lola he is less of the hawk and more of the dove.'

'Your sister is lovely, Dacio. Have you ever painted her? She's so vivid that she makes me feel like a water-colour.'

'You?' he laughed, and played his toes against her toes. 'If you knew anything about painting you would know that the vivid colours are more tiring to the eye than cool colours. Do you know that under the stars, in their reflection from the sea, your skin is as mysterious as the covering of a water-bud. You are the girl I should like to paint dressed in a slip of silk from your bare shoulders to your knees.'

'Like a harem slave?' she quipped, but her fingers dug deep in the sand with the realization that if Lola guessed they were together she might mention it to

Dom Duarte. She experienced a feeling of consternation mixed with defiance. The chemistry of these Latins made the most innocent action seem meaningful, as if design and not loneliness had brought about this starlight swim with Dacio.

As if Dacio guessed the trend of her thoughts, he leaned a little forward and said teasingly: 'What is your opinion of the man who rules Vozes do Mar? Do you consider him a tyrant who likes women to be demure and obedient?'

'I think he finds it a bit infuriating that I am not in the habit of bending the knee to any man, not even a *duque* with a pedigree of great distinction and power to go with it. I don't tremble at his wrath or blush all over at his smile. I,'- she filtered sand through her fingers and made a little pyramid of it, 'I don't think he likes me very much, but he knows Gisela does like me, and that is the important thing.'

'How can you be so sure that you aren't liked by him?' Dacio studied her face, washed clean and pure by the sea, with little hollows under her cheekbones, and eyes too candid to hold the secrets of a sophisticate.

'A girl can always sense these things,' she replied.

'Then your senses must have told you that I—like you.' He scattered the pyramid she had made and smiled directly into her eyes. 'On the other hand it isn't so easy to tell whether I am liked by you. The English girl is direct in some matters, but strangely reserved when it comes to her feelings. It is, indeed, a paradox that our Latin girls should be bodily guarded and yet be less shy of letting their eyes reveal their emotions.'

'Latin eyes are very expressive,' she said. 'You said yourself, Dacio, that the hawk's eyes of the *senhor duque* are more dove-like when he looks at Lola.'

'Do you envy the favour she finds in the *senhor*'s eyes?' he asked, teasingly.

'I'm not the envious sort, thank heaven. I was taught by my grandfather to count my blessings, which may sound old-fashioned, but it's something I believe in. A sound body and mind are prizes beyond a pretty face.'

'A very Puritan outlook, Rosary, but right now you look far more of a naiad.' Dacio's look travelled from her tousled hair to her bare shoulders, and down her slender body to her bare and sandy feet. 'You are not cold? If so I will fetch your wrap.'

'No—in any case we must go home soon. It must be quite late.'

'Stay a little longer, until the *senhor* has seen Lola to the door of the villa.'

'Doesn't he enter for a nightcap?'

'No—a man cannot do that if a girl's guardian is absent, and he is not yet her official *novio*. Our rules of courtship are quite strict, and a girl's reputation can be ruined if she allows a man to break those rules.'

'Then you and I must have broken a dozen in the past hour,' Rosary laughed. 'What a good thing I am not a Latin girl. If we were seen my reputation would be in shreds, alone with you like this, in my bathing suit.'

'You might be so compromised,' he said deliberately, 'that I would be obliged to marry you without delay.'

'How awful for you, Dacio!' Her eyes danced in the starlight.

'*Deus*, it would be thrilling if you and I were forced to marry by the edict of Dom Duarte! Shall we allow ourselves to be discovered?

'No!' She leapt to her feet as if stung, gave him a startled look, and then fled to the *caseta*. She knew he was giving chase even though she couldn't hear him on the soft sand, and she ran breathless into the little beach house and slammed the door in his face. Lord, that was all she needed, to be compromised into marriage ... forced into it by the feudal laws still prevalent on this island. She snatched her wrap and quickly put it on, belting it tightly about her waist. She slipped into her sandals, regardless of the sand grains between her toes, and parcelled her dress and underclothes under her arm. Then she hastened out of the back door of the *caseta* and ran all the way up the path to the grounds of the *palacete*. Out of breath and with a stitch in her side she hurried through the gardens, where statues lurked like pale figures, and trails of leaf and flower brushed her face like ghostly fingers.

When she reached a side entrance that led into the hall by way of an arched corridor she had to pause to catch her breath. Night enshrouded the palace and overhung its turrets. From here no lights could be seen and she breathed a sigh of relief. She could slip in unobserved and be safe in her room within three or four minutes. Silently, feeling the sand grating against the soles of her feet, she made her way along the corridor and tried the door to the hall. Her heart slumped, for the handle turned back and forth with the impotence of a handle attached to a bolted door.

She might have guessed that at this late hour the various doors leading into the *palacete*, with its various treasures, would be bolted against possible intruders. She stood biting her lip. If she banged on the door and made herself heard by one of the servants, the incident would be bound to be repeated to the *senhora*, who liked to know all that went on in and around the precincts of the Governor's residence. She would demand to know why Rosary came to be locked out, and the end result would be an argument. A refusal on Rosary's part to be treated like an adolescent who must account for her every movement.

Rather than face the inevitable inquisition Rosary decided to return to the *caseta*. Dacio would by now have left, and she would sleep there and pretend in the morning to have gone out for an early swim. It was known that she sometimes did this, and she would avoid having to explain how she came to be locked out ... like a little cat who had been out on the tiles!

Upon arriving back at the beach house, after a stumble on the dark path which grazed her arm, she found the place deserted and quickly entered, closing and bolting the door behind her. She switched on the light and after securing the back door she felt more at ease. She also felt rather hungry and found in the drinks cabinet a small barrel of biscuits, which she dipped into as she set about making the lounger as comfortable as she could. There were cushions and a rug, and after she had dressed she felt warmer. She tried not to think of the dark beach all around the *caseta*, but when she turned out the light and sought her makeshift bed, she could hear the rustling of the surf, and the whispering sound made by the fronds of the palm trees as a breeze blew in over the water.

She snuggled down under the rug and her wrap, and had to smile at her own British craziness. If she had gone sedately to her room after leaving the salon, and if she had not impulsively asked Dacio to go swimming with her, she would at this moment be tucked up cosily in her bed at the palace. Safe under its turreted roof and not alone like this, with strange night sounds whispering at the doors and windows.

She felt the throb of her bruised arm as drowsiness

crept over her. Something in the air of this island had an odd effect on a sensible career girl, and never before had she played a Chopin *étude* with such a rare understanding of the music.

As the tree-frogs croaked in unison with the rippling surf, she drifted off to sleep.

CHAPTER SIX

SUN and ocean splashed the beach as Rosary came out of the *caseta* and stretched herself after a somewhat restless night on the lounger. She took deep lungfuls of the fresh morning air, and was uncertain of the time because she had left her wristwatch in her bedroom last night, when she had collected her swimsuit. The surf flung itself high up the sands, and the sun was swinging in an arc across the beach, like a golden blade.

It would be about six o'clock, she decided, which would give her ample time to stroll back to the *palacete* with all the casualness of the early riser who had gone for a swim and was returning with hunger for the coffee and rolls which the chef would be preparing. The day always began quite early at the residence, with the arrival of the *senhor's* secretary at eight o'clock, and the *senhora's* supervision of the cleaning, bed-making, dusting and cooking. For each day there was a different menu, and everything had to run smoothly in order to cope with the people who had appointments to see Dom Duarte.

Rosary made for the path which snaked upwards among the trees, and she glanced at her arm and saw that it was now darkly bruised ... a memento of an evening which would have been totally without significance had it occurred back home in Sussex!

She made her way around a tree that was bursting with flower, and one of the great passion-blooms swung against her cheek and spattered dew in her eyes. She paused to brush away the moisture and when she fully opened her eyes again someone was standing on the path ahead of her, facing her, motionless in white trousers and a black polo shirt, leaning slightly on a black stick.

She stood shocked, unmoving, for he was the person she had hoped above all to avoid, and already he was searching her with sharp eyes that in the morning light were like ebony dipped in ice. Her heart beat quickly and her knees felt weak. She had to speak, and she had to sound as casual as possible.

'*Bom dia, senhor*. The water's grand this morning. You ought to try it.'

'You are saying you have been swimming, Miss Bell?'

'Yes,' she replied, even as a tiny warning bell rang in her brain, and he regarded her with eyes that accused even as they ran over her, from her wicker sandals to her crumpled dress, upwards to her hair. In an instant her heart thumped and each nerve in her body seemed to be a separate alarm signal. Her hair wasn't wet, or even damp. It was tousled and uncombed, and she knew from the flare to his nostrils that he wouldn't believe her if she said she had worn a cap. He *knew* she had not been swimming this morning.

'Why do you bother to lie to me?' he asked coldly, and as he spoke he came towards her, limping slightly, and then suddenly he raised his stick and slashed the head off a passion-flower. There was a rain of petals and dew, and Rosary winced, as if he had struck her. His eyes glinted as they followed the flight of her hand to her mouth, holding back a cry. When he stood over her she could feel the anger vibrating in him. Such anger made her afraid, for it told her that he knew about last night.

She wanted instantly to rush away, to be among

108

other people, so he would be forced to control his temper. She could pass him on the path if she moved quickly enough ... but even as she moved he caught her by the arm with his free hand and half swung her against the tree that was heavy with its burden of passion-flowers.

That little cry of fear escaped her and she looked at him with the shaken look of a girl who had never before in her life been treated so savagely. Her hair had flung itself across her face, and the bark of the tree acted like barbs that clung to the thin material of her dress. Her great brown eyes impored mercy of a stern face and cold eyes.

'Last night,' he said grimly, 'Gisela was stricken with one of her nightmares and I heard her cry out and I went to her. She was upset and she wanted your company, so I went to your room to fetch you. You were not there, Miss Bell. Your bed was undisturbed and had not been slept in. I at once looked for you, and when it became apparent that you were not to be found at the *palacete*, I telephoned Senhorita Cortez to ask if you were at the villa. She said no, but she thought you might be in the company of her brother.'

At his mention of Dacio, and the way he looked at her untidy hair and her crumpled dress, not to mention the bruise that his fingers had touched when he had flung her against the tree, made a scorching flush run all over her body. It left a flare across her cheekbones and sparks in her eyes.

'You have been out all night!' he accused.

'And what do you imagine I've been doing, Dom Duarte? Roaming the tiles like some immoral little cat?' The words would not be controlled and her indignation was such that she could have hit him, lashed out like a little cat at his scornful mask of a face. How dared he judge her, and accuse without justification? She hated him for looking at her as if she offended him.

'I demand to know what you have been doing!' Suddenly his hand was gripping her shoulder and his lean fingers were grinding the fine bones beneath her skin that bruised easily.

'You're hurting me!' she spat at him, but when she tried to twist away the pain intensified, and his look was that of an inquisitor who would torture the truth out of her.

'You have been in the company of Cortez, haven't you?'

'And what if I have?' she said defiantly. 'What are you going to do about it, *senhor*? Dismiss me from your precious island ... expel me like a criminal because I have a perfectly normal desire for a little freedom when I am not tutoring Gisela? Is it then a crime under Portuguese law for a girl to take a swim at night?'

'So it was last night that you went swimming?'

'How clever of you to guess, Dom Duarte!'

'You are an impertinent and foolish young woman who deserves to be spanked!' The flare of his chiselled nostrils told her the extent of his fury, and the bite of his fingers warned of the Latin violence that could master even him, the Governor of the island who should at all times be in control of his passions. 'You will tell me how you spent the remainder of the night ... I demand to know!'

'Your demands are insatiable,' she retorted. 'I must be discreet, demure and deferential at all times. I am English and free, but I must pretend to be a Latin girl, chained by the wrist to male authority. I am over twenty, yet I am treated as if I'm an irresponsible child!'

'And I suppose by Cortez you are treated as a woman of the world?'

'Are you curious, *senhor*, or are you collecting evidence that will prove me guilty of fast behaviour?'

'I am warning you, *senhorita*, that if you persist in answering my questions with impudence, I shall treat you as you appear to want to be treated.'

'And how is that, *senhor*?'

He stared down into her eyes and she saw again those tiny flickers of tawny fire. 'If you think, Miss Bell, that it is safe to provoke me, then you are very much mistaken. If you would like a demonstration of how unsafe it is, then just persist for five minutes more in acting the liberated female returning from a night of free love.'

'It is you,' she cried, '*you* who choose to think I spent last night in Dacio's arms!'

'Only because I am goaded into it. My first concern is that you might have been hurt ...'

'Do you really expect me to believe that?' She gave a laugh, which turned to a cry as he gripped her arm and studied the bruise that was dark against the paleness of her skin.

'You did not have this when you played the piano last night, so it must have been inflicted after you left the salon and disappeared for hours on end.'

'If you are thinking Dacio did it, then you are mistaken. I—I fell over on the path to the beach and knocked my arm against a tree. It was dark ...'

'You were running away from the young man?'

'No – I found I was locked out of the *palacete*, so I came back to the beach and spent the night in the *caseta*. And I spent it *alone*, Dom Duarte.'

'I know,' he said coolly.

'What? You put me through this inquisition and now you tell me that all along you knew I was alone?'

'Naturally. But there comes a time, Miss Bell, when headstrong young women need to be given a dose of medicine which might help to cure them of rash behaviour. You flounced out of the salon last night with all the pet of a *diva* who has not been praised as highly as she believes she should be. You play quite beautifully, Miss Bell, but even in that you are swayed by impulse and emotion. You won't be mastered by the dictates of the music ... or by those of a man, will you?'

In all fairness he was right about her playing, and he was overwhelmingly correct when he said that she wouldn't bow down to the dictates of a man at any cost. She tossed her head. 'How did you know I was alone at the beach house?'

'I sent two of the menservants to search for you, and again I telephoned the Cortez villa. This time Cortez himself answered my call, and Alfredo found the *caseta* locked and the marks of small sandals leading through the sand to the door. He carried a torch, of course. He hasn't eyes that see in the dark, and when he reported back to me I advised that you be left alone to sleep until the morning.'

'And when morning came you came looking for me in order to lecture me?'

'Don't you think you deserve a lecture? I hired you to be Gisela's tutor and companion. When she needed you last night you were not available. It is unfair to charm someone into becoming dependent upon you, *senhorita*——'

'I am not a female Svengali,' she broke in. 'How was I to know that Gisela would have a nightmare? I didn't even know that she was subject to them.'

112

'She has been so since her mother died.' He paused, and his fingers slid away from her shoulder, and his eyes left her face to brood upon the shimmer of the sea below the path on which they stood. The scent of the passion-flowers was distilled as the sun broke through the trees and dried the dew on the clustering petals.

'I think,' he went on, 'that last night her nightmare was triggered off by my own recent accident. Gisela has not your independent spirit, Miss Bell. She needs to be secure in the affections of those she loves. Be always within call another time, if you wish to keep your position as tutor to the child.'

'I am not to be dismissed, then, for my breach of conduct?'

'It cannot really be helped,' he shrugged, 'that you respond to the impulses of your British blood and your sense of adventure. I, too, have felt the call of the sea on a starlit night ... but I am curious as to how you persuaded the young Cortez to return to the villa ... like a good boy?'

Such was her relief at the sudden lessening of tension between them that she relaxed against the tree and as she remembered how she had bolted from Dacio she broke into a smile. 'He said if we were caught alone, *senhor*, you might insist that I marry him. Knowing how strict you Portuguese can be when it comes to the protocol between the sexes I decided that I didn't wish to be married against my will.'

'Such a procedure would hardly suit the young man in England, eh?' Dom Duarte leaned on his stick and the look he gave her was a sardonic one. 'Whoever this young man is he wasn't quite wise to let you out of his sight. He could not have known that Vozes do Mar has on certain people the effect of a full glass of *vinho verde*, which can go to a young head like champagne.'

'Yes ... I mean there is magic here. A lost-in-time atmosphere.' She spoke almost with shyness, for it seemed that only in a temper had they really talked, and it felt strange and confusing to allow him into her thoughts. 'It's hard to believe that beyond the sea and the mountains there is a world in which people fight with weapons, and trample carelessly on all the ideals of the saints and the reformers. I think if I were Portuguese I should never want to leave this island.'

'But you are not Portuguese.' His eyes flicked her hair, the fair strands of it tousled about her triangular face that without being beautiful had a charm of its very own. A dash of spirit about the mouth and chin, shading to a fey quality when it reached her cheek-bones and her large eyes with their oblique corners. 'You are a girl without artifice, Miss Bell. You say what you think, and this is a quality which we Latins find a little disconcerting.'

'You prefer to wrap everything in silk ... or steel,' she dared to say.

'That is the Saracen in our blood,' he agreed, and in his eyes there lurked a smile, a curious smouldering together of those tawny lights.

'And the Saracen in you likes women to be submissive to your wishes, *senhor*.'

'It makes life a little smoother for a man to bear, *senhorita*.'

'But to be entirely placable is to be entirely boring,' she retorted. 'And you don't quite convince me that you don't enjoy an argument with a woman.'

'We call it a duel of words,' he slightly mocked, as if her reference to herself as a woman amused him deeply. Yet she was but a year or so younger than Lola, and he seemed to take seriously the remarks and feelings of the Latin girl. It could even be that he was planning to make Lola Cortez his second wife, for no man so vital as this one could stay solitary for ever; nor could he remain always in a state of penance. Rosary bit her lip, for the one and only thing she regretted saying to him was that he should never forgive himself for the words which had helped to kill his wife.

Life was complicated ... she had never known how deeply so until she had come to live among these people who lived a great deal of the time on their emotions.

'I—I should be getting back to the palace,' she said. 'Gisela may require me——'

'She will ask where you were last night. You will of course tell her the truth.'

'Yes, *senhor*. But what of the *senhora*? She will think——'

'She will be told that Alfredo and I found you alone and asleep at the *caseta*.'

Rosary stared at him. 'You said Alfredo found me——'

'Naturally I was with him.' Dom Duarte's face was quite unreadable; that mask of bronze that forbade questions. 'I have a second key to the beach house and the door was unlocked so that I might make sure you were all right. You were sleeping, but the rug had fallen to the floor. I covered you up, and then I left, locking the door again. I have while you are in my employ a responsibility towards you.'

'I suppose you have.' She flushed slightly. 'I seem to be causing you far more trouble than a Portuguese tutor would. I—I suppose I ought to say I'm sorry, but in England an employer wouldn't be so concerned about a straying tutor.'

'That is one of the effects of female liberation in your country, Miss Bell.' He gave her a sardonic bow

115

to emphasize his words. 'But as a Latin I don't yet regard a girl of twenty as my equal in wisdom ... ah, your eyes flash at me a look which says I have not always been wise. This is true, and if I can make mistakes how many more can a mere girl make! And now shall we go and have breakfast? You must be feeling hungry.'

'I am,' she agreed, and as she fell into step beside him she was aware of his height. He was very much taller than Dacio, and the other men she had seen about the island, and this intensified his air of authority. Perhaps long ago the blood of some captured Anglo-Saxon girl had mingled with that of the Saracen ancestor from whom sprang the Montqueiros, passing down the centuries the look he had of a proud dark hawk.

They came to the palace gardens and walked among the high and scented camellia hedges, the bushes of geranium and banks of deep-toned azalea. They crossed the *patio* tiled with the raised designs that caught the sunlight and glittered with oriental beauty. Above were the balconies that enclosed the rooms in intricately twisted iron.

Rosary's eyes were as startled as her heart ... why had she never noticed before these subtle hints of the east in tilework and iron, and the incense of camphor-trees and weeping peppers? Small birds of paradise flew about in the trees and winged about the hanging lamps in the cloistered archways. Suddenly she felt so out of place in her crumpled dress and uncombed hair that she couldn't wait to get under the shower in her private bathroom and wash from her skin and hair the sand grains that still clung to her. No wonder this man of cultured taste had looked at her with such offended eyes.

'I must go and get changed before I eat breakfast,' she said, and she stared at a mass of moon-daisies and avoided his gaze. 'If you had decided to send me away this time, *senhor*, then I shouldn't have been surprised. I did behave impetuously——'

'Quite! And be assured that there are times when I feel I should dismiss you. Look at me when I speak to you!'

She reluctantly did so, but her mouth rebelled against the reproof in his voice. She pushed from her eyes a strand of her truant hair and a ray of sunshine caught the action. 'You are a disturbing influence, Miss Bell. A young catalyst, I think, rather than a little cat. Now go into the house and have your breakfast.'

She fled, hastening through the door that last night had been locked against her. She ran lightly across the hall and up the stairs, glad that she reached her rooms without being seen. There with an acute sense of relief she stripped off her slept-in clothes and was soon under the shower and lathering herself with almond oil soap. Now, with the warm refreshing water cascading through her hair and down over her body, she could reflect on her talk with Dom Duarte, and the amazing fact he had revealed without direct intention.

Last night he had led the search for her, and he had found her sleeping in the *caseta*. The rug had fallen from her, he had said, and he had covered her up.

She blinked the water from her eyes, stepped out of the shower and rubbed herself down with one of the huge soft towels that were always folded over the warming bar. Against his will he had revealed another small facet of his complex personality. He could be concerned for even a tutor, and he could be kind ... but he could also demonstrate that a steely thread of the master ran through him. A little shiver ran through Rosary as she recalled his slashing of the passion-flower with his stick.

In the circumstances she was lucky not to have been dismissed from her job, for he had rooted out without any effort the cause of her rebellious behaviour. She had played really well last night, but all he had said was, *'Obrigado.'* As cool and polite as if she had recited *An Ode to a Primrose*! instead of playing the Chopin *études* which involved technical complexities only a music student could be aware of; she had seen young male musicians go white with vexation at not being able to master some of those subtle, beautiful traps laid by the master of the piano, Chopin himself.

Had it annoyed the *senhor* that she should end her recital with a piece of music invented by herself? He had known, of course, and that was why he had asked her in such smooth tones to name the composer.

As Rosary buckled the slim belt of her short doeskin skirt, and pulled her soft green shirt into place, she heard her bedroom door open and when she turned to look Gisela was standing there, rather pale and unsmiling.

'Hullo, my dear. I'm ravenous for breakfast and shan't be more than another minute.' Rosary felt almost a guilty quickening of her nerves as she buckled her still damp hair at the nape of her neck, and decided not to apply lipstick but to look the scrubbed and shining penitent at the breakfast table. 'Isn't it a lovely morning, Gisela?'

'Where were you last night?' the girl demanded, leaning back sulkily against the door. 'I wanted you and you couldn't be found.'

'I went for a swim and like an idiot I got locked out.' Rosary spoke nonchalantly, for she wasn't going to be 'tried' a second time for what, after all, had been only a minor crime. Much as she tried, she couldn't react like a Latin and these people must come to terms with the fact that for twenty odd years she had been behaving like an English girl and only for a few weeks had she been here, among people whose customs and restrictions were new and strange to her.

'You were with Dacio,' Gisela accused, and in that moment her likeness to her father flashed like lightning across her face, but her eyes were stormier, her temper less controlled. 'I suppose you like him better than you like me because he's a man! I suppose you wanted him to make love to you!'

'Nothing of the kind, Gisela!' Rosary was sparked to anger herself. 'I seem for ever accused of being a flirt by members of this household. I begin to think that I should put my hair up in a bun and wear a pair of big horn-rimmed spectacles, not to mention a sack of a dress!'

'You'd still be too pretty not to be noticed,' Gisela muttered, and then suddenly she ran to Rosary and threw her arms around her, almost squeezing her breathless. 'I'm frightened of losing you, that is why I am mean this morning. I—I know that as one grows up, young men do become important, and I shall try not to mind too much if you care for Dacio. He is handsome——'

'Gisela, I am not in the least in love with Dacio Cortez.' Rosary smiled and stroked her pupil's dark hair. 'We're friends, that's all. It really is possible for a young woman to be friends with a man, even though you Latins disbelieve it and attribute only romantic reasons for a girl's enjoyment of a man's company. I had friends among the students I trained with and found it stimulating to argue with the male of the species. I also found that I was cleverer in some ways

119

than the lordly creatures, and I certainly never bothered to flatter any of them, unless I admired this one or that for his musical talent. Now, before I buckle at the knees for the want of nourishment, let us go down and eat breakfast!'

Friends again, they sped laughing along the gallery and down the stairs, where they were brought up short by the appearance of Dom Duarte from his study. He was dressed impeccably in grey, a sure sign that he was going out on business.

'You look brighter this morning, *pequena*,' he said to his daughter. 'Good morning, Miss Bell.' His smile was bland and courteous, and showed not a sign of their recent battle of words ending in a truce. 'I am going into town and if the two of you will quickly eat breakfast I will take you both with me and we can lunch – after I have attended to a certain matter—at a restaurant. After all, it is Saturday and life should not be all lessons.'

Gisela stared at her father. 'Do you mean it, *senhor*?' she asked, pleased and amazed, and a little flushed beneath the smooth olive of her complexion.

'Have you ever known me, Gisela, to say anything I did not mean?' The look he gave his daughter was teasing. 'A small outing to make up for the nightmare last night.'

Gisela glanced eagerly at Rosary. 'You want to go?'

'Well——' Rosary was a trifle uncertain and her eyes met the *senhor's* as if seeking his assurance that she was wanted. 'It would be nice, but I don't want to be in the way——'

'Miss Bell, I did mention that I would take both of you to town,' he said, looking suave. 'We will choose an open-air restaurant so that you won't need to dress with more formality. I shall be waiting in the car for you both.'

He limped away in the direction of the courtyard, and Gisela caught like a happy child at Rosary's arm. 'Let us quickly eat! He doesn't like to be kept waiting too long and we don't want him to go without us, do we?'

'No,' said Rosary, but as she sat down to hot rolls and jam and creamy coffee she had the sure feeling that having shown her the stern side of his personality Dom Duarte was now going to prove how disarming he could be. The prospect was daunting, for she didn't doubt that his charm was matched by his autocracy.

'I hope this skirt and blouse will do for a run into town?' she said to Gisela, when they had taken the edge off their hunger.

'You look nice, and very English.' Gisela wiped jam from her lips and jumped to her feet. 'Are you ready?'

'Yes—I'm just finishing my coffee, but if we're going where there are shops I must go upstairs for my bag.'

'Then do be quick! I will go and sit in the car with my father.' Gisela dashed off as if she expected to have this unexpected treat snatched from her. Rosary went upstairs to her room, where she combed her hair into a chignon and applied a little make-up. She wanted to look as cool and poised as possible, and as she sprayed on a little of her Tweed perfume, she prayed that she wouldn't say or do something which would rekindle that spark of discord which seemed to smoulder between herself and the *senhor duque*. It was something she had never encountered before ... this chemical reaction of her spirit in opposition to a man's.

Arriving in the courtyard she found the chauffeur waiting beside the grey limousine, with Gisela and her father seated together on the wide back seat.

'Please to join us, Miss Bell.' The *senhor*'s gaze

121

flicked her hair and her softly reddened mouth as she stood there by the door which the chauffeur held open; she knew that something glimmered deep in his eyes as she stepped inside and felt the deep carpet underfoot and the plushy softness of the wine-coloured upholstery. Never in her life had she travelled in such a handsome car, which seemed to glide on the air itself as they sped along the road which bordered the *palacete*. The morning was filled with sunlight and the sound of birds, and for a mile or more the car ran beside the boundary wall of the residence before branching on to the public highway.

'I don't believe you have yet seen a lot of our township, Miss Bell.' Dom Duarte spoke with a smile of such charming courtesy that Rosary was left speechless for a moment or two. Was this really the same man who had thrown her against a tree and spoken so bitingly to her only a couple of hours ago? It was really unfair of him to be able to switch so adroitly to courtesy while she was still smarting from his attack, and feeling rather bruised where his fingers had gripped her, under the green silk of her shirt that made her skin seem so white in comparison to his and Gisela's.

Gisela wore a lemon-coloured shirtwaister that contrasted brightly with the soft olive of her skin. Her eyes were sparkling and she looked really pretty.

All of a sudden Rosary relaxed. She knew that the *senhor* thought her an infuriating young woman with a will of her own, and somehow the knowledge added zest to this outing. She would pay him back by being so demure that he in his turn would be disarmed, and to start the ball rolling she gave him a smile that Cibby always called her melting one. It was a smile which started in her eyes and spread slowly to her mouth, so that it took on the likeness of a slowly opening flower.

'I am wondering, *senhor,* if it will be possible for you to show us the historic houses and buildings of the island's township. I am sure some of them must be many years old and adorned with those colourful tiles such as are used in Portugal itself. They depict legends and the voyages of your Portuguese explorers, don't they?'

He half quirked an eyebrow at her request and gave her what she termed to herself 'an old-fashioned look'. 'After I have completed my business it should be possible for the three of us to take a tour of the antique houses left intact over the years,' he said. 'Are you becoming interested in the history of our island, *senhorita?*'

'How can I help it, *senhor?* I am sure one of your own ancestors must have been responsible for discovering Vozes do Mar ... of even naming it, perhaps.'

'Have you been studying our family records and bound letters in the library?' he asked.

'No, *senhor,* but I have the feeling your family has its roots deeply embedded in the history of the island, and firmly bound up in its future.'

'None of us can be certain of the future,' he said, 'but it is a fact that a Montqueiro was the discoverer of the island and its first Governor. As he listened to the sound of the sea from the deck of his caravel, as the water rippled to and fro against the shore, he seemed to hear it whispering and in his log book that very night he wrote that the new acquisition of Portugal should be named Voices of the Sea.'

'A romantic notion, *senhor.*'

'Yes, *senhorita,*' he agreed, half mockingly. 'We are a people in whose soul dwells the illusion of happiness, heard like a whisper in water and never fully grasped.'

'Aren't you happy?' Gisela caught at his hand and pressed it to her cheek, and with a little laugh he turned the palm and kissed it.

'I speak in the abstract, little one. The very young, like yourself, can grasp at a joyful hour as if it were tangible. I am afraid adults have to ask the reason why this moment they are glad, the next moment a little sad.'

'I could not bear it when you had your accident.' Gisela looked at him as if for ever she would absorb his face into her memory. At nine years old she had learned that loved ones were mortal, and she clung to his hand as her eyes clung to his features. 'I was so afraid ... one of the nuns at the school used to say that the departed call the living to them!'

'It is over, Gisela!' He spoke firmly. 'The accident was entirely my own fault, and we have Miss Bell to thank for risking the flames on my behalf.'

Abruptly he looked at Rosary, and though his eyes were inscrutable he was smiling slightly. 'I had not forgotten that you came to my aid.'

'I—I'm glad your injuries were not more serious, *senhor*.'

'I'm rather glad of that myself, *senhorita*,' he said drily.

CHAPTER SEVEN

THEY entered the old *palacio* of administration, now used as a museum, by a picturesque gateway wrought into the many intricate patterns employed by Moorish craftsmen. Long ago the walls would have been pure white, but now they were heavily patched with lichen and sprawling vines, and bent in almost a bow of welcome was a catalpa tree—the tree of heaven—casting shade as they passed beneath its branches.

There were no other visitors but themselves and it seemed to Rosary that they were entering a place half haunted, lost in the past, for the inner patio was dark green with creepers and the fountain that was like a miniature minaret no longer played its liquid music, and its tilework gleamed with a certain malevolency through the mosses that cloaked it. There was a *chafariz* attached to the wall, used long ago for filling the household pots, a gem of antiquity, which awakened in the ready mind of Rosary a picture of gazelle-eyed girls tripping there in their bare feet, veiled to the eyes, to drink from its spout.

They entered the hall of the *palacio* through a doorway chiselled in a smooth oval out of the stone, above which perched a black raven, a pet of the museum-keeper perhaps, which gave a croak but otherwise did not stir, watching them intently as they studied the relics and treasures from another time, the Saracen armour that was fearful in itself, the costumes and jewellery of Portuguese nobles, the beautiful hand-made dolls and the fans that had flattered the Latin language of the eyes. There were gemmed weapons and exquisite scent bottles, and the two girls hung over them with the enthralled feminine worship of lovely things that had been handled long ago by lovely women, living half-captive lives.

Their feet echoed across the tiles of the floor, an arabesque of patterns that glowed like the old lost colours of an eastern carpet. From the ceiling hung lamps enclosed in delightful cages of wrought iron, studded with gleaming stones that would have shafted a myriad of jewel colours down upon the faces of the women and men who had gathered here in another time, clad in velvet and brocade.

The walls were panelled in *azulejos* that depicted the colour and spectacle of *festa,* both pagan and religious. The fun of grape-treading, and the full-sailed ships in which the Portuguese captains had sailed on their voyages of discovery.

The tile pictures, mainly in gold and indigo blue, were so detailed, so full of story, that Rosary could have spent the entire day just wandering around and absorbing the history and strange charm of this place.

Suddenly the raven croaked loudly and she turned with a quick smile to eye the bird. 'The raven of St. Vincent,' she said, and felt Dom Duarte quirk an eye at her, as if surprised that she knew a little Portuguese history.

' "*And his eyes have all the seeming of a demon's that is dreaming,*" ' she quoted the words, still looking at the bird of dark plumage, still looked upon by the man whose own darkness was so intensified by the grey smooth suiting that he wore. ' "*Tell me what thy lordly name is on the night's Plutonian shore!*" '

'He is an apt guardian, eh, of a place such as this where every "*silken sad uncertain rustling of each purple curtain*" thrills "*with fantastic terrors never felt before!*" The *senhor* quoted the lines in a deliberately deep voice, and he seemed to know the poem as well as she, who loved it for its rhythmic structures, and the thrill of terror that ran through the words ... words written on a dark night, perhaps, by a man gone mad from love.

They went from the hall out through another deeply cut archway into a courtyard where worn steps led down to a sunken garden of broken marble figures and a pool covered in water-lotus, whose wide leaves would harbour at night a thousand croaking frogs. Garden birds chirped in the tangle of wild vines, and the air was redolent of herbs gone to flower.

Gisela tucked her hand through the crook of Rosary's arm, for there was a sinister air about the pool and the tiled square of paving set round with urns and obelisks. Rosary noticed that Dom Duarte was gazing around him with narrowed eyes, his nostrils flared, as if he sensed the odour of a ghost!

'Long ago,' he said, 'a duel was fought here. The woman involved ran in front of her lover and received the thrust of the rapier in her heart. Here she died, by the pool, in her lover's arms.'

Rosary's eyes met the *senhor*'s in the moment that his glance flashed from the pool to her face, and she guessed instantly that a Montqueiro had been the lover. She followed his gaze to the *miradouro* attached to one of the slender towers overlooking the garden, a lady's balcony enclosed in a mesh of delicately wrought iron, a pretty cage for the girl who would have been brought all the way from Portugal to be married to a man she had probably never seen. The husband she had not loved ... and here, perhaps, she had met and found a short-lived happiness with the man she had died for.

'What happened, *senhor*?' She had to know the end of the story, for now she could feel the presence of the ghost who lingered in this garden; she saw the water-lotus stir and spin as if fingers touched them and a lizard which had been lying so still it might have been a green stone suddenly leapt high into a tangled bush of red camellia.

'For a long time the Montqueiros were banished from the island,' he said, 'until its economy began to slump. We make shrewd Governors, but we are not always wise in matters of the emotions. And now if you two girls have seen enough we will go and have lunch.'

'I've loved it here,' said Rosary impulsively. 'The old *palacio* teems with history, but I don't think you encourage tourism, do you?'

He shook his head emphatically. 'There is now plenty of work for the islanders, the farms, the fruit groves and the sea provide our food, and there are also the vineyards, the cork forest that was planted in my grandfather's time and the pottery works. We like to be self-supporting, and tourism would rob us of our individual way of life. Encourage profiteering, and those ugly hotels that spoil the coast of Portugal itself? No, *senhorita*! While I remain Governor of Vozes do Mar there will not be an influx of brash visitors from other countries. Besides, our largest beach is the Bahia de Roches, and its waters can be dangerous, and the rocks are there to protect what sand is left. My own beach is a private one.'

As he shot these words over his shoulder, he led the two girls out to the forecourt where his car waited. He told the chauffeur where to drive them. He seemed now to be withdrawn in manner, as if he regretted letting Rosary, a stranger from another country, into a dramatic secret connected with the Montqueiro fam-

128

ily. It was strange how much of the past haunted these people in whose blood ran mixed passions and the *saudade* that found a certain pleasure in sad love.

She, being young and thoughtless at times in her youth, had broken into his mood of almost enjoyable melancholy with her talk of tourism. Of course, the island must remain untouched. Its beauty lay in its isolation from the commercial race. She understood this, yet once again she had been driven to express a view which would antagonize him.

Her gaze dwelt on his hand, clenched over the handle of his stick, lean-fingered and expressing in equal measure a strength and grace and a certain violence held in check. She had angered him, and she had vowed only to disarm him.

How early, she thought, must begin the training of the Latin girl in finding her way among the twists and turns of the complex nature of the Latin male. Never in Lola's company had she ever seen him anything but relaxed and gently amused. Lola did not jolt him with the forthright questions of a British girl. She knew in her shapely bones the art of flattering with lace fan and velvety eyes. A wry smile twisted Rosary's lips. She couldn't picture herself flirting from behind a fan with this man, or ever feeling the touch of his hand in tenderness.

This thought startled her and she turned at once to Gisela and spoke at random of the dolls and jewels they had looked at and admired during their visit to the museum.

'I loved the collar of topaz,' said Gisela, putting to her nose the little flower of balsam she had plucked. 'They seemed to me exactly the colour of your eyes. Father, *minho*, do you not think that Rosary has eyes the colour of topaz?'

Rosary felt herself flush and she prayed he wouldn't answer, for his answer would surely hold a sardonic jeer only she would be aware of. Her prayer was answered, for in that instant the car turned into the parking space beside a large café, its canopied tables set out on a plaza with a view of the sea. Quite a number of people were already lunching at the tables, and heads turned and eyes followed the large grey car with the small flag of the Governor on the bonnet, and the crest of caravel and hawk on the door.

The head waiter led them to their table, with the proprietor in smiling attendance at Dom Duarte's side. Rosary felt the eyes of women diners studying her figure and her casual clothes, taking in her hair that was uncovered and very fair in the sunlight; shocked, no doubt, that she should accompany the Governor in such informal attire. When they took their seats she was aware of him bowing his dark head courteously in the direction of these women and their escorts. She saw the fine Latin teeth flash at him, and the fine eyes ... the *senhor duque*, the man in command, attractive and most eligible in the eyes of those seeking marriage for themselves, or with a daughter they would be overjoyed to have him notice.

He seemed with a flick of his eyes to notice everyone, but not by a movement of a facial muscle did he betray his awareness of what lay slumbering in the glances directed at him. He was supremely self-assured, aloof as the distant mountain peaks ... the perfect aristocrat lunching with his only child and her companion.

'What would you like to drink, Miss Bell?' he asked. 'Gisela is fond of passion-fruit juice, so perhaps you would like the same?'

'Mmm, please, *senhor*, with ice.'

He gave the order for their drinks and something rather more potent for himself. Menus were handed around the table, a large and satisfactory shield against the quizzing eyes, behind which Rosary took refuge and studied the deliciously named soups, the main courses, and the desserts steeped in the syrups and sauces made from the tropical fruits of the island.

Suddenly her sense of humour banished that slight embarrassment since Gisela's comment on the colour of her eyes. 'The menu itself is eatable,' she laughed.

'You have an appetite?' he queried. 'Shall I request that the *hors d'oeuvres* trolley be wheeled to our table?' And before she could answer him he was snapping his fingers and the trolley was being whisked to them, its white cloth laden with dishes of grilled sardine, smoked ham and salmon, slices of egg, stuffed olives, giant shrimps and baby oysters.

'Take your choice.' He obligingly held a plate while she did so, and knew him to be amused as she took an assortment of everything.

'It all looks so delicious,' she said, adding mayonnaise to the side of her plate. 'And your island air seems to give me an enormous appetite.'

'The island is not mine,' he drawled. 'I am merely the keeper of the keys. And now, Gisela, are you going to follow the example of Miss Bell and have a helping of all these good things?'

'*Sim*—and I do wish you would call her Rosary. When you call her Miss Bell it sounds so formal, and as if she were quite old.' Gisela grinned at him, pulled a face at the oysters and heaped her plate with the sardines, plump and silver and gleaming with oil. 'Did you notice how everyone looked at us when we arrived? How hot I'd feel in a dark suit and a hat and high-heeled shoes! Like Rosary I am always going to

131

be casual. It's much nicer. The food and the sunshine are so much more enjoyable when one isn't formal.'

'When you grow up, child, you may wish to be exactly like other Portuguese young women.' A waiter had brought *paté* for the *senhor*, with fine pieces of golden toast wrapped in a napkin, and a small pot of butter. 'As birds are led by instinct on journeys that would kill a man, we are led by the age-old patterns in our natures. What is natural for the Senhorita Bell is not always correct for others. If the *senhoras* at the nearby tables were clad as she, with the hair in a slight disarray, they would look untidy rather than casual. The Latin has in his and her personality a certain natural formality, something connected with the features, the bearing and the attitude of mind.'

'All of which,' Gisela informed Rosary, 'means that when I grow up I shall be expected to conform to the correct pattern of behaviour. Don't you consider that I have a strict parent?'

Rosary glanced at him as he ate *paté* on toast and drank from his glass of wine, and surprisingly enough she agreed with everything he had said.

An Englishman could get away with a sports shirt and an open collar, and look ready for cricket on the green, or some punting on the river. But if a Latin male opened his collar and discarded his jacket he looked as sensuous as the devil! It was the colour of his skin that gave him a warm look, combined with the thick darkness of his hair, and often he wore a medallion on a chain about his neck, placed there when he was a young boy and unremoved for the rest of his life. Sometimes it was a crucifix meshed in the dark hair of his chest ... utterly pagan in the eyes of a woman!

A great deal of difference did exist between the Anglo-Saxon and the Latin, and being among these people had become for Rosary a voyage of discovery. She realized how much she was enjoying herself! It was a novelty to be so different from the other women at the café tables, and though at first she had felt shy of looking around at the other people, now she did so and met several pairs of very dark eyes, obviously curious about her ... especially in relationship to Dom Duarte.

There was a woman with silvery hair crowned by a toque of shining dark feathers, and when she raised her eye-glasses to study the English girl, Rosary dared to give her a smile. Immediately in response the handsome head inclined towards her, and Rosary felt as pleased as a puppy patted on the rump. The woman was undoubtedly a personage, who seemed to dominate the young men and women who lunched with her. Perhaps they were the sons and daughters of the matriarch?

'That is the Marquesa del Ronda and her family,' said Dom Duarte, whose observant eyes missed very little of what went on around him. 'She is visiting her sons from Portugal; they are the owners of the largest vineyards, and you will be meeting them when they give the annual *festa* to celebrate the fame of their wine. It is always a lively affair, and this year, Gisela, you will be old enough to attend, and to wear a long dress. There will no doubt be visitors from Portugal and it will be exciting for you.'

On their way out of the café the Marquesa and her family paused beside the *senhor*'s table in order to exchange a few words with him. He arose and kissed the old lady's hand, and she gazed up at his face before turning to smile graciously at his daughter, 'You have grown, child, since last I saw you.' Then the shrewd eyes were fixed upon Rosary. 'You have remarkably bright hair, *senhorita*. Is it natural?'

'Certainly.' Although Rosary answered smartly, she wasn't annoyed by the question. She knew from her years with Cibby that the elderly considered it their privilege to be as frank as they pleased.

'You had best beware, Duarte.' The Marquesa looked tiny but indomitable as she gazed up at him. 'I recall that your grandmother on your father's side was very fair. She came from Austria, did she not?'

'By way of the Viennese ballet, Marquesa.' He spoke blandly and looked perfectly unruffled by the implication in her words. 'She danced her way into his heart, and as I am sure you remember there was a scandal when he married her in opposition to his family's wishes.'

'You Montqueiros,' she tapped his hand with her glove, 'were always attractive and never quite predictable. You must marry again, Duarte, and still the tongues that wag about you. You must realize that you cannot remain solitary and without a son to follow you. There has never yet been a Montqueiro who has failed to pass on his name, his looks and his dash of the devil. See to it, Duarte! Perhaps before the *festa* so that you may introduce us to the fortunate young lady.'

'Marquesa,' his smile was faintly sardonic, 'you are almost the only woman I know who dares to say outright whatever is in her mind.'

'And who,' she demanded jealously, 'is this other pert creature? I say pert in her case, but I am an old friend who saw you baptized and who has watched you at play in your bath.'

He laughed, a resonant sound that rang above the clatter of cutlery and conversation. Something almost boyish in it that made Rosary blink her eyelashes ...

the laugh and the image of him in his baby bath were almost too much for her, and she quickly took up her wine glass in case he caught her staring at him in amazement. Yet why be amazed? He had not been born a fully grown man with a disconcerting amount of authority ... and the most unexpected charm.

'You must allow me at least one secret,' he said to the Marquesa, and once again he bent his dark head and kissed her tiny ungloved hand. Laughing a little, she went on her way, followed by her well-groomed sons and their pretty but rather subdued wives.

Rosary followed the group with her eyes, and she decided that the little Marquesa would be somewhat intimidating if one were in close contact with her. That was the risk which Latin girls took when they married a man whose mother was the head of the family.

'It must be a relief for Loreta and Mira when the Marquesa returns to her *quinta* in Portugal,' said Gisela. 'They are so much gayer when she is not here on a visit.'

'She was very beautiful,' said Dom Duarte. 'Such women do not surrender to age or youth, and they possess an armoury of wit and self-assurance gained from their many years of captivating men. Loreta and Mira must stand up to her and look her in the eye— just as our Miss Bell did.' He quirked an eyebrow at Rosary. 'I am pleased you did not permit her to annoy you, but I saw your chin take its fighting tilt.'

'Why not, *senhor*, in defence of something of my own which is not artificial. I suppose by comparison to your raven-haired women I am an oddity.'

'My child, they are not my women,' he drawled.

'They would like to be——' The words leapt impetuously from her lips, and she flushed at the way he

135

looked at her, half mockingly, with a hint of speculation.

'People are always saying you should marry again,' said Gisela, with a note of jealousy in her voice. 'Why don't they mind their own business? They must know that you could never find anyone to compare with my mother. They must realize that your heart is buried with her.'

Rosary's heart beat with a strange quickness when Gisela said these things, and his reply seemed as if it would never come. She knew of the guilt he felt in relation to Isabela, but was it really true that he had loved her so much that remarriage was out of the question? Yet it was true what the Marquesa had said, he had an historical name to pass on; he had estates, pride, a shrewd governing brain. He had a young daughter who should have a mother before she became too possessive of her father.

'The heart dictates and duty directs,' he said carefully. 'Who can tell, Gisela, what I may feel one day about this matter of an heir? You are old enough, child, to understand my dilemma and my duty. I cannot make you my heir, but I can love you very dearly.'

Gisela's head was bent over her plate and she wouldn't look at him. He was all she had, and Rosary knew how much she adored him. It would wrench her young heart in two if he should ever take another wife, and Rosary felt sure he would wait until Gisela was a little older, more understanding of the demands and urges of adult life. In a year or two he would still be an extremely virile man, and Gisela would be seventeen and a young woman, perhaps by then in love and betrothed herself.

'We are all in our various ways *almas captivas*.' He

reached across and squeezed Gisela's hand, and the gleam of antique silver at his cuff caught the light and seemed symbolic of the steely pride welded into the Latin backbone, the centuries of arranged alliances which led, inevitably, to a secret gnawing hunger for love rather than a fulfilment of that hunger.

'And what,' he asked Rosary, 'holds your soul in captivity?'

'This gorgeous sweet,' she said lightly, indicating the golden fritters smothered in strawberry syrup on her plate. 'Now I know why the ladies of the harem grew so plump in their captivity.'

'Such a fate would have been beyond your bearing, I think,' he said, a deep gleam of amusement in his eyes. 'You were meant always to be a free-spirited Anglo-Saxon . . . a child of nature.'

She kept thinking of those words as the car took the coast road and they followed the sea, the beckoning glitter and the blue beauty of it all. Below the road she could see the jutting rocks, cascading with green seaweed. Yes, how true it was that she responded to natural sights and sounds; they were the music of life, but something else was the substance, the intangible thing called love, the invisible and potent power that all at once took shape in the form of another human being.

She stared at the sea as the car sped homeward to the *palacete*, and all down her arm, all down the side near to Dom Duarte but not touching him, she seemed to tingle as if electricity were alive within those few inches of space.

The feeling, the awareness was rather terrible . . . she had never been bodily aware of a man before, and so suddenly acute was the sensitivity of her skin that when he abruptly moved the position of his injured leg, the fine hairs at the nape of her neck seemed to creep with the abrupt fear that he had been about to touch her. It was minutes before she could relax, and when they drove into the courtyard of the palace she was out of the car before the chauffeur could open the door, leaving Dom Duarte to follow with Gisela.

In the hall she saw the Senhora de Ardo emerging from her *sala* with a friend, and they both nodded coolly as she greeted them and hurried on her way upstairs.

She had to be alone in order to sort out her confusing thoughts, and glancing swiftly downwards she saw the *senhor* engaged in conversation with the two women, while Gisela had picked up her kitten and was fondling him. Rosary hurried on and upon reaching her suite she entered and closed the door behind her with a feeling close to the relief of having eluded a pursuer.

She stood breathlessly with her back to the door, aware of the quick beating of her heart, of an emotional turmoil never felt before.

No ... this couldn't be happening to her, what she had seen happen to other girls. Student friends who developed long spells of silence while a troubling magic shimmered in their eyes. Or they became unbearably gay, as if the world could not contain their bubbling joy.

Rosary felt bewildered ... she had not a thing in common with the man, and she knew there were times when he found her about as appealing as a pain in the neck. Oh, heavens, how was she going to face him again when the very thought of his arrogant looks and his lean grace of body made her feel such a confusion of the nerves ... it was like music played discordantly when she longed for it to be played dreamily.

She ran distracted hands to her hair and walked slowly to the dressing-table, where she stood and stared at her face in the mirror, as if half fearful of seeing her secret written plainly on her features. The face that gazed back at her was shocked, but apart from that she looked much the same. She had always thought her eyes too large, her nose too small, and her mouth too wide. She thought of Lola Cortez, whose face was a perfect oval set with regular features and dusky Latin eyes.

A rueful smile curved on Rosary's lips. What a trick her own emotions had played on her! Dom Duarte endured her for Gisela's sake, and was somewhat amused by her independent antics ... thank goodness he had been unaware of her startling awareness of him in the car! That distinct fear, half desire, that he let his arm travel around her!

In the days that followed she avoided being a moment alone with him. He had work to catch up on, so it was only in the evenings, at dinner, that she saw him. At the end of the meal he would excuse himself and go to his study, or he would leave the house to call on someone. He was polite to the edge of coolness, and it was a relief, and at the same time rather unbearable to be treated to an aloof smile, or a brief question regarding Gisela's progress as a pupil.

She was growing up, learning what it felt like to be at the mercy of her emotions. She was scornful of these emotions and told herself she was reacting like some meek and lonely governess in a novel, ready to become attracted to her domineering master because there was no one in her life to care about her.

Rosary reminded herself that she had Cibby, to whom she could run for protection whenever the need arose. There was Erick, who had shown very plainly that he was attracted to her. She really had no need to be so foolish as to feel an acceleration of the pulses whenever she heard a deep Latin voice giving orders about the *palacete*; nor should she feel this craving to run like a hare whenever she caught the sound of his slight limp. He had discarded his stick, but the limp persisted to remind her that she had said an outrageous thing which he would never forgive.

It was now high summer and to avoid the heat of the afternoon she took to the woods and wandered there beneath the cool and scented shade of the pine trees and the gnarled old corks that must long ago have taken root from seed dropped from the pockets of the Portuguese sailors who had come ashore with the Montqueiro who had discovered and named Vozes do Mar. It was a name like music, and as she took aimlessly the twisting paths through the woods, with the thick shade of the trees holding at bay the hot blue dazzle of the sky, she found a certain pleasure in being alone with her disturbing thoughts.

She knew that certain of these paths led to the villa in which Lola lived with her brother, so it was no great surprise that one afternoon she should meet Lola, out with a small basket and clipping from the forks of the trees the tiny orchids that grew wild in the woods. She looked cool and lovely as a flower herself in a dark pink dress, with her hair drawn back from her face and folded into a double knot.

They did not immediately greet each other and seemed to be assessing clothes, mood, their motives for being here ... it was as if quite suddenly a sort of enmity had replaced their former cordiality. Rosary became a little embarrassed by the silence and she plunged her hands into the pockets of her pants and assumed a nonchalant air. 'It's something I can't get over,' she said, 'seeing orchids growing wild like this. Fancy being able to decorate the home with them.'

'Would you like to return to the villa with me for a cool drink?' Lola asked, and her glance as it passed over Rosary might have been lazy but for the brilliance of her pupils. 'You have never been to the villa and it is really quite nice if rather small. Duarte always tells me that I have the Latin woman's gift for making her home her world.'

Her casual and yet deliberate use of his first name went through Rosary like a small arrow. It emphasized more than anything else that Lola was a friend of his and not an employee; it implied a companionship such as Rosary would never know. The tender word, the exciting undertone, the promise of things to come.

'I——' Rosary was almost at the point of refusing Lola's invitation when she realized that she mustn't appear to be the slightest bit envious. 'I should love a cool drink. Thank you for asking me.'

'We go this way.' They continued along the path until they came to an ornamental gate in a wall. Lola opened it and they entered the garden of the villa, a gem of formality, with rose-hung pergolas, neatly tiled benches and well-kept fuchsia hedges. Not a petal or a speck of dirt lay on the paved paths to the veranda, shaded by a striped awning. There beneath the shade were rattan chairs with jewel-coloured cushions, and a circular rattan table. Nothing seemed disturbed or out of place, and Rosary thought irresistibly that it was like a picture in a glossy magazine.

The villa itself was as pretty as paint, with its curly tiles, curly iron grilles around the windows, and its tubs of well-trained plants beside the long windows leading into the house.

'Take a chair,' said Lola, 'and I will fetch the fruit

juice from the cooler. Would you like some biscuits also?'

'No, thanks. A long cool drink is all I want.'

'Are you quite certain that is all you want?' Lola gave Rosary a long cool look, and she seemed to infuse her words with a double meaning. Rosary felt the jolting of her pulse and she wondered if the Latin girl sensed in her an emotional awareness of the man who must often have sat on this veranda ... right here, perhaps, his long legs stretched across the pale pink tiling.

'The heat makes me thirsty,' she said, looking about her casually. 'You have a well ordered garden, Lola. Do you manage it yourself?'

'Yes. It is only small and passes the time for me ... until I am married. Then I shall be too occupied in other ways to be able to manage a garden.' Lola gave a soft laugh, and then with a scarlet orchid held to her lips, as if in self-reproach at giving away a secret, she walked into the house and left Rosary alone to mull over her significant words.

Rosary stared at the sun that turned to falling diamonds the water of the fountain in the centre of the garden, and it was amazing how unsurprised she was.

Lola would make an ideal wife for Dom Duarte. She would revel in his position, and his title, and enjoy every moment of being the mistress of the small palace that was enormous compared to the villa, which she obviously found a little too confining. She would be the envy of every woman on the island ... but Rosary herself felt no semblance of envy. She felt numb, after the first quick dart of pain.

CHAPTER EIGHT

WHEN Lola returned carrying a tray of refreshments, Rosary was seated in a rattan chair, her fair head at rest against a deep gold cushion. 'How tucked away and peaceful the villa is,' she said.

'Dacio finds it a little too peaceful.' Lola smiled as she poured their drinks. 'I am quite certain he will return to Lisbon when I am no longer his responsibility. Are you sure you will not try a biscuit? I made them myself.'

'Then I will have one.' The iced morsel was delicious and Rosary took another. 'I'm afraid I can't cook anything more ambitious than bacon and eggs.'

'Instead you play music, and you do it extremely well.' Lola sat back in her chair, her silken legs gracefully crossed to reveal her fine-boned ankles. 'It will be nice for Gisela to be able to play, but of course she will never possess your skill. Do you plan a career as a music teacher?'

'It would be interesting——' Rosary tinkled the ice in her glass of lime juice. 'I do get satisfaction out of imparting what I have learned to other people.'

'But of course you will want to marry.' Lola's gaze dwelt on the English girl while her fingers played with the golden bracelet on her left wrist. 'Tell me, do you find Portuguese men attractive?'

'It would be foolish of me to say no.' Rosary smiled slightly, for how could she help but know that Lola had a specific person in mind? 'I think most Latin people are good-looking; a combination of fine eyes and very good bone structure, not to mention the raven hair. As a lover of music I suppose I'm attuned to physical beauty.'

'Our men are great charmers—some can even cast a spell over a woman.' Lola's fingers now caressed the glass her hands were holding. 'Duarte has such fascination, don't you agree? His eyes have a magnetism that might make it impossible for a woman to refuse him whatever he asked of her ... I know how much he might demand, or sacrifice, for Gisela's sake. It would be a pity for you if he demanded that you remain her companion until she is grown up. You should escape now, before he steals away your youth, that appealing freshness you have. Duarte is a ruthless man when it comes to having his own way.'

'I expect it's true to say that most men like their own way,' Rosary murmured. 'I like this island, and I have grown fond of Gisela. No one is forcing me to stay here. I have enough will of my own not to allow that.'

'Yet today in the woods you seemed a little unhappy.' Lola's gaze was velvety dark and curious. 'We are friends. You can tell me what is troubling you, if you wish to do so. Perhaps the Senhora de Ardo has been unkind again?'

'No. I think Dom Duarte has convinced her that being English I can't be expected to behave like a Latin *duena*. No, I'm not unhappy. Why should I be?' Rosary gave the Latin girl a frank look, for not by the shadow of an eyelash would she reveal to anyone the source of her slight melancholy. Everyone had to go through an attack of infatuation at some time in their life, and she would recover soon enough, and would most certainly leave the island if Lola's marriage looked like taking place before she recovered her senses. She couldn't imagine sharing a house with the bride of Montqueiro!

'When one is young——' Lola shrugged her slim graceful shoulders. 'The heart is vulnerable, and our nights are starry. It did cross my mind that you might have—well, allowed yourself to be kissed—or not kissed?'

'How very Machiavellian is the Latin mind,' Rosary smiled, and she decided to be a little cunning herself. 'Are you afraid I may have been led up the garden by your handsome brother? I must confess that I find him charming, but we are both employed at the *palacete* and we abide by the *senhora's* rules since she found us laughing together.'

'I see.' Lola swung a slim, sandalled foot, as if relaxation would not be truly hers until the act of marriage made Dom Duarte hers; and she must know that he would make her wait rather than risk making Gisela unhappy. 'Dacio is my brother and I am so accustomed to him that I forget he is not the brother of other girls. It was very daring of you to swim alone at night with him.'

'He was the perfect gentleman.'

'I am glad for your sake.'

'I am glad for my own.' Rosary stretched her arms and rose to her feet. 'Siesta will soon be over and I must be getting back to my duties. In the first cool of the evening Gisela and I practise at the piano. The keys grow so sticky during the daytime.'

'Do you find our climate at all enervating?' Lola's smooth olive skin looked cool against the filmy material of her pink dress, and not a glossy hair of her neat head was out of place. 'I have heard that very fair-skinned people feel the heat.'

Rosary stood beneath the shade of the veranda, hands at a boyish angle in the pockets of her pale tangerine slacks, and slightly amused by her own lack of poise in contrast to Lola's. She recalled what Dom Duarte had said about the great difference between the Anglo-Saxon and the Latin ... and it was like the contrast between the camellia and the daisy, which grew where it willed, running wild among the green grasses. But the camellia had to be nurtured and cared for, and kept within the boundaries of white walls and sculptured archways.

She let her smile have its way, and it was tinged with a little irony. 'Mad dogs and English girls go out in the sun regardless,' she said. 'We are a restless nation and have no gift for looking ornamental. Thank you for the cool drink, Lola, and the little chat. I gather one of the Marquesa's sons is giving a sucking-pig party on Saturday evening; a sort of *festa* to which we are all invited. I shall see you there?'

'But of course.' Lola's gaze slipped over Rosary. 'If you have not a party dress to wear, then perhaps I can lend you one of mine? We are both on the slender side——'

'No—it's kind of you, but I am only the tutor and not expected to look too glamorous.' The very idea of wearing a dress of Lola's, in which Dom Durate may have seen her, was objectionable to Rosary. As if the future mistress offered the employee a discarded garment!

'*Ate a vista.*' She sped away, running through the garden to the gate that led into the woods. She told herself that Lola had meant only to be kind, but there had been a hint of condescension in the offer which made her cheeks tingle. And aroused her battling spirit! Tomorrow she would go into the township, to the Avenida Rey, and buy the prettiest dress she could afford. On Friday evening she would wash her hair in lemon shampoo, and at the party she would be as gay and stunning as she could be.

She came out of the woods into the fading gold of the afternoon. She could see below the grounds of the *palacete* the gilded scrolls of the sea, and she heard the cries of the seabirds as the welcoming breeze blew over the land.

She loved the turn of the day, which seemed to hold elements of the dramatic, the mysterious and the subtle. Night whispered just around the corner, preparing to clothe herself in dark velvet and diamonds, and the scents of a hundred flowers. The party on Saturday would be her first real *festa*; she had missed seeing the wedding which Dacio had promised her, and she was no longer sorry. She didn't want to know any more what a Latin wedding was like; it would be too evocative of the ceremony that would one day take place between Dom Duarte and the girl she had left dreaming on a quiet veranda. The girl who wore on her wrist the golden bracelet of Latin betrothal.

Restless, seeking an outlet for her mixed emotions, Rosary walked across the courtyard and in through the windows of the room in which she studied with Gisela. She walked to the small piano and sat down at the keyboard and she began to play ... the sun had died away and the room was filled with shadows when she became aware of the tang of cigar smoke and her fingers were arrested on the keys.

'Don't stop.' The deep voice came from behind her, near the window. 'Play to the end.'

'It is ended ... almost,' she said, and she sat still in the gloom and felt the music and her dismay tingling through her body. How long had he been there, listening as she poured her secret out through her fingertips into the passionate, lyrical notes of the song composed by Liszt? Did he know the song? Would he interpret her rendition as an expression of her personal feelings? She didn't dare to look at him. She didn't dare to find out.

'You must love that song very much,' he said, and his cigar smoke came drifting to her, brushing her senses almost like a touch. 'You played it, *pequena*, from the heart ... and I was here to listen instead of the young man for whom it was meant. Such a pity.'

'It wasn't meant for anyone,' she said. 'I merely felt like playing some Liszt. I—I hope you found it enjoyable——?'

'"Eternity in your arms,"' he murmured, and he came forward into the room until she felt his height and his darkness right behind her. 'Do you really expect me to believe that you were not thinking of a man during that intense performance?'

'I am sure you take it for granted that women spend most of their time thinking about men,' she rejoined. 'My grandfather taught me the song.'

'You are being evasive, *senhorita*.'

'And you are being inquisitive, *senhor*.'

He gave a soft, slightly dangerous laugh above her head, and all the time the shadows grew denser and the scents of the garden were wafted into the room by that blessed breeze. Rosary longed to leap to her feet and to rush away into the dark garden, but she knew instinctively that he was tensed for that very action.

'It's dark—I hadn't realized how the time was passing. I should get washed and dressed for dinner——'

'Stay as you are.' His hand rested briefly on her shoulder. 'My aunt has taken Gisela to the home of her friend for the evening. We are alone and will dine together in a while. Relax after your *tour de force*.'

'But'—she swung round on the stool and in the gloom she saw the glint of his eyes—'I had no idea

Gisela was going out tonight!'

'It was a sudden decision. This friend of the *senhora's* has teenage nieces and it will be good for Gisela to be with them.'

'I see.' Rosary tensed. 'Are you becoming afraid that your daughter is having a little too much of my company? There is a remedy for that; my six weeks' trial is at an end next week.'

'Do stop leaping to conclusions.' He laughed lazily and strolled to a table on which stood a lamp. He clicked the switch and light pooled him, leaving Rosary in shadow by the piano. He wore a dark velvet smoking jacket and as he bent to stub his cigar, the definition of his profile was outlined against the silken shade of the lamp. It had a strong masculine beauty that almost made her cry out from the thrill of wonder and pain that ran through her. He straightened and she watched the movement of his lean hand over his thick black hair, and she wanted her own hand to follow the same route, wending its way down his lean cheek to his throat, his hard-boned shoulder, to his heart that was given or promised to a girl of his own race and his own instincts.

The intrusive thought of Lola brought Rosary to her feet. 'It will be tedious for you, *senhor*, dining alone with me. I can have a tray brought to my room——'

'You are as unflattering to me as you are to yourself,' he drawled. 'It can never be said that we have ever found each other's company dull. I, at least, find our conversational duels most entertaining; I am never certain when you are going to scratch me, and when you do scratch me I am never certain how I shall retaliate.'

'I am never certain of that, either,' she retorted. A

tiny, nervous smile pulled at her lip, for she wanted to be alone with him as much as she wanted to resist his persuasion, and his fascination. She could lock her door upstairs and refuse to join him for dinner ... but oh, how she would regret afterwards her denial of his subtle, charming, nerve-shattering company. His appeal to her senses (which dispelled all sensible reasoning) had become compelling; a combination of physical harmony and mental alertness.

Lola had warned her that he was hard to resist ... he was impossible to resist.

'I—I can't dine in trousers.' She backed to the door. 'I must go and put on a dress.'

He shot a glance at his wristwatch. 'I give you exactly half an hour in which to make yourself presentable.' He bowed his head with a slightly mocking formality, and she flew like a wild young bird across the hall and up the stairs, feeling as if a velvety paw had lifted a moment to let her escape. She shivered to herself as she made her way along the gallery, which felt cool and empty and seemed to underline the absence of the *senhora* and Gisela. How terribly easy it was to say of girls in love that they should have more sense of restraint than to give in to their feelings. There was a glory, and a terror, in giving in to Dom Duarte ... even to dine with such a man was an excitement out of the ordinary.

Rosary closed her door behind her, but she didn't lock it. His marriage to the lovely Lola would lock out all other women, soon enough.

With only half an hour at her disposal she swiftly showered, sprayed cool cologne from her throat to her ankles and slid into brief lingerie. She then studied her wardrobe and decided to wear a sleeveless dress made of several panels of vari-coloured chiffon, with a

150

narrow mother-of-pearl belt. It was a youthful, un-sophisticated dress, and after combing her hair she let it curve on her shoulders, and she applied to her lips some pale, shining pink colour.

She studied herself in the mirror and for a panicky moment she wondered if she looked too showy ... she had last worn this dress at a student dance, and she certainly didn't wish to give the impression that she was expecting dinner with the Dom to be a party affair.

In the silence she heard the striking of the clock that stood on the gallery, antique and demanding, warning her that she had no more time to waste on her appearance. Snatching up a chiffon handkerchief, she walked from her suite ... when she reached the stairs her fingers clenched on the chiffon, for he was down in the hall, by the door that led to and from the wine cellars. She made no sound as she stood there, bracing herself to go down, and he turned as if his senses were always on the alert and he glanced up at her and his eyes, passing swiftly over her, disturbed her nerves and her emotions more than ever. He seemed not to miss a detail of her dress, her bare arms, and slim legs in sheer nylons. Then he was looking at her hair, loose and silvery about her young face that sought so frantically to look cool and composed.

He came to the foot of the stairs and he carried a long-necked bottle in his hand. 'You look the spirit of youth,' he said. 'Perhaps I should offer you fruit juice instead of wine?'

She stood with a slim foot poised on the stairs, knowing she must descend or retreat to her room. Tiger-eyes sparkled in the lobes of her ears; the little jewelled earrings which had belonged to her mother. With a sudden little gesture of bravado Rosary tossed

151

her head, making them sparkle all the more as she went down to him. She smiled gaily, acting the woman of the world.

'I shall be most disappointed if you don't give me wine, *senhor*,' she said. 'I'm not a child, you know.'

'No, not a child, nor yet a woman.' He continued to stand there as she drew nearer to him. 'You are at the stage when "Your slim gilt soul walks between passion and poetry." '

'Oscar Wilde!' she exclaimed, and her eyes were wide as a child's in that moment, and then her lashes were lowered with the secretiveness of a woman. 'You seem to know a lot of poetry, *senhor*.'

'The Portuguese are fond of it,' he said casually. 'Shall we go to the *sala*? I have ordered our dinner to be served there tonight. Two people at that long table in the dining-room seem like strangers before the meal is half over.'

Her heart made a soft thunder in her breast as she walked with him across the glowing tiles of the floor to the rosewood doors of the *sala*. It both frightened her, and excited her, that tonight he didn't wish to be aloof and alone at the head of the table, which even with four people seated there seemed too grand, isolating one from the other, with silver candelabra and flowers in between.

They entered the *sala*, lit by lamps, and with birds and flowers worked in silk thread on the brocade curtains and upholstery of chairs and sofas. A circular table had been laid for dinner, with two chairs facing each other.

She wanted to look at him, to question his eyes, to ask with her own eyes why it pleased him to dine like this with his daughter's tutor. Tiny flickers of alarm zigzagged through her body. She had heard tales of men of wealth, who had whims and fancies which they satisfied and then coolly dismissed from their conscience. Men who honoured the woman they meant to marry, but who thought it merely a game to seduce a girl who was foolish enough to walk like a fly into the carefully spun web.

She heard the closing of the doors behind him, and felt his silent tread across the Indian carpet that was sensuously soft under the thin soles of her evening shoes. She tautened, and wondered if he meant to explore her unawakened passions.

Rosary swung to face him and the tiger-eyes glittered against her pale, untouched skin. 'What sort of a girl do you think I am?' She blurted the words, untrained as yet in the art of being subtle.

His eyes narrowed as he looked down at her. Then he glanced at the table laid for two, at the lamps that cast small pools of gold and ruby light on to the cushioned sofas. Suddenly, wickedly, he smiled as she had never seen him smile before. 'Quite often an infuriating one,' he replied. 'Right now your agile young mind is grappling with several reasons why I should ask you to dine alone with me, and that tilt to your chin tells me that I have been cast in the role of dangerous Latin with seduction on his mind. Am I right?'

'It is always inclined to cross a girl's mind, especially when she knows——'

'Knows what?' he broke in swiftly.

'Oh, that she has nothing in common with the man and is merely a form of amusement.'

'You consider that it would merely amuse me to seduce you?' He was looking directly at her, a slightly mocking smile on his lips. 'The amusement, *pequena*, will be in holding you on tenterhooks, keeping you in suspense as to my intention ... ah, how large grow your eyes! Did you fondly imagine that once the subject was mentioned the danger would decrease? How innocent you really are! This sort of frankness between a man and a woman only increases the fun.'

'I—I think I will have that tray in my room!' Rosary went to brush past him, and with a quick movement he caught her wrist in his fingers and prevented her from leaving.

'You surprise me,' he drawled. 'I didn't take you for a coward.'

'I'm not,' she flung at him, and the indignant movement of her head set the tiger-eyes dancing in her earlobes. 'I'm not afraid of you——'

'Perhaps you are afraid of yourself?'

'Why should I be?' She defied his eyes, and her own riot of emotions as he held her so that the chiffon panels of her dress were caught like moth wings against the dark velvet of his jacket. 'Do you consider yourself so irresistible, *senhor duque*? Have you practised before your *senhor* rights on other amusing creatures like myself ... oh, don't, you'll break my wrist!' She cried out as his fingers tightened, gripped, until the bones of her wrist seemed about to snap in two. 'You are ruthless ... Lola told me you are!'

'So! You have been discussing me with Lola?' His teeth snapped whitely and his dark face came down close to Rosary's, menacing and yet still with that quality of masculine beauty that thrilled through her very bones. 'I hope it was an interesting and enlightening conversation?'

'Extremely so. I know the betrothal is not yet official, but girls like to share secrets, and I saw the bracelet on her wrist.' His closeness was making Rosary breathless ... oh, how dared he behave like this! He was playing with her like a hawk with a bird, perhaps in a reckless mood because at last he had committed himself to the marriage that everyone expected of him ... the marriage that would upset Gisela, and disturb the beautiful ghost of Isabela. He perhaps felt driven to take out on someone his doubts and his angers, but why pick on her? It was so unfair of him ... and she loved him so!

She loved him even as she hated him for being so cruel and mocking ... she almost fell as suddenly there was a tap on the door and he let go his grip on her.

The doors opened and the dinner trolley was wheeled into the room by a manservant. Rosary stared past the man into the hall ... the doors of the cage were open and she could flee this moment and Dom Duarte would not stop her in front of his servant. She was as tensed as an arrow quivering in the bow, poised to fly from him.

'Come, *senhorita*,' his voice was deep but not demanding. 'Don't let the food get cold.'

She looked at him, but now his face was an inscrutable mask, and he was holding ready her chair for her, while the manservant hovered, ready to serve them from the array of dishes on the trolley. On the table the wine stood ready, and the camellias nestled their creamy cheeks together on their bed of fern. The lace of the cloth was intricately Portuguese against the gleaming wood of the table. The lamps burned softly, and like a prisoner of a dream she walked to where he stood holding ready her chair and she slipped into it. When he took his own chair she studied his face through her lashes to see if he mocked her capitulation, but his features were as if shaped by a chisel and set in bronze, and his attention was upon the wine as he drew the cork; he tasted it and then almost filled the flute glasses.

'This was bottled and put down in my grandfather's time,' he said, when the manservant had left them, closing the doors and leaving them alone together. 'It was wine distilled from the grapevines his bride brought from Austria. Taste it.'

She did so and found it delicately sharp-sweet, like a kiss. 'It's very nice,' she said.

'It's a little more than that.' He ate a wing of pheasant and drank again from his glass. 'Did it surprise you to learn that my grandmother was a Viennese ballerina?'

Her glance skimmed his shoulders and she thought of his height, which had always surprised her in a Portuguese. 'I rather had the feeling, *senhor*, that somewhere along the line a certain element not quite Latin had crept into your ancestry. You are the tallest man on this island.'

He smiled abruptly. 'It has its advantages. Will you have some more green peas ... another wing of bird?'

'I have enough, *senhor*, thank you.'

His eyes skimmed her face. 'Your appetite is usually a hearty one. Are you still nervous of my motives in arranging this dinner for two?'

She shrugged her shoulders. 'I have committed myself to your motives, *senhor*, so I suppose I must take the consequences.'

'Ah, come,' he quirked an eyebrow, 'if you submit without a fight then you rob the game of half its appeal. More wine?'

'No—yes,' she added defiantly. 'It might help to numb my feelings, for I have already learned that to fight with you is to get bruised.'

'Bruised?' he echoed. 'Show me!'

She extended her wrist and there against the pale

156

skin was the mark of his fingers. 'I am not made of plastic, *senhor*. I can be hurt, you know, and it isn't fair of you to think I can be used. I'm not a member of the permissive society because I happen to work abroad far from my family ... not a very large one, consisting as it does of only my grandfather.'

'Child, do stop!' He gave a laugh that was half a groan, and suddenly he was upon his feet and striding round the table to her side. He took the hand she had extended to him and he examined the bruises he had caused. 'I am a brute, eh? A ruthless tyrant, who amuses himself at your expense. You hate me, eh?'

'Yes,' she said, and pulled her hand free of his, as if his touch was detestable rather than desirable ... and the extent of that desire of hers was truly amazing, all things considered. It made her eyes blaze up at him, for somehow, no matter how, she had to find protection from him, a shield against his devastation of her feelings.

'When I first came here you said you would be like a guardian to me, and you told me to try and behave like a Latin girl. I have tried to abide by your rules, *senhor*, but you seem tonight to be breaking your own.'

'Do I, Miss Bell?' He gazed for a long intent moment over her head, and then he inclined his own head in agreement. 'Please relax now and be serene. It is just that tonight the *palacete* is filled with a black memory which I have tried to dispel by playing the devil. Each year this happens and you are right, I have tried to use your youth and your innocence to try and hold at bay the dark phantom of memory.'

He returned to his place at the table and his face wore a brooding look as he refilled his wine glass, and looking at him she suddenly knew why he had sent

Gisela to play and talk with young people; why a sort of devil did seem in possession of him tonight.

As compassion gripped her, she no longer had any armour against him, or wanted it. 'Grief was never a reasonable emotion,' she murmured.

He glanced up from his contemplation of his wine, and held her in the deep-set, alive and searching gaze of his eyes. 'Don't call it grief,' he said. 'You were right the last time when you called it conscience. It is exactly six years to this day that my wife was killed, and all day I have been remembering how she died ... she who loved luxury and beautiful things ... shining things, like gems and the well-groomed coat of her horse. She married me to have them, and I married her, a young man bedazzled by her beauty.'

He tossed back his wine and the action had something reckless about it, and for a moment it was as if the youthful Montqueiro sat facing Rosary, his strong mouth sullen and disillusioned.

'You have been to the gallery to look at her portrait, eh?'

'Yes, *senhor*. Your wife was strikingly beautiful.'

'The artist, like all other men, was in love with her ... unlike me, who had then lived with her for seven years, they were unaware that she lacked humanity, which is an awareness of the feelings of others. Love is when the heart unlocks itself, but she kept hers for ever guarded, like the jewels I gave her. The strange, deep yearnings that are love slowly died in me, until even desire turned to stone. Can you bear to stay and hear why we quarrelled that day ... six years ago today?'

'If you wish to tell me, *senhor*.'

'I think I do wish!' He rose abruptly to his feet, towering there, still with something devilish about him in the lamplight. 'Come away from the table ... the left food and the dregs of the wine!'

He walked away, to the windows, where he stood framed by the long brocade curtains, lean hands thrust into the pockets of his black velvet jacket, a tie of dark silk against the whiteness of his shirt. Rosary went and sat on a sofa, and though apart from him, her entire being seemed to reach out to him. As she gazed at him, her arms at rest on the back of the sofa, her posture was young, but her eyes offered the understanding of Eve ... of Venus herself.

Though he denied it something of his youthful love of Isabela remained and would always remain, part of him, and part of Gisela.

'That morning at breakfast,' he said, 'she asked me to ride with her. She said she had something to discuss with me. Why deny that even then I was hopeful of something taking a turn for the better in our marriage? I don't deny it, but it was an empty hope. Gisela was then nine years old, springing up and no longer a toddler. Isabela had an almost pathological desire never to look or grow a day older, but a growing daughter reveals that the mother is a little older each month, each year. Isabela had decided that she didn't like this evidence of her maturity in front of her each day and she wished me to enrol Gisela in a boarding school in Portugal. I refused! I told Isabela in no uncertain terms that Gisela would remain at home with us until she was eleven. Time enough then to send her to school. One word led to another. We quarrelled as never before ... "You might as well know," I said, "that I intend to have a son from you as well as a daughter." Immediately she slashed at me with her riding whip, and then she tore off on the back

159

of the horse, whipping the poor beast as she would have liked to whip me. Maddened herself, she made the animal mad, and he threw her, and as he danced with pain he kicked her and she died, still beautiful, still quite young, and hating me.'

The last words fell away into silence and he was so very still that when at last he moved the movement startled Rosary. He came slowly to where she sat and he held out his hand and after a shy, wordless pause she gave hers to a clasp that left her defenceless.

'Forgive me for hurting you,' he said, 'but now, perhaps, you understand my demon? Do you?'

'Yes, *senhor*, I think so.'

'You are not too shocked?'

'No,' she shook her head, 'only sad.'

'For Isabela?' The golden lights glimmered deep within his eyes, the embers of the love which Isabela had killed with her coldness. Looking up at him Rosary wanted to reach up to him, to pull his face close to hers and kiss away that sardonic, almost weary look.

'Sad for all three of you,' she said, and because of what she felt her hand tensed within his, and he looked at it and still with that sardonic air he bent his head and kissed her wrist.

'Yes, a child should have a mother,' he said. 'I wonder if I asked you to play once more tonight you would oblige? Something to dispel the shadows, eh?'

'If you wish, *senhor*.' She rose to her feet and her hand slipped from his, bringing close to her side the kiss that lingered on her bruised wrist. They walked together to the larger salon and he opened the grand piano for her, lit the candles and turned out the main lights.

'*Les Sylphides*,' he murmured, and his eyes flicked

her ashen hair in the candlelight. 'You know the music, of course?'

'Of course.' Her smile was shy and swift, and she was both glad and a little regretful when he retreated into the shadows to listen to the music that evoked, perhaps, a boyish memory of his grandmother, a dancer in a misty white dress, a sweet ghost that did not torment him.

Rosary played on and on for him, until suddenly, stridently, the telephone rang in the hall. He excused himself and went to answer it. When he returned his expression by the glow of the candles was unreadable. 'Aunt Azinha and Gisela have arranged to stay the night at her friend's house,' he said. 'My aunt has a fear of night-time driving, and so I have agreed to the arrangement.'

'It will make a nice change for Gisela, *senhor*.'

'Quite so.' He began to wander about the room, picking up ornaments and quizzing them, and then putting them down again. 'It has not been such a nice change for you, eh, dining with a man of unpredictable moods? Tell me, are you looking forward to the *festa* at the weekend?'

'Immensely. It will be my first real chance to listen to the *fados* and to watch the dancing.'

'Dancing and music are the pleasures of the gods.' He stood holding a little figurine and Rosary saw the glimmer of his teeth in a reflective smile. 'Love is the third pleasure, if one ever finds it. Do you miss the young man in England?'

The question sprang at her, softly and dangerously as a springing cat. *What young man?* she almost cried, and then she recalled the white lie she had told about Erick. 'Oh,' she said, 'of course.'

'How shy the British are of speaking their love,' he

mocked. 'The Liszt song was far more expressive of your feelings. How would it be if I arranged for him to fly to Vozes do Mar for the weekend, so that you might enjoy the *festa* together?'

'No——' She sprang to her feet. 'No, he wouldn't be able to get away from the orchestra. *Senhor*, please leave my personal feelings alone! I don't question yours!'

'Mine, Miss Bell?' His gaze was directly upon her through the candle glow and his height, his danger, seemed intensified.

'Yours—with regard to Senhorita Cortez.' The sudden tiredness of spent emotions swept over Rosary, making her reckless. 'I hope I proved a satisfactory stand-in for her tonight. *senhor*? Thank goodness I have not been so guarded from life as a Latin girl, otherwise I might have been shocked to learn that love can be a hurtful thing I am sure you wouldn't want to disillusion the woman you are going to marry!'

The words rang out in the silence of the room, and then in the electric pause that followed Rosary ran to the double doors and flung them open with a sort of desperation. She expected any second to feel him breathing down her neck. and it wasn't until she was halfway across the hall, with the baroque stairway looming ahead of her, that she realized he hadn't moved. He had let her go as if too contemptuous to be angry with her. As she went upstairs she dragged her feet a little, rather like a tired adolescent going home from a party she wasn't sure she had enjoyed. She watched the pale glitter of her evening shoes against the darkness of the stairs, and felt the soft swing of chiffon against her legs. Her mood was pitched between excitement and tears, and when she reached the head of the stairs she paused to gaze at the archway that led into the picture gallery.

Suddenly she felt a compulsion to look at the face of Isabela, to see again the beauty which had bewitched Duarte.

CHAPTER NINE

ROSARY pushed aside the velvet curtains over the arch-way and switched on the wall lights, so arranged to shine on the paintings. Somewhere a window was open and as she made her way along the gallery the perfume of datura wafted in from the gardens.

Montqueiro eyes seemed to follow her from the portraits, and the sound of her own footsteps was somehow intrusive, for everything was so quiet, so enshrouded by the moonless night.

The gleam of a red gown and white arms drew her to the portrait which she had last seen on Dacio's work table. Now it was hung and the colours had been so revived that the raven hair and creamy skin of Isabela were almost touchable. Her dress and her jewels gleamed richly, and her dark eyes seemed to meet and hold Rosary's. They held a subtle little smile, as if she mocked the artist who had painted her with such admiration.

The minutes passed, one after the other, as Rosary studied the flawless face, the long line of the neck en-circled by gems, the hands whose fingers had that curious plumpness of greedy hands. Suddenly a cold shiver ran through her and she turned away from the portrait. It was too perfect a beauty, with a flawed soul.

Reaching the velvet-hung archway, she turned out the lights and slipped silently out of the picture gal-lery ... and walked unaware into a pair of arms that reached out of the dimness and closed around her, making a prisoner of her.

'So you had to go and look at her!' Dark eyes blazed down at Rosary, too stunned for the moment to move or speak. 'You had to find in her beauty the brute that I am, eh? This much a brute . . . and this!'

She was swept painfully close to him, and as her head reared back so that she might speak, might let him know that she didn't condemn him for wanting a warm and giving woman, his mouth came down on hers as if he revenged himself on her.

His lips were warm and hard and scornful in their taking . . . his left hand raked upwards into her hair, gripping the pale silk of it, and his right arm was cruel in its strength as it locked her to him, from her breast to her hips. Savagely, deliberately, he kissed her until in her maddened attempt to get away from him she was kicking his ankles.

'You little wildcat!' Still he gripped her hair and stared down at her white, almost desperate face, that of a girl swept for the first time into the deeps of a man's angry passion. The silence stretched, and then was broken as his arms slid away from her and the cool night air along the galley came between them, scented with datura. 'Tomorrow I shall doubtless be walking with a stick again,' he said drily.

'Oh—your ankle!' Free of him, she backed away, but into her eyes leapt instant contriteness, the memory of him pinned beneath an overturned car. 'I didn't think——'

'Nor did I.' He gave her a sardonic little bow. 'Kicks for kisses would seem appropriate in the circumstances. *Bom noite*, Miss Bell, and let me add that there will be no need for you to lock your bedroom door. A wrenched shoulder from forcing it open, and a battered ankle, would really be too much for even Casanova.'

Again with a bow, and something of amusement at the way she had fought him, he turned on his heel and walked away. She stared after his tall figure, and having known his fury she wondered, with a swift acute wonder, what his tenderness was like.

Madness ... she ran her fingers through her hair and felt her tingling scalp, and ran all the way to her room. Crazy ... to love him, and to hate him at the same time.

She leant from her balcony and breathed the pervasive scent of Angel's Trumpet. The night seemed heady with it ... her senses rocked and swam with datura, and the lingering ache of Duarte's mouth on hers.

Cibby, what shall I do? She pressed her cheek to the cool stonework and she hungered to be a child again, protected and directed by her grandfather's wisdom. Should she go home ... now ... next week, before it became too unbearable to see Duarte each day and to know that each week brought nearer and nearer his marriage to Lola? When she had mentioned the betrothal bracelet he had made no denial of being the donor. When he had kissed her it had been from anger, not desire.

When would he let it be known that he had decided to marry again ... at the *festa,* as the Marquesa del Ronda had suggested?

Rosary had looked forward to the *festa,* but now she had a dread of it. Was she a good enough actress to greet with a smile the official announcement of the Governor's engagement to Lola, who was so lovely, so Latin, so ready to make the perfect wife for him? Wearily she walked into her bedroom and removed her chiffon dress, the little tiger-eyes from her earlobes and the gay little slippers from her feet. She wandered about her room preparing for bed, and with her ruffled silvery hair and slightly shadowed eyes she looked very young, and yet had never felt so adult before.

What would she have done had she been more a woman of the world? Would she have fought Duarte, or given in to his furious kisses? As there rushed over her again all those alarming sensations aroused by his lips on hers, she buried her face in her hands, almost as if she prayed for the strength to withstand this sudden assault on her emotions by a man who had kissed her to punish her, and who by now would have quite forgotten those wild moments on the threshold of the picture gallery.

For her it had been the threshold of discovery ... when she had kicked him, she had kicked to be free of her increasing longing never to be free of his lips, his arms, his lean and dangerous body. She plunged out the bedroom light, but couldn't erase from her mind every feature of his face ... or blot from her body a sense of need unknown until now; an aching desire to be wanted by him. She lay staring into the darkness and it was a long time before she fell asleep.

In the morning she felt more composed, but was glad when she went down to breakfast to find that he was already at work in his study, and she had the patio table to herself. She was drinking a second cup of coffee when Dacio arrived for his day's work. As he came through the arched entrance he paused to give her a rather searching look. 'All alone and just a little blue?' he asked.

'You may join me for some coffee and then I shan't be alone,' she said gaily.

He came and sat on one of the low walls that rambled around the patio, and she rang the little bell and Manoel brought another cup and saucer to the table. She poured his coffee and gave him a smile as she handed it to him. 'If the weather stays like this for the *festa*, then it will be wonderful. I am told that people are coming all the way from Portugal for the celebration. It will be very interesting for me, my first real chance to see the islanders in their traditional costumes.'

'It will certainly be an occasion for Lola.' Dacio's gaze dwelt on Rosary's face, which in the morning sunlight was paler than she realized, with still a hint of shadow about her brown eyes. With a supreme effort of will she forced herself not to look away from Dacio; compelled herself not to betray any emotion other than friendly interest.

'I saw your sister yesterday and she told me she would soon be leaving you to your own resources. Her betrothal bracelet is very beautiful.'

'Lola was always determined to marry a man who would give her the good things in life.' He plucked a small flower from the cluster that overhung the wall, put it to his lips and with a careless gallantry he tossed it to Rosary. It fell on the table by her hand, but she didn't dare to pick it up. Her hand would crush it ... she could feel in her fingers the urge to crush something. Yes, Duarte could offer all this, but surely for a second time he wasn't going to find himself bound to a woman who wanted *things*! Rosary thought of Lola at the villa yesterday, her emphasis on the fact that the place was small and she looked forward to a much grander house.

'Don't you want the flower?' Dacio murmured. 'You aren't a girl who prefers gold bracelets, are you?'

'No.' She shook her head. 'I've been eating honey and my fingers are sticky. But, Dacio, I am sure Lola is terribly in love with ... him?'

He laughed softly. 'You also place love above rubies, eh?'

'I should hope so, if one is to find any real happiness in this life!'

'Do you think you could love me?' he asked, almost casually.

'Don't jest about it,' she said, and her voice shook a little, for she was learning the hard way that love was a serious matter and not a game. 'Just because Lola is soon to be married you mustn't get in a panic for another housekeeper.'

'You little *diabo*!' Immediately he was on his feet, and with a stride he was around the table, and Rosary cried out as he gripped her arms, where someone else had left bruises, and dragged her to her feet. He shook her, and then quickly bent his head and kissed her startled mouth.

'*Bom dia.*' The voice was smooth and cold as ice. 'I am about to drive into town and wondered, Miss Bell, if you have some shopping you would like to do. I am informed by telephone that Gisela is now going to a picnic, so you have a holiday.'

Rosary's feelings were impossible to describe as she edged away from Dacio ... his kiss had meant nothing, but the fact that Duarte had witnessed it was mortifying. What would he think of her? She, who had kicked his sore ankle in her desperation to escape his kisses! With Dacio she had been passive in her surprise, and also unafraid of him, but Duarte wasn't to know that. He had observed a girl submitting without a struggle to a young man's kiss, on a sunlit patio, surrounded by flowers and the music of bees.

All she could do was to accept politely his offer of a lift into town.

'I will go and fetch my handbag, *senhor*.'

'Don't run, Miss Bell. I am not going immediately.'

Her eyes brushed his face, a polite mask of lean distinction, with a hint of scorn about the lips that last night had been so close to hers. He wore a white suit, with a pale tan shirt. He looked ... oh, she didn't dare to think of how he looked. All she knew was that he belonged to someone else, and she, Rosary, was the one who cared madly for him. Yes! Madly! So that it wouldn't have mattered to her if he were a boatman rather than the Governor of the island.

He made polite and impersonal conversation as they drove along in the car which had replaced the Porsche. When they reached the Avenida Rey he didn't offer to pick her up for lunch, but said he would be waiting to drive her home at three o'clock, outside the Administration building.

'I am sure you can amuse yourself until then,' he said.

'Of course, *senhor*. I wish to buy a dress for the *festa*, and then I might have a look around the old *palacio* again.'

'You must have some lunch,' he said briskly. 'I fear I shall be tied up until this afternoon, but you are not a young woman who needs to lean upon a man, are you?'

'No, *senhor*.' For the first time that morning she met his eyes, and found them as impersonal as his face. 'I shall find a harbour café and eat lobster salad, and strawberries and cream.'

He frowned slightly, and his eyes flicked over her, taking in her bright uncovered hair, and the sleeveless dress she wore, cut halfway to her waist at the back and deliciously cool and short. 'I should prefer that you don't choose a café frequented by the fishermen,' he said curtly.

'Why, are you afraid I shall flirt with one of them?' She spoke the words with a painful rush of feeling, for his glance criticized her dress ... her entire person, and it was hard to endure when she longed ... oh, for the unattainable.

'I have warned you before,' his cutting tone of voice made her flinch, 'that Latin men have a fire in them that you would find hard to extinguish if you roused it uncontrollably with your careless disregard for convention.' Suddenly he put an arm around her waist and just about swept her into the biggest department store on the *avenida*. His fingers snapped and a saleswoman in a sedate dark dress came running to attend to his demands.

'I wish to buy a coat for the young lady,' he said. 'Something in a light material—tussore, perhaps!'

Rosary was overwhelmed by him, ordered not to say a word as a selection of coats were shown to him. One of them was silvery grey, with a high mandarin collar and full sleeves. 'Try it on,' he said to her, and with a mutinous set to her lips she did so. She hoped it wouldn't fit her, but it fitted perfectly, and had that light and glamorous feel of an expensive garment.

'That is the one,' he said decisively. 'Please to put it on my account, and also——'

'No!' Rosary gave him a fierce look that stopped the words on his lips. He would not pay for her dress for the *festa*, even if he was determined to buy the coat, to cover sedately the arms and neck of his daughter's tutor.

'Very well.' He inclined his head. 'I should like your promise that you will wear the coat when you leave the shop and go and have lunch.'

'If you insist.' She forced a little laugh to her lips.

'How very conventional you Latins are—in public!'

Instantly he guessed her meaning and as she saw the tiny danger signals leap to life in his eyes she tilted her chin and dared him with a look to lose in public his well-controlled temper. She knew, as the saleswoman and the other shoppers couldn't know, that he leashed that leaping temper only seconds before he gave a brief bow and left the shop, allowing the doors to swing sharply behind him.

A momentary silence followed his departure, and then people began to speak again in low tones. Rosary felt sure they were speaking about her; she felt their glances on the tussore coat and for a moment she almost panicked and dashed through the swing doors in the wake of Duarte. He was arrogant enough not to care that people might gossip about his every action, but Rosary cared, and she turned quickly to the saleswoman. 'The *senhor* was kind enough to buy me the coat for my birthday.' She spoke so her voice carried, and after all it was only a white lie; her birthday was only a week away. 'He's very generous to the people who work for him.'

'Indeed he is, *senhorita*. Firm but never the tyrant.'

'No, never the tyrant.' Rosary smiled slightly. 'I should now like to see some evening dresses, and this time I am treating myself.'

'Has the *senhorita* a particular colour in mind?' As they walked to the lift the silk coat rustled softly and expensively, and glances of unveiled curiosity followed the English Miss with the silvery hair. She felt her cheeks warming up; it was quite a new experience for her to be thought a *femme fatale*.

The morning passed and the dress she finally decided on was an intriguing blend of white and pale green silk, very simple in design, but with a sweeping skirt that made her seem tall and willowy, and gave her a much needed sense of assurance.

Dacio had intimated that the *festa* was going to be a special occasion for Lola, which must mean that her engagement was going to be officially announced. When that moment came Rosary was going to need all the courage that her resilient youth and a pretty dress could bring to her aid. A gay smile must be her shield, and the garment of silk her armour.

After arranging to pick up her dress around three o'clock, Rosary left the shop and made her way along the palm-lined *avenida* towards the noisy, bustling market-place. Here the streets were narrow and stepped, wending their way down to the colourful harbour, where below the long cobbled sea-wall the fishing boats with their high prows were drawn up on the sands.

Rosary stood by the sea-wall and watched a picturesque old fishing boat bringing in the crab and lobster pots, alive with the clawed creatures. Peddlers of fish, cheese and golden loquats carried their wide baskets on their heads, and the clatter of wooden sandals on the cobbles mingled with the talk and laughter of people haggling around the market stalls.

She felt an eager longing to be part of all this, to have a stake in the island, an assured future among these pleasant and happy people. But it was a forlorn hope. Nothing on earth would keep her at the *palacete* when Lola became its mistress. It wasn't that she disliked the Latin girl ... it was that she loved the Governor.

'Love is a devil', she thought, and with a rueful smile she glanced at her wristwatch and realized that the lunch hour was upon her and she must find a quiet café where she could eat without feeling conspicuously alone. The smart café where she had lunched with Duarte and his daughter was out of the question. It was far too expensive, and too many of his friends lunched there.

On impulse she approached one of the *varinas* who stood resting her basket of fish on the harbour wall, the bright sleeves of her blouse bunched up around her muscular arms. '*Bom dia, amiga,*' Rosary greeted her, and went on to ask if she knew of a nearby café that was secluded and inexpensive.

The *varina* looked at her with a friendly curiosity, running her dark gaze over the sunlit hair of the *Inglesa,* studying her features that were so different from those of her swarthy self. She gestured along the harbour to where the colour-washed houses were situated. If the *senhorita* was on her own, then she would find it pleasant to eat at the *quinta.* She would locate it quite easily, for it was a whitewashed house set within a garden of fruit trees.

'You are kind.' Rosary thanked her and proceeded in the direction of the houses. Soon she came in sight of white, thickly crusted walls, and an ornamental gate leading into a garden where tables were arranged under the fruit trees. The *quinta* itself had a picturesque jumble of red-tiled roofs, casement windows and deep doorways framed in cascades of a bougainvillea.

Rosary stood entranced by the place, and pleasure was swiftly followed by a stab of regret. How she would have loved to lunch here with Dom Duarte, beneath those custard-apple trees, with their enormous leaves gold-flecked and shading the table which stood within sound of the trickling water of the irrigation wheel. She removed the coat he had bought her and hung it over the adjacent chair; it made the chair seem less bare and unoccupied.

A young waitress came to her table and with a smile of welcome she handed her a menu, from which Rosary selected ice-cold cream soup, and lobster salad to follow, with a glass of wine. She then sat breathing the scents of the garden ... how peaceful it was after the bustle of the harbour, and there were no bold young fishermen to ogle her and call out those Latin compliments that always sounded so risqué. The other tables were mainly occupied by young couples intent on each other; the girls' *duenas* appeared to be lunching together at other tables.

The waitress served her cream soup, and she seemed to look at Rosary with sympathy in her eyes. Rosary gave her a gay little smile, as if to deny that it didn't hurt, or matter, that she had no attentive Latin to look at her as if she made his sunshine.

The lobster meat was removed from the shell for her and arranged on a bed of crisp lettuce; with it were slices of tomato and cucumber, a delicious sauce, crusty bread and sweet butter. Her glass of amber-coloured wine made her feel almost carefree, and the sweet wild strawberries and cream that followed made her think of childhood holidays and roaming the Devon hills with Cibby, whose affection had been all-sufficing until she came to Vozes do Mar and discovered another kind of love.

After lunch she roamed the *quinta* gardens instead of going to the museum, and discovered a little domed gazebo set round with great ferns that drooped against its walls, with blue passion-flowers climbing its roof. She was about to enter when she caught the murmur of a male voice and the soft laughter of a woman. She quickly retreated and told herself ruefully that the *quinta* was a place for lovers and she was an intruder

... anyway, it must be almost three o'clock, for she had dallied over her lunch, and she ought to be getting back to the shop to pick up her dress.

She glanced at her wristwatch and saw that the hands stood at two-thirty. Ample time for her to stroll back to the shop and meet the car outside the Administration building.

A slumbrous siesta quiet lay over the town, and the harbour looked so deserted that it was unbelievable it had been so busy a couple of hours ago. On the beach some fishermen lay sleeping in the shade of their boats, and the sun and the sea had merged into a dazzling glow. The palm trees along the Avenida Rey were as becalmed as everything else, their fans spread green and still against the blue sky. She arrived at the shop and entered through the swing doors. She went up in the lift to the dress department, where to her relief she found a girl crouched at the feet of a display model, busily stitching the hem of a white satin gown.

Rosary explained that she had come to fetch a dress she had bought that morning. It was already wrapped and labelled for her. The girl nodded and went to fetch it, and Rosary stood looking at the lovely white gown on the display model. It had long tight sleeves with crystalled cuffs, a high neck with a crystalled collar and a long full skirt with a train. It was quite stunning, and quite obviously a wedding gown.

When the girl returned with Rosary's dress box, and knelt again to continue with her stitching, it seemed the most natural thing to ask who the lucky bride was to be. The girl glanced up with a smile. 'The material was sent from Portugal, *senhorita*. The dress has been specially made for the marriage of the Senhorita Cortez ... she will make a lovely bride, I think.'

'She will indeed,' said Rosary, and she said *adeus*

and felt curiously numb as she left the department store, as if the pain would be too hard to endure if she gave in to it. She walked back along the *avenida* without noticing the heat or the stillness, and when she came in sight of the Administration building she pinned a smile to her lips and was determined to look as if she had enjoyed every moment of her shopping, and her lonely lunch in a garden made for lovers.

She saw the bronze-coloured car standing at the kerb of the paved entrance to the handsome building, with its façade of gorgeous *azulejos*, and stone lions guarding the steps. The only sound as she made her way to the car was that of the water falling into the marble basins of the fountain that stood in the forecourt, splashing down over the mermaids and the huge conch shells. A long shadow slanted in the sunlight, and Rosary's heart beat fast as Dom Duarte came unhurriedly towards her.

'I—I hope I haven't kept you waiting,' she said, 'I had to return to the shop to collect my dress.'

'Ah yes, the intriguing dress for the *festa*.' His eyes smiled a little as he took the box and put it on the back seat of his car. 'You had a good lunch, I hope?'

'Terrific! Why didn't you tell me, *senhor*, about the *quinta* where they serve meals in that lovely garden? A *varina* directed me there and I found the place enchanting.'

'But you must also have felt rather *sozinha*.' He murmured the word with a rather wicked emphasis. 'It is the local meeting place for courting couples ... did you not notice?'

'Of course I noticed.' She gave a gay little laugh. 'I expect you sometimes go there yourself, *senhor*.'

'And why should I go there?' he drawled, and she felt his narrowed gaze upon her face as she slipped into the passenger seat. To avoid answering him, she pretended not to have heard him, and busied herself removing the tussore coat.

'I feel rather hot, *senhor*. Would you put it on the back seat for me?'

'You do look a trifle flushed—have you been walking about in the hot sun?' Abruptly the back of his hand was placed against her forehead and the electrifying shock of his touch ran all through her, and she jerked away from him.

'I'm perfectly all right.' Panic made her speak sharply. 'You don't have to treat me like a child who hasn't sense enough to look after herself. If I feel hot, then it's your fault! You bought the coat and insisted that I wear it, as if bare arms are some sort of an affront to your dignity. If I offend your dignity so much, Dom Duarte, then I think it might be a good idea if I leave next week. You gave me six weeks in which to prove myself, and you obviously disapprove of everything I do. I—I can't stay on those terms—I want to go home,' she ended, on such a shaky note that she stopped speaking, in case her voice broke altogether and she gave way to the misery which had invaded her since seeing that beautiful white gown in which Lola was to be married.

'You know,' he said, looking rather dangerous with his narrowed eyelids, and his mouth drawn thinly around the words, 'you should never have left that young man in the first place. It is he whom you wish to rush back to—and don't bother to make a denial! You lunched at the *quinta* and saw the young couples there holding hands, and now you are all on edge for the man in your own heart. So be it!' He snapped his fingers decisively and strode round to take the driver's seat. The engine purred awake and they moved off

178

rapidly through the slumbrous town, heading up the slope that overlooked the sea.

It shimmered through a heat haze ... and through the tears that Rosary battled with, in silent desperation. With every bit of her heart she longed to deny the lie to which she had committed herself ... but if she told the truth he might guess how she felt about him, and that would be equally unbearable. To be pitied by him would be worse than being struck by him!

'You will, of course, stay for the *festa*?' He spoke abruptly, after about ten minutes of silence, and a sudden slowing down of the speed which had carried them for some miles along the headland. 'It will be something for you to remember when you are home again. A fitting farewell, perhaps, to my silver slave.'

'Your what?' she exclaimed, twisting around to look at him with amazement, the tears gone from her eyes to her heart.

'Gisela said it once.' A smile flickered on his lips. 'The night she had her nightmare and I was angry because you were not there. The child said you were not my "silver slave" or anyone else's. You would appear to have infected my daughter with your notions of independence.'

'Then it's just as well that I'm leaving, *senhor*. It wouldn't do for you to have a rebel on your hands when the time comes for *you* to select a husband for Gisela. All this selective mating might be good for the bone structure, but it can't always be good for the heart.'

'I see.' His drawl was menacing. 'Now you take it upon yourself to take our mating habits to task. You, who have been among the Portuguese only a matter of weeks.'

179

'Does it always work, *senhor*, to marry from the head rather than from the heart?'

'To be ruled by the heart can be a mistake.' He spoke with sudden harshness and suddenly the needle on the speedometer was swinging from fifty to sixty, and up into the seventies. The knuckles of Duarte's hands stood out like porcelain under the brown skin and the car sped along so fast that the sea below the narrow road was a dazzling blur. Rosary flung out a hand and gripped the handle of the door beside her, and she had fearful visions of the car hurtling off the edge of the road.

'I'd rather like to get home to my grandfather in one piece,' she gasped. 'Really! There should be a law against quick-tempered men who drive!'.

As she spoke the tall gates of the *palacete* loomed ahead of them, and to her relief the needle began to fall back on the speedometer and as they turned in between the gates he said in a low, threatening voice: 'Miss Bell, I beg of you to stay out of my way during the rest of your stay on Vozes do Mar. The next time we are alone I shall not be responsible for my actions.' The car pulled in smoothly beside the front steps and even as the engine cooled, he gestured curtly at the door beside Rosary. 'Please leave me! I am not coming in!'

She opened the door and slipped out of the car. 'Thanks for the lift,' she said flippantly, and she ran up the steps and along the terrace, not pausing to collect her coat and her dress box. He would have them brought to her later on by one of the maids; right now she wanted only to obey his injunction that she stay out of his way. She heard the car start up, reverse and go off down the drive where it turned into the small lane that led to the Cortez villa. Rosary tried not to feel hurt or envious, but the blessed numbness was gone and all she could think of as she ran upstairs to the cool, calm sanity of her bedroom was that she had no place at all in his life. He had thrust her out very finally with those last few words.

'Stay out of my way ... or I shall not be responsible for my actions.'

His annoyance with her had turned to actual dislike, and to wipe her from his mind he had gone to Lola ... right now he would be holding the Latin girl in his arms, soothed by the velvety murmur of her voice. Like all men he wanted flattery and not the sting of truth, especially when it was delivered by an English girl in his employ. Rosary couldn't suppress a shiver as she remembered the hard grip of his hands on the wheel of the car, the taut control of his face when he had told her to leave him.

Tiredly she kicked off her shoes and walked through the soft pile of the carpet to her bed. She lay there, staring at the ceiling with eyes that ached from too much sunshine, and the effort not to cry. The clock ticked softly beside her bed, and each minute was ticking her out of the *palacete*, off the island, and back home to Surrey. How strange its green hills would seem after the sun-baked sands, and vine-clad terraces of Vozes do Mar. How awful it would be to wake each morning to a day that did not hold one or two glimpses of a tall, dark, impeccably clad man whose sardonic smile she had grown to love so much.

She stared at the revolving shadow of the fan, like the waving legs of a giant insect, and in a while the movements acted like a narcotic and she fell asleep ... to awaken suddenly in darkness some hours later. Even as she sat up her bedroom door was thrust open, the light was switched on and Gisela was running eagerly to her bemused figure on the bed, full of the picnic and her new friends ... swooping on the dress box the maid had brought to Rosary's room and clamouring for it to be opened so that she might see the new dress.

'I can't wait for the *festa*, can you?' Gisela played with the bow that tied the box, and her eyes shone. 'I shall wear the traditional costume which belonged to my mother when she was my age. It's all so exciting and there will be so many people there. You will love it, Rosary!'

'I'm sure I shall.' Rosary spoke with a little touch of irony that was lost on the younger girl ... and then she caught her breath as she realized that Gisela knew nothing of the marriage announcement that would surely be made at the *festa*. It would come as a shock for Gisela, and Rosary could only suppose that Dom Duarte considered this the best way to deal with the problem of letting his daughter know that he was taking a second wife. The excitement and the gaiety would soften the blow; make it seem part of the festivities, a happy thing that would enrich both their lives.

'May I?' Gisela pulled off the bow and lifted the lid of the box. She took the dress from its soft wrappings and gave a gasp of delight. 'You will look beautiful in this, Rosary! You will outshine all the other girls with your silvery hair and your white skin. Every young man will want to make love to you.'

Rosary had to laugh. 'I'm glad you like my fine feathers, but I'm sure I shall not outshine Lola. She is a stunning person, with those big dark eyes and that glossy black hair.'

'She's no different from other Latin girls ... except my mother, who was really beautiful.' Gisela tossed her head, and cold fingers clutched at Rosary's heart. 'Tia Azinha's friends remarked that Lola is wearing a betrothal bracelet of engraved gold, which must mean that she has found a rich man for herself. Everyone knows that she wants a rich and important husband ... I was always afraid that she was after my father, the way she was always cooing over him.'

'Gisela...' Rosary bit her lip. 'You like Lola, don't you?'

'Not particularly.' The girl stroked the silk of Rosary's dress. 'I much prefer Dacio. He's far more honest ... he's rather like you, Rosary. He says what is in his mind, but Lola only smiles and—and looks sort of like a cat who has licked the cream.'

The description was so apt, but Rosary had never felt less like smiling. Dom Duarte couldn't think of springing on his daughter the fact that he was marrying Lola ... yet what could she do about it? The very thought of speaking to him on such an intimate matter made her flinch ... stay out of my way, he had ordered, and she must do so, and hope to heaven that Gisela would accept the inevitable fact that he was the important man whom Lola was to marry.

'Do hurry, *festa* day!' Gisela danced across the carpet of Rosary's bedroom and with a laugh of happy anticipation she bowed herself out of the room.

CHAPTER TEN

THE grounds of the wine *quinta* owned by the Ronda family were so overflowing with people that it was like a country fair, this *festa* that made welcome the wine in the autumn.

Moonlight shone in laughing eyes, the scent of wine already in the vines mingled with the smoke drifting upwards from the big open fires over which the sucking pigs were crackling in their shiny skin. Bands of musicians strolled about in their colourful costumes, quickening the pulse with the music of their guitars. Coloured lights glowed among the trees, and many of the women were dressed in the traditional costume, the full skirt flaring with colour, the lacy, full-sleeved blouse, and the medallion earrings embossed with saintly profiles. Rosary could almost imagine that the centuries had slipped back, especially when she saw the wine workers arriving with their shiny dancing boots hung round their necks to keep the dust of the roads off the buff or canary yellow leather.

The girls arrived with camellias in their hair, and the young men wore their best frilled shirts and dark velvet trousers, and these good-looking young couples made it seem very much a *fête d'amour*.

The day before Dacio had asked Rosary if he might escort her to the *festa* and she had accepted his offer in such a heartfelt way that his eyes had gleamed. They still held that gleam, she noticed, as she strolled with him about the grounds of the *quinta* and they watched the fandango dancers whirling and stamping to their hearts' content. They drank *vinho tinto* together and ate cheese and fruit from the food-laden tables.

He had just introduced her to the fruit of the *maracuja*, the passion flower. The fruit to look at was rather like a green tomato, but it wasn't at all sour and tasted rather like a mandarin with a hint of raspberry flavour.

'The *maracuja* is rather like a woman.' Dacio smiled at her and looked dashing in his black velvet suit that fitted him as closely as a matador's. 'It's a deceptive fruit, hiding its tasty sweetness in a cloak of green.'

Rosary wore a swathing of green chiffon about her shoulders, and she smiled at Dacio's meaningful remark. She knew that just lately he found her a bit of a mystery, and instinct warned her that now had come the moment for telling him that she was leaving Vozes do Mar on Monday; taking the small steamer that would call with the mail and the various goods ordered from Portugal.

He fell silent after she had spoken, and then suddenly he drew her in among the trees, away from the crowds, and the sudden glimpse she had of a tall figure in dark suiting walking beside the Marquesa, with Lola and several of the smart visitors from Portugal walking at the other side of him. Gisela was at the *festa* with her two young friends, and as Rosary felt the grip of Dacio's hands on her wrists, she felt a little shaft of pain quite unconnected with the artist. Soon, now, everyone would know about the forthcoming marriage of Dom Duarte do Montqueiro Ardo ... Gisela would know, and Rosary had to find her and be with her when the announcement was made.

'Let me go, Dacio.' She attempted to pull away from him, but he had no intention of letting her go and he leaned over her like a dark moth above a flower, for there was a flower-like quality to her in the white and pale green dress, with the chiffon filming the paleness of her arms and her slim neck. Her hair was piled into the soft ringlets on the crown of her head, and a shaft of moonlight through the foliage of the trees made it gleam like pirate silver. Her eyes looked huge, raised to Dacio's face in pleading, and her mouth was her only feature that showed any colour.

'Not from this place, nor from the island,' he said. 'You need a Latin husband, *amanta mia*. A man who will bring you the gold of his fire to match the silver of your charm...'

'Please...' She twisted away from him, and the chiffon flowed down her body like a mist, intensifying, somehow, the virginal quality about her. 'Don't spoil the *festa* for me, Dacio. I shall never see another.'

'You will see a thousand more if you...'

'No!' Though it hurt, she dragged her hands free of his and ran off so swiftly that the chiffon floated from her shoulders and was left behind among the trees clothed in vines, at the feet of the young Latin who was so attractive, but not for her.

Not for Rosary the love of a Latin... she who loved too much the man she had avoided for two long days. Not a word had she exchanged with him, and as she sought among the throng for Gisela, there was a sudden hush as a young man leapt upon a great broad wine cask and began to sing a *fado*, the traditional song of the Portuguese, one of lingering passion and a hint of sadness.

Tears sprang to Rosary's eyes. This was for her a goodbye song, a lament she could never express, yet which her heart echoed as the passionate notes trilled out from the masculine lips... to die, to be lost in the hush that preceded the delighted applause. The young man stood there smiling, a hand on his hip, and then he leapt down to rejoin his girl, who with Latin grace took the camellia from her hair and fitted it into his buttonhole.

Rosary continued with her search for Gisela, and suddenly noticed her by one of the vinewood fires, eating pork from a plate and laughing with other young people. She looked pretty and carefree in her costume, with its velvet bodice and flounced skirt, and scarlet dancing boots. It seemeed rather fateful that she would hear she was to have a stepmother wearing the costume which had been her mother's. The thought spurred Rosary to her side. 'There you are, Gisela. I can see you're having a wonderful time.'

'Yes ... and doesn't my father look handsome? I think if the Marquesa was a younger woman she would make a play for him. Look! They are going up on to the veranda, where a microphone will be fitted up so the Marquesa can give her traditional speech of welcome to the *festa* and wish upon the future wine the best of sweet health and body.'

Rosary's eyes softened as they dwelt on the young and eager face of Duarte's child ... she might have stayed for Gisela's sake, but he had accepted without an argument her decision to leave. He had even made it plain that her presence had become an annoyance, and she hoped that from where he stood upon the veranda, there among the Rondas and their friends, with Lola close by, he couldn't see her beyond the leaping flames of the bonfire. If he saw her, his features would show what he felt. They would freeze into a bronze mask, cold of all warm feeling.

The Marquesa, looking frail and yet wonderful in a beautifully made prune-coloured dress, with a pale beige mink wrap about her shoulders, and with careful make-up outlining her features and her amusingly malicious eyes, spoke for several minutes about the *festa* and how happy she was to see so many of her friends. Happiness and hard work made good wine, she said, and good wine added a sparkle to life.

After the warm applause at the end of her speech, she turned to Dom Duarte, and Rosary felt herself go cold from head to foot as the Marquesa added that their Governor had an announcement to make, which would make sparkle the eyes of a certain young woman known to them all.

Rosary reached for Gisela's hand and the girl gave her a little enquiring smile, and then returned her attention to her father, who now stood in front of the microphone, which was partly concealed by a splash of bougainvillea, the lovely purple plant that grew so lushly all over the island. He stood there, tall and in command of the crowd, smiling a little. 'Wine and romance seem to go together,' he said, and Rosary felt the wild beating of her heart as he turned deliberately to Lola Cortez, lovely and Latin in her gold brocade dress, with a pale lace mantilla framing her glossy hair. She gazed back at him and her eyes seemed to hold his gaze for an interminable moment, then she smiled and seemed to look at the many firelit faces with a hint of arrogance. Rosary bit her lip, and her fingers tightened upon Gisela's ... surely she had seen that look of Lola's before ... on the portrayed face of Isabela, whose self-love had left no room for love of a man.

'You all know Lola Cortez,' Dom Duarte went on. 'This beautiful young woman has lived among us for several years now, and graced our island with her presence. Tonight, as we enjoy the gaiety of the *festa*, it seems appropriate that as your friend, *amigos y amigas*, as well as your Governor, I should have the pleasure of telling you that within a few days the

Senhorita Lola will become the bride of'—he paused, and his eyes were glinting as he swept a hand in the direction of a portly and distinguished man, slightly silvered at the temples, who stood next to the Marquesa—'the Senhor Mateo de Randolfo, the President of the Nacional Banking House in Lisboa.'

Once again loud applause broke out, and then it was announced that everyone must have wine to bless the good health and happiness of the betrothed couple.

'So that's him!' Gisela exclaimed. 'Well, I must say he looks rich, but he isn't very young, is he?'

Rosary stood there speechlessly, and then had to pull herself together as Gisela asked anxiously if she was feeling all right. 'You look terribly pale, Rosary. Are you faint?'

'N-no. I'm a little confused by all the noise. Darling, I'm going off for a little walk by myself among the trees, where it's quiet. You will be all right with your friends?'

'Yes—but perhaps I should come with you?' Gisela drew Rosary's icy hand to her cheek. 'You feel so cold, like a statue. You should have some wine—shall I fetch you a glass?'

'All right, if you wish.' Rosary waited until Gisela was out of sight among the laughing, chattering throng of people, and then blindly she turned and ran ... ran until the trees gave shelter from the storm of emotion which had assailed her when she saw Duarte place the hand of Lola in that of the distinguished visitor from Portugal. The relief had been almost as hard to endure as the acceptance of her own dismissal from his life. She knew with her every instinct that Lola would have loved to be his wife ... she had accepted this other man on the rebound. Someone she had always known, perhaps, who would give her riches if he could not give her the excitement of being the Governor's Lady.

Finding herself out of breath, Rosary stopped running and rested her slim body against a tree. But for the moonlight through an opening in the foliage she would have been in darkness. She had been arming herself for days against the announcement that he was to marry Lola ... now she was totally disarmed by the news that he was to marry no one. It could not alter the fact of her departure. She could neither stay to see him the husband of someone else, nor could she stay to be unloved by him.

She plucked aimlessly a sprig of trailing blossom, with which all these trees were clothed to enhance their beauty. She breathed its perfume, and heard in the distance the sound of music as everyone danced for the bride-to-be.

But for that distant music everything here was strangely still and quiet. When a gecko suddenly chanted in a bush Rosary very nearly jumped out of her skin. She should go back, for Gisela would be searching for her, but a strange lassitude held her immobile where she was, the trailing blossoms soft-petalled against her shoulders. Alone like this she didn't have to smile and parade a false gaiety. She didn't have to pretend that it would be easy to take that steamer on Monday at noon; to stand at the rail and watch Vozes do Mar recede into the distance until it became a blur and then a misty blank, where life would go on as if she had never been a part of it for six world-turning weeks.

She sighed ... and then stiffened as something rustled among the trees, and a few seconds later took shape as tall, dark and unmistakably masculine in the shaft of moonlight.

'So this is where you are hiding yourself.' The voice was deep, even a trifle concerned, shattering the thin veneer of her composure. 'Gisela was worried about you, so I came to find you.'

'I—I'm all right.' She spoke defiantly. 'Do I have to account for all my actions? Didn't you tell me to stay out of your way?'

'Yes, I said that—for your own good.' He came several steps nearer to her and her face revealed itself as very pale, with that hurt quality which the moon reveals and which the daylight conceals with its busy, brash disregard for love. 'Are you not enjoying the *festa*? I saw you earlier with Lola's brother, smiling and eating supper with him. Has he now found another companion?'

'I expect so,' she said, for never for a moment had she taken seriously Dacio's talk of love and marriage. 'Latin men and women belong together. I am the outsider, and quite soon you will be rid of me, *senhor*.'

'Yes.' He spoke harshly. 'It is better so.'

'Much better,' she agreed. 'Gisela is young and will soon forget me, though it will be nice to remember that she rather liked me.'

With these words Rosary made to move away from him and as she did so the trailing blossoms caught at her hair and hooked themselves in the silver slide that held the soft curls in place. She paused to free herself and at the same time Duarte stepped nearer to help her. How it happened that she found herself in his arms she never knew, but suddenly his arms were more binding than steel bars, but unlike steel they were unbearably tender.

'Gisela told me you were close to fainting after I made my announcement that Lola was to marry Mateo. Tell me something,' Duarte forced up her chin

191

with his fingers and pinned his gaze to hers, 'did you think that I was to be the bridegroom? Come, be as honest as you always are! You have never yet shirked a truth when it needed to be told.'

'It did occur to me——' Her heart was beating so fast that the words shook themselves out of her lips. 'She came often to the *palacete* and it seemed a reasonable assumption.'

'It was never reasonable.' Again that harsh note rang in his voice. 'You knew of the hell I suffered with Isabela. Did you really believe that I would—no, Lola has never been more than the pretty sister of the man I employ in my picture gallery. A Latin girl well versed in the art of charming a man, as Isabela was. But I was young then, unversed myself in the art of knowing a woman. What a pity that you and I did not meet—ah, but if we had met sixteen years ago you would have been a toddler with a mop of silver hair.'

'Why'—Rosary swallowed in order to ease her dry throat—'why should you have wanted to meet me, *senhor?*'

'Because then I should not have wasted my youth on a miserable marriage—now the years have gone, and youth belongs to youth, and I send you home to the young man who awaits you in your own country.'

'There—there is no young man,' she said faintly. 'There never was——'

'But you told me——' Duarte stared down into her eyes, great orbs in the moonlight, wondering, shining a little, but not daring to believe yet that they could let flood into them the hunger and the giving. 'Why did you say such a thing? You always were so truthful that I was bound to believe you.'

'I had no other way of protecting myself——'

'Against me?' he exclaimed.

'Against my feeling for you.'

'What kind of feeling?' Now he gripped her, now he was insistent, and the implacability of his face was giving way to a look that was almost vulnerable. The mask of restraint was slipping, and Rosary was seeing the lonely man that dwelt inside the commanding Governor of Vozes do Mar.

Her courage flooded back, her spirit of adventure revived, the touch of daring that lay in her chin and her lips gave utterance to a single shattering word.

'Love,' she said simply.

In the silence a breeze rustled through the trees and the scent of flowers was strong, as if they stirred at the magic of the word.

'Love?' he echoed. 'For me?'

'Yes.' She stood very still in his arms, waiting for him to thrust her from him 'I—I didn't stop loving you just because you told me to stay away from you. It hurt, but——'

'Enough!' He said it savagely and with a savage tenderness his face pressed hers and his lips found hers in a blind movement of longing. Held by his kiss, her arms slipped of their own will about his neck and her fingers buried themselves in the thickness of his dark hair. If his kiss never ended then he need never tell her that he was only giving way to his loneliness.

Inevitably, because they had to breathe, his kiss did end, and with a little sigh, half pleasure and total fear, she buried her face in his shoulder. She wanted never to leave the warm, strong arms, but if she must, then she wouldn't do it in tears ... until she was alone again.

'I had to tell you to stay away from me, *amor sinha*. I could no longer be near you and not want you. I could no longer look at you and not love you. I could no longer think of you as my daughter's tutor—you who are so much nearer her age than mine. My silver slave, you made me feel a satyr each time I found myself alone with you.'

'You made me feel your slave, *senhor*, each time you looked at me.'

'And you don't like it?' he asked drily.

'As a matter of fact,' she took a deep breath and looked up at him, 'it's the most exciting emotion in the world.'

'You are so young.' He stroked her hair with a lean, caressing hand. 'It would not be fair—but then again it would not be human, eh, to send away my silver slave!'

'It would be hell!' she gasped.

'You would rather stay, *pequena*?' he murmured.

'That would be heaven, Duarte.'

'Then let heaven be ours, my Rosary.'

The bridal music played among the trees, and the heart of the English girl sang of love and joy, there in the arms of her Latin lover.

DEAR PURITAN

Dear
Puritan

"We are all relics of our past, of the ancestors who made us," said Don Delgado de Avarado, explaining to Romy why pride and honor and his own good name made their engagement necessary.

Romy admitted their situation was compromising, but she had no intention of marrying him. The old-world charm and customs that had first drawn her to Mexico suddenly seemed to threaten her freedom!

CHAPTER ONE

THE train thundered into the sunset as if it were heading for the gateway to the sun itself. A golden glow lay over the landscape and turned to purple the tips of the Mexican mountains. The wheels of the train made a rhythm to which Romy Ellyn set her own words as she sat beside the window in her private compartment and watched the flight of a great bird across the vivid sky. An eagle with outspread wings, strong enough to snatch a young animal from the *sabana*.

It was all so excitingly different from Lovtanet Bay, where Romy had spent her childhood and her growing up. There with wings as grey as the sea gulls had swooped in the sky and seals had lounged on the rocks only a short distance from the beach. To remember the bay was to think of Lance and the many happy hours they had spent in the water and the caves where long ago smugglers had stored their loot. Now he meant no more to her. He had married her cousin Iris, whose father had made a fortune from the canning of fish.

Holding on to her smile when Iris flaunted her engagement ring, Romy had agreed to be a bridesmaid, but a week after the wedding she went away to Bristol to study for a post at the Museum of Childhood, which appealed strongly to her. It wasn't long afterwards that she had to face another blow when Nonna, her grandmother, died suddenly and peacefully in her sleep. Fond of the girl who had been thrown upon the mercy of relatives at an early age, Nonna had left her a legacy, and also a letter sealed in the old-fashioned way with red wax.

When the letter was handed to Romy, she saw the instant gleam of curiosity in the eyes of her aunt and her cousin. 'Well, open it,' Iris said, blonde and pretty in her dark suit with a collar of fur. 'You and Nonna were always huddling together and whispering secrets. Perhaps she's left you a bit of country nonsense on how to catch a man.'

Romy, too upset by the loss of Nonna to care any more that her cousin's tart remarks could sting, carefully opened her letter and read it in silence. 'Each of us,' Nonna had written, 'has a longing when young to visit a faraway place. Go wandering for a while, Romy. Don't hold back, or let yourself be persuaded that the legacy I leave you should be hoarded for a rainy day. Go chase a rainbow, girl. Go with eagerness and courage, and my love.'

'Well,' Iris urged, 'what does the old girl have to say?'

'That with my legacy I'm to take a trip ... abroad.'

'And will you?' Iris shot a complacent smile at her husband Lance, as if to emphasise the fact that she had taken him away from Romy. 'Paris is nice in the spring, and so is Venice. Lance and I simply adored Venice and all those romantic palaces, and you could probably find a girl-friend to go with you.'

'I shall go alone.' Romy gazed at the letter and never had she felt so sure of what she wanted. 'I shall go where it pleases me to go, and I shall spend every penny Nonna has left me. I shall buy some really smart clothes, and with the rest I shall have fun.'

'On your lonesome?' Iris drawled.

'Yes, all on my own ...' And even alone Mexico City had been fascinating beyond words, and she had visited many intriguing museums and made sketches of the costumes and playthings of Mexican children. Now by train she was bound for Xerica, where she would stay for a week, and then journey on to Vera Cruz to catch a steamer for England ... and home.

What a sunset! It was as if that golden globe had been dropped into a furnace and drawn out again. Somewhere along the train bells rang to warn the passengers who wished to dine that the meal would soon be ready.

It had been an added expense to take a private compartment, but Romy wasn't regretful. Few women seemed to travel alone, unescorted, in this part of the world, and the men had such a dark and dangerous look about them. She arose from her seat and washed her face in her private washbasin. She was no bread-and-butter miss who quaked at the knees very easily, but it gave her a sense of security to have a compartment she could lock before going to bed, and a tiny pearl-handled automatic which she had bought in Mexico City in a quaint side-street shop.

She brushed her tawny hair, which was not kept in order unless she pinned it into a large soft knot at the nape of her neck, a style which exposed her temples, the clear line of her jaw, and the smallness of her ears. Romy was a girl not formally pretty, but it showed in her features that she had pluck, tenderness, and a ready sense of humour. It still hurt a little that Lance had only been playing with her youthful feelings, but not so deeply that she couldn't enjoy the climate of Mexico, the history of its colourful people, and the quaint villages surrounding the golden churches built by the Spanish conquerors. Romy met her own eager green eyes in the wall mirror and was glad she had spent Nonna's legacy in this way. It would always be a holiday to remember; something to brighten the lonely evenings when she returned to her bedsitter in Bristol.

Right now the train was travelling through the heart of the country, and Romy felt exhilarated and hungry as she made her way along the swaying corridor to the dining-car. A man was walking ahead of her, and there was something about his apparel, the way he carried his head and shoulders ... a supple, lordly air ... that made Romy catch her breath and slow her footsteps. She hoped he would enter the dining-car without a backward glance, but just as he reached the door he paused to gaze from the corridor window at the passing scenery bathed in the glow of the setting sun. Even as Romy was debating a hasty retreat to her compartment he must have caught a glimpse of her leaf-green dress and her tawny hair.

He swung right round to face her and after that there was no escaping him. He gave her a brief, courteous bow. 'Good evening, *señorita*.' He remembered her, as she remembered him, and she felt again that odd sense of shock as she met his bronze-coloured eyes under the level black brows, saw again those powerfully sculptured features and the skin of dark gold. The face was utterly masterful, and it belonged to Don Delgado de Avarado y Valcazar, a Consul of this country, and a man of considerable power and wealth, whose estate she had been told ran to many hundreds of acres.

'So we meet again in yet another unexpected way.' He spoke faultless English, with an accent that carved each word. 'Did you enjoy the remainder of your stay in Mexico City?'

'Very much, *señor*.' She smiled politely and hoped he didn't detect the nervous tremor in her voice. Because of the circumstances of their first encounter, and because of the autocratic appearance of the man, she felt strangely on edge and wished he would proceed to his table. She had not seen him at lunchtime and supposed that he had boarded the train at one of the infrequent stops.

203

'I shall escort you to your table.' He proceeded to do so, making instinctively for the table on which stood a bowl of small white orchids, the kind that grew wild and were known as Little White Nuns. 'I would invite you to dine at my table, *señorita*, but a friend will be joining me to discuss business. Perhaps afterwards you would take coffee with us in the club car?'

It was a request, and yet at the same time it was an order, and as Romy stood there, a cool contrast to his darkness, a small flame of defiance flared within her. 'I intend to have an early night, *señor*. Thank you all the same for the invitation.'

He met and held her eyes that were the cool green of mint, but instead of insisting he inclined his head and crossed the aisle to his own table, treading the floor of the swaying train with ease and assurance.

Romy sat down and turned her gaze to the window, and as the day darkened she felt the quickened beating of her heart. She hadn't dreamed that she would ever see the man again; had even parted from him in Mexico City with the hope that their paths would not cross in the future.

It had been hot that day, with a blazing warmth flooding down from the blue sky, intensifying the the earthy smells of the city and its teeming crowds. Romy had spent half the day in the cool halls of the museum of Aztec art, and on her way out the ground had suddenly heaved beneath her feet. Alarmed, she had clutched at the air and would have fallen down the steps if hands strong and sure had not saved her. 'It's an earth tremor! Quickly, out of the way of this tall building, all this glass!'

Confused, frightened, she had found herself sheltering with a stranger beneath the arch of a stone doorway. For several minutes the ground had pulsated and hot waves of heat had wafted up from the street pavements. Traffic had come to a standstill amidst the blare of motor-horns. People had run in various directions, seeking shelter and looking scared. Then gradually everything had gone still again, until the life of the city resumed its normal pace.

With a gasp of relief Romy had thanked her rescuer, who wore a suit of impeccable white and a shirt only a few shades darker than the tan of his face. He asked the name of her hotel and snapped his fingers for a cab. One drew into the kerb and he handed her into it ... and followed her. On the journey through the streets that no longer pulsed with these strange waves of energy he talked about the Aztec arts, and all the while there was a look in his bronze eyes that said it wasn't wise, or circumspect, for a single young woman to be roaming a foreign city on her own.

It was the desk clerk at the hotel who told her the man's imposing name, and that he held a high position in the diplomatic service. He had also been famous in his youth as a daring *espada*.

Now in his middle thirties, the Don had lost

none of his matador grace and danger, and because he had such an odd effect upon her nerves Romy smiled with extra charm at the young waiter who came to her table. She ordered a roast leg of chicken, creamed potatoes, and long beans. He had a little English, so it wasn't difficult to make conversation with him.

'The *señorita* likes the flowers?' he asked shyly.

'They're lovely, perfect miniature orchids.' And she was aware as she spoke that Don Delgado glanced across the aisle, his black brows joined in a frown as she fondled the Little White Nuns. She felt again that tiny flare of antagonism as she defied the disapproving look in the Latin eyes.

'And does the *señorita* wish for a glass of wine with her meal?'

'Yes ... a glass of champagne would be very nice.'

'The *señorita* is celebrating?' The waiter had noticed the direction of her gaze as she ordered champagne and he cast a swift and curious glance at the distinguished figure of Don Delgado, who had now been joined by a soldier in a dashing uniform.

'Perhaps I am,' Romy smiled, for to be young, and on holiday, was something to celebrate.

She enjoyed her dinner, especially the peach waffles and cream, and at the end of it she slid past that table wreathed in good cigar smoke and hoped she was unnoticed. '*Vaya con Dios, señorita,*' mur-

mured a deep voice, and at the same time she felt
the flick of bronze eyes over her face.

'Goodnight, *señor*.' She hurried on her way and
heard behind her a mutter of enquiry from the
cavalry officer with whom Don Delgado dined. She
had to admit that she admired the uniform. It was
rather romantic that in this mechanised age, horse-
soldiers should still patrol the vast grasslands of
Mexico and the fawn-coloured deserts.

She closed the door of her compartment behind
her and began to prepare for bed. Clad in her nightdress and robe, she stood at the mirror and brushed
her long hair that curled slightly at the ends. It
was Nonna who had persuaded her not to have
her hair cut short, and Romy smiled a little as
she reflected on the amusing facts and fancies of
he grandmother's girlhood in a country vicarage.
Nonna had once told her that there was something
a bit diabolical about a very attractive man and
that if she ever met one, and the moon was full and
shining, she was to cover her eyes and drop a curtsey to the moon.

'How will that protect me?' Romy remembered
how she had laughed, and how she had thought to
herself that she was safe with Lance, that she
knew him too well to be hurt by him.

'Who's talking about being protected?' Nonna
had said in that dry way of hers. 'It's luck you'll be
needing if you ever meet a devil of a man.'

Romy turned away from the mirror and pulled
aside the curtain that covered the window near her

bed, which the porter had made up while she was at dinner. What she saw from the window made her catch her breath in surprise; a torrent of rain had followed that wild-gold sunset and the wheels of the train had drowned the tumult. It fell in a solid sheet and Romy could hear the wind whistling past the train, racing it through the dark night.

She gave a little shiver and quickly closed the curtain. She swore to herself that she had not been looking for the moon, but when she opened a magazine before settling down for the night it was not a model arrayed in the latest fashion which she saw but a dark-browed autocrat who disapproved of self-reliant women.

It was disturbing that they should meet again. After that encounter during the earth tremor she had carefully avoided the Aztec museum and the Diplomatic quarter where he might be run into again. Being of an independent nature Romy was far from keen on dominating men who had old-fashioned ideas about women travelling alone and seeing something of the world.

Chaperones had surely gone out with the whalebone corset, which like some awful chastity belt had kept women securely in their place ... no doubt the kitchen and the nuptial bedchamber!

Romy buried her nose in her magazine, and heard in the corridor the chatter of people on their way to bed. Beyond the train windows the clamour of the rainstorm had not diminished, in fact it seemed to have increased in fury, and once again that tiny shiver of alarm ran through her slender frame.

Mexico was certainly an unpredictable land, and her people seemed of a similar disposition; their smouldering warmth surely held its own changes from charm to danger. The train rushed on through the wild night, and Romy tried to ignore her nervous tension. In the morning she would have breakfast in her compartment and avoid seeing Don Delgado for the remainder of the journey.

She gave a little yawn and folded her magazine. She glanced at her travelling clock and slipped out of her robe. Time for bed and, she hoped, a dreamless night. She turned down her sheets and plumped her pillows, and then remembered that she must bolt her door. As it was a sleeping compartment there was only one entrance, and without bothering to slip her feet into her mules she padded across to the door and was about to slide the bolt when there was an abrupt tap upon the panels.

Romy was staring at the door when with equal abruptness it opened and she retreated as a masculine figure strode into her compartment.

'What are you doing?' The words broke in quick alarm from her lips. 'How dare you come in here!'

There was only one person on the train who was so outrageously confident and golden-skinned; only one person in the world who could make her feel so immediately unsure and immature.

'Get out this instant!' The words rang with a Victorian indignation she might laugh at later on, but right now she was shocked that Don Delgado should come marching into her private domain dressed in a dark silk robe and pyjamas. What did he take her for, because she travelled alone? Fury tingled through her from the roots of her tawny hair to the soles of her small bare feet.

He didn't say a word for at least a minute, and his expression was unreadable as he stood there with the overhead light shining on his black hair. Then he glanced around her compartment with a casual air, as if contrasting its sombre panelling with her pale youthful skin and her single silk garment.

She felt the hammering of her heart as those remarkable eyes of his missed not a detail of her appearance. They dwelt with a disturbing intensity upon her hair, a cloud of tawny gold about her shoulders, tendrils clustering about her temples and intensifying the clear green of her indignant eyes.

'What do you want, *señor*?' she demanded.

'From the look in your eyes, *señorita*, you have decided what I want, and as you are a headstrong young woman travelling entirely alone you might well have cause to look alarmed. In this country girls who go about alone are asking for the attentions of men.'

'Which doesn't say very much for Latin males,' she retorted. 'In my country women are free to go where they please, and they don't have to be afraid that every man will accost them.'

'Perhaps that is because your countrymen play cricket on the village green instead of learning the art of bullfighting.' Small fiendish lights played in the Don's eyes. 'A Latin is taught from a boy that once he can master a bull, and then a woman, he is indeed a man.'

'I'm quite certain, Don Delgado, that female independence is to you like the flickering cape to the bull. Well, I am one woman who doesn't intend to be tamed by you, so please leave my compartment before I ring for the porter. I am sure your Latin sense of honour would hate a scandal.'

'It would be appalled.' A smile flickered on the firm, yet well moulded lips. 'You amuse me, *señorita*. You travel so audaciously alone in a strange country, yet a man has only to make the mistake of entering the wrong compartment and you are ready to cry wolf. A Latin girl with a *duenna* would have no need to be so afraid.'

'Are you suggesting that I get myself a *duenna*?' It was Romy's turn to smile scornfully. 'Chaperones went out with the bustle and the boa in my country.'

'But you are not in your country at the present moment.' His voice was as deliberate as his gaze. 'You are in Mexico.'

'I am well aware of that.' Her eyes flicked his lordly face, and she felt a panicky urge to snatch up her robe. Never before in her life had a man so disconcerted her, and she wanted to hide herself from those worldly Latin eyes with their deep glimmers of mockery. 'As it happens, *señor*, I prefer my own company and I would be grateful if you would bow out and leave me alone.'

'I embarrass you, eh?'

'Is it so surprising, *señor*? What if I screamed and aroused the other passengers?'

'You are not the type ... you are much too reserved to give way to hysterics at the sight of a mere man.' He spread his hands in a very Latin way and his hint of a smile revealed that he knew all about women and their reactions. He turned to the door. 'I will say once more *vaya con Dios* and leave you to your own company, which you so much prefer.'

'Don't you mean *vaya con diablo*?' she murmured irresistibly.

He swung her a look as his hand touched the door-handle. 'Travel with the devil, eh? Is that how you regard me?'

Her silence was her answer, and during that endless pause a heavy gust of wind launched itself at the windows and walls of the train, and a rumble of thunder seemed to fill the air. Romy pulled her gaze from the Don's and cast a nervous look at the rattling windows. She could not repress a shiver, and was unsure which unnerved her the most, the torrential rain outside, or the man who had invaded her privacy.

'Are you afraid of storms?' he asked. 'Are the rains and the wind less tempestuous in England?'

'Our climate is a bit more moderate.' Her green

eyes dwelt on his face with a flash of curiosity. 'You speak such perfect English that I believed you had been there.'

'One day I shall go there. I am intrigued by a country which allows its young women such a dangerous amount of freedom. Perhaps you come to Mexico because you are intrigued by the more restrictive ideas with regard to women?'

'Mexico is colourful and historical, Don Delgado. Women in seclusion, guarded by elderly *duennas*, have all my sympathy.'

'You would doubtless have theirs, so young and alone, and at the mercy of strangers. To them it would seem that you had no one at home who loved you and cared what became of you.'

There wasn't anyone who really cared what became of her, but she wasn't going to admit such a painful truth to this man. It really was none of his business.

'In England girls are reared to stand firmly on their own two feet ...' The words had hardly left her lips when Romy was thrown off her feet ... the train gave a frightening lurch, its wheels screeched on the tracks, and then it rocked as if giant hands had taken hold of it. Romy gave a strangled cry as hands caught hold of her and dragged her close to a hard chest. Everything slid, fell, shattered ... it was as if the destruction of the train was imminent, and as the lights blinked and faded, the sense of doom was horribly intensified.

'Oh ... heavens!' Romy clung to her only support in a reeling world, this stranger who in another place, upon a similar occasion, had offered the shelter of his arms as the earth rocked.

CHAPTER TWO

THE train had run into some obstacle and by a miracle had not piled up, one carriage upon another. It had tilted and flung people willy-nilly.

Romy and the Don had been flung upon her bed, to become muffled in the covers and the folds of her silk robe. When the lights struggled on again Romy felt a sense of fear not entirely connected with the mishap to the train.

'Eyes of the Madonna!' She was held to the bed as Don Delgado raised himself and gazed down at her in the dim light. Her eyes were wide and densely green in her white face. Her nightdress was half off her shoulder, and every nerve in her shaken body was aware of the closeness of him. She was close to panic in his arms, and then to her acute relief he released her and slid off the bed. His black hair was slicked back with an impatient hand as he planted his feet wide and braced himself against the slope of the floor.

'My theory about you is proved, *señorita*, you are not the screaming sort.' Those fiendish little glints were alive in his eyes again. 'There has no doubt been a landslide on the railway lines and by a miracle not a headlong crash. However, the situation is obviously a grim one, so if you are now feeling a trifle less shaken I will go and ensure that not too many people are injured.'

'I ... I feel all right, *señor*. Yes, please go and assist ...'

He bowed ironically and made his way to the door. He took hold of the handle and pulled. He shook it, pushed and coaxed, and thrust a shoulder hard against the door. When after several minutes it refused to yield, he cursed softly in Spanish. 'The door has jammed! The angle at which the train has come to a halt has dislodged the mechanism and we are firmly locked in.'

'Oh no!' Romy knelt on the bed—as if in supplication—and watched in alarm as Don Delgado fought to open the imprisoning door. 'I have a nail file ... will that help, *señor*?'

'I need a crowbar.' He swung round to face her and his teeth showed themselves in a smile of grim humour. 'I suppose you don't happen to have one beneath your pillow?'

'Hardly.' She could feel her heart hammering from the double shock of the crash and the closure. 'D-don't you carry one of those knives with all the gadgets attached?'

'I am not exactly a schoolboy, which fact you have doubtless noticed, and if I carried a knife it would not be in the pocket of my dressing-gown.' He swept his sardonic eyes over her kneeling figure. 'I fear you are going to need all your British courage. We are without doubt locked together in your compartment and there is no way of knowing when we will be released. Those in charge of the train will attend first to those who have been hurt, and it may take until daylight for all sections of the train to be checked.'

'Daylight?' Her slim body went tense with shock. 'You can't mean that we have to stay together ... all night?'

'I have no axe.' His teeth seemed to bite out the words. 'No iron bar with which to break open the door.'

'Are you quite sure that it won't open.' She looked at him almost accusingly. 'Please do something, Don Delgado!'

'What do you suggest?' He quirked a sable eyebrow and seemed to enjoy the predicament in which they were placed. 'That I pray the ground might open so I can return to the nether regions? You may blame me for walking into your compartment by mistake, but don't look at me as if I arranged for the train to run off the rails.'

'There's no need to be sarcastic.' Her eyes flashed. 'I realise the gravity of the derailment, but I refuse to believe that we are trapped here until the morning. If we bang on the window or yell out someone is bound to hear us and fetch help.'

'If you will just listen a moment, *señorita,* you will hear there are people in other carriages calling for help. We are fortunate not to have been injured.'

'But a rescue squad will surely arrive before morning?'

'Perhaps.' He shrugged his shoulders and leaned against the door that had somehow locked them in. 'I would point out, however, that we are in the wilds of Mexico. and I predict that it will be some time before aid arrives for even the injured. There is in the nature of the Latin a tendency towards fatalism. That what is to be, will be. Destiny. The hand of chance. Taking hold of this train in the stormy night and stranding its passengers in the middle of nowhere. Listen to the wind ... it cries above the voices like a banshee.'

Yes, it mingled with the cries of distress and made everything seem like an awful dream ... yet no face in a dream of Romy's had ever looked so alive and forceful as Don Delgado's, as he stood there looking at her, his wide, silk-clad shoulders against the door that imprisoned them. 'A country as vast as Mexico,' he said, 'still retains many of the old beliefs. In many ways it must seem strange to an English girl, whose parents were very unwise to allow her to travel through this country as if its deserts, its volcanoes, its extremes of climate did not exist. Did they think it a soft, green land? Did they believe its people tame? Did they not realise that in an unpredictable country anything might happen to a young woman unescorted?'

Romy huddled on the bed like a small girl, and though she could hear the clamour of the other passengers on the stricken train, it was only Don Delgado of whom she was utterly aware. She could feel herself trembling, and she knew that most of it was caused by the man who calmly informed her that she must spend the night with him.

It was the first time in her life that she had been so intimately alone with a man, and there was nowhere she could run to escape him. His darkness, his lean matador grace, his powerful personality ... they combined to make her acutely aware of her own youth and innocence. He made Lance seem like an unfledged boy!

'I can take care of myself.' She spoke with a bravado she did not feel. 'I have been doing so, oh, for years. This trip is my first real holiday. I work for my living; I'm not a pampered socialite.'

'I never supposed you were, *señorita*. You are far too amiable towards young waiters, far too eager a tourist, far too interested in the Indians and their history to be a globe-trotting sophisticate.' With a lean, expressive hand he took a slim leather case from his pocket. 'You permit that I smoke?'

'Do you need to ask, *señor*?'

'But of course. There are women who object to the smoking habit.'

'But do you take heed of any woman's objection?'

'If it pleases me to do so, otherwise no.' He took a thin cigar from the case, and his seal ring of heavy gold caught the dull light and revealed itself as a heavily carved family ring, probably dating back to the days of the Conquest. As his lighter flared and he projected smoke from his nostrils, his face was stamped with a Latin autocracy. There was not a tinge of copper in his skin. He was a descendant of a line which had never intermarried; their cream-skinned brides chosen from the Iberian convents in Spain, where girls of good family were kept in seclusion until the time was ripe for the arranged marriage to take place. Then the girl, in the close company of her *duenna,* would travel to Mexico to be married in one of the golden churches to a man she had never met before. It was a romantically barbaric custom, the giving of a girl to a stranger who might be cruel or indifferent.

Aware that she was staring, and yet unable to drag her eyes away from the Don's face, Romy felt all these thoughts racing through her mind. Don Delgado de Avarado y Valcazar was like tempered steel that might be cruel, and there slumbered in his eyes a fire that might frighten a girl.

The fine smoke of his cigar tendrilled its way to the ceiling, and he watched it lazily.

'We are bound by circumstances to spend tonight in each other's company,' he said, 'so I suggest you relax and try to stop regarding me in the manner of a white mouse which expects at any moment to be attacked by a large and rather wicked cat. Please to put on your robe—I can see you are trembling—and we will attempt to make the best of the situation.'

'Do you really think it will be hours before someone ... *señor,* what about your friend the cavalry officer? Won't he look for you?'

'If I know Javier he will be helping those in real need. He is a dedicated soldier, and he will assume that I am busy doing my share to help the unfortunate. I only wish I could be of use, but fate has decreed otherwise.'

'I didn't ask you to come blundering in through my door.' Romy tied the sash of her robe in a tight knot. 'It isn't my fault that you're here. I was all ready to go to bed and was about to bolt my door for the night.'

'Now destiny has bolted it,' he drawled, 'and you have company, whether you wish it or not. Have you a pack of playing cards in your overnight bag?'

'Yes.' She gazed at him wide-eyed. 'I like to play solitaire.'

'A game for the lonely. Are you a lonely person, *señorita*?'

'I have no *duenna*, *señor*,' she said demurely.

His smile was a brief flash of strong teeth against the skin that was like golden leather. 'May I have the cards?'

'Of course.' She reached for her bag, then noticed that with her toilet articles it had been flung to the floor when the train came to its precipitous halt and the contents had spilled out. Don Delgado, who seemed to possess a catlike sense of balance, stepped across to the bag and one by one he picked up her scattered belongings and gave each an amused glance. Pretty trifles that looked lost in his hand, like her lacy handkerchief and a tiny ivory charm, which he studied for a minute, his cigar clenched in his teeth, his eyelids lowered against the smoke.

'You are superstitious?' he asked.

'I suppose most people are, *señor*. You seem yourself to believe that fate takes a hand in most things that happen.'

'I am a Latin and so I have my beliefs in the machinations of fate.' As he spoke he studied the snapshot which had fallen from her wallet, then he glanced at her with a sudden intensity. 'This is your brother?'

'No.' Her heart gave a thump beneath the silk of her robe, which was a soft rose colour and not unbecoming. 'I have no brothers.'

'A cousin, perhaps?'

'My only cousin is a girl.'

'I see.' He dropped the snapshot into her bag, snapped it shut, and handed it to her. 'I think everything is safe, including your passport and papers ... this tiny gun I shall keep in my pocket for the time being. It is a pretty-looking toy, but dangerous in the nervous hands of a girl in company she does not seem to care for.' His smile was diabolical. 'Now with your permission, or without it, Miss Ellyn, I will take a seat on the foot of your bed and we will play a game of cards.'

Romy watched, with a certain feeling of helplessness, as the lean hands dealt the cards. The Don's face in the dim light had a fascination she could not deny, but he was right when he said she was uneasy in his company. He had walked in here at at fateful moment, and whether she liked him or not, she had to endure him until daylight came. Her only consoling thought was that when the morning came and he was released from her compartment she need never see him again.

She picked up her cards and fanned them ... the king of diamonds stared at her and for some odd reason she thought of the Don's first name. Delgado in Spanish meant light, but his hair was so very dark, and his brows and lashes cast shadows on the autocratic planes of his face.

Light ... Lucifer ... dark angel.

'Please to begin, Miss Ellyn.'

She didn't bother to ask how he knew her surname; his keen eyes would have noticed the name on her passport. Almost deliberately she tossed away the king that she held.

'That is a dangerous card to treat so carelessly.' Romy felt the flick of the Don's eyes. 'Do you want to lose to me?'

'We are only playing to pass the time,' she retorted.

'And you can't wait for daylight to come fast enough, eh?'

'I shan't be ... sorry.'

'I hope indeed that you won't be ... sorry.' His glance took in the tawny hair clouding about her young face, and a sardonic smile edged his lips. Beyond the fast closed door of the compartment a good deal of shouting activity was still in progress ... Romy and the Don were part of it, and yet curiously apart from it. They were a pair of hostile strangers, forced to spend an entire night together.

As their game proceeded Romy was intensely aware of the dark figure at the foot of her bed, watching her from beneath those rather heavy eyelids, everything about him so forceful and male and mockingly aware that he made her feel about as composed as a moth on a pin. Whatever would Iris and her aunt have to say if they could see her now ... what would Lance have said, if he had really cared for her?

This is real, Romy thought wildly. I really am trapped in the compartment of a train with a man who looks as if he has always had his own way. Suppose he reached out and dragged her into those strong arms ... if she screamed no one would take much notice, they would think her just another hysterical passenger.

'What an expressive face you have,' drawled the Don. 'Right now you are wondering what you will do if I become amorous. It might be amusing to find out ... please, *señorita,* don't jump out of your pretty English skin. When you do that you really give yourself away as a total innocent. And I think a rare puritan. It really was astute of that young waiter in the dining-car to put White Nun orchids on your table.'

Don Delgado studied Romy, and there was a mocking kind of gravity in his eyes that made her want to throw the word Devil in his face. She tensed herself for a sudden move from him, and she very nearly did scream when he did move his hand, to the pocket of his dressing-gown for his cigar case.

'I shall smoke,' he drawled, 'just to soothe your nerves.'

'My nerves are perfectly all right,' she rejoined. 'But it isn't every night of my life that I'm involved in a train disaster, forced to spend hours with a stranger, and subject to his sarcasm because I happen to have English ways instead of those of a Latin girl. It must be nerve-racking for you, Don Delgado, to have to spend the night with someone you obviously despise.'

He regarded her through the smoke of his cigar and that ironic little smile tugged at his lips. 'You leap to conclusions that are not justified, *señorita*. Latin girls are a lot more cautious, but in a crisis they are often less than calm. You did not scream when the train ran into trouble, yet you almost did so when I reached for my cigar case. Tell me, do you take me for a libertine?'

'If I am as naïve and innocent as you think me, *señor,* then I am bound to be suspicious of you.'

'Why me in particular?'

Her eyes were fastened upon his face and all that she had to fear was surely written there. He was far too striking and subtle not to be a man who could—when he wished—bend any woman to his will. She closed her eyes in order to shut out that handsome and dangerous face, and it was only a few seconds later that her tired young head drooped on the pillow and the playing cards fell from her hand. She went quietly to sleep, the tang of cigar smoke drifting to her nostrils, unaware of the moment when the Don arose and wrapped the coverlet about her. In her sleep she murmured something and he bent his dark head in order to catch the words. When he straightened up he was frowning slightly and his heavy-lidded gaze dwelt on the handbag whose contents he had picked up from the floor of the compartment, whose privacy he had also invaded.

Romy was fast asleep when a hand touched her shoulder and aroused her. She opened her eyes and lay a moment, confused by her surroundings and by the rather stern face that met her gaze in the dawn light. The events of last night began to filter back to her mind and her emotions, and before she could stop herself she shrank away from the touch of Don Delgado's hand.

'Ambulances are here.' His black brows joined in a level line above his bronze eyes. 'Before long men will start to check on the occupants of these compartments. Miss Ellyn, we must talk!'

She struggled into a sitting position. 'What more is there to talk about, *señor*? Look, it's morning ... soon the men will have the door open!'

'Almost too soon, and there is something I must say to you which I have saved for this last half hour we will be alone.'

Her eyes dwelt on him, wide and hazily green from sleep. She watched as he took a seat on the side of the bed, and the thought struck her again that in his personal relationships with women he must be overwhelming. For the first time she wondered if he was a married man ... if so how would he explain last night's escapade if it reached his wife's ears?

'I am glad that you managed to get some sleep.' As he spoke he was studying the heavy gold ring he wore and the seal carved upon it. 'You have doubtless heard that we of Latin blood have strong feelings of honour?' he said, somewhat drily. 'If that does not sound too old-fashioned to a modern-minded English girl?'

'I have heard something of the sort, *señor*.'

'Well, it happens to be a fact,' he crisped, 'and the night we have just spent together places both of us in a situation of the most awkward ... I should not care to be labelled shameless, would you?'

'Shameless ... ?' Romy forced herself to meet the Don's eyes and their expression caused her heart to give a thump. 'But we did ... nothing. We played cards and you told me about your country. We have only to tell the truth ...'

'This is one of those occasions when the truth, I fear, would sound like a tale we had manufactured in an attempt to save our faces.' The ring on his hand gleamed almost malevolently as he indicated his dressing-gown and dark silk pyjamas. 'Because I am clad like this it will be assumed that I came to your compartment with the intention of staying the night, or part of it. Then when the train ran into misfortune I found myself forced to remain here because the door had jammed. All very logical, and damning.'

'But you are a Consul,' Romy protested. 'Your word is surely your bond?'

'In Latin eyes, *señorita*, a man is judged first and foremost as a man.' A grim little smile played about his lips as he scanned her face and saw its increasing alarm. 'It really was indiscreet of you to travel alone in my country. Such an invitation to trouble would not be presented by a Latin girl; those of good family travel always with a companion and if last night's mishap had occurred in front of a witness, neither of us would be in jeopardy.'

'I ... I don't care if I am taken for a liar,' Romy said defiantly. 'Your people can believe what they like. *I* know the truth and that's all I care about.'

'It may be all you care about, Miss Ellyn, but my code is not quite so elastic.'

'If your Latin rules are so rigid, then why do Latin girls have to be chaperoned as if they aren't to be trusted? It would seem, *señor*, that you people are all too ready to believe that men and women aren't to be trusted on their own. Well, I'm English and I don't make eyes at men over a lace fan, or invite their attentions because I have the safeguard of a *duenna*.'

'Tell me, *señorita*,' he leaned forward and his gaze was so sardonic as to be downright devilish, 'if we were in your country, right now, and the situation was the same, that we were locked together in a railway compartment, would it really be believed that I spent last night at the foot of your bed?'

'I don't see why not!' She spoke with a bravado she didn't really feel, not with those sardonic eyes mocking her, and informing her that not everyone had her own innocent sort of mind. 'In any case, it would be shrugged off, not treated like a point of honour which must be remedied at all cost. I am sure, Don Delgado, that you have not lived such a blameless life that one so-called indiscretion will be held against you.'

'A man's indiscretions, Miss Ellyn, are not usually on display as this one will be when that door is forced open and I am discovered here with you ... to all intents and purposes your lover!'

'My lover?' she gasped, and her green eyes were shocked as they raced over his face, which in the struggling morning light was made even more sardonic by his unshaven chin, and by the overnight disarray of his usually well-groomed hair.

'Perhaps you had better break my neck, *señor*, and call me a victim of the crash.'

'*Qué brava*, are you not?'

'I try to be.' She thrust up her chin even as her hand crept to the neck of her robe and clasped it to hide her white skin and the pulse that throbbed there so nervously.

'And you like it that people admire your British courage?' His eyes had narrowed in a rather dangerous way, as if each small action of hers was aimed against that infernal honour of his.

'Yes, I like it.' She was finding also that she enjoyed defying this Spanish autocrat. 'I suppose you prefer girls who submit to your will without even a struggle?'

'It does save the energy for better things,' he drawled, and tiny fires were flickering behind those dense black lashes that surrounded his unusual eyes. 'A Spaniard likes to be held in high esteem, Miss Ellyn. He has a deep, inborn sense of decorum, as instinctive as the proven courage of the British. He finds that his conscience is not easy to live with if he fails to fulfil a duty.'

'I have read *Don Quixote*,' she murmured. 'Surely you aren't saying that a Spaniard would go to such extremes to prove himself honourable?'

'He would go beyond them, Miss Ellyn, and he has often done so. Each of us is a relic of the past, of ancestors who made us. Your hair and your eyes are a living proof that you have a Celtic heritage. Mine is linked to the Knights of Santiago, and the wars against the infidels.'

'You mean,' her green eyes blazed, 'that your ancestors burned at the stake those who rebelled against their laws!'

'Perhaps.' He shrugged. 'You with your green eyes might be descended from a sorceress. Who knows? The only certainty is that in a very short while we are going to be found together in a most compromising way.'

'Then we must shrug it off,' she said. 'Just as you have just shrugged off those poor devils your ancestors burned.'

'Sweet breath of life,' he said with dangerous softness. 'Are you quite such a child that you don't see the consequences of last night and being so alone with a man of my age, my position, my blood? Look at you! It would take a saint to believe that we played card games throughout the night.' He said it bluntly, almost brutally, and brought wild colour storming into her cheeks. 'Miss Ellyn, you are altogether too tempting a young person for the truth to be believable. You give the eyes a little too much pleasure!'

'Am I supposed to be bowled over by the compliment?' Her cheeks burned as his eyes swept over her. 'I thought you looked a devil in Mexico City, now I know you are.'

'Not such a devil, *señorita*, that I took advantage of your ineffable innocence and made of you what people will call you ... if I don't redeem your good name by telling everyone you are the young woman I am going to marry.'

CHAPTER THREE

'*Marry you ...?*'

It was as if a thunderclap shook the train, but in reality it was the railway engineers shunting the train back on the lines. It shuddered a moment and then steadied, and Romy had a curious sensation

230

of giddiness.

She stared at Don Delgado in a dazed way. 'You tell me I must become engaged to you, just like that! People in my country fall in love before taking such a step.'

'There is little time left for falling in love.' His tone of voice held the essence of irony. 'The train has been righted and any minute now that door will be forced open and we will be found together ... in a mutual state of undress!'

'I ... I must dress!' Romy looked desperate ... the compartment was filling with daylight and she could hear deep voices in the corridor, those of the rescue workers.

'Where will you dress?' The Don asked the question with a wicked courtesy. 'In front of me?'

Romy caught her breath and realised in an instant that it was far more intimate for a woman to dress in front of a man than to be lightly clad in his presence. She seemed to burn from head to toe as the Latin eyes dwelt on her with a worldly awareness of her innocence.

'Now do you begin to see how things are? We are male and female, and our every action, imprisoned as we are, is made a thing of guilt. The only way we overcome the guilt is to be a man with his prospective bride when that door is opened.'

'Y-you can't be serious?' Romy wanted to be scornful, but his expression warned her that he was not joking. 'You are *serious* about all this? You mean what you are saying?'

'Every word, Miss Ellyn.'

'But it's so drastic. How can I pretend to care for you ... to have a feeling of affection for someone I hardly know?'

'Affection?' he queried. 'What a very tame word.'

'It's a better word than blackmail!'

'Blackmail, Miss Ellyn? What I am suggesting is a betrothal in place of a scandal. Surely your family would be most affronted if they heard you had been disgraced by a Spaniard in the wilds of Mexico?'

'I have no family.'

'So!' He slowly raised an eyebrow. 'Now I understand why you please yourself and take little heed of your safety in a strange land. Why would you not tell me before that you had no parents? Did you really believe that I would take advantage of you?'

'Aren't you taking advantage when you suggest that I become your fiancée? How do I know that you will set me free afterwards, to go my own way? For all I know an engagement in Mexico may be as binding as a marriage, and you are the last man on earth I should wish to marry.'

'*Gracias.*' He stood up and gave her an ironical bow. 'What a pity we have no witness to prove our mutual antipathy, but as things are no one will believe that such angelic lips can be so unkind.'

'Do you really care what other people believe?'

'As Consul to this part of the country I have to care. An adventure with a woman is all very well, but not on my own doorstep. A pity for both of us, but I refuse to dishonour my own prestige.'

'You speak like a man who places pride before anything else,' she accused. 'I am sure my feelings are of little account to you.'

'On the contrary, I am making amends for my blunder of last night, when I mistook this compartment for that of my friend. Surely you would prefer to be thought my fiancée than a girl of light morals, the English girl who spent a night of love with a Spaniard on a train.'

'There was no night of love!' she gasped.

'In the eyes of everyone else it will seem so. What a drama they will make of it, with railway victims in other carriages, and the train half derailed. Two people who snatched at romance during a train wreck.'

'The train has not been wrecked!'

'Our reputations will surely be wrecked if you refuse to listen to good sense.' His voice roughened and abruptly he reached for her hand, which was plucking restlessly at the bedcover. 'I do assure you that my *hacienda* in the Valle del Sol is quite lovely, for all its age. It should appeal greatly to your vivid imagination.'

'You present your valley home like a bribe, *señor*. A toy to make a sulky child behave herself and obey.'

'I can see that compliance to a man's dictates does not come easily to you, and that tells me something very significant.'

'Really?' She tried to free her hand from his, but

his grip was like a vice, strong and on the edge of being painful. 'Won't you tell me what is so significant and not keep the secret to yourself? Oh, you're hurting my wrist!'

'I think before you are much older, *chica*, I shall spank you. Latin girls are taught to have some respect for the man they are to marry.'

'You are not that man!' she broke in. But even as she spoke her qualms of unease were growing stronger. His powerful fingers were holding her hand and the contact made her feel as defenceless as the child he called her. She was alone in a strange land whose codes were far more rigid and unforgiving than those of England. She knew just by looking at the Don's proud face that he belonged to one of the notable families of the region; people interwoven into the history of the country, to whom scandal would be like poison.

'Let us understand one another,' he said crisply. 'This engagement will take place because circumstances decree that it should. But we are not forced to love one another ... though you have a certain *buen angel* charm which is your own downfall, and mine. If you lacked such charm I could walk away from you ... as it is I must protect you.'

'And do you expect a demure acceptance of such a great honour?' Her green eyes were defiant, and yet a shade of terror lurked in them. 'Do you really think I'll be sacrificed to save your blushes?'

'It is your blushes I am saving, Miss Ellyn. Last night at dinner you were given White Nun orchids.

Would you prefer scarlet roses for a scarlet woman?'

'Y-you have a cruel way of putting things, Don Delgado.'

'I am sorry if I am cruel in what I say, but we Latins are a realistic race of people. We have also a saying; resist Fate and darken your own eye. Is it not much nicer, when all is said and done, to be held in esteem by other people? You fondled the small white flowers the young man gave you ... to-night a young man might ask you for some of those kisses you are reputed to give so freely.'

'Don't ... please.' She was startled by her own degree of shock ... men were cruel in that way, if they thought a girl an easy target, and even with Lance she had been shy of being kissed. Perhaps she was idealistic, but something within her wanted a man's kisses to be associated with a fond love. Perhaps instinctively she had always known that Lance was rather shallow ... and to be thought shallow herself was something she could hardly endure.

'It's true,' she murmured. 'I have to bow down to your wishes ... oh, but I can't! We're almost strangers. You are a Spaniard, with ways and customs so different from my own!'

'It will at first be bewildering for you, but we have no choice ... do you hear? They are battering the door!'

And as the flames of a new day lit the sky and stabbed into the compartment, the lock of the door was forced to yield, and a workman and a railway official were standing there in the aperture, taking

235

in with curious eyes the girl in the bed, and the dark personage who towered at the side of it, hands thrust into the pockets of his heavy silk dressing-gown.

'Don Delgado!' exclaimed the official.

The Don inclined his dark head as if they had just met politely on the street. '*Buenos dias*, Inspector. I hope there is not too much trouble with the line, and no one seriously injured?'

Though he spoke in Spanish, Romy knew from the calm tone of his voice that he was determined not to seem embarassed. The Mexican workman was staring at her, and instantly the Don snapped out an order that made the man retreat from the compartment. Her cheeks flamed. She felt instantly the force of Spanish protectiveness ... the Don had decided her fate, and though she hardly understood his language she could sense the meaning of his words.

'The young lady is my betrothed. We are on our way to my *hacienda* to announce that we will be married in the family chapel. I came last night to wish my *novia* goodnight, then the crash occurred and the door became jammed.'

The words were spoken, the fatal announcement was made, and Romy's hand slowly clenched the sheet as consternation cleared from the Inspector's face. 'Everything is understood, Excellency. And everyone will be most happy for you.'

'*Gracias.*' Don Delgado did not glance at Romy, and for about five minutes more he and the official talked rapidly together, no doubt about the trouble on the line. Then she caught the Spanish word for breakfast, which she knew, and a moment later, with a polite and smiling bow the Inspector withdrew and closed as far as possible the shattered door.

Then the Don turned slowly to gaze at Romy. 'It is done,' he said, speaking now in his impeccable English, with that accent which stressed certain words in a rather disturbing way. 'You are now my bride-to-be, and not a soul will dare to breathe a word against you. Come, try to smile. The Valle del Sol is not the nether regions!'

Because he was so adept at reading her mind, the panic went racing through her veins and she hardly dared to look at the man who was claiming the right to call her his intended bride. Heavens, how would she feel if they were not pretending?

'I should like to know your first name,' he said. 'I noticed your surname on your passport.'

She swallowed dryly. 'I was christened Romola, but when I was almost three years old I was left parentless and relatives took charge of me. My grandmother always called me Romy, and I rather like it.'

'Yet Romola has something Latin about it.' Then at the glance she gave him a sardonic gleam sprang into his eyes. 'Don't be afraid, I shall not try to make of you a Spanish girl. I prefer originals to copies, and there is much that is original about you.'

'Is there ... all I know right now, *señor*, is that my

mind is in a turmoil and I'm rather afraid of you ...'

'Come, *niña*, you kept your head most admirably last night, and there is no reason to think you will lose it in the future. We are only playing a game, so try not to look such a reluctant fiancée.'

'Were many people hurt last night?' she asked.

'About a dozen, but not seriously. The driver of the train was admirably quick in sighting a fall of rock on the lines. The heavy rains had brought it down. Engineers are now busy repairing the damage caused by the derailment, and I am told that passengers will be disembarked after breakfast to await transport to take them on to Xerica.'

'I am bound for Xerica,' she said eagerly.

'You were bound for that particular place, but not now.' He spoke decisively. 'I have ordered breakfast to be brought to you, then you will dress and we will leave the train together. My *hacienda* is about ten miles from here—I should in the normal course of events have left the train at the next station—and I shall try to arrange some means of transport for us.'

'You are very determined, *señor*, once your mind is made up.' She smiled with a certain wistfulness. 'I feel rather like a twig bouncing on a tempestuous stream. Do we have to go through with your drastic proposal? Can't we say that we had a fearful tiff and called off the ... marriage?'

'If I were not the Consul of half this territory, then a lovers' tiff might be easier to arrange. *Por cierto*, for both of us this is a serious matter. You saw the way those men looked at you! Did you enjoy the feeling?'

She gave a little shudder. In Mexico City she had known from the air about this man that he was someone notable. On board this train he was Excellency ... he could not be seen to have spent a night with a young, single English girl and not be talked about. Her own notoriety would precede her to Xerica, and to Vera Cruz, and already she had found that Mexican men were bolder in their approaches than Englishmen. She would in their eyes be the scarlet woman of the Don's graphic description.

'You must accept the turn of events,' he said. 'The rainstorm, the wrecking, and soon the haven of my *hacienda*.'

'The Valley of the Sun,' she murmured. 'It sounds like a place of Aztec worship.'

'Long ago the valley did belong to the Aztec people, and the *hacienda* is built upon the site of one of their pagan temples.' His hands moved expressively. 'Strange that our first meeting should take place outside the museum where you were studying their customs. Do you remember? You had made sketches and you showed me some of them as we drove in a cab to your hotel.'

'Yes, I remember.' How could she ever forget? His face and his voice had lingered in her memory for days afterwards. She told herself it was because they had met at a dangerous moment, while the earth shook and the many windows of the tall cubic building shimmered in the hot sunlight.

How could she have known they would meet again ... that here in the very wilds of Mexico she would be thrown upon his mercy, a victim of his pride and the prejudices of this unknown land.

'So after breakfast I prepare myself to go with you ... to the Valley of the Sun, *señor*?'

'Yes, *niña*.' His eyes held hers and the smile that edged his lips added to the subtlety of his face. 'Please try to look as if the prospect appeals to you, and not as if the Devil himself proposed to take you to his domain. The valley is an evocative place, and I have the strong impression that your relatives in England are not exactly congenial. Why do you brood ... because of the young man in the photograph holding aloft a tennis racket?'

Words clamoured through Romy. She wanted to deny the lack of affection in her aunt's home, and was wildly tempted to say that she loved him and *must* return to him. Then she saw the adamantine set to the Spanish jaw, the glinting of the bronze eyes, and that strange new fear of another person held her in its grip, numbing the words that sprang to her lips. She had loved Lance, in a girlish, idealistic way, but now he was the husband of her cousin, and gone forever was that feeling of youthful worship. She knew now that he had just been pleasant to be with as a playmate. Good at tennis, swimming, and horseback riding. Charming and gay, and popular with everyone. She hated to admit what her heart knew, that he had married Iris so he could run his own riding school. Romy could not have given him that.

'Lance was just a friend,' she said.

'He must have been close to you, if you carry his likeness?'

'We knew each other from children. He had no sisters so he taught me how to swim and ride.'

'Ah, you can ride! Excellent. We have horses at the *hacienda* and I like them to get as much exercise as possible. Their strain is Arabian and you will enjoy their swiftness. You see,' his eyes were mocking, but also fleetingly indulgent, 'I shall not be altogether the tyrant.'

'I should hope not,' she said, with a flash of spirit. 'I am going with you for your sake as much as for my own.'

'Do you know what name the Spanish give to our type of engagement, *señorita*?'

'Something pretty strong, I imagine.'

'They call it Iberian rape.' He quirked an eyebrow. 'Which means that everyone believes we have eloped and made love before taking the marriage vows. A very dramatic thing to do in Latin eyes, and hard to live down if the man fails to offer his name to the girl.'

'What if the couple swore on oath that they had not ... made love?'

'Few Spanish men would risk their reputation as a *novillo*.'

'And what is that, *señor*?'

241

'A young bull.'

'I see.' Colour stung her cheeks. 'So in order to boost your prestige, that of the daring *espada* and the ardent lover, I must hand myself over to you and your family ... rather like a sacrifice on those temple stones your home is built upon.'

He considered her way of putting it, and then with a brief smile he inclined his head in agreement. 'Perhaps so, but I don't play this game of make-believe entirely from self-interest. I have my family's integrity to think of. Don't mistake me. Latin people are not narrow-minded. A man may have his affairs of the heart, but with an experienced woman, not a girl who is young enough to look seduced. My name would be mud among those who work for me, and a thing of scorn to those of notable family. Ah, they would say, has Don Delgado taken to seducing young visitors to our country? *Ay, Dios,* it would not be a pretty thing for members of my family to hear from the lips of their friends.'

Romy studied his proud face and realised that it would be anathema for him to be labelled a seducer. He would sooner sacrifice his personal happiness than have the clinging mud of gossip thrown at his imposing historic family name.

Never leave the highway for the byway, flashed through her mind. *There you might meet the Devil himself.*

At that precise moment, just as she was on the verge of crying out that she couldn't even pretend to be his fiancée, there came a tap upon the door. *'Espere un momento.'* The Don bent over Romy and took her hand. 'I know your thoughts, *señorita*. Your eyes reveal them all too clearly. Have courage and don't try to fight the unkind fate which has caused us to be trapped like this. You are not, remember, the only one who has to pretend to be in love.'

'I ... I couldn't possibly love you!' The words broke from her.

'But I hope you can eat the food I have ordered for you.' His face was unreadable as he carried her hand to his lips and kissed the slim cold fingers. The next moment he swung on his heel and left her, and the waiter who carried in her breakfast was the young man who had been so kind to her. This morning his eyes evaded a meeting with hers. He placed the tray on the table and poured out her coffee, then with a distant little bow he withdrew from the compartment.

Romy sugared her coffee and took a look at the food beneath the covered dishes. Eggs and crisp rashers of bacon, hot rolls and butter, and a jar of honey ... but no chaste white flowers for the *señorita*.

Romy ate the food quite hungrily, as if her body and nerves needed the nourishment in order to tackle the problems that lay ahead of her. She drank her coffee, and after fixing a chair against the door she washed and dressed herself in a leaf-green linen suit. Her shoes had slender high heels that added to her height and her dignity. The mirror reflected the gravity of her face framed by her hair in a soft madonna style. Her new clothes, bought with part of Nonna's legacy, gave her a certain elegance which she had lacked at Lovtanet Bay, where she had roamed about the shore and the moors in casual jeans and jumpers. She had been the young cousin who often felt unwanted in her aunt's household, and now as she looked back she guessed why Aunt Madge had been so snappy with her. She had set her cap at Lance for her own daughter, and with hard cash she had bought an attractive, easy-going son-in-law.

Romy gave a sigh. Growing up in this world meant learning about other people, and trying not to be hurt when they turned out not to be the godlike creatures you thought them. She missed Nonna. She had no one, now, to whom she could turn for a word of wisdom.

What would Nonna have said about Don Delgado? 'Aye, wickedly attractive, my girl. Watch out for that moon and turn your silver, for you're going to need all the luck you can muster.'

Romy felt that she was going to need all her courage as well. She gazed critically at her own reflection and saw a girl with wide, enquiring green eyes, and features that were alive and sensitive. Don Delgado had said that she gave pleasure to the eyes, therefore no one would believe that he was not her lover.

She saw terror darken her eyes at the bare

thought, and she wondered if she could possibly escape from the train and find some means of getting away from him. She glanced out of the window and saw a lot of activity going on. Vehicles were at the track side, and people were standing about in anxious groups. Some of them were holding children, others were eating a sandwich or wandering aimlessly about.

She could surely lose herself among all these people, and could afford to pay anyone with a car, or a van, to take her to Xerica. She snapped the locks of her suitcases and swept a last look around the compartment which still seemed to hold images she would sooner forget. She made for the door and pushed aside the chair that secured the broken lock. The door swung open ... to disclose in the corridor a suave figure clad in a white shirt, cavalry breeches, and knee-high riding boots with spurs at the heels.

'There you are!' The Don flicked his eyes over her stunned face. 'I have borrowed my friend's horse and we shall ride to the *hacienda*. Our luggage will be collected later ... come with me!'

'No ... please let me go on to Xerica!'

But her plea was something he chose not to hear, and in a stride he reached her side and took her by the arm, with fingers that felt like iron. 'Come, we must be on our way.'

She wanted to struggle free of his demanding grip, but people were watching, aware and whispering, as she was led from the train and across the track to where a black and prancing horse was held by a man in a rather dishevelled uniform. For the briefest of moments she met his dark and sympathetic eyes, then the Don had lifted her into the saddle and with a supple bound had joined her and taken the reins. She at once felt his nearness, his muscular warmth, his infernal control over her and the stallion.

'We will see you later on, *amigo. Hasta la vista.*'

His friend the cavalry officer stood away from the horse and gave them a salute. '*Muy bien, hombre.* Good luck!'

They were off with a clatter of hooves, the breath catching in Romy's throat as a hard arm swept around her and held her firmly and inescapably.

CHAPTER FOUR

ROMY had heard of girls forcibly abducted while alone in foreign lands, but she had believed the tales far-fetched. She had never dreamed that such a thing could really happen, least of all to herself. Yet here she was on the saddle of a black horse, being carried across a country of rocks and shadows and savage sunlight, held within the circle of a man's unyielding arm.

She felt the trained muscles beneath his skin, and despite her fear of him she was impressed by his handling of the stallion, which was sleek and mettlesome. The wind across the *sabana* carried the tang of wild mountain plants, isolation, and mystery. The long vistas were broken suddenly by strange hills, clumps of cacti, and waving miles of esparto grass, which grew in places as high as the haunches of the stallion.

It seemed to Romy as if they were leaving civilisation behind and entering a region ruled over by the burning sun, the swooping golden condors, and the man who said she must pretend to be his chosen bride. All chance of escape had slipped away from her and her destination was firmly controlled by Don Delgado.

Her eyes smarted from the blaze of the sun and tears clung to her lashes as she followed the flight of a condor with outspread tawny wings.

'You had better tie my bandana over your head.' The Don spoke abruptly, breaking the silence between them. 'Take it from my neck.'

'I'm perfectly all right,' she assured him.

'Do as you are told, *niña*. Fair-skinned people feel the hot sun rather more than we swarthy Latins.'

'But you aren't ...' She broke off and twisted around in his arms so she could untie the bandana from around his neck. She had been about to say that he was golden-skinned, but in the nick of time she had bitten back the words. It would have been mortifying to reveal that she had noticed his attraction. He might well have laughed at her.

As she untied the scarf she saw the flare to his nostrils as he breathed the wild and spicy air, and she noticed how his eyes glinted as he surveyed the landscape. She wondered, just out of idle curiosity, if he had ever felt about a woman as he felt about the territory over which he had charge.

'Does that feel cooler?' he asked.

She adjusted the scarf over her hair and murmured her thanks.

'Say *gracias*,' he urged. 'I think you must learn to speak my tongue. *Gracias* is one of the loveliest words in Spanish.'

'I am grateful for the scarf, *señor*, but I am not Spanish, remember.'

'True, you are no demure dove despite the name of Romola.' As he spoke he deliberately tightened his arm so that she felt the iron muscles, the hint that she was at his mercy right now and had better do as she was told.

'This is all a bit melodramatic,' she said stiffly. 'Riding off with a girl as if this were the eighteenth century.'

'Have you not yet realised that in many ways Mexico is still a land of unchanged customs, whose people have their roots in a tempestuous past? Look around you at the strange rocks, at the cruel flower with its spikes. You love this land or you hate it, *niña*. There is no middle course.'

'May I ask, *señor*, if you call yourself a Mexican?'

'Not entirely. I was born in Spain where I grew up and was educated. My parents made a runaway marriage and they came to Mexico to live at the *hacienda* owned by the Avarados. The marriage

248

was not a happy one and six months later my mother returned to Spain to the *estancia* of her father, where she gave birth to me. I grew up among matadors and bulls, for my grandfather bred fighting bulls for the arenas. I enjoyed going into the arena as a youth and I made quite a name for myself, but my mother saw the necessity for me to have a more lasting career and I trained for the diplomatic service. When my father died in an accident the *hacienda* was left to me and it was suggested that I become Consul of the region.'

He paused as if to let his words sink into her mind. 'I enjoy my work and my position here, Miss Ellyn, and I cannot jeopardise either for the sake of a foolish girl who took a journey alone and invited the devil's eye.'

'Your eye!' she retorted.

He laughed in that dangerously quiet way and she felt again the hardness of his encircling arm. It was as if the devil in him enjoyed inflicting this physical closeness which she disliked and shrank from.

'*Guapa*, you are going to be an amusing fiancée if not an affectionate one.'

'I hope you don't expect affection,' she said icily. 'I very much hope you don't expect me to parade false hugs and kisses in front of your family and friends ...' There she broke off as the horse shied in alarm from the great winged shadow that swooped suddenly above them, casting a feather that glinted like gold and then flying off with arrogant

249

grace. Romy was thrown back against the Don by the startled jerk of the horse and gripped bruisingly as he controlled the animal and urged him back into the rhythm of the ride.

When Romy recovered her breath and her ribs no longer ached, she asked if his mother lived with him at the *hacienda*. 'She is going to be surprised, *señor*, when you present an English girl as your fiancée.'

'Latin women, Miss Ellyn, are extremely tolerant when it comes to the peccadilloes of their offspring, that is if they are male.'

'You mean ... like everyone else she will assume that we spent last night as ... lovers?'

'You must be prepared for that. I am my father's son as well as hers and she will accept with gracious resignation that having committed Iberian rape I did at least bring the girl home as my bride-to-be.'

Romy turned her head slowly and looked into his eyes. They were wickedly amused, and she felt a swift inclination to slap his face. He had placed her in the most awful predicament of her life; she either submitted to his game of make-believe, or she became labelled as the girl he had seduced on a train. He wasn't even apologetic about all the trouble he had set in motion when he had walked into her compartment in his dark silk pyjamas.

She told herself furiously that his Iberian lordship needed a lesson, and he would learn from her that she was the one female who wasn't going to swoon at his feet.

Some time later they came in sight of the grazing grounds of the Valley of the Sun, an undulating *pampa* where the sleek cattle roamed and bent their heads to the rich grass. The Mexican horsemen who tended the cattle wore the *ruana*, a picturesque cloak that swept the sleek haunches of their mounts. They looked colourful and swaggering and they saluted the *dueno* as he rode past, and their sloping eyes dwelt with interest on the girl who rode on his saddlebow. It was a very Latin thing, a girl arriving like that with the Don. Some of them galloped closer, and as Romy sensed their curiosity she yielded ever so slightly to the man who had authority over them.

'Don't be afraid,' he mocked. 'They can see that you belong to me and are merely curious. The *vaqueros* prefer their own handsome girls with glowing copper skins.'

'Don't you prefer such girls?' Romy asked, with bravado.

'I am not a *vaquero*,' he crisped. 'Thank your stars I am not, because on that train last night I should have paid scant attention to your girlish pleas and made wild love to you. Do you imagine a *vaquero* would worry about slanderous remarks?'

'Hardly ... but if I had been alone with one of them last night I should not this morning be in the position of having to pretend that I want to marry you, a man I don't much like.'

'I hope you are not assuming that I like you?' He reined in the horse as he spoke and they were stand-

251

ing on the rim of the valley, so immense and wildly beautiful that Romy was lost for words. How lovely and limitless was the valley, and despite the doubts and fears which had brought her here, she would be able to explore it all on horseback. A tiny shiver of irrepressible delight ran through her.

'Are you so afraid now you are here?' asked the Don. 'I felt you shiver as if with apprehension.'

'It's the strangeness of everything.' She wouldn't admit how much she thrilled to the Valley of the Sun. She would be outwardly frozen, unstirred by the vista of coffee and cocoa bushes shaded by the immense leaves of banana trees. High above them stretched the great *sierras,* holding in their shadow the glitter of a lake.

'It is bridged.' He pointed with his riding whip. 'On the other side is the *hacienda.*'

'Your own moat and castle,' she murmured. 'Is there a tower awaiting your reluctant fiancée?'

'As a matter of fact there is.' He sounded amused. 'An *atalaya,* as we call it. A lookout across the lake and the land.'

'And what do you look for, *señor?*'

'In the old days it was bandits, but now they have gone rather out of fashion.'

'Have they really?' She spoke with a soft note of meaning in her voice.

He laughed with equal softness, and then he prodded the horse with a spur and they broke into a gallop that soon brought them in sight of the lake and the bridge that spanned it, stretching narrow and dangerous-looking across the wide expanse of sunlit water. Don Delgado set the horse at the bridge and when they were halfway across Romy saw how deep and current-licked was the lake. A person would have to know it well to swim in it or go boating on it.

She wondered if the Don often did so, when free of the duties that must take him all over the widely scattered villages and farms. It was his job, no doubt, to settle disputes among the Spaniards who had settled here; to see they were well rewarded for their labours, and to ensure that all went well with their families.

It had been ironical of fate to make her share a night with a man in a position of authority and power; someone who could not afford to become involved in a scandal.

Now they were across the lake whose shores were hung with wild flowers and mosses. Papaya trees curved on the shore and scented creepers sprawled in the tropical warmth. The silence was intense, without even the sound of a cicada. Only the hooves of the horse broke the silence as they cantered in through the entrance of the *hacienda,* which soared above them into a great arch, its pediment emblazoned with the family device ... an eagle with a dove-like bird in its talons!

'I take it you are unsurprised by the device?' The Don spoke as she stared at the pediment.

'I half expected something like it,' she replied.

'There is a legend in our family that an eagle

mated with a dove and a Spaniard was born.'

'Poor dove!' she found herself laughing. 'What a very formidable egg to hatch!'

'You must laugh more often ... green eyes were not made for tears.'

They cantered into the great stone patio, with walls as high and sun-gold as those of a pagan temple, weathered by wind and time, with palm trees and a turret rising above the patio, steps of twisted iron leading up to its parapet. It was like a minaret, with trailing plants down its walls and gnarled pomegranate trees clustered at its base.

Everything was so still, smouldering with the noon heat and the scents of aloes and coral-bush. Beyond the main patio were archways that mirrored fountains and flagstones, and the rambling walls of the *hacienda*, with red-tiled outbuildings clustered here and there. Then all was cloistered and cool as they came to the patio around which the family rooms were situated. Water tinkled in a fountain set with tiles blazing with colour, and upon slabs of cool stone were set great jars holding juniper and orange trees.

The place was Spanish poetry in stone. Romy imagined the scarlet swirl of a flamenco skirt against the old gold walls ... there was an undeniable magic to the Don's home which she could not deny to herself. Even a certain grace to the way they arrived, a man and a girl seated together upon a black horse.

He took his arms from around her and slid from

the saddle, and after hitching the reins to an iron ring in the wall he reached for her. As she was sitting sideways it was awkward for her to dismount and she was obliged to slide down into his extended arms. Her green eyes were blazing their resistance to him, and all through her slim body there ran the shock of physical contact with him. It was like an electrical charge, from which she still tingled after he released her. She knew from the sardonic smile on his lips that he had felt her antagonised reaction to him.

'I hope, Miss Ellyn, that my home at least will appeal to that cool artistic nature of yours. Do you think that it might?'

'It's a little too early to say. First impressions can be misleading, and you must make allowances for the fact that all this is very different from what I have always known.'

'I intend to make a few allowances,' he drawled. 'Your cheeks are flushed ... would you like to taste our water? It is piped from a mountain stream and very refreshing.'

'Yes, I am rather thirsty after that ride, and the sun seems to have grown hotter.'

'It's noon and the sun is high.' He approached the fountain of *azulejos*, on the rim of which rested a conch shell. He filled it from the fountain and brought it to her. 'Here you are, little *gato de monte*, slake your thirst and be welcome at the *hacienda*.'

She took the shell and drank the water, which

felt delicious as it cooled her lips and her throat. 'I ... I should like to know what you called me, *señor*.' She handed him the shell, which he immediately refilled and drank from. When he looked at her the lids of his eyes were half-lowered over his bronze eyes, and it was a curiously disturbing look.

'You are like the little mountain cat,' he said. 'On the defensive and quick to scratch. You make me wonder what you are like when you purr.'

'What nonsense!' She tossed her head. 'Are all Spanish people fond of talking in such exaggerated terms? Human beings don't purr.'

'On the contrary, *niña*.' He leaned against the colourful rim of the fountain, a striking and masterful figure in surroundings that suited him so well. 'There is a dash of the primitive in all human beings which our airs and graces and our clothes conceal.' His eyes flicked the leaf-green suit in which she looked so willowy. 'Our responses to each other have their roots in the law of the jungle, the sea, and the air. Perhaps in England you failed to realise this, but here in this remote valley you are bound to learn that I speak the truth.'

'Are you warning me about something?' She flicked the red scarf from her hair, which shone in the sun about her slender neck. 'Are you insinuating that I may expect primitive behaviour from you?'

He stirred, there against the fountain, and the spurs at the heels made a little chiming sound. Even his eyes held the full force of his Latin personality, the fire, the temper, and the glinting humour. He made no answer to her question, and his silence was far more disturbing than any words could have been.

'Y-your bandana.' She held it out, flaming silk to a bull. 'You must have patience with my fears, *señor*. It isn't every day that a girl is informed that she must masquerade as a stranger's bride-to-be.'

'Many Latin girls marry strangers,' he said, and as he took the scarf his fingers nipped hers, deliberately. 'But no doubt you have been reared to the romantic belief that love should come before the marriage.'

'I should imagine it helps, if two people love each other,' she said.

'Love? What a puny word it has become when people talk so lightly of loving a dress, a pet, or a picture. What has love to do with the battle of the senses that can rage between a man and a woman? "With love" is printed on a birthday card!'

'What a cynical viewpoint!' Romy backed away from him and didn't care if she annoyed him. 'Someone must have caused you to be disillusioned. Is that why you can regard me without any feeling?'

'I don't know, *niña*, that my feelings are unaffected when I look at you. Your colouring makes quite a contrast for a man who is accustomed to brunettes with dark eyes. Did the young man in the photograph never tell you that you have the hair and eyes of a small cat?'

'I don't like to be called a cat, thank you!'

'How do you think I feel about being referred to as a devil? Scratch a Spaniard, Miss Ellyn, and he will retaliate with a slap. He enjoys a fight, and regards a woman as an exciting opponent.'

'More exciting than a bull, *señor*?'

'Indubitably.'

'I suppose because a woman is more defenceless.' Suddenly as she looked at him Romy became aware of a feeling of curiosity; in the deep opening of his white shirt there gleamed a gold crucifix against the dark hairs of his chest. Had that strong body ever felt the cruel thrust of the bull's horn? Was that golden torso scarred in any way? Few *espadas* escaped without injury ... not that she cared if he had ever been hurt? It was just hard to imagine him at the mercy of anything ... except his over-riding pride.

'Yes, I have felt the *cornada*,' he drawled, reading her eyes. 'It was inflicted by a brave bull, I am glad to say, and you will be pleased to hear that it hurt like the fires of damnation.'

'I'm not so hard-hearted, *señor*! But on the other hand you must admit that it's a cruel sport.'

'It is a form of conquest, and to a woman all conquest is cruel. Even when a woman is to marry, she has this deep-rooted sense of being conquered, of having the sanctuary of herself invaded and mastered. All life, as I have so recently pointed out, is deeply primitive under the veils of perfume, polite talk, and civilised clothing. At the core of us we remain Adam and Eve.'

'And I suppose all this is the Garden of Eden?' Romy said pertly. 'I don't notice any apple trees, so I hope I'm safe from temptation?'

'Latin people believe that it was an orange which the woman offered to Adam, and if you consider it, *niña*, it would seem more than likely. Orange blossom is the traditional flower for a bride, and the fruit of the orange is much sweeter than that of the apple.'

'But you don't believe that love is sweet, *señor*.'

'Quite so.' His smile was slow and wicked. 'It is more like the *quemadero*, a flame which burns fiercely.'

'It sounds most uncomfortable, but then I have heard that Latins have a liking for martyrdom. English people prefer kindness and comfort, and as you have pointed out more than once I am very English, despite my name. Nonna, my grandmother, once said that my mother took the name from a novel.'

'Romola,' he murmured. 'You will have to grow accustomed to my using it, for I can hardly refer to my prospective bride as Miss Ellyn.'

'And just how long must we keep up the masquerade, Don Delgado?'

He stood there considering her question, beating time with his whip against the coloured tiles of the fountain. Romy felt that her heart beat in time to that whip, for what was a mere girl and her feelings to a man in whose blood ran the sacrificial pagan-

259

ism of the bullfight; who had faced the hoofs and horns of fighting bulls?

'Surely not longer than a week?' The words escaped from her in the tense silence he had created. 'I have to return to England, to my work and my studies. I can't stay here in Mexico indefinitely. I am not financially free to do so.'

'While you stay here at the *hacienda* you are not obliged to worry about money. Tell me, is your work in England so exciting; is your home life so congenial?'

'I like my work, and I live away from home in a bedsitter.'

'What on earth is a ... bedsitter?' He slowly raised an eyebrow. 'Is it possible that it is what it sounds like, a room in which you have a bed and a chair and a table?'

'There is no need to be so superior because you have an enormous house with countless rooms in it,' she said stiffly. 'You are fortunate, *señor*, but I am quite happy with my one room. I am happier there than ... anyway, it's my business. The arrangement we have come to does not include a résumé of all my past life and my expectations for the future.'

'Just tell me one thing, *niña*.' His whip hissed softly against the *azulejos*. 'Does your future include the young man who smiles in such a carefree way in the photograph you carry?'

Again she was tempted to tell a white lie, but honesty prevailed. 'That photograph was taken before he married my cousin, *señor*. He was a friend, that's all.'

'Then there is little of real importance which calls you back to England.'

'There is my job!' She had to fight that helpless feeling of being at the mercy of this man's relentless logic; his determination to have his own way regardless of her desires. 'If I don't return to the museum when my vacation is up, then I shall lose it.'

'There are plenty of museums in Mexico,' he drawled, as if the matter of how long she stayed here was already settled in his mind. 'I have a certain influence and can always arrange for you to work among the relics of the past, if that is what you wish.'

'You always manage to sound so sarcastic about my wishes,' she stormed. 'Please remember, Don Delgado, that you are not my *real* fiancé and I don't have to take orders from you. I don't even have to go through with this crazy masquerade ...'

'Don't you?' A whisper of a whiplash was in his voice and he had moved away from the fountain before she realised and she winced as he caught her by the wrist. 'How do you imagine you will get away from the valley now you are here? Do you suppose anyone would invite my wrath and take you? Here at the Valle del Sol we are miles from what you probably think of as civilisation, and I am in complete authority. Do you really suppose I would introduce you as my fiancée only to have you walk out on me? Surely you know me a little better than that, even though our acquaintance is not yet of very long duration.'

'Yes, I know you!' She fought to twist her wrist free of his fingers and only succeeded in hurting herself, and this of course was fuel to her fury. 'Y-you are a tyrant and a bully. You are so used to bulls, that women are easy targets for your cruelty. I said before that I didn't like you ... now I begin to hate you!'

'Ah, now we really begin to know each other.' With an adroit movement he jerked her close to him and held her locked there, bodily, while his eyes looked down mockingly into hers. 'No man is sure he has made an impact upon a woman until she cries out that she hates him. You see, *chica*, to a Latin a woman's indifference is far more intolerable.'

'Y-you are intolerable!' She beat at his chest with her free hand and then stopped and blushed vividly as she felt his warm skin and the gold crucifix and the shock of touching him with her bare hand. 'I wish I had never come to Mexico ... since meeting you my holiday has gone all wrong.'

'Come, *señorita*,' his eyes held hers with wicked insistence, 'your holiday is not yet over and anything might happen in the future. You might even grow to like it here in the Valley of the Sun.'

CHAPTER FIVE

'DELGADO, *mio*!' The voice was deep and sweet, and Romy was released abruptly as the Don swung round and went striding across the patio to where a slender figure had appeared from the interior of the house.

'*Madre, qué gracia tiene!*' He embraced the woman and then kissed her on each cheek. There was love and delight upon the woman's face, and hands with flaming rings reached for his face, clasping his head, tears shining in her magnificent eyes. 'My son, how good to see you, and looking so fit. I have counted the hours, and when one of the Indians brought the news about the train I was worried. You were not hurt . . . no, I can see you are fine. Delgado,' the dark eyes flashed in Romy's direction, 'I see you have brought a visitor. You must introduce me.'

Romy felt the beating of her heart as Don Delgado and his mother walked across the flag-stones to where she stood near the fountain of *azulejos*, a slim and uncertain figure, about to be introduced as the bride-to-be of a man she hardly knew.

'*Madre*,' now he was standing tall and dark in front of Romy, 'I wish you to meet Romola Ellyn, whom I met in Mexico City and who has kindly consented to become my wife.' He reached for

Romy's hand and gripped it warningly. '*Amada*, I wish you to meet my beloved mother, the Doña Dolores.'

Romy had never been confronted by such a moment, when she must smile and force herself to look as if Don Delgado was the one and only man in the world. His mother obviously thought so, and she seemed such a charming woman that it would be a pity to disillusion her.

'I am so pleased to meet you,' Romy murmured, and with each nerve in her body she was aware of lean fingers holding captive her fingers, and of his mother's eyes searching her face in instant bewilderment.

'Did I hear you correctly, *hijo mio*?'

'Romola and I travelled together on the train, *madre*. She has agreed to become my wife.'

'You are pledged to each other?' Doña Dolores glanced sharply at her son. 'But what of Carmencita? She is here at the *hacienda* ... you knew from my letters that she would be here, and everyone thought ...'

'I cannot help what everyone thought.' His fingers tightened upon Romy's and she shot a look at him and saw how haughty he looked. 'I do my own choosing when it comes to a wife, and if you don't say something nice to Romola she will feel unwelcome and unhappy. She is English, *madre*, and extremely sensitive.'

'Of course you are welcome, my child.' Doña Dolores smiled with her lips, but her eyes revealed how unwelcome was her son's engagement to a foreign girl. She must in her own youth have been a stunning Latin beauty; now in middle age she was rather like a severely beautiful nun, with a small exquisite rose hung on a chain around the neck of her grey silk dress. Her black hair streaked with silver was parted in the centre and looped into a heavy coil at the nape of her neck. Her rings intensified the beauty of her hands, and there was in her carriage, and the way she held her head, that same look of pride that her son possessed.

Yes, she had charm, but Romy could see that like Don Delgado she would be equally demanding. She had also his look of culture and aloofness, and Romy began to understand why he had been so insistent that there must be no scandal attached to his name.

'So, my son, you return from the Embassy the *amante* of a pretty English child. Forgive me if I seem rather overwhelmed. You gave nothing away, Gado, in your letters to me.'

'Our decision was a sudden one, *madre*. You might say that our feelings took possession of us and *presto*! we found ourselves engaged.'

Doña Dolores gazed intently at Romy. 'My dear, you still appear to be swept off your feet by this son of mine. You work at the Embassy, perhaps, and met him there?'

'No ... I was touring a-and we met in Mexico City during an earth tremor. Don Delgado swept me off beneath a doorway. I had never felt such a strange thing as a tremor before and I didn't know what to do.'

'So ... a *turista*. You like Mexico?'

'Yes, in a bewildered sort of way.'

'Just as you ... like my son, eh?' A smile came and went in the deepset eyes, reminiscent of the faint scorn with which Don Delgado had treated Romy's reaction to him. 'It must have been nerve-racking for you when the train almost crashed last night?'

'Don Delgado was with me ...' Romy broke off, furious with herself for blushing because the innocent truth had taken on such a guilty meaning, here in this country where a woman's honour was lost if a man was seen in her room at night.

Doña Dolores swept her eyes over her son's face. 'Then you plan to marry very soon, Gado? Here at the *hacienda* in the family chapel, perhaps?'

'We will think about it,' he replied, gripping Romy's hand as it gave a nervous jerk. 'And now, *madre*, I think Romola would like to have some refreshments while a room is prepared for her. Our luggage is at the train and I will arrange for someone to go and collect it.'

'*Lo que tu quieras*, Delgado.' For the span of a moment his mother looked as if she might weep or grow angry; she had obviously made hopeful plans with regard to his marriage, only to have an English girl introduced into her Latin household. With a restrained smile she asked Romy if she would like to enjoy her refreshments in the patio. The flash of

266

jewels on her hands was a subtle expression of her quiet anger as she indicated cane chairs and a table set beneath a pergola of wild golden cassia.

'It is cool there, *niña*. Perhaps you will take a seat while I tell Ana the cook to make a fresh jug of *sangria*.'

'Yes, take a seat.' The Don led Romy to one of the deep, fan-backed chairs, and it was a relief to relax into it. 'I will go with *madre*, if you will excuse me, and attempt to reconcile her to our engagement.'

'It would be better to tell her the truth,' Romy said hopefully.

He met her upraised eyes, mint-green in the shadow of the cassia, and wildly troubled. 'You are English and have not lived all your life with the many prejudices that embroider our Latin way of life. The Latin woman lives a secluded and rather guarded life, and it is important to her that her home and her children are never exposed to dishonour. This may sound outdated to you, Romola, but it remains a fact among my people. I cannot shrug off the implications attached to our night alone in the private compartment of a train. I must let it be seen that I wish to marry you.'

'Your mother doesn't wish it ... she made that very plain.'

'She was taken by surprise ...'

'Who is Carmencita?'

'Do you care who she is?' He quirked an eyebrow. 'Are you a little jealous as well as curious?'

'I'm far from jealous, *señor*! I just think it a shame that she and your mother must be made miserable because of our masquerade.'

'I have known Carmencita since she was a child. She is like a young niece of whom I am fond, and *madre* like all mothers would like her son to marry the angel who is known rather than the stranger who could be a Circe.'

'Do you think your mother takes me for a Circe, *señor*?'

'Very probably, as she refuses to take me for a devil.' He swung a branch of cassia against Romy's hair and studied the effect of the contrasting golds. 'Unlike yourself she is blinded by love.'

'Go away,' Romy said entreatingly. 'I have had enough of you and would like a little peace for a while. Go to your mother and assure her that I shall try not to be a bother.'

'*Niña*, she will expect to be bothered by the girl I am supposed to be infatuated with. She will be persuaded after last night that our marriage had better take place as soon as possible, so beware!'

'Y-you really have placed me in the most awkward situation.' Romy, driven by the impulse to express her fury with him, slapped the cassia spray out of his hand. 'And please don't flirt with me!'

'When I start to flirt with you, you will really know it.' A little flame burned in his eyes and menace purred in his voice. 'You had better beware of provoking a Spaniard, especially the one who in the eyes of everyone else is your beloved *amante*. It would not surprise my mother or my staff if I were seen to chastise my tawny-haired, green-eyed *amiga*. With such attributes you cannot help but have a temper, eh?'

'I am sure you can be ruthless,' she retorted. 'The way you have dragged me here against my will is proof of that.'

'Come, *chica*,' he mocked, 'I didn't exactly drag you. I am sure you enjoyed certain moments of our ride as much as I did.'

'Such as?' She dared him with her green eyes to say she had enjoyed being held bruisingly close to him during that ride.

'Why, when we saw the golden condor,' he said mock-innocently. 'And when we arrived at the valley and you saw the lake for the first time. I heard you catch your breath, or perhaps I felt it. I sense that beauty appeals to you almost as much as it appeals to me ... can you deny this?'

She wanted furiously to deny the appeal of the *hacienda* situated as it was in a wild and wonderful valley, but his gaze was too penetrating, he read her eyes and saw that she was captivated by all this Spanish poetry in stone, tumbling flowers and sun-warmed tile. Her heart leapt and her pulses hummed just to look at the lion-gold beauty of the rambling house, whose walls had absorbed into their stonework the sunshine of centuries. Its ornate ironwork had surely come from the forges of old Castile many years ago, its Moorish-looking belfry held echoes of the desert blood that ran deep in the Avarados, and the shadows of window grilles and hanging lamps were as detailed as Spanish lace; strong as the ironwork were the rambling scarlet vines that burned against the golden stone. Each pendant leaf and weighted petal seemed to hide the heat-tranced cicadas and lizards, moving secretly with a flick of a tail or wing.

'To me this place has become the sweet breath of life.' The Don stood tall beside the chair in which Romy sat, a strong, vital figure in his riding clothes. 'It is built and cultivated as if it were a piece of Spain itself . . . in the twilight when the chapel bells ring and the trumpet vines breathe out their scent in the dusk, it becomes Spain for me. I was born on Spanish soil, *señorita*, and my roots felt torn when I first came here. You will feel strange for a while, but in time . . .'

'You speak as if I had come to stay, *señor*!'

'You think so?' The look he gave her was baffling, the lids of his eyes half lowered over the irises of bronze. Then he gave her that brief bow that reminded her of old court manners and the sweep of an invisible cloak. She watched him stride away, his dark head brushed by vines that trailed over one of the archways leading into the cool interior of the *hacienda*.

She sat very still until the fall of a petal upon her hand brought her out of her reverie. She knew now why his face had haunted her in Mexico City; even then she had had a premonition they would meet again, and from the moment she had seen him on the train, looking so much the haughty Señor d'España, she had known that Nonna's 'devil of a man' had crossed her path in no uncertain manner. As Romy put the fallen petal to her nose she had the feeling that Nonna would have regarded her dilemma with a great deal of wry interest.

Not even Nonna could have guessed that her legacy would lead Romy into the wilds of Mexico, into a masquerade she was committed to now she had met the Doña Dolores, who now approached her across the patio carrying a tray. She set it down on the cane table, and then sat down facing Romy. 'Have you ever tasted *sangria*?' she asked. 'Ours is made from a family recipe and is very refreshing.'

She poured it from the jug into long glasses and ice tinkled as cool against the glass as the words she addressed so politely to Romy. She uncovered a little dish of sweet cakes, and her eyes dwelt on the girl her son had brought home with him, taking in the red-gold hair that framed the green-eyed face with its blending of humour, compassion, and rebellion.

'You must forgive me, Señorita Ellyn, if I say that I think my son has been trapped by an unusual face. I don't want to play the embittered mother, but I always hoped that Delgado would marry a girl of his own people. A Latin girl born to understand a Latin man.'

'Are Latin men so different from other men?' Romy was trembling inwardly with nerves, but she forced herself to appear calm as she sipped her

271

sangria, which tasted of wine and spices. She felt a rebellious stirring within her that the Don's mother should think an English girl unworthy of her precious son.

'They can be more demanding, more cruel and passionate than other men. They can also be most attentive and courteous, and you would not be the first young woman to fall a victim to the Avarados charm. No petticoat ever ruled one of them, though I understand that English young women like to please themselves.'

'I do please myself, *señora,* and I intend to carry on doing so.'

'Even when you become the wife of my son?'

'We are not yet ... married, *señora,* only engaged.'

'My child, you must know that you are already as good as married! Gado told me before I brought the *sangria* that you and he were together all last night, shut in your compartment which the engineers had to force open. He said the men saw you with him, and he is so well known, so respected, that he is under obligation to make you his wife.'

'I beg your pardon, Doña Dolores, but there is no obligation involved!'

'*Señorita,* my son must have told you that from the moment he called you his intended bride the people of this region would expect the marriage to take place. He not only governs here, but as a family we are traditionally proud.' Doña Dolores rose gracefully to her feet. 'I will not believe that you were not ambitious to marry a man who has every reason to believe that he will soon rise to the position of Ambassador. What girl could resist the title of Ambassador's lady?'

Colour flamed in Romy's cheeks. 'Whatever you believe, *señora*, I am quite innocent of enticing your son into my compartment. He entered by mistake...'

'A very fortunate mistake for you, Señorita Ellyn. Please to finish your wine and cakes. I will send a maid to show you to your room.'

The *señora* walked away, leaving Romy almost on the edge of tears. So that was what everyone would think, that she had deliberately set out to entice the Don because he was a man with a spectacular future. It was unbearable ... despite its beauty this whole place had become unbearable and somehow or other she had to get away! She jumped to her feet and looked wildly for the way out of the maze of patios. She was too unhappy to think sensibly; she knew only a compulsion to escape from the *hacienda* before she saw Don Delgado again. Perhaps there was someone who would help her. She had money in her bag and could not believe that the men employed here were so afraid of the *dueno* that not one of them would take payment for helping her to get away. From what she had seen of the herders they hardly looked the nervous sort ... in fact they looked decidedly devil-may-care, and the Don had enjoyed telling her that if he had been one of them last night she would have been treated with scant respect.

This recollection brought her up short as she was running out of the *hacienda* under the great main archway. It was impossible! She couldn't bring herself to ask one of those *vaqueros* to take her to Xerica. She glanced around wildly and her heart leapt. A rather dusty station-wagon was standing in the shadow of the high wall, and as luck would have it she could drive; had been taught to do so because her aunt had liked to be driven to the shops and to her bridge parties.

Romy made a dart for the parked wagon and to her intense relief the key had been left in the ignition. She climbed in, started up the engine and swung out on to the sun-hot road. There might be a map she could study later on, but right now she was intent on putting as many miles as possible between herself and Don Delgado.

It would surely be more of a relief than a rebuff for him to find her gone. Neither of them had wanted this involvement and she was severing it in the neatest way possible, with no more pretence, no more unjust suspicion that she had behaved like a Jezebel. A flash of temper tightened her hands on the wheel and her speed increased, making a blur of the grassy *sabana* she and the Don had crossed on horseback.

'*Hasta la vista,*' she murmured, as the wagon sped over the bridge and the valley gradually receded behind her. It was beautiful, but not for her. It was a place she might have enjoyed, but not as the girl whom everyone thought of as the Don's bride of dishonour!

The petrol gauge dropped quite suddenly, in the middle of nowhere, and the wagon ran on for only a few more yards before grinding to a halt at a roadside whose desolation was almost complete. High above in the late afternoon sky circled a couple of big-winged birds, whose cries were curiously distinct in the silence.

Romy sat tiredly, with her hands still clasping the unresponsive wheel of the wagon. There had been no map in the dashboard and she had known for the past hour that she was lost, and with increasing dread she had watched the arrow of the petrol gauge and had tried to believe that before the tank dried up she would find herself on a main road with other traffic.

Her hopes were dashed. Twilight was falling, the warmth of the day was fading away, and she was stranded in the wilderness. It was no use telling herself that she should never have come to Mexico in the first place; that she would have been far wiser to have gone to Venice with a friend. No, she had desired to show Iris and Lance that she was heart-free and independent, and look where it had landed her! Far from civilisation, with nothing warm to drink and a gnawing place in her stomach, which had last seen food at daybreak.

Daybreak ... when the Don had insisted that she

go with him instead of staying with the other passengers.

Everything was his fault. He was the cause of all her woes. But for his overwhelming pride and ambition she would be warm and fed in a hotel at Xerica, not stranded like this. Romola Ellyn, English spinster of twenty, likely to be found one day a bundle of bones on a road leading to nowhere!

She fiddled with some knobs on the dashboard. Mexican music wafted from the radio, but now the engine was dead a chill was creeping into the wagon. Romy shivered and decided she had better take a look in the back to see if there was a rug. She climbed out on to the darkening road and stretched her limbs. The sky overhead was turning grape-blue in the afterglow of the sunset. Never before in her life had she felt so physically alone, and so in need of a hot cup of coffee. Bleakly she had to face the fact that it had been crazy of her to drive off in the wagon ... if she had kept her temper, and her head, she could have enlisted the help of Captain Javier when he arrived at the *hacienda*. He at least had looked sympathetic and friendly.

Romy sighed and told herself that regrets would not keep her warm through the coming night, and opening the rear door of the wagon she climbed in and looked for a rug. She looked in vain and finally sat there wrapped in her own arms, listening as something howled across the miles of cactus grass; watching through the window as the moon arose, full and tinted faintly blue. The moon tonight had every reason to look blue for her; it suited her mood, lost as she was, cold and hungry, and nervous of the surrounding countryside with its creatures that might come close to the wagon as the night drew on.

An hour later Romy was actively shivering and rubbing her feet and hands to keep a little warmth in them. Who could have believed that so dazzling a sun could leave the night so cold! She felt miserable enough for tears, and wondered in her misery what Don Delgado had said and done when he had found her gone. He had declared that morning that having named her his fiancée he would never allow her to walk out on him. Would he then come searching for her?

Tiredly she rested her head against the seat back and curled her legs beneath her. The night would pass more quickly if only she could sleep, and in the morning, in daylight, she would not be so afraid to cross those fields in search of a habitation. There must be people around somewhere, houses concealed by the undulations of the land. In her crazy haste to get away from the *hacienda* she had probably passed houses without noticing them.

She closed her eyes and tried not to feel the draughts that were stealing into the vehicle. She prayed for sleep, and it came at last in the form of broken dreams and a creeping numbness ... then in the very depth of night she seemed to dream of clattering hoofs, the chink of harness, and the rumble of voices speaking words she could not grasp. She

277

seemed to feel arms around her, lifting her, and a cradling warmth into which she snuggled. Her pillow felt a little hard and she gave it a drowsy thump and settled her head more comfortbly. In the dream that didn't quite leave her a throaty growl of a laugh seemed to waft against her ear.

Moments of deep sleep can seem like hours, and Romy awoke abruptly from those moments to find that she was no longer in the chilly wagon, stalled by a roadside. She was in a fast-moving, comfortable car, wrapped in the heavenly softness of a vicuña rug, and held for double warmth in a pair of arms that were all too real, her head at rest against a muscular shoulder.

'Oh . . .' She stared upwards and in the rays of the ceiling light she saw a set of features that might have been carved from fine teak, with shadows cast beneath the high cheekbones, eyes that brooded upon her face, a diabolical slant to the brows above them. 'You, señor!'

'Yes, señorita. Who else but I would bother to search for such a foolish runaway? My men, who searched with me, think me foolishly fond of you. Only you and I know the real truth of that, eh? We made a bargain and I will see that you keep to it; you will stay at the hacienda until I say you can go.'

'I . . . I might have guessed that I couldn't get away from a . . . a devil!' She might, in fact, have been grateful to him for finding her and making her feel warm and alive again, but he had to speak arro-

278

gantly; he had to let her know that only out of pride had he looked for her. 'What tale did you tell your *vaqueros*? That I went for a drive and mistook my way in a strange country?'

'I told them no such thing. They are of Spanish blood. They know that girls become frightened and behave irrationally on the threshold of marriage. They know you are English and not accustomed to having a master.'

'You will be lucky if you make me bow down to your every wish, El Señor!' She tried to look as scornful as her position in his arms would allow; she lay as tense and unyielding as a plaster figure. 'It wasn't fear of you that made me run away. It was being labelled a Jezebel by your mother ... she believes I chased you because I'd like to be an Ambassador's lady. The very thought of any such thing scares the breath out of me, and I am only too glad that our engagement is a charade and nothing more.'

'A charade, yet you ran away today.' His eyes held hers intently in the low, down-slanting light that reminded her of last night, those moments of panic on her bed, when if his face had come any closer to her, his lips might have touched hers and might not have withdrawn. It made her feel like fainting to even imagine those firm yet passionate lips taking and holding hers.

Suddenly, for all its smoothness, the sleek car was bouncing over the bridge that spanned the lake, and Romy felt the grip of the Don's arms like the grip of fatality.

'You will make me a promise,' he said, and there was a ring of steel in his voice; a glint of it in his eyes. 'You will not run away from me again ... this can be a dangerous country, and the next time you might fall into hands less patient than mine. Whether you know it or not, you are a most attractive young creature ... a wild young dove, whose purity I should not like to see tarnished. Do you understand me, *niña*?'

'Yes,' she spoke rather faintly, 'you are very explicit, *señor*.'

'Were you afraid, alone like that in the wagon, as if in the depths of nowhere?'

'It was the coldness I found most unbearable ... how can it be so warm by day and so cold by night?'

She shivered at the memory of those cold and lonely hours, just as the car swept beneath the great arch that bore the insignia of the eagle and the dove. In her tiredness Romy's thoughts were strange ... when he spoke of her purity did he mean to possess it himself? Doves were a pure white, yet they were also amorous birds ... did Don Delgado think of her like that, his arms around her as the driver halted the car in the courtyard of the *hacienda*, where lamps cast pools of light along the wide verandas?

Suddenly Romy could bear no more talk, and closing her eyes she pretended to be exhausted as the Don stepped from the car, then reached for her and carried her indoors. His booted feet rang on the tiled floor as he strode with her to a staircase. The stairs were not steep and soon he paused in front of a door ... Romy peered at him from beneath her lashes, the Spanish eagle bringing home the English dove and depositing her upon a great soft bed in a room redolent of sheets taken from lavender, beeswax polish, and the oil like incense burning in the lamps at each side of the bed.

Romy opened her eyes. 'Goodnight, *señor*. I shall be all right now.'

'Is there nothing you wish?' He spoke in a soft drawl, as if he read her thoughts in her great sleepy eyes.

'Only one thing,' she swallowed dryly. 'I'd love a pot of coffee, if it isn't too much trouble at this time of night?'

'You shall have it within ten minutes,' he promised. His smile was subtle as he regarded her, then with that brief bow that was both courteous and slightly mocking he withdrew from the bedroom and closed the door behind him. Romy slowly relaxed and watched a moth clinging with quivering wings to the bowl of the lamp at the left side of her enormous Spanish bed. The shadow of the moth was enlarged in its agony upon the smooth white walls of the room. It looked almost like a bird ... a dove, perhaps.

CHAPTER SIX

DESPITE her adventure Romy slept deeply and awoke to such a brilliant flood of sunshine that she knew the morning must be well advanced. She felt guilty, and then remembered that she was supposed to be the Don's fiancée and could be lazy if she wished.

She sat up in the vast bed that made her feel so small, and for the first time she took notice of her room. Yes, the walls were a sunlit white, with beams of a rich honey colour, and a crucifix of chased gold attached to the wall facing her bed. There were delightful things of beaten silver and mother-of-pearl on the wide dressing-table, and palatial cupboards for hoards of clothes! The floor was the same honey colour as the ceiling beams, scattered with creamy vicuña rugs. Red geraniums were banked in alcoves at either side of the wide, iron-grilled window.

Made vulnerable this morning by her recapture of the night before, Romy fingered the beautiful edging of lace on her sheets. By daylight she saw that gold-leaf glimmered in the deeply carved patterns of the woodwork of her bed. and the immense coverlet was of rich scarlet silk.

She didn't know whether to smile or to be awestruck. She, Romy Ellyn, always the outsider in her aunt's house, had slept in a gold and scarlet bed that might long ago have been slept in by a Spanish queen. She wouldn't doubt it. The very look of Don Delgado was an indication of how old and proud was this family whose roots were deep in Spanish soil and its history of past glory and conquest. It was no wonder he was masterful; a man whose pride could not bear the stigma of scandal; a man ambitious to be Ambassador.

Romy slipped out of bed and felt the silky tickle of the rugs as she went across to the window, that opened like doors on to a balcony that immediately put her in mind of a large birdcage. As she stepped into it she seemed to hang suspended above the patio below, and because this place seemed to have such an odd effect upon her imagination she felt again like a captive dove.

A reflective smile quivered on her lips, which curved into a startled oval as below her balcony there came a sudden clatter of hooves and the appearance of a horse and rider making for one of the stone archways.

Then as if he had senses always alert the rider glanced upwards and saw Romy before she could retreat into her room. The sunlit flash of his eyes caught and held hers, and the black sheen of his hair was like the sheen of the horse he sat upon. The white silk of his shirt threw into contrast the deep gold of his skin. He raised his whip and saluted her ... like some knight of old about to go jousting for his lady.

'Buenas tardes,' he called up to her, in his deep voice with its Latin intonations. 'I hope you slept

283

well and did not dream that you were still lost in the wilds.'

'I had a good sleep, *señor*.' She was vividly conscious of being seen by him in her nightdress; it wasn't the first time he had seen her so lightly clad, but the garment was diaphanous and the sunlight was revealing. 'I ... I must get dressed ...'

'Of course you must.' His eyes were amused as they flashed over her. 'Let me say first that you look as if I had caged you ... don't, *niña*, make any more attempts to fly away. Remember what I said to you last night. The *sabana* is a wild place and some of my hawks have a liking for chicks who are so unfledged. Come down to breakfast when you are ready. I shall join you now I am back from my ride ... I have been looking at the bull calves.'

'Are you preparing them for the fighting ring?' She shuddered as she spoke, for his own strong torso beneath the white shirt bore the scars of his own fighting days. Her eyes flicked over the wide shoulders tapering to a supple waist and she felt a stab of emotion, almost as if it hurt her to think of that perfect male body tossed by a bull upon the hot, hoof-trampled sands of a noisy arena. How reckless of any man to dare to face such a duel ... but then she had heard that Spaniards were fond of a game of chance.

'My bulls are for breeding and for the market,' he called up to her. '*Señorita*, don't be too soft-hearted about life and its rather cruel ways. A grilled steak never hurt anyone, and I have watched foot-

284

ball matches in which men have had legs broken from the kick of a so-called sporting opponent.'

And having had the last word he cantered off through the archway, and Romy knew without seeing it that a sardonic smile clung to his lips. She returned to her room and indignantly told herself that she was indeed a little fool to ever feel a moment of pity for such a high and mighty devil. She supposed that like most *espadas* there had been a flamenco dancer to stroke his cheek and flatter his nerve while he recovered from his wounds!

Romy explored her room and upon opening the door adjacent to it she found to her delight a bathroom tiled in black and white, with an enormous tub of luxury proportions, a shower enclosed in glass walls, great pink bath-towels, and flagons of tangy-smelling salts and talcum.

What girl could resist such a Bathsheba bathroom after years of sharing one with a cousin who never cleared up the water or the powder which she splashed over everything? Like a child with a new and shining toy Romy ran the taps and scattered a cloud of crystals into the steam, which immediately turned to a most enticing scent. She allowed her nightdress to fall around her ankles and stepped with delight into the deep tub. Rather shy in company, she often sang when alone, and the tiled resonance of the bathroom echoed to the warmth of her voice, most Celtic when she sang an old melody of Nonna's, just as her eyes were too green to be truly English.

Half an hour later she was clad in a lemon dress with a white collar that revealed the slim white line of her throat and the taut young bones of her shoulders. Her hair, still a little damp from her bath, she twirled into a Psyche knot and secured with a tortoiseshell comb which she had bought in Mexico City. Her eyes did not need the addition of makeup, and her skin had a pale honey glow. As she applied pale pink lipstick she wondered, not without a shrug, what the Don's views were on cosmetics. His mother was far too dignified and lovely to need them. Would he decide that his masquerading fiancée must discard the little paint that she wore upon her lips? Immediately in the mirror her green eyes held rebellion as she thought of his tendency to give her orders.

And now to breakfast.

She met in the hall downstairs the young maid who had brought coffee to her room last night and who had kindly helped her to bed after her ordeal. This morning, with only a few words of English, she semed to understand what Romy required and with a smile in her Latin eyes she led the English *novia* to where El Señor awaited her, in a small patio tucked away from the main bustle of the house.

He arose at her approach from a table set for two beneath a juniper tree, and he had changed his riding clothes for a suit of cool fawn with a thin chalk striping. It was tailored with the perfection he seemed to demand of all things, the shirt and tie beneath as crisp as his greeting.

'At last! Did you return to your bed for a nap?'

'No.' She gave him an indignant look. 'I took a bath and lost track of time.'

'Hoping I would have eaten and gone by now?'

'You shouldn't have waited for me. I'm sure you must be starving.'

'You should know by now, *niña*, that when I make a promise I keep it, I said I would eat with you ... do you object?'

'No ...'

'It will make things easier for you if you are seen to enjoy my company and I am seen to enjoy yours. Come,' a wicked glint came into his eyes, 'try and look a little more *enamorada*.'

'I feel sure, *señor*, that you have given everyone ample reason to believe that you enjoy my company ... after the other night!'

'The memory burns, eh?' He was laughing low in his throat as he drew out her chair. Romy slipped into it, feeling him close to her and avoiding his eyes and their mocking awareness of how she felt about him. 'Was the comfort of your Spanish bed better than a night spent uncomfortably in the back of a stranded car?'

'Of course,' she had to admit. 'Was your mother annoyed with me for causing you the trouble of a search?'

'As it happens I was a trifle annoyed with her.' He sat down facing Romy and his eyes missed not a detail of her appearance. They lingered on her hair, drawn back from the youthful hollows of cheekbone and temple. 'I have taken the liberty of ordering breakfast for you.'

'You seem to like taking liberties where I'm concerned, *señor*.'

'Men are notoriously bossy, as you know,' he drawled. 'Mmm, you are very slender, but I don't think you breakfast on a slice of toast and a cup of dark coffee. Am I correct?'

'I thought Spaniards took a frugal breakfast.'

'Many do, but I find that the air of the *sabana* gives me an appetite when I ride. After we have eaten we will go and select a horse for you. Please to give me your hands.'

'Why?' She looked as startled as if he had asked for her lips.

'Believe me, *niña*, I am not about to kiss them or to put rings upon them, not just at the moment. Come, your hands!'

She extended them reluctantly and felt the lean warmth of his fingers closing around them. 'Now you will grip my hands,' he ordered.

She did so, feeling the steely strength of his hands and the hard band of the ring he wore.

'Ah, *bueno*, I think you will manage Duquesa without too much trouble. She is, you know, the most beautiful mare this side of Mexico, bred in a direct line from the Arabian horses the Avarados first brought to the valley.'

'You are proud of everything you own, aren't you, Don Delgado? Are you not taking a chance in letting me ride one of your best horses? As I learn the terrain I might ride off ...'

'Into the arms of one of my *vaqueros*?' He looked amused, and yet there was a warning glint in his eyes, which turned at once to a suave politeness as a manservant carried a tray to the table and began to serve their meal. Romy watched wide-eyed the plates of delicious-looking sausages, kidneys, eggs, ham, and soufflé potatoes.

'I shall never manage all this,' she gasped.

Yet she managed quite well, and even ate the delicious slice of pumpkin which ended the meal. She sat back replete. 'I really was hungry!'

'You had little to eat all day yesterday,' he said, and he was lighting one of his thin cigars as he spoke, looking very much the dark-browed *grandee* who knew better than Romy what was good for her. He made her feel curiously like a child who had not been properly protected until his advent into her life. Fed, and sun-warm, her nostrils filled with the combined scents of the juniper tree and his masculine cigar, she was not unaware of a treacherous response to him. He was so diabolically attractive, as assured of a woman's needs as only a worldly man could be, and into the bargain he looked and acted as if like everything else at the *hacienda* she belonged to him. To a girl who had never really belonged to anyone it was an attitude which had a dangerous appeal.

She glanced away from him, disturbed with herself for liking even for a moment her rôle of *novia* to Don Delgado.

'What are you thinking?' he murmured.

'Why, don't you know, *señor*?' It was a daring thing to ask in the circumstances. 'I thought you could read my mind so easily.'

'No, only when you look at me, and right now you are studying every aspect of the patio except my part of it.' He puffed cigar smoke at a hovering bee. 'Do you find the patio to your liking?'

'It's very old-world and traditional, somehow lost in time.'

'Does it therefore not fit in with your modern ideas?'

'*Señor*, my ideas are not so outrageously modern as your tone of voice suggests. I admire old and lovely gardens, and houses steeped in history. I am not a superficial person, gliding from one thrill to another and quickly bored. Would I work in a museum if I were all that modern? You said yourself ...'

'Yes, I know what I said. It's just that as a Latin I don't like to see so young a woman travelling all alone. Is it true what you told me? There is no one, no relative, no lover, who cares what you do and where you go?'

'Not since my grandmother died. It was her legacy which enabled me to take this trip to Mexico. She left me a letter suggesting that I travel to a faraway place just once in my life.'

'And why Mexico?'

'I ... don't really know. It just seemed more

exotic than Europe.'

'It seemed to call to you, eh? Perhaps because your mother named you Romola, which has a Latin sound to it. So you were three years old when you lost your mother?'

'I ... lost both parents. They left me in the care of a baby-sitter while they went to dine at the home of my father's employer. It was foggy when they left, and on the way home a lorry ran into their car and they were both killed instantly.' She drew a sigh. 'Nonna always told me they loved each other very much, so in a way it was good for them that they should die together.'

'You are very romantic, *señorita*.'

'No,' she denied. 'I'm being realistic ... why should people in love be parted, with one left to grieve and to be lonely for years?'

'Have you ever been in love, Romola?'

'No ... yes, a little.'

'Calf love, of course,' he drawled, his gaze half-veiled by the lids of his eyes. 'With the young man in the snapshot. Well, it is good that you have got those slight pangs out of your system.'

'Why?' She looked at him because she had to. 'What business is it of yours, *señor*?'

'We are engaged ... betrothed, as my people call it.'

'We are pretending and you know it! There is nothing remotely romantic between us. I find you overbearing, and you find me foolish.'

'Don't get into a panic.' His eyes filled with those

wicked glints that made his bronze gaze seem alive with hidden fire. 'Like most men I have the desire to be loved ... why then should I desire you when you declare that you hate me? I should have to force you to accept my kisses, would I not?'

Her eyes found his lips before she could prevent them ... he had such masculine lips, the kind that would kiss without compromise, making a girl feel his passion to the marrow of her bones. He would be a masterful lover, demanding complete surrender from his partner. He would be passionate ... but would he be tender?

'I am reading your eyes,' he said wickedly.

Instantly she jumped to her feet and turned to caress a cat who drowsed on one of the low walls of ornamental rock. The Don was infuriating! With merciless charm he coaxed her into a mood of revelation, and then when she least expected it he mocked her youthful fear of him. He knew that a man like himself had never crossed her path before and he was enjoying the situation in his own sardonic way. Playing on her terror that he would make the demands of a real *amante*.

The cat arched its tortoiseshell back beneath her fingers and she heard it purring ... it was not unlike the sound that came into the Don's voice when he chose.

'Come, we will go to the stables and I will introduce you to Duquesa.' He took her by the wrist and for the sake of dignity, which he had ruffled enough, she walked with him through the maze of arches until they came in scent and sound of horses and a long line of stone-vaulted stalls. Dark-haired men and boys were at work among the stalls, polishing leather saddles and brasses, grooming the glossy-coated animals, and forking hay from a great stone loft.

Each man gave the *dueno* a respectful greeting, and in passing them Romy was far from unaware of the glances they gave her and each other. She caught their knowing smiles and wished the Don would release her wrist from his inescapable fingers. Last night she had obviously tried to run away from him, and this morning he was letting everyone see that she was firmly in his keeping again. A tingling pressure seemed to run from his fingers into her bones, and she was glad when they came to the stall marked Duquesa and he released her wrist. He glanced into the stall, and then turned sharply to one of the stable hands and spoke to him in rapid Spanish. Romy herself could see that the mare's stall was empty and she realised that the Don was demanding who had taken her out.

Then she heard the name Señorita Carmencita and a quick glance at the Don's face told her that he was deeply annoyed. He was about to say something more when a young woman in a riding-habit appeared in the stable yard, leading by the reins a superb, cream-coated horse who was limping badly.

Don Delgado's frown was like thunder as he strode towards the horse and caught at the reins. The girl, who wore an Andalusian type hat at a

293

rakish angle, gave him a defiant look. Her eyes were carved at an attractive angle in her narrow, pretty, pale-golden face. 'It is only a sprain, Delgado. There was a rabbit hole and Duquesa cantered into it ...' The girl's eyes flickered over Romy, and back again to the Don, who was smouldering with anger. She tilted her chin and the stiff-brimmed hat fell to the back of her neck, the strap stretched taut across her throat.

'*Dios mio,*' she forced a laugh, 'you look as if you might strike me! Have I done something so terrible?'

'You took out Duquesa when I had given explicit orders that I wished the mare left in her stall this morning. You told Carlos that I had changed my orders, and now you return with the mare in this condition. Explain yourself!'

'I wished to go riding and Duquesa is the prettiest horse in your stable.' The red lips pouted and appealed. 'I have a liking for her.'

'You have a liking for your own way,' the Don snapped, and it was then that Romy realised she could understand every word of the tirade and that Carmencita had spoken first in English as if to impress upon Romy that only a certain intimacy between herself and the Don could make him so angry. And the girl was alluring in her purple habit, with a froth of cream lace in the opening of the jacket, and tiny gold rings in the lobes of her ears. Her hair had a bluish sheen to it, and it was drawn back so tightly from her narrow, pointed face that it had the gleam of silk.

She and Romy were as unalike as two girls could be, and looking at her Romy could understand why Doña Dolores had desired her for a daughter-in-law. She was from the crown of her silky head to the heels of her high-arched feet as Latin and fiery as the Don himself.

With a Spanish imprecation he turned to the limping mare and took her foreleg gently into his hands. As he felt the tendons she nuzzled his shoulder with her honey-coloured nose, and he spoke to her in deep purring Spanish, a lovely creature he had obviously pampered and couldn't bear to see in pain.

'Return to the house, Carmencita, and be good enough to show the way to Romola. I shall stay to attend the mare.'

'You forgive me then, *amigo*?' The girl smiled audaciously.

'No,' he said shortly. 'You are a spoiled child and should have a sound spanking. Go with my *menina*, and please not to sprain her leg or I shall be furious with you.'

The girl looked consideringly at Romy, taking in her slender body and legs, and the style of her dress. 'I have been curious to meet *la Inglesa*, whom everyone is talking about. Come, I will show you the way and we will become acquainted.'

'In a moment.' Romy went up to Duquesa and fondled her bowed head; she was quivering slightly, a highly-strung creature who had been used by a rider in a bad temper, someone whose fond hopes had been dashed by the Don's meeting with an English girl. For a fleeting moment Romy met his upraised eyes and she was almost tempted to give him a smile of sympathy.

'Run along,' he said to her. 'Accidents will happen, as you and I discovered on a train journey.'

His words chilled her and she walked away from him with Carmencita, whose Latin audacity could not be dented quite so easily as Romy's sensitivity.

'You look quite upset,' said the girl. 'You British people are so silly about animals. It is a wonder that you can love a man who used to be a matador ... you are madly in love with him, of course. No woman can be near Delgado without wanting him for herself, and you have been very clever ... for someone who looks as if she has never been kissed.'

They reached the patio in which stood the fountain of *azulejos* and as they faced each other Romy wanted to tell the girl that she was welcome to the man who had disrupted her life and forced her to masquerade as his fiancée, but even as the words rushed to her lips she thought of the way his favourite horse had been mishandled. This Latin girl was not only spoiled, she was also inclined to be cruel, and Romy decided that she needed a lesson.

'Whatever you say makes little difference, *señorita*. I am the Don's *novia*.'

'Everyone knows how you came to be his *novia*.' Carmencita swung her riding-whip in a meaning way. 'But you are not yet his wife. Not a soul in the

296

valley welcomes you as the future mistress of the *hacienda*. They scoff at the idea. To them you have no re, no sign of passion, no streak of lightning. You are no woman for the *dueno*!'

'I was woman enough on the train.' The words left Romy's lips before she could stop them ... Carmencita stared at her, then with a sharp flick of her whip she flounced across the patio, where she paused in one of the carved archways and studied Romy. Suddenly her laughter pealed out, mockingly.

'Oil and water don't mix, *Inglesa*. Fire and ice are not happy together.'

She disappeared into the cool shadows of the house and Romy was alone but for the play of the fountain. She turned to gaze at the sunlit curves of water, and then she tautened as she heard the approach of masculine footsteps, firm and brisk on the tiles of the patio. They came closer and closer, and when they had almost reached her she swung round and found herself looking at the dashingly uniformed figure of Captain Javier.

'*Señorita*,' he smiled with his dark eyes, 'how nice that we meet aagin!'

'How very nice to see you, Captain.' She was delighted to see him, for at last there would be someone at the *hacienda* who would not treat her with hostility. She liked the reassurance of his uniform and had not forgotten how tousled and tired he had looked after a night of helping the train passengers who had been shocked and hurt. 'I hope you have 'come to stay for a while.'

'But of course.' He glanced around at the *hacienda* and there was a look of pleasure on his sun-burned face. 'I have no real home except the officers' quarters at Fort Riera and it always make me happy to be a guest here. This time I am extra pleased because of the duty I shall perform.'

'And may I ask what it is, Captain?'

'Has Delgado not told you?' A smile flashed beneath his slim black moustache. 'I know, he is rather inclined to have his mind made up before consulting others, but that is his way and always has been. Like the tide to the beach he is not to be turned from his purpose.'

'Please,' she appealed, 'you have me in suspense. What duty has the Don devised for you, while you are on leave of all things!'

Luis Javier raised his eyebrows and laughed at her with a hint of indulgence. 'He has asked that I give to him his bride at the wedding between you. A duty I shall perform with some pleasure ... and some reluctance.'

'He ... has asked you to do so ... in actual words?' she gasped.

'Yes, he made his request when he borrowed my horse so he could bring you to his home. Are you not pleased? I assure you it will be an honour for me.'

Romy could only gaze at the Captain in speechless surprise. Don Delgado had no right to go this far, dragging his friend into the masquerade and

298

pretending an actual wedding was planned. She was angry, yet at the same time she hesitated to blurt out the real truth to Luis Javier.

As much as she wanted to say it, something held her back from a revelation of the truth ... that in order to safeguard his diplomatic career Don Delgado had forced her to pose as his fiancée. That never ... never would she dream of marrying him.

CHAPTER SEVEN

No matter what the Don had intimated to his friend there could be no marriage without a willing bride, and soon Romy was able to laugh at the idea of the proud Don Delgado dragging a bride to the altar. In any case Doña Dolores was still very cool towards her and not so graciously ready to accept an English girl into her household as the Don had predicted. In her, as in her son, there ran a streak of iron obstinacy and though it made Romy's visit an awkward one, it also provided the loophole through which she could slip ... her English ways being so out of tune in such a Latin household.

There was one thing she could enjoy without reserve, the rambling, golden beauty of the *hacienda*, which in itself occupied acres of land on which stood the farms and stores and adobe houses of the many people who worked for the family. In every way possible it was run as if it stood upon Spanish soil. Its very odour seemed redolent of Spain, a blending of spices, coffee beans, and the carnations which stood in antique vases upon the carved sideboards and tables, whose sheen was like that of rich dark sherry which in the evenings picked up the glow of chandeliers.

Romy wished she were an artist so she could paint the *hacienda*, but she could sketch its patios, the flower-draped walls and lovely old fountains that splashed and gurgled. When she returned to England the sketches would provide a memorial of her strange visit ... she wished to make a sketch of the Don, but was too reluctant to ask him to sit for her. She tried sketching him from memory, but the subtle expressions of his face eluded her. No matter how she tried, she could not depict what lay behind his varying expressions; the essential man was too composite, too complex for her amateur talent. Yet still she tried to capture him, and one afternoon, when she thought everyone at siesta, he came silently behind her and discovered her at work upon his likeness.

'*Nos lametamos.*' He breathed the words as he leant over the back of the tiled bench upon which she sat absorbed. 'What a *mal hombre* I look! Is that how you see me, *mujer*?'

She turned a startled head and stared into his half-amused, half-searching eyes. 'Oh ... I didn't hear you, *señor*. I ... I'm trying my hand at some sketching, but I'm afraid my ambitions are greater than my expertise. Y-you have a difficult face ... oh, you know what I mean.'

'Do I?' He strolled around to the tree that shaded the bench and leaned against the many-branched trunk. It was a magnolia tree and it threw into relief his intense masculinity. He wore a shirt ruffled like a *gaucho*'s, and his trousers fitted his hips and his long legs like a dark skin. With his face partly shadowed by the tree, and clad as he was, he took on the look he must have had as a matador. Romy felt an ambitious aching to sketch him as he was, but with a slight smile she admitted defeat and closed her sketching book.

'You are too much an enigma,' she said. 'You would need to be painted by Velasquez.'

'You pay me a compliment, Romola. The first to pass your lips.'

'I merely state a fact. You are intensely Spanish, *señor*. Of a people who seem to remain as they must have been in the days of the Conquest and the golden galleons.'

'Proud, cruel, and intimidating, eh?'

'You said it, Don Delgado.' Her smile flickered to him and away, like a moth uncertain of where it should settle.

'How much do you know about the Spanish?' he asked curiously. 'Only that which you were taught in the schoolroom?'

'Only that, and the things I have seen for myself since coming to Mexico. When the Spaniards conquered this land they made it very much their own, didn't they? They imposed their beliefs and their religion upon the Indians. They strike me as a very imposing nation.'

He laughed deep in his throat. 'In other words we have the grand manner, eh? *Grandeza*. We like to rule and despise humility. But we are also able to bear great pain and sadness. Like everyone else we have our good side as well as our black. We are kind to young things.'

'But cruel towards animals ... oh, I know you are proud of your stable, *señor*, but you have fought bulls and killed them.'

'To fight a bull a man must be brave, or don't you agree?' He spoke half mockingly. 'That great angry creature can spit fire, believe me. His breath scorches the cape as he thunders by, and do remember that I was young at the time. Foolish just like yourself in entering an arena to face an opponent so much stronger and wilful.'

'You refer to you and me, of course, *señor*.'

He inclined his black head and his eyes slipped over her youthful figure in a white silk shirt and a scarlet skirt embroidered with yucca flowers. Her hair hung loose to her shoulders and she might have been a teenager ... but for the sudden flash of feminine fear in her eyes as he stirred like a panther in the sun and came to her with his graceful, silent strides, those of a man in the prime of his vigour and his awareness of the deep, almost primeval differences between a man and a woman.

In the moment when their eyes met, man and

woman aware, she saw in him not the *grandee* but the smouldering of this land, the free sky of the eagle, the *sabana* of the strong bulls and the wild winds.

'I want to show you my land from the top of the *atalaya*. You wish, of course, to come with me?'

'Have I a choice, *señor*?'

'You have, but it would be foolish to deny yourself such an experience for the sake of opposing me. I promise not to take advantage of our supposed relationship. Come,' his smile was not promising as he reached for her hand. 'It is such a clear day that we shall see for miles, as far as the blue peaks of the *sierras*.'

'I'll come, but you don't have to lead me there as though I'm a child.' She jumped to her feet and evaded the touch of his lean dark fingers, and as she walked with him towards the slender shape of the watchtower, flaring sculptured into the sky like a minaret, she felt the Don's sardonic side-glance.

The tower stood in its own tiled court, surrounded by palm trees and arcades that intensified its Moorish look. The cicadas shrilled softly in secret places, and at the corners of the patio wall were attached dwarf towers and stone lamps. There was a seductive air about the place, as if lovers might have trysted here when darkness fell; adding to Romy's apprehension in being alone with the master of it all.

Each time alone with him was strangely like the first time ... he was forever dangerous, subtle, unpredictable. They were close now to the fluted masonry of the tower and there beyond the meshed lace-iron door was a winding staircase, leading away up to the eagle's eye view from the rooftop.

'I shall go ahead of you,' said the Don, and there was a purring note in his voice which made her conscious at once of the brevity of her scarlet skirt and the slender bareness of her legs. Colour tingled in her cheeks as she climbed the stairs behind him, the sunlight striking hot through the arabesqued openings as they finally reached the balcony that overlooked the miles of *sabana* and the hot blue water of the lake.

Romy caught her breath as she stood beside the Don at the iron rail of the balcony and took in with wondering eyes the extent of his land and how tiny everything looked from this height. The white-walled villages in the valley looked like clusters of toy houses, the bull herds that sprawled beside the streams looked as tame as lazy dogs, while here and there the coloured cloak of a herdsman revealed him at rest beneath the shade of a tree.

The scene from this height was idyllic, and Romy had to admit that any man who ruled like a lord over all this would in the end develop a sense of power.

'Whenever I come up here,' he said, 'I feel a sense of peace, as if I had taken wing from my cares and responsibilities for a while. I fold my wings like an eagle and rest.' He smiled and rested his elbows on the parapet rail, and Romy's eyes were upon his profile as he scanned the valley in which grew the green acres of coffee and cocoa. Now while they were alone had come the moment when she must know why he had told Luis Javier that his duty would be to give away the bride ... she had no intention of being the Don's bride!

'Señor ...'

'Yes, *niña*? Is there something you would ask of me?' He spoke lazily, like a man who didn't wish to be bothered by serious matters just at present. 'Look at those peaks beyond that stab at the sky ... they are like the abode of the old gods ... ah, you should see them when it storms, when the thunder bounces from peak to peak, booming like anger in the throat of a god. The lightning slashes open the clouds, and the rain falls fast like the passionate tears of a goddess. At other times the peaks seem wrapped in a velvety stillness ... the love night of the gods.'

'I want to ask you something ...' She stood braced beside him, unnerved that he should be talking of love. 'Will you listen to me and give me a proper answer a-and not evade the issue?'

'*Niña*, I never talk of serious matters during siesta. It would be most unlike a Latin to do so. A Latin feels all things intensely and there must be a time and an hour when he can relax and not be bothered by argument or busines. Come, give me my hour of pretending that I have only the cares and concerns of a *vaquero* at rest in the shade with his *sombrero* at tilt over his eyes.'

'Would you really wish to be a *vaquero*?' She looked sceptical. 'You with your ambitions!'

'My ambitions, *señorita*?' He turned lazily to look at her. 'I have duties which I accept regardless of what I should really like. I envy the man who possesses but a horse and a saddle and the sun above his head. He is free; I am merely a master.'

'You love mastering people!' She gave a laugh. 'I can't imagine you riding the *pampa* at the tail of the bulls, or saluting another man as your *dueno*. You like giving orders too much.'

'I sound most charming,' he drawled. 'And only a short while ago you paid me a compliment and I thought you had become a little defrosted in our warm climate. I wonder what it would take to melt your English coolness? The treatment perhaps of a *vaquero*?'

'W-what do you mean?' Her impulse was to back away from him, but when she did so she found herself literally cornered in the iron hold of the balcony, which curved to the shape of the *atalaya*. With a step the Don had pursued her and she was trapped by his tall figure, and by the wicked glints in his eyes.

'Shall I tell you by what rule the *vaquero* lives? Fruit is sweet, but one must eat it or it perishes. Flowers are lovely, but they must be plucked or they wither on the stem. Well, *mujer*, what do you say to that?'

'Y-you don't leave me much to say.' Her eyes clung unwillingly to his smile that hinted at many things; the outline of his muscles showed under the thin silk shirt, and she knew him to be as intensely passionate and wilful as the men who rode for him. 'Except that you might want to seduce me because everyone thinks you have already done so. You like subtle games, and the one you are playing with me must be very amusing.'

'Amusing ... strangely pleasurable.' His fingers touched her hair. 'You flutter like a tawny moth on the edge of the flame ... you wonder what it would be like.'

'I do nothing of the kind ...'

'Ah, but you do, *chica*. Never were two people so opposite in temperament as you and I, and opposites attract like lightning to the lonely tree.'

'You seem to like making profound remarks, Don Delgado, but they are not always the absolute truth. You told Captain Javier that he was invited to our wedding—of all things—and now he believes that he is to give away the bride. There will be no wedding because you can't have one without a bride!'

'How very true.' The Don's look was mockery incarnate. 'But Luis, having no family of his own, holds ours in such high esteem that I could not let him think that I would compromise your honour and my own without redeeming it. I told him with a careless laugh that he could give away my bride when I married ... I named no names, *señorita*.'

'But all the same he believes I ... I am to be your bride!'

'We have a saying, Romola. "Don't run for cover before it rains."'

'Meaning I am getting into a panic?'

'Are you not? We have another, which tells a man not to look into the future but to enjoy tonight's moon, wine, and woman.'

'I am glad, *señor*, that the saying applies to the night-time.'

'It can just as well apply to the daytime. I am enjoying the sun, the view, and the girl who flatters me by being afraid of me.'

'I ... I'm not afraid of you!'

'Then your eyes are liars.'

'Th-they match the deceiving person you have turned me into!' Tears started to her green eyes and set them shimmering. Romy didn't enjoy deceiving his mother, whom she admired for her grace and beauty despite the coolness received in return. Romy, who could not recall her own mother, had always missed the special kind of love a mother gives and she had often witnessed the touch of a jewelled hand against the Don's lean cheek; the indulgent smile when Doña Dolores poured his wine or helped him off with his riding-boots. It was not easy for Romy to live a lie, yet because these people were Latin and aware of passion they would not believe the truth ... that Don Delgado had not made love to her during the night he had spent with her.

As he studied the tears in her eyes, his dark brows drove together in a frown. 'What are you asking with those tears, that I let you go? *Mi Dios,* a person would think that I mistreated you. Only today I was looking at papers and things in the family vault and I came upon something which might amuse you. I planned to give it to you this evening; a small token for being a good girl.'

'Don't speak to me as if I'm a child,' she stormed, brushing away angrily a tear that fell to her cheek. 'I don't need bribing ...'

'A bribe, you say!' In an instant his features had a look of menace, and pain shot through her bones as he gripped her by the shoulders and pulled her with sudden fierceness against him. His hand curved like a talon around the nape of her neck and her head was held immovably as he bent and took her lips and kissed them for a long time without any mercy or tenderness. His kiss was a total punishment, and yet even as he hurt her, Romy was aware of his arm like a shield between her vulnerable body and the iron of the balustrade. Even as her head spun she was conscious that he held her so she was moulded to his body rather than bruised against real iron.

'That time you drove me almost too far.' He muttered the words as he pulled his lips from hers and his gaze scorched the colour back into her cheeks. 'Now I have given you something to cry about.'

'Y-you have given yourself away as a brute!'

'Were you ever in any doubt of it?' He held her with cruel ease as she tried to wrench herself out of his arms. 'I really believe you would leap this balustrade to escape from me ... such a long and painful fall, *mujer*. Much harder to take than even my kisses.'

'It really gives you pleasure to play the devil with me, doesn't it?' Her eyes blazed into his, filled now with temper instead of tears. 'All your life you have had your own way and now you must have it with me, a-and I hate you for tricking me into coming up here. I hate your tower, your house, and everything about you!'

'To be sure,' he drawled. 'We have already covered that ground and the spikes of the cactus flower have already scratched me. You know, *mujer*, you really don't need jewels with eyes such as yours.'

'I can do without your flattery!'

'I only say what is true. Flattery has the ring of a false coin.'

'You have placed me in a false position, so your flattery ought to match it.'

'*Santina amada*, you really hate to be the fallen angel in the eyes of everyone. Well, there is a remedy, but I am sure you would sooner suffer...'

'Yes,' she broke in, 'I'll put up with anything sooner than marry a man I don't love, or ever could in a thousand years!'

'The point is taken, *chica*.'

He spoke soothingly, as if to a child, and this infuriated Romy. 'I hope it hurt you!'

'But how can a man of iron and ambition be hurt?' he queried, with a quirk to his eyebrows. 'Only those with feelings can have them wrung ...

310

do I seem broken-hearted?'

'You seem always a mocking devil, where I am concerned.'

'And what would you like me to be ... attentive like Luis and stunned by your emerald eyes?'

'I ... I could hit you!' she gasped. 'You make me furious with your taunts, as if I am the one who compromised *you*. I shall be thankful when I can bow out of this farcical engagement and return to the cool sanity of England, where people don't cry "rape" just because a man is seen in his pyjamas with a girl.'

'How unexciting for the Englishwoman that equality with men has turned the bedroom into a public room.'

'It might be unexciting, *señor*, but you people are prudish about such things because you can't seem to trust your own passions.'

'I consider that I was very much in control of mine on the night in question.' He lounged back against the iron railings, scrolled to match the wall openings of the *atalaya*, and with lazy movements of his hands he took a thin cigar from his case and watched her above the flame as he lit it. His features looked even more chiselled as the smoke played over them. 'But only because you seemed young and frightened, not because I am a saint who finds green eyes unbeguiling. I begin to wonder if some of your insistent dislike of me is based on feminine disappointment that I didn't take advantage of your innocence. In fact you couldn't hate me more, could you?'

She just looked at him, racing around in her mind for words that might pierce the leathery gold of his skin. He gazed back at her, the lids of his eyes drawn down against the smoke of his cigar, taking in the youthful purity of her face, the delicate definition of the bones beneath her English skin, and the slightly rebellious look of the lips he had so recently kissed. 'Angel and tyrant, you and I,' he drawled. 'I could do no more than bring you here to the *hacienda*. It would, believe me, have got around that you were seen in my company in a locked bedroom. Even had I no reputation of my own to consider, you would have been pestered by men in Xerica. Mexicans live for *amor*, and you are pretty.'

'Lots of English girls look as I do,' she rejoined, resentful that his Spanish eyes could bring the colour to her cheeks. 'I'm not unusual.'

'Here in Mexico you are. You stand out like a tawny moth among tiger moths. Like a lily in a garden of poppies. If you don't know it, then you are younger than I believed and too modest to be let loose on the world. A cloister would be a better place for you than a train speeding through the Mexican desert.'

'I managed to avoid trouble until you walked into my life. When I first say you in Mexico City ·I hoped I'd never see you again.'

'Even your honesty is angelic.' He gave his deep purring laugh. 'I wonder why you were afraid to see me again? Did I make so deep an impression as we stood in a doorway and the earth threatened to open beneath our feet? If it had, *chica*, we should have been buried alive to remain immortally clasped in each other's arms. What an escape you had!'

'I agree.' She leaned her arms upon the balcony rail and gazed at the rolling freedom of the *sabana*, and she felt a smile pulling at her lips. If other people could hear them when they were alone like this there would be no question of scandal because who could believe they were ... lovers? Love was surely composed of sweet whispers and adoring kisses ... swift battles and breathless surrender.

'It all looks so peaceful,' she said, 'yet one senses a smouldering quality.'

'The climate of a country has much to do with the temperament of its people. Mexico is a hot country ... England is a cool one, eh?'

'My country has unexpected moods, *señor*. Sometimes we are lucky enough to have several weeks of blazing sunshine, but I prefer the autumn when the countryside is all shades of rusty red and sultry gold, and the sun seems to wear a smoky veil. Gorgeous, and all tangy with bonfires and fallen leaves. Secretive, rustling, with starlings strung out across the sky as the twilight begins to fall.'

'You speak with nostalgic affection, *señorita*.' His gaze was reflective as it dwelt on her face. 'We at last have something in common ... I often think of Spain and the south where I grew up. I remember the young bulls being driven across the plains and the drovers sculptured against the darkening sky. I remember the gypsy songs and the scent of bitter oranges. Can it be that distance makes the heart feel fonder, and scatters roses where nettles really grow?'

'You really would disappoint me if you weren't cynical, *señor*.' She flicked him a look as he lounged beside her, exhaling his cigar smoke in a manner too nonchalant to fool Romy. His stillness was too alert, like that of a swift and supple leopard. It might be the sunshine, or it might be anything that lurked behind his half-closed eyelids, and Romy was wary and trying not to show that she could still feel his hard kiss on her mouth ... a tormenting reminder that he could master her whenever he wished.

A wind stirred across the *sabana*, the first hint that the heat of the day was giving way to the coolness of the approaching sunset; it touched Romy's hair and the side of the neck, and reminded her of the long evening meals at the *hacienda*, when the various relations of the Don and his mother emerged from the suites tucked away all over the house, dressed in immaculate evening clothes, talking with animation, and kissing each other as if they had not met for days.

Romy had not known that such a feudal system still existed in the world, that a man of means should give home and board to the relations who wished to accept it. It amazed her, and amused her, and also made her own position in the household a pivot for speculation and rather embarrassing questions.

Tia Texeira had been quite scandalised to find that she had no box of silk and lace fripperies for her *luna de mielo*, and Romy had all but retorted that a honeymoon with Don Delgado was the last thing she looked forward to.

It caused her nerves to panic just to think of being a prisoner in those dark golden arms, and she was about to make an excuse to leave him when something cast a large shadow and there was a beating of wings directly above the balcony. The great bird hovered, then suddenly swooped as if to fly in over the rail ... as its talons gripped the rail the Don caught hold of Romy and dashed with her towards the stairs. He then snatched an iron lantern from the wall and heaved it at the eagle, which flew off with a cry, its wings spread wide against the deepening blue of the sky.

Romy stood breathless on the stairs, while Don Delgado remained at the rail and watched the eagle out of sight. Then he swung round and came striding to Romy. 'You have gone quite pale, *chica*.' He stood looking down at her. 'But I agree that eagles can be terrifying.'

'The talons, and the eyes ... so primitive.' Romy stared into the Don's eyes, then as if he might swoop upon her she turned and ran all the way down the winding stairs without pause, arriving out of breath in the patio where Doña Dolores was taking tea with two of the aunts.

'Romola, will you join us for *merienda*?' Rings glittered as a slender hand hovered above the teapot.

The request was polite and the thought of tea was inviting, but Romy wished only for the cool white walls of her room and its closed-in balcony.

'Thank you, *señora*, but not just now.' Romy's eyes shone green and delicately pointed against the pallor of her face, and she fled again as Don Delgado strolled into the patio. He would explain about the eagle and they would no doubt smile and shrug and say how timid she was to be the *novia* of a Spaniard.

She reached her room, across which the rays of the sunset were slanting, burning softly against the white walls and the golden crucifix. Romy sank across her bed and buried her face in the lace and scarlet cover. She was trembling from the reaction of the eagle ... and not a little from the Don himself.

Try as she might she couldn't forget the touch of his hands, the feel of his arms, and the fiery pressure of his lips. She was becoming frightened of what he wanted ... there seemed too much truth in the accusation she had flung at him, that he would not be satisfied until his seduction of her was a reality.

She must get away from him ... soon she must find some way to slip out of his reach ... at present he was playing with her, but there would come a day, an hour, when the mocking smile slipped out of his eyes, and his arms became her prison of warm, living gold.

Her heart thumped and a quiver ran all through her slender body. Never again would she venture into his ivory tower, where even in a *guaybera* and narrow slacks he had a look of lordly assumption over her person. Even with her eyes tightly closed she could still picture his face, which had the strength of sculptured gold, with long brows which seemed to tally with the strong line of his nose. His lean jaw was implacable ... it was his mouth that gave him away as a passionate man.

His mouth which had taken hers almost with ravishment.

CHAPTER EIGHT

THE wind had risen all of a sudden and by the time Romy was dressed for dinner it was rasping across the golden miles of *sabana*, and beating against the stone walls of the *hacienda*. She had already experienced an earth tremor in Mexico, and tonight a whirling wind had arrived, so that maids had spent the past hour running from room to room fastening shutters and throwing sheets over the furniture.

As Romy coloured her lips she felt the dust with the tip of her tongue and grimaced at her reflection in the mirror, which was lamplit owing to the switched off electrical supply. Wires and poles could be torn down and the roofs of the barns were thickly thatched and a fire could cause damage and death to the livestock. The Don had given his orders ... lamplight for the bedrooms, candlelight for the dining table!

Romy looked herself over in the mirror ... Spanish people were so meticulous about their own appearance, and she honestly believed they would sooner go hungry than not have a smart suit or dress to wear, and a good piece of jewellery, whether it be a diamond brooch in a *mantilla* or gems at the cuffs of a speckless white shirt.

Romy wore this evening a limpid green dress with an oval neckline, and she wore also several dabs of her precious *Blue Grass* perfume. Her satin high-heeled shoes were the same colour as her dress and she felt rather chic, and looked coolly English with her tawny hair clipped into soft swirls at either side of her jawline. Across the lids of her eyes she had applied a slight hazing of silvery green. It wasn't that she was trying to look glamorous; she needed to appear in cool control of herself, in contrast to the confused young creature who had fled from Don Delgado that afternoon.

As she turned from the mirror she met the wrinkle-faced gaze of a lizard which uttered a small strange cry from its perch on top of the wardrobe. Tonight many tiny animals would take refuge from the wind inside the strong walls of the *hacienda*, and as Romy listened to the wind she couldn't help but feel a sense of security herself, enclosed within the walls which had withstood the variations in the Mexican weather for several centuries.

There was even a romantic isolation to the place ... like a castle of olden days it held all the members of a single family, and all the retainers of that family. They were shielded by its great roof and watched over with authority by the Don ... she alone held an equivocal position in his house.

But Romy didn't want to think about that and she tried to stem her thoughts by crumbling a biscuit for the lizard and lingering in her room until she heard voices passing in the corridor. Now she could go down and not be caught alone by the Don. He was always first in the *cuarto de estar* to greet everyone, and tonight Romy wanted not a moment alone with him.

As luck would have it she met Luis Javier and they made their way downstairs together. 'Is this wind likely to get worse, Captain?' she asked. 'I'm thinking of the coffee and cocoa bushes and the damage likely to be done.'

'The plantation is shielded by the valley walls, and these winds sometimes sound more furious than they are.' He shot her a smile. 'Anyway, it feels good to be here at the *hacienda* and not out riding in it. The company is fine and we shall eat an excellent dinner and drink the best of wines. What more could we ask?'

'You make it sound like a party.' And she was

laughing as they entered the *cuarto de estar*, to become immediately the focus of the Don's eyes. He stood a head taller than the other men present in the room, clad in a dark suit tailored to fit him like a glove. Above his head, shining against panelling like old silk was a gem-encrusted Aztec mask, and Romy chose to look into the eyes of the mask rather than into the eyes which swept from her hair to the tips of her satin shoes.

Everyone had been talking excitedly, with that hint of emotion which is aroused when danger lurks in the night. There were flowers everywhere, and lamps that flickered whenever the wind shook the shutters. Eyes held a glimmering brightness and lace fans moved restlessly ... everyone was enjoying the danger, and yet there was also fear in the air. Tonight the women's dresses were gayer, and Carmencita looked almost like a lovely Indian girl in her frilled blouse and flounced skirt of flamingo pink. Her hair shone like watered silk and was arranged into intricate loops and twirls and plaitings, so that her slender neck seemed as if it might snap under the shining weight. Her long lashes curled away from her almond eyes as she stared at Romy. In the lobes of her ears hung gleaming gold earrings.

Romy caught the message that flashed in the Latin eyes. She, Carmencita Revelde, was made for a man such as the Don, and she would do anything to take him away from an English girl who seemed always distant with him.

320

'How charming you look, Carmencita.' Romy meant every word, but the Latin girl refused to return her smile. Her dark eyes smouldered with resentment as they took in the tawny fairness and green-clad slimness of the girl who had come as a stranger to be the *dueno*'s bride.

'*Silencio, por favor!*' The Don was holding up his hand, and at once the chatter died away. 'I have something to give to my *novia* which I have only just found in the family vaults. I wished to make the presentation in private, but I have been so busy all the evening that the moment slipped by. Romola, will you come to me?'

Romy's cheeks burned as all eyes turned to look at her. She couldn't move and was ready to hate him for paying her such deliberate attention in front of his family. Of all the eyes upon her, it seemed that his mother's were the most intent. She knew, as Romy knew, that he was fastening more tightly about her the arms that didn't really love her. Never before in his life had any female opposed him as she did, and he was subtle as an inquisitor in his punishment.

'The Doña Romola appears to be reluctant.' Carmencita gave a taunting laugh, and the golden hoops swung against the creamy-gold of her bare neck. She would have leapt to claim whatever he had to offer, and Romy wanted to cry out that she was welcome to his gifts.

All at once he moved and strode gracefully towards Romy. He wore his most charming smile, but deep in his eyes there glittered that look of a leopard about to leap upon its prey. Romy's eyes implored him not to come any closer, but already he was towering above her, his chin jutting firm and hard above her head. 'Please to give me your hand, *amiga*. Come, don't hide it behind you as if I mean to bite you.'

She longed to defy him, yet she yielded to him because all the family watched and it would have been humiliating to be forced by him to surrender her hand. He took her wrist in his supple fingers and she felt their pressure against her racing pulse. His eyes flicked her face. 'So nervous of me?' he murmured, for her ears alone. The look she gave him was defiant as he locked about her wrist a bracelet of gems almost the same shade of green as her eyes. Her heart missed a beat ... Spaniards did not give rings, they gave a betrothal bracelet, and Romy could tell from the gasp that ran from person to person that she had guessed what he was doing.

'And now the necklace,' he said, and she knew it would be no use to protest ... it would be like begging mercy of the wind storm that raged around the *hacienda*. 'I shall not disturb your hair too much, *niña*.' His hand swept aside her tawny hair and she was helpless to defend herself against his intention. A necklace to match the green gems was clasped about her throat, sending out glimmering sparks that shocked her as much as the brush of his fingers against her skin. She had thought he was giving her beryls, but when she looked into his half-mocking eyes she knew differently.

'My child,' Doña Dolores came gracefully across the room, surely acting out the pleasure she didn't really feel as she took Romy's face between her ringed hands and kissed her on both cheeks. 'The family emeralds become you! You have eyes that almost match their colour and their lustre. Are you pleased with them?'

Romy gave the bracelet a glance of panic, and yielded to a smile which ached on her mouth. 'It's kind of Don Delgado to let me wear such valuable jewels ...'

'They will be yours when you marry Delgado, but it is nice during the *noviazgo* for some of the jewels of the family to be displayed by the *novia,* and I am pleased that you are *guapa* for my son ... how do you say? ... good-looking, with your fair skin and shining hair.'

Romy's fair skin took a blush very easily and though she knew that Doña Dolores was being gracious because all the family watched this ritual, it was nonetheless welcome. This was a family of strong, proud, explosive passions, and it was for their benefit that the Don presented the jewels. He meant to play his part of *novio* to the very hilt, and Romy was too sensitive, too reserved, to make a fuss in front of a roomful of relatives. For the sake of his mother's pride in him she had to tolerate his air of proprietorship.

He pinched her earlobe and shot a quizzical

smile at the assembled company. 'This time I take more than the ear,' he quipped.

'And she is prettier than any young bull, *amigo*,' laughed one of the uncles. 'He was an artist with the cape, Romola, this man that you will marry. He teased the bulls to within a fraction of his torso and everybody held their breath ... Delgado, will you ever fight in the arena again?'

'No, *tio*, that kind of fighting is over now.' The Don's eyes flicked the face of his supposed fiancée. 'I enter now for a different kind of *corrida*.'

The men laughed, while the ladies smiled behind their fans.

'A moment of truth even more exciting, eh?'

'Exactly so,' drawled the Don. 'And now I think we will go in to dine before the *gazpacho* becomes warm.'

The *gazpacho* was a delicious cold soup, creamy and tangy, and served with little dishes of savoury ham, juicy olives, and sliced tomato. Everybody ate with gaiety and hunger, while the wind outside seemed with fury to hurl itself at the shuttered entrances, shaking them and whining at the keyholes, and making dance the candle flames in the candelabra of silver scrolled with Inca patterns. The interior walls of the dining *sala* were covered with a rich velvet of a startling and lovely design ... eagles and foliage and exotic fruits.

The room made a perfect setting for vivid Latin faces, high fluted combs holding the perfumed hair of the ladies, and the gleam of dark, proud, yet humorous eyes.

The Don sat at one side of the great carved table, while his mother the *madrina* faced him. The conversation was vivacious, in a mixture of Spanish and English, and each time the Don spoke in his deep voice, both musical and merciless, Romy had to admit that he dominated the company. Mysterious and ineffable was the spell he could weave, intensified by the candlelight as it stroked the proud, high bones of his face.

'We are all safely gathered in the *alcazar* of our Don.' Tio Isidro raised his wine glass to his nephew. '*Salud*.'

Covers were lifted from enormous dishes and out wafted spicy odours. Roast pork crackled as it was carved, baked onions stuffed with meat and rice were served, along with sweet potatoes and plump green beans. Everything came from the estate and every dish was cooked with the perfection demanded by the Don.

Tonight his range of nieces and nephews (he was by courtesy their *tio*) sat with their parents at the table and listened wide-eyed to the conversation. Romy had to smile a little. How feudal in some ways were these people, yet how worldly in others. No subject, however intimate, was kept out of earshot of these children, while the Don seemed to enjoy tossing them fondants, not to mention fond remarks.

He was the *dueno*, and Romy was very sure that he revelled in his status. Suddenly a silver-wrapped sweet landed in her lap, and when she looked at him he quirked an eyebrow.

'What are you thinking, Romola? That we are of the Middle Ages? That unlike more sophisticated nations we cling to family traditions and like to eat and talk and laugh together all under one roof?'

'I . . . I rather like it.' She was too honest to deny the appeal of this large, vital, good-looking clan of Spaniards, and after two glasses of the rather potent Spanish wine she might even have said that it was enormously generous of Don Delgado to give so many relatives such a good home. Even if it made him feel the grand gentleman, it was still undeniably good of him.

'Yes, Tia Felicitas,' he bent his ear to one of the more elderly aunts, who wore a silken shawl with long fringes, 'my English *novia* is in sympathy with our tradition of closeness within the family circle. She has no such family herself and has been rather alone.'

'Then, Delgado, it is good that you make her a member of ours.' Tia Felicitas gave Romy a considering look. 'We are proverbially proud, child. Our traditions survive because we honour the family and have men such as Delgado to protect us when we grow old, or find ourselves homeless. It is part of our Moorish heritage.'

Tio Isidro heard this remark and joined in. 'They gave us the bullfight, *niña*, and also the instinct to keep our women in secluded fountain courts. They gave us our music, our fear of hell and our hope for paradise.'

'You speak like a poet, *señor*.'

'A Spaniard is always a poet by candlelight ...
it brings out the lover and the mystic in him.'

She smiled into the dark and twinkling eyes and
thought that Tio Isidro had quite a dash of the
romantic Arab in him. She ate the candied green-
gage which the Don had tossed her, and dared not
look at him for confirmation of his uncle's remark.
Let him play the lover and mystic in the direction
of Carmencita, who was looking at him as if he
were the only man in the room.

Romy turned to Luis Javier and asked him if
there was any chance of going boating on the lake
when the weather settled down again. 'I've seen the
Indians fishing in the deep parts and I'd love to
sail across to that small island ... the one with the
sacrificial stone.'

'It is always deserted, Romola. The Indians won't
go near it.'

'Will you, Luis?' Her green eyes glowed in her
slender face. 'I'd very much like you to take me
there.'

'Why?' He leant a little towards her and his
eyes were serious. 'Do you think it would make Delgado angry with you, to be alone with me? Do you
look for an excuse not to marry him?'

'Yes ... he begins to frighten me ... as if he really
means ...' She bit her lip and fingered the bracelet
on her wrist, shafting its green fire into her frightened heart. 'His code of honour means more than

327

anything to him, and you must have guessed that nothing happened between us that night on the train.'

'I did guess,' said Luis in a voice as confidential as hers.

'But he insisted on bringing me here, and now he decks me out in part of the family heirlooms ... where will it all end? How will I get away, Luis, if I become too involved with this patriarchal family? A point of honour brought me here, so why can't another help me to get away? I know you are the Don's best friend ... I'm sure you wouldn't want to see him tied by Spanish law to a woman he doesn't really love ...'

Luis played with the stem of his wine glass, and a glance at his serious, duty-marked face kindled a spark of hope in Romy's breast. He was the only person here who could help to snatch her like a brand from the burning. He valued the Don as a friend, but he knew how proud he was. Romy was certain she would be sacrificed to that pride unless someone helped her, and she implored Luis Javier with her large green eyes to be that person.

'Take me to the island, Luis. Let everyone think that I ... like you better than the Don.'

'It might blemish the friendship he has for me.'

'I'm sure that it won't! It isn't as if the Don cares for me. He's playing a game of make-believe, and something must be done before we are both trapped into a marriage that would be a disaster. You know how things can get out of hand. How one wrong step can lead to another, until there is no turning back. Help me not to let that happen. I ... I know I'm asking a lot of you, but there is no one else I can ask. If I rode away he would follow me, and I don't know the country well enough to evade him. The best way is for me to hurt that darned pride of his, or to appear as if I do, then he'll let me go ... the English Miss who couldn't resist flirting with his friend.' She broke into a smile. 'There is a belief, Luis, that English girls are unable to resist a man in a uniform.'

'I think, *señorita*,' Luis raised his wine glass to her, 'that you are the sort of girl who would love a man for reasons of the heart rather than the eye.'

'You are kind to say so, Captain.'

'And you really wish me to take you to this pagan little island ... to make it appear that you like to be alone with me?'

'I like your company, Luis. There would be no real deception involved.'

'Only a blow to Delgado's pride, eh?'

'Exactly. How could such a man, who might possibly become Spanish Ambassador, take for a wife a girl of untrustworthy instincts?'

Luis looked gravely at her. 'I have a great regard for Delgado ... are you certain he is not fond of you?'

'Absolutely. He plays with me ... as you see him now playing with Loreta.'

Luis followed her glance across the table, to where the Don held the youngest member of the family in the crook of his arm while he fed her with cream cake. Her glossy hair shone against the sombre darkness of his sleeve, and Romy steeled herself against the appeal of the scene. He was a Spaniard, so he was fond of children ... he would want them when he married, but they mustn't be the offspring of a marriage resulting from a false step taken into her compartment on a night reserved by the fates for a fall of rock on the railway lines. Like the wheels of that train she and this man were heading for trouble ... unless a diversion of some sort was created.

When dinner came to an end the adults returned to the *cuarto de estar* for coffee, while the children were taken to bed by their nursemaids. First of all they had kissed everyone, including Romy, and feeling more shaken than ever she took a chair on the fringe of the family circle and tried to look as distant as possible. She wasn't one of them, and they mustn't behave as if she were, with those knowing glances at the emeralds around her neck and her wrist. She wished the evening would end so she could remove them ... she wished she had the courage to walk out of the room right now, but the Don would only come after her; she saw it in his eyes as they settled on her, there in the shadowy part of the lamplit room.

Was he remembering their hour alone on the roof of the *atalaya*, as she was? Though he looked the well-groomed *hidalgo* tonight, she kept seeing him as he had looked in his *guayabera*, whose chamois colour had been darker than his skin. When he made charming remarks to this aunt or that one, Romy was feeling again the primitive anger of those same lips on hers, kissing her as if to punish her for ever coming to Mexico.

'That wind is really too persistent,' said Doña Dolores. 'I hear a loose shutter banging somewhere and I must go and see to it. Delgado, perhaps some music to drown the wind?'

'Of course, *madre*, but first some *queimada* to help us forget that the wind attacks the *hacienda* with the fury of a locked-out soul. Tio Isidro, you will assist me with this cure for the blues?'

'Only too willingly. We need *coñac*, a lemon squeezed in the fist, brown sugar, and a bronze bowl.'

When the *queimada* was prepared a flame was applied to it, leaping azure to add a glint of devilry to the Don's eyes as he carried round the tray of glasses.

At last he paused in front of Romy. 'You look rather blue tonight, *niña*, despite the emeralds. Try some of this and try to relax ... you are as tense as you were the first time we met.'

'And with good reason,' she rejoined, hating the tremor in her fingers as they clasped the brandy glass. 'I don't want your jewels ... if it was your intention to make me feel a thorough cheat, then you have succeeded.'

'A cheat, *niña*?'

'Yes ... a miserable phoney.' Her eyes met his with rebellion in them, and a hint of pleading. 'Y-you aren't playing a fair game, *señor*. Gems of betrothal were not in our bargain.'

'Most women love jewels, especially when they match the eyes of the wearer. You should take a look at yourself. You hardly look a girl who plans to spend her life in a museum.'

'You won't alter my plans, Don Delgado.' The tremor had reached her voice. 'I ... I know that you are doing all this as a sort of punishment ... paying me back for travelling on my own and landing you in a spot. I won't apologise for something I couldn't help ...'

'Hush, *niña*. The family will think we are quarrelling.'

'I absolutely hate you!' Her eyes duelled with his. 'I warn you ...'

'I shouldn't if I were you, *niña*.' The lids of his eyes held a menacing weight to them, and then he walked away from her, with an arrogance she swore to shake to its foundations. How dared he assume rights over her that were only permissible within the bonds of a declared love and a mutual desire for union!

Romy gasped as the strong brandy raced down her throat and spread its fire through her veins. She jumped to her feet and would have run from the room, but suddenly Luis was by her side and he was gripping her hand. 'No,' he said, 'this is not the moment to run away. Look, two of the boys are going to play the guitar ... ah, and we are to have some dancing!'

A combination of nerves and brandy made Romy's legs feel weak; she wanted to lean against Luis as Carmencita ran to the centre of the room, holding her flounced skirt in her hands and revealing the scarlet heels of her shoes.

Flamenco, exciting and sensuous as only a Latin girl could dance it, her dark eyes flashing signals at Don Delgado and seeing no one else in the room ... she might have forgotten Romy until with a sudden pounce she grabbed her arm and forced her away from Luis. She dragged her to the centre of the room. 'Dance as I dance, English girl! Come, show us if you have spirit and fire!'

'Let me go!' Romy fought with the girl, and abruptly hands were beneath her armpits and she was being lifted like a doll. There was laughter. The relatives thought it just a game, but for Romy it was humiliation as the Don carried her from the room as if he could no longer wait to be alone with her. He was laughing as the music followed them, then they were alone as abruptly as they had been the focus of all eyes. A door closed with a thud and shut them together in his sanctum, a place of rich dark walls, Goyas in carved frames, and the decorative killing swords and golden capes of his *espada* days.

When he had first taken hold of her she had been too stunned to put up a fight, but now she began to do so. 'I-I'm not your plaything!' She beat at him with her hands, and when she caught the mocking sparkle of his eyes she lost all control and slapped his jaw. He merely laughed low in his throat, but when she would have repeated the slap he suddenly stepped aside with the agility he had never lost, and Romy staggered and saved herself against the edge of his desk. Her hair flew in a wing half across her face, her green eyes blazed, and her body had the slim tenseness of the swords upon the wall ... those symbols of his ruthlessness.

There was silence, so absolute it was unnerving, and then the music started again ... *no hay amor como su amor* ... no love like this love.

'The wind has dropped,' he said. 'Perhaps it listens to the music.'

Romy fought not to look at him and stared at the two magnificent Goya paintings on the wall beyond his head, one of a woman in carnation red, the other of a matador in black and gold. The flesh tones were superb, the eyes were bold, the colours alive and glowing. Everything in this room was of the very best; he selected his possessions with the keen eye of a connoisseur ...

'What is it you want of me?' she demanded. 'A total submission before you let me go?'

'A total submission I would find tedious. No, *niña*, I enjoy our scuffles; they are like the pinch of spice on the tortilla.'

'You are a devil a-and I won't be made fun of!' Romy struggled with the clasp of the bracelet, but it was firmly locked about her wrist, like the chain of a prisoner. 'Take these off me ... I don't want to wear them!'

'To take them off I shall have to come near you, *niña*, and you seem to find my proximity quite intolerable.'

She held out her arm and braced herself as he approached her with his silent tread. A shudder ran through her as his fingers touched her skin. He pressed a tiny concealed lock and the bracelet came undone, a chain of living green fire in his hand.

'These gems came originally from the jungle,' he said meaningly, and he let the bracelet drop to his desk. 'And now shall I remove the necklace before it chokes you?'

'Please.'

She turned her back to him, and then gave a little choked cry as he placed his hands around her throat and held her so that she felt the pressure of his fingers. 'You foolish child,' he mocked. 'In some ways you are not yet as grown up as Carmencita.'

He undid the necklace and released her. 'Go, run away to your bed and dream your little girl dreams.'

She walked to the door without looking back, aware that he stood and ran the emeralds through his fingers like drops of jungle fire ... the skin of her neck still felt the touch of both.

CHAPTER NINE

During the next few days Romy had no chance to be alone with Luis. The Don was making a tour of the region in order to speak with the farmers and to hear their troubles, and his friend rode with him. They would return late to the *hacienda*, tired and dusty, ready only for a cool shower, long glasses of *sangria*, and deep chairs in the shade of the patio trees.

The deep timbre of their voices, speaking in Spanish, would drift upwards to Romy's *mirador*, and secure behind its lacy iron she would listen to the sound and recognise that the two men valued each other's friendship in equal measure, and she grew uncertain of her plan of hoped-for freedom. She had no wish to turn the Don against Luis. All she wanted ...

Restless, undecided, she rode off alone the following day, not joining the other young people for their morning canter—an amusing procedure as a rule, with its cavalcade of children and ponies, the strumming guitars of the older boys, and Carmencita's bold glances at the Don's *gauchos*. Romy couldn't help but wonder what the girl's reaction would be if one of them should accept the invitation of her eyes and snatch her from the saddle. They looked capable of it, with their sun-bitten faces, wide hats shading wicked eyes, and colourful shirts.

The morning was a warm mingling of sun and blue sky; of pampas grass and prickly pear, shaped more oddly than any other plant on earth, its knobbly fingers pointing in aimless directions.

Romy made for the adobe village across the lake, where she could stable her horse for a few *pesetas* and wander in the market place. Odd and charming mementoes could be bought quite cheaply, and lunch could be made of baked sweet potatoes at a stall, and fruit bought from a pannier and eaten in the shade of an adobe wall. Papaya, plums, and custard apples ...

The siesta dream of a tourist again, her troubles held at bay for a while.

Dressed *de corto*, with her hair pinned beneath her riding hat, and wearing a shirt and narrow riding trousers, Romy felt and looked rather like a boy. She almost wished she were a boy, with the freedom to ride away, perhaps, on a Mexican truck heading for the border, without the fear of being discovered as a girl; green-eyed, fair hair spilling from the Cordoban hat, at the mercy of a man who was not an *hidalgo*.

She shivered and gave Duquesa her lump of sugar before leaving her at the stables. The mare whinnied as if to warn her that they should be making for home, but Romy soothed her and told her in Spanish not to fuss. 'The *dueno* is miles away, my angel, and today is mine to do with as I wish. Now eat your sugar and enjoy the shade out of the sun.'

The morning passed almost before Romy knew it, so engrossed did she become in the intricate layout of the village, where each narrow street led eventually to the colour and noise and spiciness of the market place. Some of the women wore the regional costume, a vermilion or black skirt banded with contrasting colour, with slitted sleeves to the jacket to show a lace blouse. Dark oiled hair was plaited into fine chain-like braids coiled at the nape of the neck. Earrings swung provocatively against copper skin, and sloping eyes held centuries of mystery and passion, and now and then a glimpse of rebellion.

Her own feeling of rebellion was like a distant thunder in her blood, there but no longer holding her in a tense grip. The spell of this place had worked its magic and she was lost in the goods piled in a heap, desirous of owning a delicate lace *mantilla* which in England could be used as a scarf at the neck of her scarlet raincoat.

Strange that she had left her raincoat behind, as if in Mexico it never rained. She smiled, and then caught back the smile with biting teeth. Because of the rain ... ah, it had poured from the heavens that night!

'The *señorito* likes, eh?'

The voice of the vendor recalled her. 'Quite well ... how much are you asking, *señor*?'

They bargained and the *mantilla* became Romy's. As she folded it and put it in her pocket she had to grin to herself. A *senorito* was a young man, and the vendor no doubt thought that the *mantilla* was a gift for a flashing-eyed *chiquita*.

Romy sauntered, acting the boy. Had she the courage to run away, now? There was a mule-cart ... but where was the driver? She looked around and became aware that the market place was becoming deserted. Shutters were closing, the time of siesta was at hand, and it would take far more cash than she carried to persuade the driver of the cart to abandon his rest while the hot sun took possession of the day.

Romy made for an old courtyard near the church and made herself comfortable on a wooden seat bowed over by a plumbago tree. She tilted her hat as she had seen the *gauchos* do, not to mention the Don himself. Darn him, intruding upon her thoughts and bedevilling her! She closed her eyes tightly, but there was his face, so vivid that she had to let her eyelids fly open so that she might be certain that he had not appeared in all his height and darkness, there against the sun, looking down at her with those mocking bronze eyes.

No, she was quite alone but for the *reinitas*, tiny birds that flew about with a shy twittering, searching for honey and pretty as paint. Little queens, perhaps the same ones who came to the patio each morning to take jam and sugar from the bird table.

Why could she never escape even in her thoughts from her graceful prison? Yes, the *hacienda* was a place of beauty and grace, roofed over with its

339

mellow old tiles and great clusters of flowering vine, planted centuries ago by the first Avarado, a captain of conquest from Spain, intent upon making his home as Spanish as possible. Luscious wine-coloured oleanders framed the family chapel, where the Don's ancestor had been married to the girl who had travelled by ship to a strange land and an unknown bridegroom.

So were matters arranged then, and even today. The Latin temperament seemed attuned to the conquest of a stranger ... the Don had said that love was just a pretty word used to express affection for a pet or a song or a favourite garment, and looking back to Lovtanet Bay she knew without a doubt that the few forlorn tears she had shed on the beach, standing there in her bridesmaid dress, had been tears of disillusion. She had not run away because of a broken heart ... she had left Bristol without giving Lance a thought ... when she tried to recall his face she could hardly do so, yet she had known him from childhood.

Life was certainly full of surprises, and she reached up to fondle a spray of plumbago and felt a sudden sharp sting as a wasp buzzed and flew off. Romy looked at her hand and saw the red mark of the sting ... the asp in the garden, she thought wryly, and decided it was time to fetch her stabled horse and ride back to the *hacienda*.

She strolled the deserted streets, nursing her stung hand as she passed the adobe houses with rough white walls hung with pots of plants and painted saints in the little niches. She walked beneath limewashed archways and was glad of the shade after the heat of the sun. A dog stirred against a wall and scratched lazily. A snatch of *quichua*, the Indian dialect, stole from a window. It made Romy very aware of the strangeness of the place, of dark eyes watching her from behind a curtain as she passed by.

She arrived at the stables and entered, breathing the tang of horses and hay. She made for the stall in which she had left Duquesa, only to find it empty! She stared and felt a stab of alarm. Hastily she glanced in the other stalls, none of which held the proud and glossy young mare, whose bridle was bright and polished, and whose pedigree was apparent at a glance.

Suddenly frightened, Romy ran to the shabby little office where she had paid her *pesetas* to have Duquesa minded for a few hours. The boy was sleeping and as she shook him awake his straw hat slipped from his head to reveal his startled face. With very little Spanish at her command Romy could only make him understand that her horse was missing by dragging him to the stall which she had rented. 'Look, my horse is gone! Duquesa, the mare I ride at the wish of Don Delgado, the *dueno* of the *valle*. Do you understand me?'

He understood who the Don was and comprehended that the horse was missing, and at once the boy broke into a spate of Spanish and looked as scared as Romy. She didn't want to believe what had obviously happened ... while the stable boy took his siesta someone had entered the stable and stolen the best horse in the place. *'Mierda!'* the boy groaned. *'Ay Dios mio!'*

Romy sank down on a mounting stone and pulled off her hat to fan her hot yet blanched face. Her hair tumbled about her shoulders and the boy stared at her. *'Una señorita!'* he exclaimed, and looked at her trousers and back again at her face framed by the tawny hair. If the situation had not been so serious Romy might have laughed at the boy's expression.

'What do we do, *chico?* Is there a police station ...' She sought for the Spanish words and made him understand, but he shook his head. The *pueblo* was too small for a station of the law.

'Then who ...?'

'El padre.' The boy grabbed her hand. *'Pronto, por favor.'*

Together they hastened down the street to the house of the local priest, and Romy prayed that he could speak English and be able to do something to help. The Don would flay her for having left Duquesa to be stolen ... but she hadn't dreamed such a thing would happen. She had visited the village before ... yes, but in the company of Luis and Tio Isidro! It made all the difference, darn it. They belonged, but she was obviously a foreigner, and presumed to be rash and foolish. Why not steal her horse, if she was thoughtless enough to leave such a fine animal in the local stable?

She and the Mexican boy arrived breathlessly at the old door set in a high wall, with a small iron judas through which the boy peered. *'Padre,'* he called through the little grille. *'Señor Cura, uno momento, por favor!'*

Romy guessed from the boy's expressive shrug that the Father was taking his siesta and they were disturbing the ritual. All the same the door was opened and there stood a sun-weathered figure in a black cassock and a straw hat. 'Carlos?' he exclaimed. *'Que ocurre, chico? Que hay?'*

The boy explained very rapidly what had happened, with gestures of heartfelt innocence.

'Dios mio!' The Father stared at Romy, then swept off his straw hat. 'Good day to you, *señorita.* The boy tells me you are an Americano visitor to the *pueblo* and that your mount has been taken from the stable where he works? This is so?'

'Yes, Father, except that I am English.' Romy was relieved almost to the point of tears to find that someone in this forsaken place spoke a language she could understand. 'I am staying at the Hacienda del Valle and I came here today on a very fine mare owned by the Don. When I returned to the stable in order to collect my mount, she was no longer there. The animal is valuable, Father, and the stable boy tells me there is no *comisaria* in the village. Please, can you help me?'

'First, *señorita,* you must come into my garden and take a chair. You are out of breath from walking too fast in the heat ... come sit down and I will

343

arrange for a message to be sent to the *hacienda*.'

'Oh, but ...' Alarm caught at Romy's heart like cold fingers. 'Can't we make enquiries first, before informing the Don that Duquesa is missing? I mean, she might only have been borrowed by someone for a ride. The person might return her, and those at the *hacienda* will be worried unduly.'

'I can see that you are worried, *señorita*.' The good Father's eyes dwelt with a glimmer of shrewdness upon her anxious face. 'Very well, I will send my servant Carlos to make enquiries, but if the mare is still unreturned by Angelus, then the Señor Don Delgado must be told. He will contact the *guardia* by telephone. I am not connected, you see.'

'You're very kind.' Romy smiled and breathed again. There was still hope that Duquesa would be found before it became necessary to inform the Don ... she dreaded his anger, the very thought of it made her legs go so weak that she was thankful to sit down in a fan-backed chair while Father Sabio, as the Mexican boy called him, went into his house to fetch his servant Carlos.

She smiled at the boy who still hovered by the door in which the judas window was set like a rather malevolent eye. He still looked rather scared, as if she might blame him for the theft, or the borrowing of the Don's valuable horse, but Romy could only blame herself. She had come here alone when she should have stayed with Carmencita and the others, and her impulse had as usual led to trouble.

Trouble had seemed to lurk at her shoulder ever since her advent into Mexico ... the eye of the Devil as the Don had called it, following her around and no doubt grinning wickedly when she walked into yet another spot of bother.

Carlos and the boy departed, and Father Sabio brought a jug of wine to the table set beside the woven-cane chairs in the shade of an old lime tree.

'You will take a glass of wine, *señorita*?'

She hesitated, and then decided that she needed something to steady her shaken nerves. 'Please.'

He sat down in the other chair and poured the wine. 'I can see that you need a little consolation after your shock. This is made locally and the wine treaders always present me with a few bottles for my cellar. It is rather a nice colour, eh? Like a topaz.'

She smiled, grateful for the wine before the questions. Also she had hurried through the assaulting sun of this semi-tropical *pueblo* and the wine was refreshing.

'Will you permit that I smoke my pipe, *señorita*?'

'Of course, Father.' She watched as he lit the carved old pipe and puffed the strong tobacco. She suspected that he knew a little more about her than the villagers; they had not met before, but he had no doubt guessed that she was the English girl the Don was rumoured to be marrying. He must therefore think it strange that she should be in fear of the man she was supposed to love ... or did it seem

345

perfectly natural to him? A natural part of Latin courtship that a Spaniard should give his *novia* a silver-bridled horse to ride, and set her quaking when the horse went astray?

'You have heard of me, haven't you, Father?'

'Yes. I had heard there was a fair-haired young woman at the house of the Don. I guessed when I saw you ... but I am perplexed that you are so many miles from the *hacienda* and all alone. It is not ...'

'Proper?' she murmured.

'But you are English, so of course ...'

'I do improper things.'

He puffed his pipe and watched from beneath tufted brows as her fingers played restlessly with the wine glass. 'I am not too old, nor too rigid in my views, not to understand the follies of the young. In any case, human beings are inexplicable, impulsive, and predestined.'

'You Latins are all such fatalists, Father!'

'Why not, child? If you had not come riding this way today, then your horse would not be missing and you would not be wondering nervously how your *novio* will react.' Father Sabio's smile was quizzical. 'He is known to have a temper to match his generosity.'

'He sets great store by the mare.' Romy gave a little shiver as she grew cooler in the shade of the lime tree and the sky began to take that deeper shade of blue as the afternoon waned. 'You wouldn't think it of a once famous matador that he should care so much for an animal.'

'Do you regard the matador as heartless?'

'Nerveless.' Her smile was shaky. 'You have an attractive walled garden, Father. I have never seen camellias so huge and velvety, not even in the gardens at the *hacienda*. You must have green fingers.'

'I like to grow things.' He arose and cut a pair of the lovely flowers growing on a single stem. He gave them to Romy with that touch of gallantry so disarming in the Latin male.

'*Gracias*.' She caressed the petals and wished she might hide away in this walled garden, but that would be cowardly, an admission that she feared to face the Don and his famous temper. What would he do? Her heart seemed to turn over. Would he be angry enough to set her free? It was what she wanted, yet not at the expense of Duquesa, whom he had trusted her to take care of.

'You have hurt your hand, *señorita*?' Father Sabio had taken hold of her hand and was examining the swelling on the back of it. 'Ah, this is a sting and it needs a little soda to take down the swelling and ease the irritation. I will fetch some.'

'You're very kind ...'

'I am pleased that in this matter I can help, child. I am not so sure about the mare. On market days we have all sorts in and out of the village and it may not be in my power to ... anyway, we will hope for the best, but if Carlos returns empty-handed ...' Father Sabio raised his own hands expressively, and then went indoors to fetch the soda.

Romy, all on edge, began to walk about the garden, which was full of birds, scarlet-tailed, others yellow-breasted with bright pink beaks, and a macaw that swept a branch with a long blue tail. At any other time Romy would have found delight in this old-world place, but the time was passing and she truly dreaded the moment when the Don came striding through that door, looking like thunder and ready to shake the breath out of her. She sank down on the coping of a fish pond and wrapped her arms about herself like a bird folding its frightened wings. A breeze stirred through the trees, rippled the water where the fish lurked red and gold, and played over Romy's bare arms in the thin silk shirt.

After bringing the soda for her hand Father Sabio had to leave for the evening service at the little church. Carlos returned with very little information beyond that a woman had heard during siesta the sound of hooves beneath her window and the jingle of a bridle. That would have been about three o'clock, a short time before Romy had returned to the stable to find Duquesa gone.

'I must now send a message to Don Delgado,' the Father said, firmly but kindly. 'Are you so afraid of him, child?'

'I . . . I seem always to do the wrong thing, Father. I'm impulsive and it makes him mad.'

'No one human is angelic, and perhaps you expect it of him, to be a saint when instead he is very

348

much a man and a Spaniard into the bargain.'

'How he is a Spaniard!' She had to smile as she doctored her sting with the soda. 'And I am English, and never the twain shall fully understand each other.'

'You may find, my child, that we Latins are attuned to the fact that women suffer in mysterious ways and seem almost to enjoy it.'

'Father!' She gave him a rather shocked look. 'How can you say that we enjoy being hurt?'

'When we are hurt, and when we are happy, we are more aware than at any other time of being fully alive. Women are by nature more sensitive and by reason of that they feel everything with more intensity. And now I will leave you in the good care of Carlos, who will cook you a meal and ensure that you have all you need.'

When the garden door closed behind the kindly figure of Father Sabio, a moth flew in and hovered on the edge of the wall. Romy saw plainly the flame cross and impression of a skull on the black body, and in her highly strung mood it seemed like a symbol of the encounter she must face later on.

Carlos served a delicious meal of baked rabbit, tomatoes, onions, and peppers, but Romy could not do it justice, though she drank several cups of coffee and made herself more nervous than ever.

She sat alone in the Father's old-fashioned parlour, with its Mexican cushions and mats, and mixture of cane and mahogany furniture. There were books and among them a copy of *David*

Copperfield. She tried to lose herself in the book, but each time the clock chimed the quarter hour, she felt her heart skip a beat.

By now they would know at the *hacienda* where she was, and soon someone would arrive to take her back to face the dueno's wrath. From the porch leading out to the garden she watched the sun burn out of the sky and heard the sound of the Angelus bell drifting along the quiet, darkening streets. Coppery golden clouds hung in the sky, and then the garden turned slowly to a place of shadows, and everything was still and waiting, and Romy was plucking the petals from her camellias without being aware of what she was doing.

The petals fell soundless to the ground, in front of the stone Virgin in chains ... and in the stillness came the soft whine of car wheels stopping in front of the house. The door had been left ajar for the caller to come in and fetch her. 'Here goes!' she thought, and finding her hands empty she plunged them into the pockets of her trousers and walked down the garden path to meet the driver of the car.

CHAPTER TEN

Their eyes clashed in the beam of the headlamps and Romy, already taut with nerves, was certain she would cry out if he touched her. She had hoped that having been busy all day he would send someone else for her, but here he was, punishing her with his presence even before he spoke a word to her.

She stood there as if enclosed in a bell-glass and the silence was deep and crushing as she waited for him to catechize her. He confronted her, dark and tall and ineffably the master of the situation, just as he had been on the train when he had insisted that she go home with him because scandal was something he would not tolerate.

It seemed as if an eternity rushed by before he turned and reached into the car for something. From the start Romy gave he might have been reaching for his whip.

'I-I'm hopelessly to blame for what happened,' she said shakily. 'It was entirely my fault ... I wanted to explore the *pueblo*, which took my fancy when Luis brought me here last week, and I left Duquesa at the local stable as if she were any ordinary horse. I'm sorry, I truly am ... and I deserve a scolding.'

'You deserve a spanking,' he drawled, 'and you would receive it, if Duquesa had not come home by herself, dragging her reins and thirsty but otherwise all right. Her pedigree cannot be hurt by how many miles she travels, only by neglect or misuse. You neglected to unsaddle the mare!'

Romy stared at him, then weak with relief she sank against the bonnet of the car. 'Thank heaven! I've been so worried ... so afraid.'

'Of me?' He raised slowly a black eyebrow and

351

deliberately took a step nearer to her.

'Y-yes.' She pressed herself against the steel body of the car and wondered in panic what form his punishment would take for even allowing his fine mare to be left in the hands of a Mexican stable boy. She had left the boy to unsaddle Duquesa, so eager had she been to lose herself and her troubled thoughts in the colourful market place. She had paid for the mare to be made comfortable ... no, there was no excuse for what she had done! Duquesa could so easily have been stolen! She deserved that glitter in the Don's eyes, and even as she shrank from him she submitted to his hands as they reached for her. Perhaps it was true what Father Sabino had said ... that women enjoyed their suffering.

Yet as his hands touched her, she looked thin, elfin, almost a slip of a boy in the car lights that cut in two the shadows all around them. The rate of her pulse beat was no secret to him as his fingers brushed her throat, fastening about her the poncho he had taken from the car!

'There, now perhaps you will stop shaking.' His fingers brushed against the thin silk of her shirt. 'No wonder you women go in fear of men when you dress like this!'

'I ... I dressed like this to ride in the sun ...'

'Without a hat?'

'Oh ... I must have left it in the Father's house.'

'I will fetch it. Get into the car and wait for me.'

Romy did as she was told, huddling down into

the warm folds of the woollen poncho, and still trembling a little from the shock of seeing him. It was such a relief that Duquesa was safe, but Romy was sure he wouldn't let her off with only a few words of disapproval. He was biding his time, awaiting his moment to take her unaware, and when she heard him returning to the car she kept her gaze fixed on the glimmer of the dashboard. He joined her inside the car and tossed her hat into the back. He slammed the door, started the engine, and backed along the lane that led into the main artery of the *pueblo*. The car became warm as the engine responded swiftly to his expert touch, and soon they were driving across the *sabana*, along the road that led inevitably to the *hacienda*.

'I am glad that you had the sense to go to Father Sabio,' he said after a suspenseful silence.

'You don't imagine I'd have tried walking to the *hacienda*?' She shot him a look and saw that his profile was stern and aloof in the down-reflecting roof light. She could tell that he was holding on to his temper, but she hadn't asked him to drive all this way to fetch her. He could have sent his chauffeur!

'I imagine you might have taken it into your head to find someone to take you in the opposite direction.'

'I hadn't enough money on me, nor did I fancy ...'

'What, *chica*?' His drawl softened meaningly. 'A tussle with an importunate Mexican? It could well

353

happen, dressed as you are.'

'I ... I was taken for a boy in the market place, and believe me I was tempted to beg a lift on a mule cart ... anything to get away from you!'

'You had Duquesa at your disposal, before you left her to wander home on her own.'

'The mare is yours, *señor*. I wouldn't steal her, and you are well aware that I don't know the country well enough to find my way to Xerica without getting hopelessly lost.'

'Xerica, with its airport of departure for England and home, eh? Shall I drive you there right now, put you on a plane, and be rid of you?'

She couldn't take her eyes from his face. 'Would you do that? No, I can see you are mocking me, playing one of your subtle games, building up my hopes only to knock them down!'

'How well you know me, but women are intuitive, are they not, about men and their motives?'

'Your sarcasm is intolerable. I knew the moment I saw you tonight that you had it in for me. You just can't resist taunting me for proving once again what an incompetent creature I am in comparison to the incomparable Latin girl. I need the keeper, in your opinion. I'm hopeless without one.'

'A mere child, less capable than the mare I trained myself to always find her way home.'

'Naturally! What is yours must have the homing intinct ... but I'm no pigeon.'

'I agree, *chica*. You are more of a goose.'

'The goose has been known to outfly the arrogant eagle!'

'But not to outwit him.'

'We'll see, *señor*.' Romy sat as far away as possible from him, wrapped in the poncho she would have been grateful for, had he not been so unbearable ... and male ... calling her a child and a goose!

Suddenly he laughed, and that too whipped at her outraged nerves. She felt the colour rise hot to her temples and she gave way to temper. 'I wish it had been Luis who came for me,' she said hotly. 'He has a better nature than you, a-and feelings more human than those you exhibit. He would realise how miserable and upset I've been, all these hours, and try to be a little kinder than you can stoop to manage.'

'You want a demonstration of ... kindness?' In an instant the brakes were applied and the car sped to a halt in the very centre of the bridge that spanned the lake. There they hovered above the sheerest drop, the waters of the lake spread beneath them, deep and dark as the Spanish eyes that drowned out all the world as Romy was caught in the Don's arms and his lips crushed the cry that broke from her. His arms and the poncho imprisoned her; she was helpless to resist the onslaught of his kisses. They were everywhere, blinding her eyes, warm against the hollow of her throat, there at her earlobes, a relentless invasion of senses she had not known she possessed.

'No!' She tried to turn her head away, but his

hand caught and held in the tawny tangle of her hair so that it hurt if she twisted away from him. He was whispering words which she sensed to be Spanish love words, and fear grew in her that she would not escape this time from what had threatened on the roof of the *atalaya*.

'Gado ... please ...'

He became instantly still, holding her within the curve of a steel-like arm, his other hand lost in the silk of her hair, so that she could not escape his gaze upon her red lips, her green eyes, her white skin.

'Don't,' she pleaded. 'Don't always blame me for what happened that night on the train. I didn't make the rain, or the breakdown. I didn't cast a spell so you would walk into my sleeping compartment by mistake. I ... I wish with all my heart I had never come to Mexico ... the place causes only trouble for me and I don't want more of it.'

Tears had come into her eyes and now they spilled and ran down her cheeks. 'Let me go away, then when everyone has forgotten that I ever came to the valley, you can marry Carmencita.'

'I don't take orders from a woman.' He bent his head and his lips brushed the tears from her face. 'I am far too much the tyrant, as you would say, to release you from my life. We are going to be married, no matter what you say.'

'Y-you can't force me to marry you. I won't, just for the sake of a scandal that never was!'

'What if there is a scandal, a real one, *chica*? I hold you at my mercy. I could do anything I pleased with you. If you tried to open that door beside you, you would fall into the lake. I should feel compelled to dive in after you and the centre of the lake is so deep that we should both be drowned. Immortal lovers, *niña*. Does it not sound romantic?'

'It sounds crazy. Gado ... I mean, *señor*, be reasonable.'

'I am being perfectly reasonable. I brought you to the *hacienda* to marry you, and that is what I intend to do.'

'But it was all ... fake. People only marry when they love each other.' She moved tentatively and at once his arm tightened into a curve of captivity. 'Y-you know I hate you.'

'It will be my pleasure to teach you how to do the opposite.'

'That's typical of your arrogance,' she said stormily. 'But you'd be wasting your time. A pupil can't be taught something she is unwilling to learn, no matter how expert the teacher ... and I am sure you are an expert, having been an idolised matador. They are, I believe, notorious for their *amors* with every pretty *señorita* who throws them a rose.'

'You make dangerously provoking remarks, *niña*, and let me remind you again that we are very much alone and having been an *espada* I am also ruthless.' He spoke the word against her ear. 'You consider me very ruthless, don't you? So what have I to lose if I teach you a lesson in love, here and now?'

'Love?' She hoped the scorn in her voice hid the tremor she could not control. 'My ideas of love are about as much like yours as ... as the sun is to the moon.'

'Really? Don't you know that in our mythology the sun and the moon are lovers?'

'They would be, in your mythology! Especially as your southern sun is an assault rather than a caress.'

'Do you then regard love as a thing of tender caresses and whispered endearments?'

'I ... I should hope it isn't as savage as your sun can be.' She sat rigid within the circle of his arm, and hoped that while they argued he would not kiss her again so closely that each bone in her body, each nerve and limb seemed to vibrate unbearably, almost to the point of pain, so that she had come close to moaning in his arms. He would like that. It was in his nature to enjoy being cruel to her.

'The soft and tender things are never as exciting, niña, as the more primitive things. The hard-shelled passion fruit is more delicious than the peach once the shell is cracked. The dragonfly that eats the moth is gorgeous. The Moors who ruled with the sword made gardens like jewels. The cactus, which we call the cruel flower, holds water for the man lost in the desert. Life, you know, would be fearfully dull if it were not enlivened by danger. If we knew what lay around every strange corner ... and what lay in the stranger's heart.'

He tilted her chin with an imperious finger and

forced her eyes to look into his, there in the intimate, shadowy light of the car, poised there on the bridge, like a wasp clinging to the rim of a water glass.

'If you were a girl who really liked everything to be cosy and narrow you would not have spent your grandmother's legacy on a journey to Mexico. And alone, *niña*!'

'That really tries your temper, doesn't it, *señor*? It's at the root of every argument we have. Your Spanish colonial nature just can't tolerate the thought of a woman being able to look after herself.'

'Can you?' He quirked an eyebrow in the mocking way she found so infuriating. 'You gaze at the world with such wide and innocent eyes, don't you? A babe in the jungle. Hardly aware yet of what life is all about, and why men and women find each other so exciting. It was your eyes I noticed that day in Mexico City. Green eyes for danger, and the earth shook. Then the rains came, and an angel or a devil's hand led me into your sleeping compartment.'

'I-I'm sure it was the devil's,' Romy said, defying him with the green eyes he had likened to the Avarado bride gems. At once his arms tightened and she felt the strength that could have crushed her body as his strength of will had crushed her resistance on the train. Now if she resisted he would kiss her with those kisses that whirled her around until she couldn't think straight, until the danger made her submit to a marriage that would leave his pride unblemished and his ambitions untouched by the breath of scandal.

Feminine instinct came to her rescue and she let herself go slack in his arms, allowed her eyes to close as if she might faint.

'Romola?' His breath stirred warm against her eyelids. 'Poor child, you look worn out, a waif of the night, in the hands of a devil you don't much like.'

Those same hands laid her back against the seat, and a moment later she felt the throbbing of the engine. The car moved on across the bridge, and the sardonic irony of his words kept revolving in her mind. A man such as the Don could never love what he called 'a waif of the night'. She, that waif, would never marry him, no matter what he did, or said, or submitted her to. She had her pride and it rejected a marriage of convenience, one that would grow roots of resentment and bear the bitter fruit of regret when he became Ambassador and his lady could not look a Latin, or behave like one. Beautiful, submissive, yet fiery beneath it all.

All the lamps in their iron sconces were alight in the courtyard and along the veranda, and members of the family were gathered in groups to await the arrival of Don Delgado with his truant *novia*. When the car came to a halt they milled around it, and it was into the arms of Luis that Romy stumbled. He looked into her eyes, read their message of imploration and assisted her into the house with a firmness that held at bay the solicitous but curious aunts. 'I just want to go to my room, Luis. I'm so weary ...'

Somehow she achieved her wish and when at last she was alone she sank across the smoothness of her bed and let her body relax at last from the tension of the past hours. Ah, it felt so good to be here, with the turbulent events of the day behind her at last, and she was almost drifting off to sleep when the beany spiciness of fresh-made coffee stole to her nostrils.

She had not heard the door open, but when she turned her head she saw Doña Dolores standing beside her bed. Romy sat up and pressed the tumbled hair away from her eyes. She had no idea how defenceless she looked; how much the stranger in the enormous Spanish bed.

'Poor child, you have had a worrying time, Delgado tells me. Let me pour you a cup of coffee, and later on when you have rested you may have a supper tray here in your room.'

'That would be nice, *señora*, though I could come down if you prefer ...?'

'Not at all.' A cup of delicious coffee was handed to Romy, made from the beans grown in the valley. To her surprise as she sipped it, Doña Dolores sat down on the foot of her bed. Her dark eyes studied the pale contours of Romy's face, around which her tawny hair was clouded. Her slender hand played with the antique pendant which hung against the silk of her dress.

'When the mare returned riderless we were all very worried here at the *hacienda*. We thought you might have been thrown.'

Romy gazed at the woman who had every reason to wish that she and the Don had never crossed paths, and yet in her eyes there seemed a look of genuine concern. Romy longed to respond to it, but she dared not believe that the Don's mother felt any sympathy for her, the interloper into her home; the girl who had disrupted her plans regarding a union between Carmencita and her son: the bringing together of two of the oldest families in the region.

'I am sorry to have caused so much anxiety.' Romy's hands gripped her coffee cup, for this was not the time to say that soon the entire family would be rid of her; that none of them need fear that she meant to marry without being loved. Such an arrangement might suit a Latin girl, but Romy was far too sensitive to be able to face even the thought of a loveless possession.

'We have not spoken together very often, Romola, but I should like you to feel at home with us. I have noticed that you seem a little *soledad*, as we say. But that is only natural for a while. Our valley has an insidious way of stealing the heart, until it seems the only place to live. Years ago, before Gado was born, I was unhappy here. I was young and wilful ... would you believe that?'

Romy studied the woman who had borne a proud and wilful son; the silver at her temples, as if painted there. The expressive eyes; the mingling of tolerance in the beautiful woman, combined with certain shades of Latin intolerance. She had eloped with Delgado's father, and because the marriage had been a tempestuous one, she now believed firmly in the arranged union. It was understandable.

A smile softened the pensiveness of Romy's face. 'I suppose to be young is to be impulsive and on the brink of trouble a good deal of the time. You must have been very young when you married, *señora*.'

A soft flush stole into the smooth olive of the *señora*'s face and her eyes held for a moment the burning memory of the wild but unhappy love she had known with her husband. 'I was too young to know anything about men. Ramon had always had his own way, here in the wilds of Mexico, and I was accustomed to the constraints of the convent. Ramon came on a visit to southern Spain; he was buying bulls for his farm and my father bred the best. We met, we fell madly in love ... the girl just out of convent school, and the dashing *gaucho* who sprang from a long line of colonial Spaniards with a dash of Aztec blood in the veins. I knew that I was meant for a man selected by my father, much older than me and of a rather serious nature. I wanted Ramon and so I eloped with him to Mexico.'

The *señora*'s fingers clenched hard on the Spanish locket, and Romy couldn't help but wonder if it held a miniature of that wild young man she had been unable to resist.

'I left Ramon within six months of our marriage.

363

For a Latin girl to leave her husband is a serious matter ... that is why I must be sure that Delgado has not made the mistake of carrying off a girl just to satisfy an impulse.'

'But you know....' Romy's heart beat fast. 'It was a matter of expediency. He cannot afford a scandal in his position.'

'Has he ... made love to you?' The *señora*'s head was elegantly poised on her slender neck as she asked the question, but her eyes were pained, as if she didn't wish to hurt or embarrass Romy.

Romy thought of his kisses in the car, so deliberate and punishing, but knew it was not that kind of lovemaking to which his mother referred.

She shook her head, and heard a soft sigh of relief escape the *señora*'s lips. She rose to her feet, and her fingers relaxed their tense hold on the locket. 'I am glad we have talked, Romola. The atmosphere seems lighter between us. We are more *simpatica*.'

'Yes,' said Romy, but she looked young and uncertain curled up on the gold and scarlet bed. She wanted to say outright that the *señora* need have no more fear of another broken marriage in the family, but words alone would not convince her. It would take action. A deed of kind, such as the one which had brought her here.

A day alone with Luis on the mysterious lake island, to which the Indians never went, should jolt the pride which had made the Don bring her home with him. It should convince everyone that such a flighty miss should be sent away again.

'Xerica?' he had mocked. 'With its airport of departure for England and home?'

'Home,' she whispered, as the door of her bedroom closed behind the slender figure of Doña Dolores, and the night breezes stirred the flowering vine which had crept from the *mirador* right inside the room, alive and scented.

Her bedsitter would seem dull and austere after the colour and scent of her Spanish bedroom ... she would miss this old, fascinating, rambling house, its walks of delight, and the golden *sabana*, but in England she would be her own mistress again and not the masquerading *novia* of a man who put pride and position before anything else. She slipped off the bed and smoothed the cover, and as the silk whispered beneath her fingers she seemed to hear again the words spoken by Doña Dolores a moment before she had made her departure from the room. 'I want above all for Gado to know real happiness and not the passion that burns out leaving only bitterness in its place.'

Romy wandered out to her vine-shrouded *mirador* and found that a moon had risen and that the night held a mystery that breathed of elemental things. Don Delgado was his father's son also, and the same passions must stir his blood and smoulder in those bronze eyes until they seemed like the eyes of a furious, graceful animal.

His mother could not know how he looked at a girl until her very soul cried out for mercy. Such a man was like this half-pagan night and its moon like an Aztec shield.

If he took a woman without loving her ... Romy caught her breath and put a hand to her throat. Someone was pacing the courtyard below the enclosure in which she stood, cigar smoke arose on the still air, so strangely still since the moon had arisen, and Romy breathed the now familiar aroma of the Don's cigar.

Long and prowling were his strides from one side of the patio to the other, and when Romy peered from among the vines she could make out his tall figure in the rays of the moon. The black velvet of his smoking coat was like the pelt of a panther, to match the way he prowled the circular patio, almost as if it were a cage from which he sought some means of escape.

The pulse beneath her fingers seemed to throb more insistently. He desired escape as much as she did. Anger with the fates, a male reaching out for some prize or compensation, had made him insist that she marry him.

A marriage of convenience ... and angry passion!

Suddenly she felt his gaze upon her *mirador* and she stood as still as a bird among its foliage and prayed that his keen eyes would not see and assume that she was spying on him. She saw the dark tilt of his head in the moonlight, the smoke of his cigar rising against the pallor of the moonglow. Did he sense that she was there? Her heart seemed as if it were trying to beat its way out of her body, and then he turned away and a moment later she heard him speaking to someone. There was the lacy gleam of a pale mantilla, the glitter of earrings, and then a girlish laugh.

Carmencita had joined him in the patio. They seemed to stand very close together for several moments ... the girl's bracelet of tiny golden bells caught the moonlight as her arm curved upwards and encircled his neck. Romy held her breath, then she retreated into her room before she saw the completion of that embrace.

She had known that no man of the Don's age and temperament could treat Carmencita as if she were a niece. The girl was as glowing and warm as a carnation on a slender stem ... she was like the song she liked to sing to the music of her young brother's guitar. *'The woman is the chalice, the man is the wine.'*

She was made, as Doña Dolores knew, for a man like the *dueno*.

CHAPTER ELEVEN

THE Don's tour of inspection ended, after which he was kept busy in his study writing reports and letters. This was a relief for Romy. It meant she saw more of Luis, who seemed attuned to her mood, which was a mixture of gaiety and determination to return to her own way of life as soon as possible.

Then came a surprise ... Luis mentioned that the

Don had received a rather lengthy telegram from the Embassy in Mexico City, and that same evening the Don asked Romy to accompany him to his study because he wished to speak with her.

'I ... was going to listen to the music, *señor*,' she said, hoping wildly that he would not insist.

His eyes insisted, warning her that he would take hold of her and march off with her in front of the family. With a little shrug, and a smile at Luis, she left the patio where the family were gathered for the evening and walked beside the Don to his sanctum. Her every nerve was tingling, and she had to fight to look composed when he opened the door of his study and ushered her into the room, with its leather floor-covering, its swords and capes, and aura of good cigars and a total lack of female influence.

He indicated that she sit down in one of the leather wing-backed chairs. 'A glass of wine might help you to relax,' he drawled, and he went to a carved cabinet and took from it a carafe of wine and a pair of stemmed glasses. As he poured the wine, Romy strove to look as if she didn't remember in vivid detail the last time they had been alone. She tilted her chin and watched his approach across the room, his features unsmiling, but his eyes so mockingly aware of her tension.

'To what shall we drink?' He handed her one of the glasses and seemed deliberately to let his fingers touch hers. Then he lounged against the high carved mantel, the family eagle above his head and in its talons the dove like a ruffled flower. 'To a journey without incident, shall we say?'

Romy stared at him. 'A journey, *señor*? Are you going away, or are you letting me go?'

'Which would you prefer?' He took a lazy sip at his wine. 'Come, don't spare my feelings.'

'Have you any?' she asked, more from defiance than a belief that he couldn't ache at heart or bleed when hurt. Looking at him in his dark suit, with the heavy silk shirt so white against the dark-gold skin, she could imagine the scar which he carried and the spell he had cast in the bullring. His fascination was the most dangerous thing about him, and clad in a fighting cape he would have quickened the heart of every woman who watched him stroll across the sand to match his quickness and subtlety against the temper and strength of a bull who faced for the first time a man who swung a coloured cape in its face.

No fighting bull was ever trained, being born a fighter. Up until its advent into the ring it was kept from any knowledge of flickering capes and the supple daring of a matador. At the *estancias*, so Romy had been told by Tio Isidro, the aspiring *espadas* learned their tricks by fighting the heifers. It was the most courageous of the heifers who eventually gave birth to the brave bulls. The bulls were sacred, like Mithras, until their entrance into the arena ... their hour of glory, and the matador's moment of truth.

'You are giving me such a strange look, *niña*.

Drink your wine and I will tell you about our trip.'

'Our . . . trip?' A sudden terror gripped her. What could he possibly mean . . . a honeymoon?

'You look on the verge of a swoon . . . please to drink your wine before I have to revive you with the kiss of life.'

'Don't you dare!' She swallowed half the wine in a gulp, and then looked at him with defiant eyes, the contours of her face revealed by the way her hair was clipped back in a silver buckle. Just as her eyes dominated her face, so did the leather chair dominate her slim figure.

'Do you now feel brave enough to hear the details of the trip?'

'Stop behaving as if this were a *corrida*. It isn't fair!'

'Stop looking at me as if I carry an invisible whip. It isn't very flattering.'

'I'm not a Latin girl, so I wouldn't know how to flatter a man.'

'No,' his eyes flicked her green-clad figure in the winged chair, 'you are certainly in no way a Latin girl. It should cause quite a lot of comment at the Embassy.'

'What do you mean? Oh, for heaven's sake stop playing verbal chess with me and tell me why you dragged me away from the music and why you keep talking about a trip. What trip?'

'The one you will be taking with Luis and myself to Mexico City.' He strolled to his desk and picked up a sheet of paper overlaid by the strips

370

of a telegram. 'There is at this time of the year a carnival in the city and a ball to round off the saturnalia. I am requested to return to the Embassy to attend the ball and to meet various officials from Madrid. I am asked to be accompanied by my fiancée.'

Romy couldn't take her eyes from him, and then to give herself courage she finished her wine. 'I gather from what you say, *señor*, that you are expecting soon to be addressed as Your Excellency? I take it that I am to be inspected to make sure you are choosing the right wife for such an eminent position? How will you explain things when I return to England ... because I intend to return! I won't be sacrificed on the altar of your ambitions!'

She jumped to her feet as she spoke and ran to the door. With long supple strides he was there before her and blocking the way with his height and his relentless eyes.

'You will come to Mexico City and you will behave as my fiancée. If you attempt to run away I shall come after you and then you will learn how angry I can be when I have real cause to be so.'

'Ever since we met you have been making threats,' she stormed. 'Is that all you are capable of, even with Carmencita?'

'Why mention Carmencita?'

'Because she is the one you should take to meet your Spanish officials. She is the girl you ought to marry.'

'When the time arrives I shall marry whom I

choose to marry, but right now I am concerned with the carnival ball. You will attend it with me and I refuse absolutely to accept your refusal to do so ... do you hear me?'

Romy heard the pounding of her heart, and outside in the patio the strumming of guitars. There was no music more evocative than Latin music; no eyes in the world more expressive than Spanish eyes. The Don held her with his gaze, and unable to bear it a moment longer she turned away from him and went to study the Goya painting of the woman in a red frilled dress, holding in her hand a lacy fan above which her vivid eyes flirted with whoever looked at her.

'We endure some things so we may enjoy others.' The Don came and stood behind Romy, whose body tensed like one of those slender swords on the wall. 'Think of all those museums, not to mention the masked ball. Surely every young woman should attend one just once in her life.'

'You seem always to be making demands of me ... if I come to Mexico City will you make me a promise?'

'I must know the promise before I commit myself to keeping it.'

'Don't ... force me to marry you.'

He was silent for about half a minute, during which time Romy was acutely conscious of his supple figure behind her, and those arms that might suddenly enclose her in an embrace that mocked her fragile inability to escape from him. 'Very well,

Romola, I swear not to force you to become my wife. I will allow your emotions to dictate their own demands and desires, and having made this oath I shan't break it.'

'I should never forgive you if you broke such an oath, *señor*.'

'Turn, *niña*, and look into my eyes. They have, you know, a truth of their very own.'

She turned slowly and let her gaze dwell on his face. He looked almost stern as he gazed down at her, and slowly her hands relaxed their grip on each other. 'It wouldn't be right, *señor*, for two people to marry without ... love.'

'I agree ... and will you make me a promise?'

'Not to run away from my supposed lord and master?'

He took note of the smile that touched her lips. 'For that I demand a forfeit. Since our first meeting I have wanted to see the effect of one of my *chaquetas* against your skin and hair. Will you oblige?'

He reached for one of the matador short coats that hung upon the wall. 'This I wore as a youth of seventeen. Come, try it on.'

'To make our *corrida* seem more real?' she asked daringly.

He held the coat and after a slight hesitation she slipped her arms into the sleeves and was surprised to find that the gold and silver stitchings made it seem like a coat of mail. It gleamed against her green dress and her tawny hair, and made the Don narrow his eyes to study the effect.

'Do I look like a youth, *señor*?'

'Are you wishing you were, *chica*?'

'Sometimes with you it would be an advantage!'

He smiled with his eyes, until they seemed to hold fire. 'Perhaps we could then have been friends, eh? But you are most fetching in the *chaqueta*. Far more so than any youth.'

'Then if you don't mind I'll take it off.' She did so and handed it to him. He returned it to its place among his mementoes and Romy noticed the suggestive rent in the side of another jacket, and when she flashed an enquiring look at the Don he quirked an eyebrow and touched his side. 'Yes, my retribution for my sins,' he drawled. 'We go to the city on Thursday morning, by aeroplane from Xerica.'

'Y-you have no heart.' Her legs held the most curious tremor as she walked to his desk and touched the ornament which he used as a paperweight, a carved hand holding an uncut topaz, barbaric and yet at the same time strangely beautiful.

'I have certain duties and I intend to carry them out.'

She dared not look at him and kept her gaze on the hand stabbed by the gleaming stone. His tone of voice was explicit, he intended to have his way and she was left defenceless.

'I am glad that Luis is going with us,' she said.

'You like him, don't you?'

'Yes, very much.'

'Much more than you like me, eh?'

374

'Yes, do you mind?'

'If I minded would I give you this? Catch!'

To her own surprise she caught the object which he took from his pocket and tossed so carelessly. She looked at it as if it might burn her and heard him laugh softly and mockingly. 'It has nothing to do with the bride gems you took such a dislike to. It is designed in the tradition of the Incas.'

It was a wide bracelet of patterned gold. 'It's very lovely,' she said. 'I ... I will accept it, if there are no strings attached.'

'Do you see any?' he drawled.

'No ...' She slipped the bracelet over her fingers and felt its golden weight against the bones of her wrist. She would dismiss from her mind how much it had cost and enjoy without asking questions its pagan beauty. 'Thank you, *señor*.'

'You are welcome, *señorita*.' He seemed to mock the formality of her tone of voice.

'May I now join the others?' The weight of his bracelet against her wrist made her feel defenceless and defiant. It was a charming token, his way of saying *gracias* because he had made her promise to carry on with the masquerade until he was ready to ring down the curtain. Always he must have *his* way.

'By all means join those on the patio.' He gave her a faintly sardonic bow, and this time she was allowed to leave the study. Her legs still felt strangely shaky as she made for the patio, where the young people were dancing the *sevillana* with gaiety and exuberance. Carmencita seemed to be on fire as she tapped her scarlet heels and whirled her skirts, and Romy was suddenly wild with the man who played with both of them as if they were mere dolls for his amusement. She found Luis and drew him to one side. 'Will you take me to the island tomorrow?' she asked. 'The Don is infuriating ... he's putting his career before everything ... everyone ... and I won't be a party to it!'

'The island?' Luis murmured. 'You seem drawn to it.'

'Yes, I want to see it, and this may be my last chance.'

'You want Gado to believe ...' Luis frowned and gazed over towards the dancing couples. Romy hung on to his answer. It was true about the island, as if some pagan voice called her to it, and there all her problems could be solved and answered.

Then Luis looked at her, just as the Don came out to watch the dancing. They were both acutely aware of that tall figure in the lamplight as Luis inclined his head and said with his eyes that he would take her to the island. He was not happy about it, but Romy felt a sense of elation as she fingered the Inca bracelet with its raised figures of sun, moon, and stars, and profiles which had the look of fierce pride and domination displayed by Don Delgado as he stood talking to his mother. Suddenly he took her slender hand and bent his head to kiss it. She touched his black hair with a gesture of infinite affection, reminding Romy of her words the other night. She wanted the *dueno* her son to find happiness with a wife he truly loved.

Refreshments were served, and the music grew dreamy. People began to drift off to bed, and soon only a single guitar was being played beneath the Spanish *encina* tree that spread its branches across the patio. Stars winked in a sky as dense as velvet, and the moon had waned leaving only a silvery shadow in the sky. The rumble of male voices still talking, and the music of the guitar, lent a transient peace to the night.

Romy slipped away unseen, running quickly up to bed, like a child eager for the morning to come.

The morning dawned golden and brilliant, and after a hasty cup of coffee and a buttered roll, Romy dressed herself in a Spanish lace middy blouse and a pair of pirate pants, and ran from the house to meet Luis on the foreshore ... she ran as if someone might pursue her, and it wasn't until she arrived at the lakeside that she realised she was wearing the Inca bracelet. She stared at it and wondered at the compulsion which had made her put it on this morning.

Then she saw the boat which Luis had hired from one of the fishermen. It has a pea-green sail and she broke into a smile as he held out a hand for her to jump aboard. She was light in her rope-soled shoes, almost gamine with her pony-tailed hair catching the sunlight.

Luis clenched her hand and studied the bracelet

that glinted with a pagan goldness. 'We have a food hamper and a flagon of wine. A breeze to carry the sail, and no cares, eh?'

'No cares, Luis.' She spoke gaily. 'Those we leave behind us for the day.'

'You are sure this is what you want?' His eyes were serious for a moment, studying her upraised face.

'I am very sure ... listen, Luis, I seem to hear that beguiling voice across the lake.'

'You are full of romantic fancies,' he scoffed. 'A dreamer who refuses to awake to reality.'

'What is reality?' She gazed about her at the wonderful beauty of the morning, with a sparkle to the water and birds on the wing. She felt like the Inca maiden of legend, being taken to the island for the sacrifice of her youth and all her secret longings.

'Come, Luis, let the owl and the pussycat be away on their voyage.'

He laughed and tossed her a papaya, succulent and thirst-quenching. She ate it as the boat sailed out across the thousand silver ripples of the lake. She shut her mind to everything but the hypnotic dance of the water. She mustn't think of the future; she must like the Inca maiden pretend that after today she would still be able to feel both pleasure and pain.

Sunshine scattered itself on the lake so that it shone like a great broken opal. 'Do you mind very much, Luis, that I asked you to take me where the

Indians never go? Are you superstitious about it?'

'It has a pagan history ... the virgins were sacrificed there to the Aztec gods.'

'How cruel were their gods.' She shivered in the sunlight, and watched as the island came in sight, long and lizard-shaped, with a hump at the centre. Luis steered in against the shingle and leapt ashore. Romy followed him and stood looking about her with eager eyes ... eyes as green as the palm leaves that waved on the shore.

While Luis was busy bringing the hamper off the boat and the rug for their picnic, Romy wandered off across the silvery sand and climbed the rocks that led to the island's vantage point. Halfway up she turned to beckon Luis ... down there on the sands lay the hamper, but he was back on board the boat and steering it away from the island.

'Luis ...' His name echoed on the breeze, and the strangest fear clutched at her heart. 'Luis ...' She scrambled down the rocks and ran to the water's edge. 'What are you doing ... come back!'

He waved to her and she could see the flash of his teeth in a smile. The pea-green sail stood defiantly against the blue of the sky, and it stunned Romy to realise that she was being left all alone on this island of sacrifice.

The palm trees waved their fans with lazy unconcern above her head and she kicked at the sand in sudden temper. 'Luis, you traitor!'

'Naughty, naughty,' drawled a voice. She swung round and there by a palm tree stood a tall and negligent figure, barefooted like an Indian, black hair agleam with water, a silk shirt open to his waist and tucked into the belt of long narrow trousers.

Romy could barely believe her eyes. 'Don Delgado!'

'None other.' He strolled towards her, flagrantly attractive and supple as a panther, a lazy smouldering to his eyes that made Romy take a step backwards away from him.

'Th-the pair of you arranged it!' she gasped. 'It was a conspiracy between you ... oh, I might have guessed! Luis is too much your friend to ever do anything ... how did you get here?'

'I swam, with my clothes around my neck like an Indian.'

'All that way?' She could feel her heart beating hard beneath the lace of her middy blouse as his eyes stole over her, so deliberately, coming to rest on the bracelet he had given her.

'Did I not tell you that if you ran away from me I should come after you?'

'But ... why?'

He slowly smiled. 'There is not a soul at the *hacienda* who doesn't know why. You alone seem innocent of the reason. Tell me,' his voice softened dangerously, 'why do you wear my bracelet when you planned to look seduced by another man?'

'It's a nice chunky piece of jewellery that goes well with my outfit,' she said defiantly.

'It goes very well with your ... outfit.' Almost before she knew it he was close to her and she was

380

tilting her eyes to look at him, at the warm, hard lips curving into a smile. She felt curiously breathless ... she wanted to run from him, but where could she go on this small strip of sand and stone to get away from him? He made her feel intolerably shy and uncertain, and as her gaze dropped away from his, she saw in the opening of his shirt the jagged scar on his right side. A feeling of faintness seemed to sweep over her, and then she was in the Don's arms, held passionately close to his golden skin and the crucifix which hung against his breast.

The touch of him, the tang of his skin, the tousled blackness of his hair, they combined to so disarm her that very little fight was left in her. She wanted to cling to him, to give love for passion, if that was all he wanted. 'No,' she breathed, 'you'd bully me day and night, make me so much yours that I'd have no freedom ...'

'Mine,' he agreed, his lips burning warm against the hollow of her throat. 'My possession.'

'Oh ... how typically arrogant!'

'Sacrificed to me instead of a stuffy museum, *mia*.'

'Th-the Ambassador's lady?'

'His lady with the tawny gold hair and the green eyes.'

'Gado ... I could never carry it off!'

'Then for you I shall refuse to be Ambassador.'

'For me?' She pulled away a few fractions to search his eyes; what she saw there made her bury her face swiftly against him. 'I couldn't let you do that. You've worked for it. You deserve it.'

'Do I, *dulce amiga*?' He crooned the words against her bright hair. 'How good of you to say so.'

And feeling him so close to her, strong and yet vulnerable, she realised the truth of what she said. He worked hard for his people, and was as generous as he was passionately just. All this she had noticed, what she had been blind to was the rather lonely man searching for love and finding it, to his chagrin, in a rebellious English girl who would keep saying that she wanted to lock herself in a museum with dead things.

'Gado, you have often called me a child.' She smiled against his warm shoulder. 'You meant I was too juvenile to be trusted with your adult feelings, didn't you? I ... I don't seem to feel juvenile any more. I feel ...'

'Unutterably sweet, dear Puritan.' His hand tilted her head against his arm and his eyes shook her heart with the look of love that burned in them. 'Did you never wonder why I travelled home on a train when I could have taken a plane? No, you are much too innocent and modest. I bribed the clerk at your hotel to tell me where you were going and when. I arranged to be on that train ... fate was kind enough to arrange the rest.'

'I always knew you were a devil,' she murmured.

'Do you mind, *amada*?' His eyes were laughing at her, but they were also loving her, and nothing mattered except that he love her. If he ever asked she would give him her soul, and perhaps she did as her lips met the sweet and dangerous ardency of his lips.

'There is one thing I should like to know, Gado. What was Carmencita doing in your arms the other night?'

'Confessing that she likes you ... that if I am to marry someone other than herself, then the "demure English Miss" should suit me well. She suits me very well.'

'She also loves you, Don Delgado.'

RAPTURE OF THE DESERT

Rapture
of the
Desert

As a solo dancer, Chrys had felt her life was fulfilled. Now, with a year off to recover from an accident, her prospects were bleak.

Then she met Anton de Casenove, a playboy-prince who seemed likely to prove a distraction. Chrys, realizing that her years of dedication to ballet had left her particularly vulnerable to men, fled from him in panic.

But how long could she resist his devastating charm?

CHAPTER I

"You have my answer," said the man who was dressed all in grey, with even a distinguished dash of it through his hair. "A year from today and you might dance again. The fall you had from those railway steps was a serious one and you might well have been killed, or crippled for life. But luck and skill were on your side and the operation which you underwent was almost a total success. It will become a complete one, if for the next twelve months you set aside your career in ballet and turn to some less strenuous occupation."

"A whole year!" The girl in the chair at the opposite side of Van Harrington's desk looked at him as if he pronounced for her a life sentence away from her beloved dancing. Indeed it was her life. Since the age of seven she had worked and slaved for love of the dance, and now at twenty-two she was a recognized soloist, and only a few weeks previous to her accident she had danced in Russia at the Bolshoi Theatre where the stage was so wonderfully spacious, so made for those dramatic ballets which were for her the breath of life.

"Dancing is all I know," she said tensely.

"Unless you wish to undo all the skilful work which has made you fit again, then forget that you are a dancer, Miss Devrel. A year is not for ever."

"You said cautiously that I *might* dance again, Mr. Harrington. Your verdict doesn't sound conclusive."

"Medical men are rather like bankers." His smile was brief but kind. "We are cautious with our hand-outs. I have given you back a sound enough body, but you must be careful not to squander your strength. You could return to your career next week, and be again my patient in four weeks. Wait a year and we will see then—"

"But a year away from dancing could mean the end

for me! Unless a ballet dancer's body is kept continually in practice there is a gradual lessening of speed and grace." Chrys Devrel drew a sigh of near despair! "If you say I must stop dancing, then I'm finished."

"Nonsense!" Now he spoke sharply, as if scolding a child. "Life has many things to offer an attractive young woman. Your heart won't easily break, but your body could be ruined for good unless you accept my advice. Well, Miss Devrel, what are you going to do?"

She avoided his stern gaze by looking down at her hands, slim and clasped together as if they sought to comfort each other. "You don't give me much choice," she said at last. "I must swallow the bitter pill of a ruined career in order to keep my bodily health. I – I'm not altogether a fool, so I shall have to abide by what you say."

"You will make me a firm promise?" He rose to his feet and came round to where she sat. Chrys stood up and she felt numb inside as he took her hands in his. "Come now, young woman, give me your word that you will not perform a single pirouette for the next twelve months."

"I wouldn't dare a single ballet step," she replied. "One alone would lead me on to dance and dance, until I dropped. That's how much I love to dance!"

"You have, perhaps, never tried to love anything else because to dance was all-sufficing. Now you have to face an alternative. Now you have time and leisure –"

"No, I shall need to work," she broke in. "The clinic and the operation took most of my savings. I have to find a job, but heaven alone knows what I'm suited for! I dare not find work in a theatre – my will-power isn't strong enough for that."

The surgeon gazed down at her, his look an effortless one, because she had dark gold hair framing a white, slender, purely-boned face. The small lobes of her ears were pierced by small gold rings, and her eyes were intensely blue. She gave an impression of being fragile, but in reality she was supple as fine silk and equally resilient.

She tilted her chin. "Something will come along, I daresay, but I can't promise to give it my devotion or my love. Thank you again, Mr. Harrington, for all your kindness."

He walked with her to the door of his consultation room. "Goodbye, Miss Devrel. As I said before, a year soon passes."

"I suppose it does,"she said, but as she left him and made her way down the stairs to the front door she knew that even a week away from the *barre* could rob a dancer of some of her skill. She smiled absently at the woman who opened the door for her, and as she stepped into Wimpole Street she felt as if it might as well have been raining instead of looking so bright and cheerful. She walked to the end of the street and there she hailed a cab and asked the driver to take her to the St. Clement's Hotel, where she was meeting her sister for tea.

Dove took life as it came and had never bothered about a career. Dove had wanted only to marry, and in a couple of weeks she would walk up the aisle and look glowingly expectant and content.

Chrys sat back against the leather upholstery of the cab and breathed the tang of cigar smoke left by the previous occupant. Life for her had become so tangled up since that awful moment at Fenchurch Street Station when she tripped on the steps there, while running to catch a train. She had fallen backwards, all the way down to the hard ground, crushing a couple of the fine, intricate bones in her spine. The pain had been unbelievable, and the fear of never walking again had been like a nightmare from which she had seemed not to awake for hours and days.

The cab swept through Soho, so unnaturally quiet at this time of the day, and made its way past a towered church that looked so old in the sunlight. She noted the time by the church clock and knew that Dove would already be up in the penthouse lounge, gazing dreamily from the wide windows, or studying that sweet and simple engagement ring of hers. With that unimpaired grace which had made it too easy for her to believe that she would soon be able to dance again Chrys stepped out of the cab and paid the driver. She felt his eyes on her face, but it meant little to her that like Van Harrington he found the bones, and the shape and the colour of her eyes, a pleasing blend.

She turned and walked into the hotel. She crossed the carpeted foyer to the express lifts and pressed the button of the one that would take her up to the lounge. Dove would be sympathetic, but she would be like the surgeon and say that Chrys should count her blessings. Her health was restored and she could *walk*. Dove would smile that dove-like smile of hers and insinuate that Chrys find a beau and enjoy the pleasure of falling in love.

There was a little twist of a smile on Chrys's mouth as the lift doors opened and she stepped out and saw her sister composedly seated on a long couch by the panoramic windows, the sun on her smooth young profile.

Dove turned instinctively as if she felt the sudden tightening of the bond between them. A smile broke on her soft pink lips and she jumped to her feet. Her hair was a lighter gold than Chrys's, her eyes a gentler blue, and the curve of her chin was less obstinate. She was the pretty sister, the more popular one with the young men of Westcliff, their home town. She had not the haughty tilt to her head that made Chrys seem too distant to touch. Her lips were not those of a passionate and talented spirit.

She was like her name, a dove, and Chrys loved her, but could never be half so sweet, or ready for the tender delights of love with a young executive who, quite literally, adored his bride-to-be.

The sisters embraced, and then a waiter came to take their order. "Tea and cream cakes," said Dove, who in a couple of years would be plump and quite unconcerned.

"Well, darling?" She studied her sister's composed but very white face with concerned eyes. "What was the great man's verdict?"

"I must give up dancing for a year, or find myself flat on my back again." Chrys spoke through forcibly controlled lips.

"Well, that isn't too bad." Dove squeezed her hand. "A year will soon go by and then you can start again, if that's what you truly want."

"I can think of nothing else to want." A thread of emotion broke through the control of Chrys's voice. Dove had never really understood her temperament; her need to find poetry and passion through the medium of the dance. Dove could only see life through the eyes of an average young woman seeking security and protection by marrying a nice, steady, loving man. Dove was not – artistic.

Chrys sighed and gazed from the windows at the panorama of London. Somewhere in that teeming city she must find another occupation and hope it would keep her busy enough, and at the end of the day tired enough not to pine after the ballet company and the people she was so in tune with. God, but it would be awful not to be among her own sort, living a life that was never dull or humdrum. There was magic in the air breathed by those connected with ballet. There was beauty of movement, and the drama of temperament.

"Heaven knows what I shall find to do!" Her blue eyes burned with resentment and unshed tears, but unlike Dove she never found it easy to relieve her feelings by weeping. She was much more inclined to give way to temper.

The waiter arrived with a tray on which stood tea things and a plate of delectable pastries. He arranged the pot and cups on the table in front of them and withdrew.

"Shall I be mother?" Dove giggled a little, for it was

an open secret that she planned to start a family as soon as she was married to Jeremy.

"Yes, do enjoy yourself and get in some practice," said Chrys, a trifle scornfully. "Honestly, Dove, have you never wanted to do something exciting with your life?"

"I consider marriage a very exciting thing." Dove poured the tea, and with a smile of anticipation she selected a cream and honey slice, almost purring with pleasure. "One of these days, Chrys, you're going to fall in love with a bump, and it will so shake you that you won't know whether you're on your head or your heels. I hope I'm around to see it happen."

Chrys stirred her tea moodily. "I just love to dance, and can't believe that any man could offer me the delight I feel when I spin across a stage and stretch my body to the very limits of its endurance."

"Heavens, it sounds such hard work." Dove forked pastry into her pink mouth. "I've never known you to relax, Chrys. In fact the only time I've ever seen you flat on your back was during those weeks you spent in hospital. D'you remember what Nan used to call us when we were kids? The Persian tabby, and the sleek alley cat! She wasn't far wrong, was she? I like comfort and being pampered. But you like to go prowling among the arty types of London, alert and sleek as any alley cat, but without the amoral temperament. Have you never been attracted to a man?"

Chrys reviewed in her mind the various men she had met during the course of her career. Some she had admired for their artistic abilities but she couldn't remember losing a heartbeat over a single one of them. "Perhaps I'm frigid," she said, with a cynical smile. "Well, Dove, have you any ideas about what I should do while my career goes to pot in the coming year?"

"Don't say it like that, Chrys! As if your life is half over." Dove stopped eating pastry like a gourmand and regarded her sister with fond, and faintly, anxious eyes. "Look, darling, there is a job you can tackle if only you'll shake off your moodiness and try to be interested in other things beside Swan Lake and being the Pavlova of the Seventies. I wouldn't mention it before you saw Van Harrington and heard what he had to say about your future –"

"A job?" Chrys broke in. "Not in that darned office of Jerry's?"

"Don't call him Jerry," Dove pleaded. "It makes me think of that strip cartoon, the one about the cat and the mouse. No, pet, this has to do with Jeremy's aunt, the one who travels a lot, and who used to go on 'digs' with her husband. It's a sort of mania with her. France one month, Scotland the next, and like as not Romania for good measure! Well, my darling spouse-to-be was telling me that she's been left in the lurch by her travelling companion, a mousy little woman who suddenly ran off with an American bartender in Paris. Jeremy said his Aunt Kate was livid. She has this journey all fixed up for the East, and can't seem to find the right person to keep her company – Chrys, the job would be better for you than some nine-to-five office routine. You'd be bound to hate that."

"And prefer being companion to some bossy globe-trotting woman?" It seemed so mid-Victorian, so absurd a role for her, that Chrys had to laugh. "Not on your life, dear sister! I'm not cut out for dabbing *eau de cologne* on an elderly brow, and reading the saga of Barchester while the train speeds through some uncomfortable Eastern landscape. I'd hate trotting round bazaars, being mousy and obedient."

"But I don't think Aunt Kate is like that at all," Dove objected. "Jeremy says she's his favourite aunt and quite a worldly sort of woman. She once wrote a thriller about the tomb of that Egyptian boy king – king of the moon, wasn't he? It was a best-seller, I believe. And she knows lots of interesting people, and helped to get refugees out of India not so long ago. You'd be bound to like her."

"H'm. "Chrys sat thoughtful, her face at its most

pensive and therefore its most beautiful; the classic, half-enchanted face of the ballerina. "I couldn't stand a fluffy type of employer, or a butch with bobbed hair. We once had a choreographer like that, and she came to my dressing-room one rehearsal morning and made a pass at me."

"No!" Dove's eyes widened to such an extent that they threatened to fall out. "Whatever did you do?"

"Told her frankly that because I wasn't sleeping around with men that didn't mean I preferred the company of a woman. She hated me after that. Those sort of women harbour grudges, unlike men who take a slap if they make an unwanted pass and then shrug it off."

"I'd be terrified of the people you've known, Chrys." Dove gave a little shiver. "Why don't you find a nice young man and do what I'm doing? Marriage isn't so bad."

"It's a tie." Chrys poured herself some more tea and added milk but no sugar. Instinctively she was still looking after her svelte dancing figure. "And meeting all sorts of people is all part of living. I'd sooner have my eyes open than closed to the oddities of life."

"Yet," murmured Dove, "you look so unworldly. A little like Undine when you dance the part. Part enchanted. In some ways I believe you shrink from love because it means sharing yourself with another person."

"Yes, perhaps," said Chrys. "Men can be terribly demanding. Even your Jeremy will expect you to live for him. He'll often take you for granted, but heaven help you if you ever show him a moment's disinterest. He'll go out on a binge, or find himself a blonde to flirt with."

"Don't you mean a brunette?" Dove smiled and touched her fair hair with her ringed hand, very much in love and incapable of finding Jeremy anything but a perfect and adoring male. It was at that moment, as the sunlight slanted through the large windows and touched the faces and the hair of the Devrel sisters, that both of them became conscious of a pair of eyes upon them.

So direct a gaze that it had to be felt, and when met, unavoided.

It was Dove, whose interest in men was more personal than her sister's, who glanced across the lounge and caught her breath so hard that Chrys was obliged to look as well.

He sat alone smoking a cigar, and the very perfection of the dark grey suit he wore made him seem illimitably foreign. His eyes dwelt on her face with not a flicker of the dark lashes, and there was something so long and lean and inimitably graceful about his body that Chrys thought at once that he must be a perfect dancer. Her gaze sped to his feet in hand-tailored shoes; long narrow feet to match the hand holding the dark cigar.

Then again his eyes were looking directly into hers and a strange shudder had swept through her before she even realized that a stranger could invade her being with his eyes alone.

She looked quickly away from him, hating herself for a coward, but aware that she had just met the eyes of a man who knew women as an English stockbroker knew the pound note!

"Chrys, you're blushing!" There was an exultant note in Dove's voice, albeit she whispered, as if the lone male might have ears as penetrating as his eyes. "Isn't he something! And fancy seeing him here at the St. Clement's."

"Who the devil is he, then?" Chrys felt annoyed with herself for letting the glance of a mere male shake her. "He's too abominably good-looking to be respectable, that's for sure!"

"Darling, do mind your voice," Dove hissed. "I saw his picture in the *Daily Star* yesterday. They say he only cares about horses, cards, and fine living. He travels all over the world, so he must be very well off."

"No doubt he's a card-sharp," Chrys rejoined.

"With those eyes he can probably strip the cards to their last diamond."

"But I don't think he's one of those –" Dove cast him a hasty glance, and at once he inclined his head, with its thick hair like smoked silver, and a quiver of amusement ran round the bold line of his lips.

"Oh!" It was Dove's turn to blush. "Oh, I do see what you mean, Chrys!"

"Humph, I'm glad you're not that innocent, for Jeremy's sake!" Chrys spoke tartly. "The damned decadent Adonis is looking right at us. He knows full well we're talking about him . . . who is he, Dove?"

"Well, as I said, it isn't right for you to call him a card-sharp." Dove was now so nervous that she was tearing a paper napkin to shreds. "He's Prince Anton de Casenove, and I really don't know whether to be thrilled or frightened that he bowed to me. He has Russian royal blood in him, and they say he attracts women like a magnet. Oh, heavens, even I can feel the pull of him, and I'm engaged to Jeremy!"

"Don't let it upset you, pet," Chrys said drily. "Both the devil and the divine have this pull on the female of the species. I'm sure if *milor* suddenly rose to his feet and came over here to kiss your hand, you would run like a pretty hare."

"And what would you do?" Dove spoke huffily. "Slap his face?"

"I might," Chrys drawled. "I'd hate to be kissed by a man with his kind of face. I can't make up my mind whether he's wickedly good-looking, or gaunt and interesting. I'm sure all that suavity is only a thin veneer over a basic savage."

"Chrys, that's putting it a bit strongly." But Dove giggled, as if it excited her own basic niceness and timidity that a wicked-looking prince should bow to her. "I wonder why he's all alone? D'you suppose he's waiting for a woman?"

"No." Chrys was amazed that she felt so sure. "He's the type that keeps women waiting. I believe he's sitting there with the deliberate intention of putting the pair of us into a flap. He's hoping we'll either make a bolt for the lift, or one of us will give him the eye in the hope that he'll come over here. I bet if I gave him the eye right now, he'd shrivel me with a frosty look and enjoy doing it. That one believes in the *harem*, not in the liberation of feminine libido."

"Would you dare?" Dove spoke so excitedly that she forgot to whisper.

Immediately, from the corner of her eye, Chrys saw that dark cigar make a downward stab into the ashtray. That devil was waiting for her to dare something. Being a foreigner he obviously believed that European women were fast, and he was waiting for her to prove him right.

As if nerving herself for that moment when a dancer runs from the wings into the many eyes of the stage lights, beyond which are the thousand human eyes of her audience, Chrys slowly turned her head so that she was looking directly at Prince Anton de Casenove. He was looking at her and there was challenge in every graceful line of him; in the way he held his haughty head and revealed his eyes by the sudden rapid lifting of his lashes

Deep grey, almost smoky eyes . . . shockingly beautiful eyes!

Never as a dancer had she been a victim of stage fright . . . but now fright took hold of her and she was the one who felt like bolting like a hare for the express lift. There was something about those eyes that stripped her of all her assurance and made her feel that she was a girl of sixteen again, who had never been out of England, and never been kissed.

With a sense of total surprise she realized that it was true about the kissing part . . . only male dancers had ever set their lips to hers, and only because it was all part of the ballet . . . Albrecht with Giselle and nothing more.

"I think we'd better be going, Dove." She looked round for the waiter and quickly beckoned him over.

Dove was looking a little let down.

"Scared of him?" she asked.

"No, but it suddenly seemed a foolish game, like a pair of schoolgirls imagining that a grown man would be interested in their nonsense. I'll pay the bill and we can be off."

Chrys avoided her sister's stare as she settled up with the waiter and pulled on her gloves. They walked across to the lift, and she knew he was still there on the black leather seat, perfectly at his ease, and perfectly aware that she was running away. She was glad when the lift door closed and she could feel the steel enclosure swooping herself and Dove to the ground floor. They stepped out and made for the swing doors leading on to the street.

They were outside and she was about to hail a cab when Dove clutched at her arm. "My parcel," she wailed. "My wedding shoes! I collected them just before we met for tea, and I've gone and left them up in the lounge. Oh, Chrys!" Dove glanced wildly at her wristwatch. "I'm meeting Jeremy and we're driving over to Hampstead to see his mother. I daren't be late. Jeremy's an angel, but Mrs. Stanton is a bit of a tartar. Look, can you go back for my shoes? I must grab that taxi and be off!"

"You are the limit, Dove." Chrys gave a rueful laugh. "You're so cockeyed about that young man that you'll lose your head before the great day arrives. Run, then, or that cab will be snapped up. The busy hour is just starting."

"Angel! I'll see you later on. The shoe box is a pink one in a Fereaux bag. See you!" Dove darted to the cab and climbed in, and the next moment it was gone and Chrys was standing alone on the pavement. It was now past five, and the shadows of the church across the road, and the buildings round about had a smear to them, they were stretching as the sun slid down the sky, going pink and unreal. Chrys tilted her chin and walked back into the hotel.

Once again she rode up swiftly to the lounge, its fittings and its carpet bathed in a pink glow as she walked across to the seat where she had taken tea with Dove. She didn't look left or right, but just kept on going . . . only to find the parcel gone!

Now she had to look around for the waiter, only to find the lounge deserted but for a tall, tall figure who was coming inexorably towards her. On his feet he was even more elegant, with that silent way of walking which she had felt was the requisite of Russian male dancers, as if the soles of their feet were padded with velvet, and springy as the paws of the leopard.

She stood very still, a tall girl herself, with coiled gold hair, pure pale features, and eyes spooned out of a pure blue sky. Her suit of tawny wool fitted her without a wrinkle, for she had learned long ago the ballet dancer's art of always looking neat. She was silent and still and strangely trapped, high above London, it seemed, with a man in whom she had detected a savage flame, uncooled by civilized living, and the sartorial elegance of the man of the world.

"Your pardon, *madame*, but can I be of service? You appear to have lost something?"

"A parcel." The words seemed to scrape her dry throat. "A pair of wedding shoes which were in a paper bag on this seat."

"Shoes for a wedding, eh?" He slowly raised a black brow. "I expect the waiter has carried them away, and if we ask at the desk they may be there awaiting collection. Shall we see?"

"I don't wish to bother you."

"It would only bother me if I could not help a bride-to-be to find her wedding slippers. Come, let us ask, and do stop looking so anxious. Are they golden slippers?" He smiled briefly as he spoke and then gestured her to walk ahead of him among the low tables to the aisle leading to the porter's desk facing the row of express lifts. She obeyed him, and felt him close behind her, head and shoulders above her, lean and lethal as one of those fine and glittering swords which she had seen in a museum in Moscow ... the type that officers of the Czarina's guard had worn long ago with their handsome uniforms that fitted them like a glove, from their wide shoulders down over the lean hips and the long supple legs.

She almost cried out when lean fingers gripped her elbow and brought her to a standstill in front of the porter's desk. "The young lady wishes to know if a parcel was found on that long seat over by the windows?" he said, and his English seemed extra striking because of his accent, tinging the words with a sort of mystery, as the golden arc of the falling sun was misted at its edges with exotic colour.

"Would this be the young lady's property, sir?" The porter took something from a shelf under his desk and transferred it to the counter. A decorative paper bag containing Dove's precious shoes. Chrys had noticed that Prince Anton had referred to *her* as the bride-to-be, but she didn't intend to correct him.

"Oh, good!" She spoke with all the intensity of relief which would have been Dove's and accepted the package from the porter, while the man at her side handed him a generous tip.

"Thank *you*, sir."

"We cannot have the young lady walking barefoot up the aisle, can we?" The prince looked at Chrys as he spoke, and once again she was made aware of how amazingly beautiful were his eyes, and utterly male in their regard despite the length of his lashes and the shadows they threw on to the high-boned contours of his face.

"And now may I escort you to the ground floor?" he asked.

"I don't want to drag you away." Her fingers clenched the handle of the shoe bag. "I really can manage to press the button that will transfer me and my shoes to the street. Thank you –"

"I am going down myself, so we might as well go together. Come!"

402

It was impossible not to go with him, and as the lift door opened and she stepped past him into the enclosure, she felt again the height of him, and the darkness, and all the exotic differences deep within his bones. The door slid shut and they were alone together . . . alone for the few moments it would take for the lift to reach the level of the ground. She felt strangely tense, and wondered what Dove would say if she could see her alone like this with the man whom she had called dangerous.

Suddenly there was a jarring sensation, taking her so much by surprise that she was thrown against him and aware in an instant of the muscular control and resilience of his body . . . so like that of a male dancer, and yet so unlike, for the face that looked directly down at her was not a mask painted on but a detailed, utterly masculine, aware and dangerous face.

"What's happened?" She retreated away from him, to the steel wall of the lift cage.

He pressed buttons, thumped the door, but there was no response. All was still and silent as he turned to look at Chrys. Then he pronounced the alarming words. "We appear to have come to a halt midway between the floors. Something has evidently gone wrong with the mechanism, so I had better put my finger on the alarm button, eh?"

"Right away," she said, and her eyes were immense in her face as they dwelt on him and watched his long, lean finger stabbing the button that would set ringing the alarm bell on the ground floor. "Oh, what a nuisance! What a thing to happen!"

"You are in a hurry, perhaps?" His eyes dwelt with total composure on the shoe bag. "You are meeting – someone?"

"Yes," she lied, when in truth she was going home to the flat she shared with Dove to cook herself a steak and to watch a television play, and maybe come to terms with the halt in her dancing career. "Yes, I have a date."

"Then let us hope that the engineers will not be too

long in freeing us from our predicament." He lounged against the steel wall, and the overhead light gleamed on his thick, well-groomed hair. "It was your sister, of course, with whom you were taking tea? She is very pretty."

"Thank you." Oh lord, she thought, it was a devil of a thing to happen, as if his dark magnetism had caused the lift to stop like this between floors. She wished he would stop looking at her, as if he knew her thoughts and was deeply amused by them. Where did she look to escape his eyes? At the roof of the lift? At the floor? At his perfect tie against the pale grey silk of his shirt?

"Tell me," he drawled, "if you are to wear the bride shoes, why is your sister the one who wears the engagement ring?"

"What?" Chrys stared at him, and felt so trapped.

"I had a Cossack grandmother and she handed on to me her keen eyesight." His smile was infinitely mocking. "I noticed while you drank tea and your sister ate cream cakes that your hands were ringless and hers bore a ring. The shoes are hers, are they not?"

"Yes — so what?" Chrys gave him a defiant and slightly annoyed look. "She's always forgetting things."

"But why did you return for them?" he asked, and his eyes suddenly held hers so that she couldn't look away. "Did you wish to see me again?"

"Really!" Chrys felt quite staggered by the suggestion. "You must have a pound on yourself if you think I came back for the shoes because I couldn't resist another look at your face. Dove had to meet her fiancé, so I — really, I'll be darned if I need to explain my actions to you. I couldn't care less about men!"

"Oh?" He arched an eyebrow in that infuriating mannerism he had, as if he rarely believed a word spoken by women. "Are you frigid, then?"

"You," she gasped, "live up to the way you look!"

"And may I know how I look in your eyes, *matushka*?"

"I'm not a child," she retorted.

404

"You speak like one if you say you don't care for men. The woman who says that cannot care much for life."

"Really?" she said again. "Are women the great barren *steppes* until a wonderful man deigns to notice their existence?"

"Why not? Can a garden grow by itself? I think not, unless you like a garden of stones."

"My likes and dislikes have nothing to do with you, *milor*." She said it sarcastically. "I shall be glad when they get this lift working again. It would have to happen—"

"You could have been alone," he cut in, "and that would have been even more alarming. As it is we can talk and pass the time. Won't you tell me your name?"

She sighed and listened for the reassuring sound of the lift's mechanism at work again, but all was still, all was silent, except for the quick beating of her heart.

CHAPTER II

"My name is Chrys Devrel," she said, above the beating of her heart.

"And mine is Anton de Casenove." He bent his head and clicked his heels, and all the time his eyes studied her face. "You have a boy's name," he added drily.

"I do not." Temper sparked in her blue eyes. "You have heard of the chrysanthemum, haven't you? If my mother had had her way I should have gone through life with that label attached to me."

"I see." A smile glinted deep in his smoky eyes, "So you are the golden flower, eh?"

"Don't mock everything I say." Her fingers tingled and she thought of Dove's remark about slapping his face. How easy to just lift her hand and accomplish the deed . . . if only she didn't feel so sure that his retaliation would be of a kind also inherited from his Cossack grandmother.

"I don't mock you," he rejoined. "I find the name most suitable for someone so lissom and golden."

The words struck her speechless and she knew that if the lift door had opened in that moment she would have fled from him like a young hare and not stopped running until she arrived at the safety of the flat, where she could shut out the world and the dangerous face of this foreign prince. But the lift door did not open, and even as she wondered how effective her fingernails would be if she had to defend herself, he made a soft growling sound in his throat that was, presumably, his way of laughing.

"How could I know that when I awoke this morning in London I would find myself tonight trapped with a girl halfway between the sky and the earth? It is quite a situation, eh? The story is bound to get into the newspapers and you may find yourself – compromised."

"In this day and age?" she scoffed. "Virtue no longer has that kind of value."

"Not even to yourself?" He spoke in a dangerously soft voice. "You think you would enjoy the notoriety of being a girl who spent hours alone in a lift with Anton de Casenove?"

"Are you so notorious?" She made herself speak lightly, but inwardly her heart flamed with a certain fear, and a touch of resentment, for she had always prided herself on being a girl who had made her way in the dancing profession without relying on the patronage of a man; whose talent and dedication had been enough to lift her out of the *corps de ballet* into the realms of solo dancing. Not once had she needed to use feminine wiles in order to advance her career.

It had always pleased her that she could go home to Westcliff and remain the nice girl her parents were so proud of. A *risqué* story in the newspapers would upset them, and she reached out nervously to press the buttons again, but nothing happened. The lift stayed static, and only her heart sank a little lower.

"Well, are you so terrible?" she demanded. "Can't you be seen with a girl without causing people to talk about her?"

"No," he drawled, "not since an irate Frenchman put a bullet through me when he caught me on the balcony of his sister's bedroom. It was a story that made all the newspapers, mainly because I survived the injury. The bullet passed through my heart."

"Your heart?" she exclaimed.

"Yes." He smiled in an infinitely sardonic way, as if really he was more angry than amused. "It is a good thing you have a sister and not a brother, eh?"

"I – I might have a boy-friend," she fenced.

"You?" His eyes moved slowly and deliberately over every inch of her face. "You told me a while ago that you didn't care for men, which is hardly the remark of a young woman in love. Tell me, Miss Devrel, do you ever make a bet?"

"Do you mean – gamble?"

"Yes." He inclined his head. "Just to pass the time shall we make a bet? It should be amusing if nothing else."

"And what do we gamble on?"

"Ourselves. If this lift is enabled to move within the next hour, then you and I will shake hands and part. But if the lift keeps us trapped until midnight, then you give me a promise that you will dine with me tomorrow night."

"Oh, I don't think that would be very wise."

"Do you always allow wisdom to be your guide, Miss Devrel?"

"I have found that it pays better dividends in the end, especially for a single girl with a career she cares about."

"Ah, so you have a career?" His eyes flickered over her, taking in the slenderness of her body, and her slim legs with the pronounced arch to her feet in the soft leather court shoes that were her one outstanding extravagance because they were hand-made. Her first *maître de ballet*, the famous Maxim di Corte, had drilled into her the good sense of always caring for her ankles and her feet. His own wife, the enchanting Lauri di Corte, never danced unless Maxim had made her slippers as supple as possible with his own hands.

Chrys smiled a little to herself as she recalled that dancing season in Venice ... the di Corte marriage worked, in her estimation, because the couple were both involved in the art of ballet. Unless a dancer found such a man, she did better to remain single.

"You smile as if you care greatly for your career."

She came out of her reverie and glanced up at the proud, slightly melancholy face, into those eyes that glinted like magnets and seemed intent on divining her thoughts. "It has been my life," she said simply. "You see, *milor*, I am a dancer."

"I know." He said it so casually. "I saw you dance in Russia about ten months ago."

She was so staggered by this revelation that she leaned back against the wall as if for support. "So that was why—"

"Yes." A lazy smile gleamed in his eyes. "I was guilty of staring at you while you took tea with your pretty sister. I recognized you, of course. You have unusually shaded gold hair, almost tawny, like a sand cat."

"Thank you," she laughed a little ironically. "It's the first time I've been likened to one of those."

"They are elusive, graceful creatures, yet capable of tearing out a man's eyes."

"Thank you again, Prince de Casenove." But this time there was a thoughtful note threading her laughter. "It's funny, but my grandmother used to refer to Dove and myself as the Persian tabby and the alley cat."

"Ah, but that description of you is not apt." He spoke crisply. "You must see the sand cat with its jewel-like eyes, and its stealth when men are about, to appreciate my simile."

"I doubt if I shall ever see one, unless the zoo has some on show." The smile faded completely from her eyes. "I mustn't dance for a year, so if the Company should go on tour to the Middle East I shall be left in England to pine."

"May one ask – ?"

"I had an accident a few months ago. I fell down some steps, and now I am ordered not to perform a single pirouette for a whole, long, empty year."

"Poor *matushka*." He seemed to mean it, but she didn't dare to look to see if that eyebrow was arched in irony. To a man such as he, who divided his time between French girls guarded by quick-tempered brothers, and the best stable horses, it could hardly seem of significance that her life felt empty because she was unable to carry on with the work she adored.

He was just a playboy prince . . . he wouldn't understand.

"You will abide by the advice of your physician?" he said.

"I suppose I must." She gave a little resigned shrug. " 'Rather a peppercorn today than a basket of pumpkins tomorrow', as they say in the country."

"Strange is destiny." And then it was his turn to shrug. "And now to revert to this little game of chance which I suggested. Will you dine with me if we are trapped in here a sufficient time for it to create an item of news in the papers? If we are seen together, let us say at the svelte Adonis Club, it will be assumed that we were acquainted when we stepped together into this lift. But if we part after the intimacy of being alone like this, with no means of escape, there will be speculation of a snide sort."

"On account of your reputation as a rake?" she said frankly.

This time his eyebrow drastically quirked. "The British are so blunt!"

"True," she agreed. "We don't wrap our proverbs in silk."

"Such a pity," he said drily. "So, do you wish these newsmen to wonder how we passed the time in such close proximity?"

"We can always tell them we played Russian roulette."

"Perhaps in a way we do play it," he drawled. Whenever a man and a woman are alone there is a feeling in the air of a silent dicing with danger. Only between a man and a woman can there exist this awareness of a thousand subtle differences, each capable of arousing a thousand subtle sensations."

A small, tense silence followed his words, and a thousand crazy thoughts rushed through Chrys's mind as her eyes skimmed the face and frame of her close companion. Beneath that impeccable shirtfront there lay a hard chest scarred by the bullet of an irate brother whose sister had succumbed to the dark, courtly, demonic attraction of this foreign prince, with Cossack instincts smouldering in his eyes, and there in the sculpture of his cheekbones and his lips.

She prayed silently and swiftly for the engineers to hurry and get this lift moving again. She strained her ears and it seemed that far below them some kind of activity could be faintly heard, but there was no vibration in the steel enclosure itself, suspended in the frame of the hotel, in which the guests would be buzzing with the news that Prince Anton de Casenove was trapped with a young woman . . . the porter at that desk upstairs would know this, and by now the information would be all over the building and someone would have been bound to notify those daily devouring hawks of a spicy bit of news.

"Are you afraid to accept my bet, in case you have to pay the price?" the prince murmured. Very deliberately he glanced at his wristwatch. "We have now been entombed for over an hour, and I have heard that when these express lifts go wrong it can be hours before they are set in motion again. We may have to spend the night together."

"I'm shivering in my shoes," she said flippantly.

"You may indeed do so, Miss Devrel, as the hours pass and it grows rather cold. I expect the fault in the mechanism will effect the heating of the lift as well. That is the trouble with modern amenities, they rely on the machine rather than on the man, and machines are quite careless about the feelings of a hungry, cold couple, almost strangers to each other, and locked together as if in space, while the world continues to vibrate around them. The situation is piquant, no?"

"Something terribly funny for you to relate at the card table next time you play, *milor*. I expect you will add a little relish to the tale, or will it be taken for granted that you seduced me?"

"Are you wondering if I will do so?" That black eyebrow mockingly etched itself against the pale bronze of his brow. "According to Freud, women of virtue are more curious than their more voluptuous sisters, and the victims of their own imaginations. What makes you think that I could be bothered to try and charm a Miss Fire and Ice? Neither element is all that comfortable, especially to a man who was anticipating a choice meal, perfectly served, within the historic Regency walls of the Ritz restaurant. By contrast a tussle with a reluctant virgin strikes me like snow across my face from the very *steppes* themselves, stinging like fire and ice."

"I'm sure," she flashed, "that you're accustomed to the type who fall at your feet like *harem* slaves, hair unbound and eyes pleading for the thousand delights of the Khama Sutra!"

Silence followed this little flash, fraught with a tension that broke in soft, indescribably amused laughter from his lips. "I wonder what I have done to deserve such a little spitfire for a companion in an air-locked lift? Perhaps I am being punished for my past sins, eh?"

"Well, I don't see why I should be punished with you," she retorted.

"Why, has your life been blameless, Miss Devrel?"

"I've worked too hard to have had much time for playing around, Prince de Casenove."

"Such a pity, *matushka*. A little play does no harm, but now you tell me that you are forced to give up your career for a while."

"A year!" She said it bitterly, as if it were a lifetime. "Everything was going as I planned, and then at Easter I was rushing to catch a train home for the weekend when my foot turned and I – I fell down all those steps." Her young mouth brooded and the fire and ice of temper and misery shimmered together in her blue eyes. "I daren't go against the surgeon's decision. I don't want to spend years on my back for the sake of yearning to dance – oh, life is so complicated at times!"

"Like the machinery of a lift," he drawled, "or the machinations of fate herself. Destiny is a woman, say the Arabs, and so she is perverse. What will you do with your life for a year?"

"Work in an office, I expect. Or become companion to some dotty travelling aunt of my sister's fiancé."

"And you relish neither of these as a means of toeing the line, let us say, until you can rise again upon your toes?"

"Hardly! A whole year away from the *barre* and the stage could ruin my line, my strength of leg, my entire future as a soloist. I might have to start again at the foot of the ladder."

"And that could be very frustrating," he agreed.

She looked quickly at his face, and felt rather shaken by his understanding of her predicament. Her eyes questioned him, and with that courtly inclination of his head he enlightened her:

"My grandmother was known as Miroslava – which means beauty. You may not have heard of her, but a Russian prince saw her dancing in a Cossack village on the steppes and she so entranced him that he took her to the city to be trained as a dancer in ballet at the Maryinsky Theatre, which was very famous in those days. She became a great favourite there until the prince, my grandfather, married her in secret. You may not know that in Czarist days a man with noble blood in his veins was strictly forbidden to marry a commoner, so Miroslava and he had to pretend to be only lovers. Then came the uprising, and because she was known to have associated with a prince, Miroslava had to flee from Russia. My grandfather, an imperial officer in the Czarina's guard, was killed in the fighting.

"Miroslava and her servant eventually reached a strange haven, a desert province called El Kezar, where they stayed and came under the protection of a true Sheik of the desert, who always treated her son by a Russian prince as his son . . . my father, of course."

"Your father was born there, in the desert?" Chrys was interested despite her inward determination to stay aloof from this man.

"Not exactly on the tawny sands," he drawled, "but in a desert house given to Miroslava by the Sheik. I believe he wished to make her his wife, but she could not forget the prince. He was her one and only love."

"It all sounds very romantic," said Chrys. "But you don't appear to be so singlehearted."

He gave a soft laugh. "Others might jump to that conclusion." He gestured at the shoe bag in her hand, with silver wedding bells printed all over it.

She had to smile herself. "Oh dear! " she said.

"You are thinking that the reporters will take me for the prospective bridegroom?"

"There is a chance of it, knowing how quickly they will leap to conclusions in order to fill the daily papers."

"Indeed I do know! And you think it would discompose me to be thought a man who has been trapped at last by the wiles of a woman, eh?"

"Won't it, *milor*?"

"In the circumstances it might not be such a bad thing if we are thought to be on – intimate terms." He pinned her gaze with his and would not allow her to glance away from him. "In this modern age what a man does with his 'girl-friend' is not a subject for much speculation. But if the young woman is a stranger to him – *comprenez-vous?*"

Only too well, she nearly retorted. She would have to be caught in a lift with a man who imposed on her such an awareness of him. Had he been an Englishman, they might well have stood here, in polite silence, until the lift was put into action again. But Anton de Casenove was everything an Englishman was not! He was far too aware of the fact that she was a female, and that in itself was disconcerting. He was too dark-browed, too mocking and worldly to be acceptable as a companion in adversity.

He was altogether too aware of how her mind was working, and the sort of thoughts his near presence was engendering.

"Will it be so hard to endure if you are taken for my bride-to-be?" he asked, in an amused tone which at the same time held a hint of menace.

"It's in my disposition to dislike being mistaken for any man's bride-to-be," she replied, and though she spoke coolly she knew that a slight panic stirred in her eyes as they ran over his crisp dark hair, strong slanting cheekbones, and bold mouth with its shades of perpetual mockery. He looked as though he might make a ruthless lover ... a man who made his own rules and lived by them.

"You have never played the game of love, with its gambits and its thrills ... its height and its pitfalls?" He drawled the words, but his eyes were intent on her face.

"I prefer to be my own person," she said icily. "Love is depending on someone else for happiness."

"And you regard that as a precarious state of living?"

"I'm afraid I do."

"Perhaps you are a little too afraid of certain aspects of life?"

"Meaning that I'm a shrinking violet from the facts

of living?" Her eyes flashed an indignant warning at him. "I hope you don't see this situation as an opportunity to put me wise!"

"You prefer to remain innocent, eh?"

"Independent is the correct word, *milor*."

"And you imagine that by remaining independent you can stay isolated from the emotions which are as much a part of a woman as her eyes and her hair. You may be able to control your hair, and even to keep your eyes from revealing all your thoughts, but are you so sure you have your emotions tamed?"

"They have not yet overruled me. A dancer is like a soldier, *milor*, discipline is her second name."

"You are still a woman," he said suavely. "And still a very young one, and life is always waiting to surprise us. Did you imagine when you came to take tea at the hotel that you would step into a lift and suddenly find it beyond your control to make it move? There are certain events in our lives over which we have no control at all. Destiny weaves a strange and varied pattern, not an orderly one."

It was true, of course. Something she couldn't argue with, but none the less frustrating.

"Are you a fatalist?" she asked him.

As he considered her question he let his gaze rove the steel-lined walls of their prison. "I believe I am," he said. "Usually when I am in London I stay at the Savoy, but this time I felt like a change, so I accepted the recommendation of a friend to stay at the St. Clement's. We might never have met had I gone to my regular hotel."

"I'm sure I would have survived such a loss to my education," she rejoined.

"You are very much on the defensive," he said, "and I saw you shiver just then. Are you beginning to feel cold?"

"I'm perfectly all right—"

"No, you are very much on edge. You know, as I know, that if we are forced to spend the night alone

415

like this, it will be assumed that you spent the night in my arms. Your tawny gold hair is truly remarkable – unbound it should reach to your waist."

"I'm not about to demonstrate!" Quickly and protectively Chrys lifted a hand to the braided chignon at the nape of her slim white neck. Her hair was uncut because some of her dancing roles called for long hair and she disliked wearing false pieces which might detach themselves during a strenuous *pas de deux* with a male partner. When released from the chignon her hair reached past her lowest rib, thick and fair, and a feature of her person of which she was admittedly rather proud.

The colour came into her cheeks that this man – literally a stranger to her – should almost threaten to unloosen her hair and make it look as if he had made love to her!

"I wonder,' she said scornfully, "if it has ever occurred to a single man on this earth that there are women who can endure to go through life without panting to be kissed and mauled?"

"Mauled, Miss Devrel?" His eyes narrowed until their greyness was lost in the shadow of his lashes. "Is that how you regard lovemaking, as an undignified wrestling match, with the loser locked in a painful hold?"

"Isn't it exactly like that?" She stood very straight against the wall of the lift, and avoided his worldly, beautiful, wicked grey eyes. From a child she had danced the magic of the ballets, where love was an enchantment, with a dreamlike quality about it. She could not believe that real life love was like that.

She shrank physically from the very thought of being captive in the arms of a demanding man, at the mercy of his wilful strength.

"I think I should hate to be married more than anything else on this earth." She said it fiercely. "I'm not like Dove. I don't want my wings clipped by any man."

"What if you should fall in love?" he murmured.

416

"Love only happens if you want it to. Love doesn't approach unless you beckon to it."

"Are you quite certain of that, *matushka*?"

"I am certain of what I want, and what I don't want."

"Then why are you so afraid to commit yourself to a dinner *à deux* with me, if we should be obliged to spend the next few hours together?"

"I'm disinterested, Prince Anton."

"No, Miss Devrel, you are afraid to put your own theory to the test. If you remain aloof from men, then you are unlikely to fall in love. But if you permit yourself the company of a man –"

"You think you are so irresistible?" she gasped.

"No man is that, Miss Devrel, but when we walk from this lift certain whispers are going to follow at your heels. People will wonder why you were here at the hotel in the first place. They will suppose that you came to call on me."

"My sister can easily repudiate that little speculation!"

"Will you wish the smoke of a little fire to drift in her direction?"

Chrys stared at him . . . and there stole into her mind a picture of Jeremy Stanton's mother, that awful, snobbish woman whom Dove was daring to take on for love of the son.

"You are a devil, Prince Anton," she said. "You know how to hit a sensitive nerve."

"Yes." The word was quietly enough spoken, but suddenly he stirred, moved, and sent rippling through the air a breath of danger as from a leopard caged.

A cage that stayed firmly suspended in mid-air, while down there on the ground people looked at each other, and knew by now from the porter on the penthouse floor that a girl was alone in the lift with Anton de Casenove . . . the man whom an angry Frenchman had shot through the heart . . . the man with a reputation as dangerous as his face.

"Come, agree to dine with me *demain soir*. Forget

for once that you hate men."

She looked at him expecting mockery, and saw instead a pair of grey eyes veiled in the smoke of the cheroot he had just lit up.

"You are very sure of yourself, *milor*," she said.

"Do you think so, Miss Devrel?" His smile was enigmatical. "Only destiny really knows what tomorrow may bring."

"It's tonight I'm worried about!"

"Is it?" he drawled. "Don't you take me for a gentleman?"

"Would you advise me to bet on that, *milor*?"

His answer was a smile, half veiled by smoke; half veiled by the dark lashes shading his smoky grey eyes ... a smile which confirmed for Chrys what she had felt from the moment she had noticed him across the sky lounge.

Under that suave veneer, that smooth dark suiting, there lurked an untamed heart in a graceful, untamed body.

CHAPTER III

"Darling, enjoy his company but don't fall in love with him!"

Those words of Dove's echoed through Chrys's mind as the cab she had just picked up sped through the gaily lighted West End to the Adonis Club on the south bank, across whose dancing terrace the breezes of the River Thames wafted.

Needless to say Chrys had scoffed at the idea of losing her contained young heart to a *roué*, no matter how darkly attractive he was; no matter how gallant he could *act* when walking out of a lift with her at one o'clock in the morning and kissing her hand for the benefit of those who had stayed to watch the rescue.

The incident had got into the daily papers, and there

had been a coy reference to the wedding bells on the bag Chrys had held clutched in her hand. She smiled a little to herself as she thought of Prince Anton and his possible reaction to the speculation of the newsmen. She didn't imagine for one moment that he was a born bachelor, but when he married he would choose someone a little more passionate than herself, she was sure of that.

She sat self-contained in the cab as it halted in a traffic jam near the Mermaid Theatre, where Tarquin Powers was starring in *Macbeth*. She leaned to the window and gazed at the large poster with his distinguished face and figure on it. Like herself that great actor was dedicated to his art ... a career in the arts did not mix with marriage ... not a marriage that involved the total involvement of the heart.

She leaned back in her seat as the cab proceeded on its way to the Club, and a street light that slanted into the enclosure revealed the cool silvery material of her dress, and the wrap of pale velvet against which her coiled hair gleamed softly. In her earlobes there were little flame-coloured gems, and deep blue were her eyes, with flying wings of eyeshadow painted above them.

It was while she was dressing that Dove had come into her bedroom and made her profound little remark. "Fall in love with *him*?" Chrys had laughed. "He's the type who breaks female hearts as he breaks in Arab fillies. He's been brought up to think of women as chattels ... objects of pleasure."

"Then why are you dining with him?" Dove had asked, reasonably.

"Because we made a bet, the prince and I. He said the lift wouldn't move before midnight, and I said it would. He won, and so I must pay the forfeit."

"Dinner at the Adonis, eh? They say it's all rigged out just like those clubs of the Georgian era, where Beau Brummel and the other rakes used to dine in alcoves with their 'ladies of the night.' "

"Thanks!" Once again Chrys had laughed, but in

her heart she had wondered what real motive lay behind the prince's invitation. "I should think he already knows I'm not a 'lady of the night' after being locked in a lift with me for eight hours."

"Chrys, whatever did you do?" For about the fiftieth time Dove had looked at her as if it were impossible to be imprisoned with such a man and emerge with her virtue intact.

"We talked," Chrys repeated. "Do I have to convince you, Dove? He's as good at talking as I imagine he is at most things, including casting doubt over a girl's good name! Do assure Jeremy's mother that her beloved son is not marrying into the family of a scarlet woman. In fact, to put it quite bluntly I couldn't imagine a man as suave as the prince enjoying love's antics on the hard floor of an express lift."

"Chrys, really!" Dove had looked quite shocked.

"Well, it was what you were wondering, now wasn't it, my pet?" It was then, with a touch of bravado, that Chrys had added the flame-coloured earbobs to her ensemble. She had bought them in Russia off a gipsy fortune-teller, who had looked deep in her eyes and warned her about a tall, dark man. She had laughed at the time, because it was so to formula – beware of the dark stranger – he will bring you love or danger!

It was as Chrys had viewed the earbobs in the mirror, and set them sparkling against her hair with a little defiant toss of her head, that Dove had announced her intention of sending a wedding invitation to the prince.

"It will conciliate Mrs. Stanton," she said. "She's a bit of a snob and his title will overwhelm her."

"Which one?" Chrys said drily. "He's also known as Zain ben Sharife, and Jeremy's mama might imagine that he'll sweep her off to his desert abode in the manner of that silent-screen actor – what was his name, Rudolph Valentino? Mrs. Stanton probably remembers him."

They had joked about it, Dove and herself, but tiny flickers of curiosity and doubt were like sparks in

Chrys's veins when she alighted from the cab at the discreetly lit entrance of the Adonis Club. She paid her fare, then turned to find a bewigged and knee-breeched doorman holding open the bowed-glass entrance door so that she might step into the Regency-decorated foyer of the restaurant.

She had specified that she meet the prince on the premises of the club, wishing for as long as possible to conceal from him the address of the Kensington flat she shared with Dove. There was no knowing what Dove might say to him if they were to meet! She was the type of girl, pampered for her prettiness, who said naïvely whatever came into her mind. She might ask Anton de Casenove if his intentions were as honourable as Jeremy's, and Chrys was appalled by the very thought of what he might assume.

He might take it into his mocking head to think she had designs on his bachelorhood!

"Your mask, *madame*."

"I beg your – a mask?" She stared at the white velvet half-mask the bewigged attendant in the foyer had placed in her hands.

"It is a rule of the Adonis Club, *madame*. Each patron must be masked."

"How romantic!" She had been about to say 'how ridiculous', but thought better of it when she saw a tall, lean, elegant figure reflected in one of the long Regency mirrors of the foyer. His evening suit was perfection, his ruffled shirt-front impeccable, his narrow feet shod by a master hand. And though he wore a black strip of velvet across his upper face, she knew his figure, and the faintly mocking smile on his mouth.

The attendant took her wrap, and the prince advanced towards her with all the silent suppleness of a duellist . . . for all the time he duelled with his eyes and his words, and perhaps his intentions.

As he came closer to her, her nerves quivered like water when a sudden breeze passes over it. Now those subtle grey eyes were appraising her through the openings of his mask, studying her dress with its shapely hanging sleeves and its design that was so simple as to be medieval. The material had been purchased in Russia, and the design had been seen in a stained window of the old Russian castle where she and the other members of the Company had danced a ballet one memorable evening.

She knew from the look in the masked grey eyes that the prince admired her dress, but all he said as he bowed his head with that flawless perfection of manner was that he welcomed her and was glad to see that she had not lost her nerve and left him to eat and drink alone.

"You must put on your mask before we go into the restaurant. Shall I assist you, Miss Devrel?"

"Are the masks in the tradition of the Regency rakes, *milor*?"

"Quite so. To be seen but not recognized was all part of the game."

"What game is that?" she asked, retreating ever so slightly as she adjusted the white velvet mask and saw his face, in the golden light of the Regency chandeliers, take on a demonic quality, partly mocking, and yet with something intent about the set of the lips and the glint in the eyes.

"The game of illusion, *matushka*. Of sadness masked in gaiety. Of devilry masked in piety. Of hate masked in love."

"I see." She stood there slim and silvery, with only the scarlet earbobs to light her pale beauty. "And what mask are you wearing, Prince Anton?"

"Only the one you see." A smile flickered on his lips as he touched the strip of black velvet across his upper face.

As she thought over his remark a teasing silence hung between them for a few moments, then a waiter appeared at his elbow and murmured a few deferential words.

"Our table is ready in the Alcove du Diable, so shall we go in, Miss Devrel?"

"Yes," she said, and felt her heartbeats under the fine taut silk of her dress as she followed the waiter to their table and felt the prince walking so tall and silently at her side. Dark velvet curtains across the doorway of the alcove were thrust aside so they could enter, and inside a table was beautifully set in front of a banquette, and a soft illumination came from the shaded wall-lights.

The alcove was private, intimate, and as she felt the admiring flick of the waiter's eyes over her person, the little jolt to her nerves told her that he thought she was the prince's *inamorata*. It was the inevitable supposition in view of his rakish reputation, and as she sat down on the banquette and smoothed her dress, she noticed there were orchids on the table. A cluster of them meshed in fern, creamy pale with a merest dusting of gold at the edges of their secretive petals.

Instinct told her that the prince had ordered them; that they weren't a speciality of the club like the face masks and the Regency satyrs and cupids decorating the ceiling of the Alcove du Diable.

"*Champagneskaye,*" said the prince, as he sat down beside her, using the Russian word with a sort of love in his voice. "And baby oysters on the shell."

He turned briefly to Chrys. "You will allow me to select your *hors d'oeuvre?*"

"Yes, if you wish to do so." She was slightly confused to find him close to her on the seat, looking so directly at her through the oblique openings in his black velvet mask. He had the kind of face that suited a mask, for it brought out the fine shaping of his lips, and the firm sculptoring of his jaw. It emphasised the mystery, and the charismatic quality of the man. Made her even more aware of his unique accent, and fascinating turn of phrase. She turned to the orchids, with their quieter exoticism, and touched her fingers to the strange pale petals rimmed with gold.

"Champagne and oysters, *monsieur.*" The waiter withdrew and the portières fell into place behind his

423

dark-clad figure. At once the sense of intimacy was provocative, made more so than last night in the lift because Chrys was wearing silk and eye-shadow and a whisper of her best perfume. And they were seated together on the soft leather of a banquette and orchids out of season were on the dining table.

"You look very lovely, Chrysdova," he said. "Like a figure which has stepped out of a medieval window in a quiet, mysterious chapel. Even your hair has the authentic styling, and the only note out of tune – ah, but perhaps I am being too personal. The blunt British are reserved about themselves, eh?"

She turned her head to look at him, provoked by his remark about her appearance. What could be out of tune when she had spent a couple of hours getting ready for this dinner with him? "What little thing displeases you, *milor*?" she asked pertly.

"These, of course." He flicked a finger at the scarlet earbobs. "You should wear only sapphires, the very darkest, with a blue flame burning in the heart of them."

"I could hardly afford sapphires on the money I earn." She jerked away from his touch, and consequently the tiny red gems danced gaily against the gold of her hair. "If it offends your taste to be seen with a woman in jewellery which has not come from Cartier, then I can leave this instant without a qualm or a backward glance."

"You will stay exactly where you are, you little spitfire." His lip quirked, but there was a looming danger to his wide, impeccably tailored shoulders which warned her to remain seated. The wall lighting slanted on to his face and he seemed tawny-skinned, and the sculpturing of his cheekbones was intensified. He had the looks of a man who could be cruel when it came to having his own way with a woman.

"No woman walks out on me," he drawled. "Later on I might grow bored and send you home in a cab, but right now I am intrigued by the look of you, and by the antagonism I arouse in you."

"I suppose it must come as a shock to you not to be turning my head with your practised charm and your sophistication, Prince Anton? Or do you have a desert name by which you prefer to be called? Somehow you strike me as a man who regards women as *harem* slaves, to be enjoyed one hour and ignored the next."

"I had no idea, Miss Devrel, that you were such an authority on the men of the East, or of the West." His drawl was infinitely mocking. "When you told me last night that you hated men, I took it to mean that you had ice crystals in your veins, but now I begin to wonder if your coolness is the result of passion spent on the wrong man."

"Men have never bothered me," she retorted. "All I have ever wanted is to dance every dramatic role in ballet, but I am sure you wouldn't understand about dedication to anything. To you, *milor*, life is a game and pleasure is your pastime. You are like Adonis, ever chasing, and ever fleeing the trap of Venus. Like Adonis you bled for love, but being also something of a devil you lived to chase and run again."

"From you?" he mocked. "After I have chased you, of course."

A scornful answer sprang to her lips, but was checked as the portières opened and the waiter appeared with their champagne and oysters. The next few minutes were devoted to the opening of the wine, the tasting and the pouring of it into the wine bowls on the long stems, ideal for collecting the bubbles at the edge of the wide rims. The small oysters, pale pink in colour, were served on the shells of giant oysters, with a mayonnaise sauce and slivers of lemon, slices of crusty bread and balls of butter.

Despite the antagonism which he aroused so readily in Chrys, she watched fascinated as the prince tasted the wine and pronounced it perfect in his flawless French; then he examined each shell of oysters to make certain they were of the very best, and finally he dismissed the waiter with an imperious yet in no way demeaning flick of his hand. He was a man accustomed to giving orders, and having them obeyed with the minimum of fuss and the requisite of perfection.

Chrys felt the stab of realization that he wasn't just anyone, and colour tingled in her cheeks as she accepted the pepper mill from him and recalled the way she had just spoken to him. Adonis – and Venus! The colour deepened in her cheeks. She had more or less implied that his looks condemned him to be a lover, whereas at heart he was really scornful of love. This placed her in the position of Venus, the one who was hungry for love!

She looked at him with a flash to her eyes, all on edge in case he should think for one moment that she saw him in the light of a lover. He returned her look with almost too much innocence, and then he raised his wine glass.

"Come, Chrysdova, drink a toast with me!"

Obediently she picked up her glass and felt it quiver in her nervous fingers.

"To the sham pains of life, *matushka*, and may you rarely know the real ones."

"It would be nice not to know them, *milor*, but –" She shuddered as she remembered the agony of her fall, the rack of pain on which she had lain in the speeding ambulance, the terror of finding her legs so useless ... until the blessed relief of that first movement all those days after the operation.

"Drink your champagne," he said quietly. "It has a way of blurring the reality of things."

She was tempted to retort that she had tasted champagne before accepting the honour of dining with him, but the moment she put her lips to her wine glass she knew that she had never tasted champagne like this before. It was like liquid gold, with a sensuous quality ... it was like everything else he demanded of life, a perfect wine.

"I see that you are a connoisseur, *milor*." By now she had fallen into the habit of addressing him in this Regency way, for try as she might she couldn't accept

Anton de Casenove as a modern man. He had the locks and the rakish dignity of those Georgian gentlemen of leisure and refined pleasure. The cut and style of his suits had a quiet flamboyance about them, and as he ate his oysters off the small silver fork, she noticed his dark-stoned cufflinks, and the seal ring on the small finger of his left hand, engraved with a strange Islamic symbol.

There was not a single item about the man that was ordinary . . . least of all his conversation.

"You are wondering, *petite*, all the time about my motive in wishing you to take dinner with me, and I wonder why you should find it a mystery when a thousand men could give you the reason in three simple words."

"But you don't deal in simplicities, Prince Anton. You are too subtle for that, and last night you didn't ask me in plain terms to dine with you. You made of it a thing of chance."

"But I had to do so." His eyebrow quirked above the darkness of his mask. "You would not be here in the Alcove du Diable if I had not coerced you. Now would you?"

"Perhaps not." She shrugged her shoulders and the silk of her dress glimmered in the soft lighting that illuminated their table; there was a gravity to her blue eyes as they dwelt on his face. "I am not a girl who goes out on many dates. My ballet régime has always been a strict one, imposed by my first important balletmaster and kept up by me. The dedicated dancer never dances out of theatre hours."

"How wistful your eyes look when you speak of dancing." The prince drank from his wine glass and studied her eyes as he spoke, the blueness of them intensified by the white mask. "Has your surgeon vetoed all dancing, or only your professional activity?"

"Oh, I'm quite fit for normal activity, but as you probably know from your grandmother, the art of ballet is pretty strenuous and I mustn't do the bending and limb stretching involved . . . not for a year!"

"A year in the desert is but a day in the city." Again he spoke in a voice almost as smooth as velvet. "So the gaieties of other female hearts are of less importance to you, eh?"

"I'm not a gay person, *mon cher*." She smiled a little as she spoke and ate her last oyster. "They were delicious . . . do you always demand the very best from life, Prince Anton?"

"It is in my nature to do so." His lips smiled beneath the mask, but it seemed to her that his eyes had the stillness of the sea when a storm has passed and left a certain melancholy in the air. "You are correct in your estimation of your own personality. Gay people are of the surface, like a frothy soda drink. You are deep . . . still waters . . . with possibilities unseen and undisturbed. No man, of course, has ever touched you, and I don't mean in a physical sense. There have been men, no doubt, who have kissed you?"

"Are you being curious, *milor*, or are you being personal?"

"Both." He reached to the wall and pressed a small button for the return of the waiter. She knew that other couples were dining close by, and yet the portières seemed to muffle all sound and it was intensely intimate to be here like this, being asked such questions by a man so worldly, and yet at the same time so primitive.

Chrys was startled by the thought . . . he wore his perfectly tailored evening suit as if it were a second skin, and yet she sensed a restlessness in him, a barely suppressed desire to wrench open the tie of black silk at his throat, to toss back his head and breathe a free wild air in a wild and open place.

"When do you return to the desert?" she surprised herself by asking.

"Soon – perhaps in a month from now."

"I have the feeling you can't wait to see and smell the sands again. You are like a sailor who while at sea longs for dry land, but as soon as he comes ashore he

428

finds himself hemmed in, restricted by the civilities of civilized living. You appear to be incredibly sophisticated, *milor*, but I believe you are really a Tartar."

He inclined his head and laughed so softly in his throat that it was almost a purring sound. "The *steppes* are in my blood and the freedom of the desert supplies my need for what I cannot have in reality. I visit Russia, but I cannot live there ... it is not my person but my spirit which is exiled from the land of my grandparents. You understand?"

She nodded, and was glad when the waiter reappeared to dispel the air of seriousness which had crept into the alcove. The waiter carried two large menu cards, but with a slightly lazy smile she requested the prince to choose for her. "You are the epicure, *milor*."

"*En effet*," he rather mockingly agreed, and for an intent moment his eyes looked directly into hers, and from that look there sped through her person the quicksilver awareness that he thought her a rather beautiful object ... something which he might desire to possess ... perhaps for an hour. Immediately her eyes went as cool as ice, and the soft shimmer of her dress was like a coating of ice over her slender figure. She sat very straight against the dark leather of the banquette, entirely untouchable, virgin as fresh fallen snow ... only the gems in her earlobes had animation in that moment.

Then he looked at the menu card and began to order their meal in his impeccable French. Fresh asparagus and Irish salmon, with tiny new potatoes ... the delicious, almost simple food of the epicure, following the richness of the oysters and champagne. Finally richness again when he chose fruits *au kirsch*, and coffee with Armagnac.

"You have wined and dined me," said Chrys with a smile that was still a little cool, "like one of those dancers of the Edwardian era, who were so underpaid that they lived almost on birdseed all day and relied on the stage-door admirers to keep them from starving to death."

"Really?" he drawled. "Is that how you regard me, as a stage-door admirer? And what did the little dancers do after the supper *à deux*? Did they pay with kisses and pleasure?"

"Very likely," she said. "But if you are expecting a similar kind of repayment then you are in for a disappointment, *milor*. I dined with you because I lost a bet not because I needed the food, delicious as it was."

"I am pleased you found the food to your liking, at least." There was a quirk to his lips as he raised the cognac glass, but a faint angry flare to his nostrils as he breathed the aroma of the Armagnac. "You are a cool one, Miss Devrel. You need the lash of love to break the ice around your heart."

"All I need," she retorted, "is to find a job in which I can bury my feelings for a year, until I can get back to the thing I love. There are different sorts of love, and you as a man of the world must know it."

"Perhaps." And then very curtly he broke the epicure's rule and tossed back his cognac in a single gulp, as if it were vodka. "You find physical fulfilment in dancing ... you find love in the applause which your dancing receives. That is because you have not yet met love in the guise of a man ... ah, you think it couldn't happen?"

"I am making no bets with you, Prince Anton." She gave a slight laugh. "All my life I have wanted only to be a dancer, unique like Markova, poetic and perfect in line and action. I dare not love –"

"Ah, what a significant word, *matushka*. Does your heart warn you that you might love a man with a greater force than you love the dance?"

"No," she denied, "not at all. Men are all alike. They want a slave, a meek and willing keeper of the home and the hearth. Their egoes demand that the domestic slave produce a child, and then another, ensuring that the slave is doubly enslaved. Oh, I know for girls like Dove, my sister, this is a kind of heaven on earth, but I – I'd stifle if my body and my soul were tied to the stove and the cot, and the demands of a man!"

"You shuddered when you said that, *matushka*." He leaned a little towards her, and there was a danger to him, and a subtle knowing quality that made her cry of the heart seem the cry of a child who had yet to grow up. "Are you afraid of lovemaking? Afraid it will dispossess you of your 'slim gilt soul' in your slim, white body?"

"Stop it!" Her words were a whisper and a cry. "You have no right to speak to me in such a way!"

"And why not? There are women who find their excitement in such conversation."

"I don't." Her eyes blazed through the openings of her mask. "All I want right now is to go home!"

"Don't be a child," he rejoined. "The night is young and I intend first to dance with you, and then to take you for a long cool drive. For once in your self-contained, planned and passionless life you will let someone else rule you, if only for a few hours. Now relax from all that tension which is making your pupils dilate and your heart beat too quickly for comfort. Relax!"

She stared at him a moment longer, then gradually she leaned back against the soft leather of the banquette. "I – I had an idea you could dance. It's in the way you walk."

"I am very fond of the pastime." He leaned back himself, his *demi-tasse* of coffee in his lean, well-shaped hand. "With a grandmother such as mine there was always music in the house and she had me taught all manner of dancing when I was a child. Miroslava was never a woman to displease, for her smile was as lovely as her anger was terrible. A true Cossack woman, composed of honey and iron. Anyway, I liked to dance, especially as I grew older and could tango and foxtrot with attractive girls."

His lips smiled nostalgically beneath the black rim of his mask. "I did not go to public school. I had a tutor until I went off to college who had been a Guard's officer; a rake with women, but with a brilliant mind. He and Miroslava between them made a man of me before I was sixteen." His mouth as he spoke those words became a dangerous one, with a glint of hard white teeth. "*Leben seele* was the motto of my German tutor. Life is soul, and soul is life — so live it! I have lived, *matushka,* and you can also say that I have died."

She gazed at him as if mesmerised, and his face in that moment had a cruel dark beauty. He was everything her training, her upbringing and her instinct fought against. She wanted to leave with all her mind, yet her body was excited by the thought of dancing with him. Oh, how long it had been! Weeks since she had known the heaven of music in her limbs and the delight that only dancing could give her. She would have wanted to die if they had told her at the clinic that she could never dance again . . . and now had come the moment when she could dance again, if not as a ballerina, at least as a woman.

A woman . . . in the arms of Anton de Casenove!

CHAPTER IV

"WELL, have I set your mind somewhat at rest, and made your feet impatient to dance?" he asked abruptly. "I hope your *cri du coeur* is no longer that I take you home?"

"You learned well from your tutor, didn't you?" She gave a rueful little laugh. "Even as you give a woman what she wants, you lay on the lash."

He shrugged and finished his coffee. "I grew up among Arabs, who regard women as mettlesome as horses. It does only harm to feed a woman and a horse with too much sugar."

"The comparison is hardly flattering. I hope you don't think, *milor,* that I shall trample all over you in my friskiness on the dance floor?"

"That is hardly likely, *matushka*. I saw you dance at the Bolshoi – and it occurs to me how my *baboushka* would have enjoyed that. She would indeed find a cool angelic creature like you, Miss Devrel, enjoyable to shock."

"You are speaking of your grandmother?"

"Yes. She would say to you 'the key to life is love of it' and tell you there is no harm in tasting the wine of every experience, so long as you avoid the dregs." He moved his mobile hands in an expressive gesture. "It is being alive that counts, whether it brings pain or gives rapture. Desire itself is a crucifix – ah, but you have your heart fixed on dreams not on reality."

"At least I harm no one with my philosophy," she said.

"But is it any fun for a girl to be so miraculously virtuous? What has held the men at bay? Ah, but you don't need to tell me – it is that cool hauteur, that tilt to the chin, that threat of the sand cat in your eyes that exactly match the darkest sapphire. Do you wish to dance with me?"

"I dislike modern dancing," she said, even as anticipation leapt alight in her veins and there was a tingling in her toes racing upwards through her slim dancing legs.

"So do I, *matushka*. Do you want more coffee, or are you replete?"

"Quite replete, *milor*. It was a splendid dinner, thank you very much."

"*Bon*." He rang the bell for the waiter, and while he was engaged in settling the bill and commenting favourably on the food and wine, Chrys took a swift look at her face in the tiny mirror of her powder-case. She ran the tongue of her lipstick around her lips, and tried to be as composed as her companion would allow. She knew he was looking at her, watching each of her movements with those smoky eyes that held elements of the dramatic, the mysterious, and the subtle.

They were eyes that would look terrible in real and overwhelming anger ... eyes that would smoulder with all the passions of his fierce inheritance when he held a woman in his arms.

Soon ... quite soon he would hold her in his arms when they danced. As the waiter held aside the portières and they left the alcove she could hear the dance music drifting from the terrace which overlooked the oldest, most historic river in England. The river upon which the carved barques of royalty had sailed to and from the palaces; to gilded and gay receptions ... and to the block, and the dark-masked axeman at the royal Tower.

A tremor ran all through Chrys as they stepped on to the terrace and she saw the masked couples dancing so close in each other's arms. The atmosphere was seductive, with the river running by and glimmering in the dim light of the lamps along the balustrade of the terrace. The orchestra was concealed so that the music seemed to be in the air itself rather than played by musicians.

Chrys tautened as an arm encircled her waist and she was drawn so inevitably against the smooth dark suiting of the prince, against the lean suppleness of his body, her limbs and her body responding to him at once, as if he were her partner in a *pas de deux* instead of her partner in a foxtrot.

Anton de Casenove was a devil without a doubt, but in his blood and his bones ran the inheritance of rhythm from Miroslava herself, and he danced like an angel. The wonder of it was like a magic igniting Chrys so that within seconds, no more, they were dancing as if they were one person. He had all the mastery, all the control of some of her best ballet partners, with that wonderful strength in the legs, that instinct that guided a girl through the most intricate steps. And the foxtrot could be wonderfully intricate, and inexpressibly evocative as the music played ... a music from another time, when war had swept Europe and sons and lovers had choked in the mud of battlefields, where soon masses of poppies had grown as if to defy death with their scarlet beauty.

"Poor butterfly,
                    In the blossoms waiting. . . ."

Chrys was lost in the music as it went from one past melody to another; it was an incredible delight to be so in step with this man who so antagonised her at other times. His guidance was so sure and strong so that her body knew instinctively that it could enjoy the fabulous pleasure of dancing without a moment of fear that suddenly the disintegrating pain would flare in her spine and her legs would give way beneath her.

She was in a kind of heaven and when at last the music ceased she came down to earth almost too abruptly.

"No –" The word broke from her in protest. "I want to go on and on –"

"No!" He spoke firmly and led her from the terrace. "You have danced for an hour and that is sufficient."

"It was so perfect – oh, please, Anton!" She spoke his name almost unaware. "Please, let us stay! Let us go on dancing!"

"You mustn't overtire yourself." Now they were in the foyer and he removed the mask from her brilliantly blue eyes and looked down into them . . . unseen by her because she was still in that rapt, enchanted mood in which dancing always left her. It was as if she stood in the wings of a theatre as the applause died away and the curtain fell for the last time . . . strung to go on, to dance and dance until her body ached and her toes were on fire.

"Come, we will go for a drive!" Her velvet wrap was clasped about her shoulders, and something soft and scented brushed her cheek. With a little shiver of realization she saw the prince being helped into a topcoat, and felt under her hand the curled petals of the orchids which had decorated their table. Now they were pinned to her wrap, and the prince was unmasked and looking at her with intent and glinting eyes.

"They are bringing round the car," he said, and very casually he took a blade-thin cheroot case from his pocket and opened it. He selected one of the dark Russian cheroots, and immediately the foyer attendant was at his elbow flourishing a lighter. Smoke jetted from the imperious nostrils and the faint, strange perfume of the orchids was drowned in the aroma of the cheroot.

"Is it late?" she asked.

"Not too late," he said enigmatically.

The attendant held open the door and they went out into the night air, cool against her skin, golden from the tall lamps along the embankment. In the kerb there stood a long, racy car in a bronze colour. Chrys hesitated and stood by the tonneau of the sleek car, a pale, silvery figure with questions in her eyes. "Where are we going?" she asked him.

"Somewhere – anywhere. What does it matter? You are not Cinderella who has to be gone by midnight, are you?" A quizzical smile gleamed deep in his eyes as he regarded her in the amber light. "All that finery will not turn to rags, I trust?"

"My sister will be wondering about me."

"Why, because you are with a man of uncertain reputation?"

"Something like that. Dove is the anxious sort."

"A dove by name and nature, eh?" He glanced at his thin gold wrist-watch. "It should not unduly ruffle her gentle feathers if I take you for a spin in my new car? It was delivered this morning and I am having it shipped to the Middle East in a few days, so I wish to enjoy it like a new toy. Don't you like it?"

She turned to look at the rakish lines of it, and saw that the top was back and that the upholstery was leopard-pelted. A smile touched her lips. There was a streak of the exhibitionist in *milor*.

"It's very sleek, and has an air of danger about it," she replied. "It suits your personality."

"Is it my dangerous personality, *matushka*, which makes you hesitate to take a drive with me?" His voice

436

had softened to that husky purr and he had drawn a little nearer to her, silently, until suddenly her wrists were locked in his fingers. "You danced with me. You enjoyed that with every nerve in your body. Do you think I don't know? That I didn't feel your pleasure?"

"I – I hadn't danced for so long." Her eyes met his, resistant and deeply blue; her breath quickened. "Yes, it made me happy to dance."

"Will it make you less happy to drive in an open car with me?" he quizzed her. "My hands, this time, will be occupied with the wheel, and my thoughts with the road and the other traffic."

"You make me sound a prude." She gave a slight laugh and pulled free of him and went to the car. She opened the door and slipped inside . . . he was too tantalizing to argue with, and she didn't really wish to end yet this fascinatingly dangerous evening. Being with Anton de Casenove was like being on the edge of a volcano, or within range of the unpredictable temper of a leopard. She gave a little sigh and settled down in her seat . . . but he danced divinely, the devil, and she could dislike no man who moved as if his muscles were of silk and steel. Her artistic nature was at the mercy of his lean and fascinating grace . . . she wouldn't think of the *roué* in him which had climbed forbidden balconies.

They drove away from the Adonis Club, and the night wind blew the soft hair from her brow. A half-hour spin with him wouldn't hurt, she told herself. He wasn't to know that Dove was spending the night at her fiancé's home, where discussions regarding the forth-coming wedding were to be held with the forthright Mrs. Stanton presiding and directing in a way which Chrys would have rebelled against, had she been the bride-to-be.

She smiled a little to herself . . . how easy on the system to be malleable like Dove, but she would sooner have her own flashfire temperament and independence. It wouldn't suit her to be a dove by nature.

"It is a fine night," said the man at her side, who drove the Rapier as he did everything else, with the skill, verve and style of the man who feared no one, not even Destiny herself. "On a night such as this in the desert I would be riding instead of driving. Can you ride, Miss Devrel?"

"Yes." It was faintly disconcerting the way he switched from the informality of calling her 'little one' in Russian back to the formality of her surname. "Dove and I had riding ponies when we were quite young. My father has always worked for the local council and my mother liked us to have 'nice things' and to be a little more privileged than she was herself when a girl. You understand?"

"Indubitably." There wasn't the faintest hint of mockery in his voice and he sounded quite kind. "You have a nice mother . . . my own was selfishly gay and in the divorce court long before I had my first long trousers."

"I'm so sorry." She cast him a sympathetic sideglance, but his profile was as hard and fine as that upon a bronze coin. She knew at once that he had long since ceased to regret the legal loss of his mother, but she felt certain that he had never tried to fight the gay and wilful instincts inherited from her.

"Are you wondering about my father?" he asked, and the car sped smoothly along as he spoke, and the street lights were less clustering, as if they were heading out of London. "He was a finer man than I am, who devoted much of his life to the Sheik's people, and who died one hot *khamsin* day when the North African campaign was in full swing. He was decorated for bravery, and his memory is cherished by the people of El Kezar. They expect me to live up to him, of course, but quite frankly I am not a saint. I sometimes think that if he had given to my mother the devotion and the passion which he gave to the Oasis, she might never have looked at another man. He married her, placed her upon a pedestal, and then was surprised when she toppled into

438

the arms of a French artist who came to North Africa to paint the Ouled Naïl dancers, and the Arabian cavalry, and all the wonders I remember from my boyhood. Much has changed, of course. The province is now state governed, and the fruits of the Oasis are so heavily taxed that profits are a laugh. But I still have the house in which Miroslava lived as a Sheik's friend. The house called Belle Tigresse! "

"What a provocative name, *milor*." Chrys looked at him, and then at the wide highway along which they were travelling so swiftly, so smoothly that the engine made hardly a sound. It was as if the engine of the car was wrapped in velvet . . . the same velvet that seemed to enwrap the surrounding fields. Her heartbeats quickened. She wanted to ask him to head back to London, but she was strangely afraid of him and his unpredictable nature. If she showed fear of him now, he might dash the car into the nearest lay-by and give her every reason for being afraid. She strove to sit calmly beside him . . . she sensed that he was waiting for her to panic . . . this *beau tigre* of a man!

"It is a provocative house, *matushka*. All of white stone, you understand, with one entire wall and tower enshrouded in scarlet bougainvillaea which Miroslava had planted . . . perhaps to remind her of her passionate Prince Ivanyi, who died in his white uniform, cut down by sabres on the steps of the Czarist palace the first day of the uprising. *Magnifique! Come il faut.*"

"I think it terrible," she retorted, "that a man and a woman should be parted in such a tragic way! "

"Ah, there speaks the romantic! And now, *matushka*, I have discovered in my devious way why you remain the ice maiden who has never melted for a man. You are looking, yourself, for a *preux chevalier*."

"I am doing nothing of the sort, *milor*. A man would interfere in every way with my career in ballet. He would expect me to make *him* my career! "

"But you might fall in love with a dancing partner," drawled the prince, and still the car sped smoothly through the night, on towards the coast, it seemed, with London now left far behind them. Chrys cast a rather wild look behind her, and her hair flew in a gold wing, breaking loose from its chignon as the wind soared towards her. She gave a gasp, half fear, and half delight to be travelling along like this, in a swift car commanded by a man who drove fast but who broke not a rule in the driver's handbook. It was as if he had an instinct for going through life on the knife-edge of danger. . . only once had he come to grief, and that had been through a woman.

Chrys thrust the loosened hair from her eyes and wondered briefly if love had blunted, for once, his instinct for enjoying danger without having it touch him?

"Male ballet dancers are as dedicated as the females," she said. "To dance in ballet is to be at the mercy of the dance. Of course, there are one or two exceptional marriages within the world of ballet, but they are love matches in the grand tradition and would survive despite the demands imposed by the régime of the dance. Famous male dancers such as Lonza and Dantoni are also famous for their love affairs, and though it's marvellous when one is lucky enough to have the Panther for a partner, a sensible girl avoids becoming involved emotionally."

"Sensible!" muttered the prince. "What a very British word it is! Like hotpot and pudding with gravy! Well, tonight I am teaching you that too much sensibility will blunt your natural sense of gaiety. Ah yes, it is there, the gaiety, like small blue devils in the eyes. You desire with one half of you to enjoy this drive without inhibition, but the primly obedient and dedicated half of you is terrified that the wind is combing out your hair into the wild silk which you have been taught to keep meticulously neat and orderly. What is this dance régime? Some sort of novitiate, for which you take vows of devotion and sublimation?"

"Of course not!" She had to laugh, albeit with a touch of nerves and temper. "There are rules attached to everything, but you are a natural rebel, *milor*, so you wouldn't understand. To love something is to be enslaved."

"But you would rebel against enslavement to a man," he argued. "You prefer the inhumanity of pirouettes upon the tips of your toes, and the arabesques that would seem like torment to your audience. You know, I have heard Miroslava say that for hours after dancing she has lain in a torpor of sheer exhaustion, with every muscle aching and in revolt against the merciless demands of the dance. Do you really think that a man would put you through such torment in his arms?"

Chrys tautened where she sat, and stared at the dark shapely profile of the prince, outlined now and again by the infrequent tall lamps at the roadside.

"W-what are you implying?" she asked, and she felt the shock in her body, and heard it in her words. What did he mean? And where was he taking her?

"Oh come, Chrysdova, you are not that unworldly."

"Look, if you are planning some sort of a – a seduction –"

"As if I would?" He laughed in that purring and infuriating way, as if laughter were an inward thing and never a bellow; a secret to be shared with himself but never with her.

"You would, if you felt like it!" Anger and nerves shook her voice. "Where are we going? To some hideaway you have in the country, where you take your ladies of the night? I'm warning you – if you dare to touch me I'll tear out those devil eyes of yours!"

"I'm sure of it, little sand cat." But still he softly laughed as if illimitably sure of his own strength and his practised ability to overcome the resistance of a mere woman. "We are on the road to Kent, which is very attractive at this time of the year, with the fruit on the trees and the sunrise so colourful over the Bay of Sandwich."

"Kent!"

"Yes, do you know it?"

"I know that never in my life have I met anyone with your gall! Turn the car this instant and take me back to Kensington!"

"It sounds like a song," he rejoined, "from the music halls, *hein? 'Take me back to Kensington as quickly as you can. Oh, Prince Anton, you are a naughty man!'*"

"The word 'naughty' when applied to you," she stormed, "is about as appropriate as calling a tiger pussy! I want to go home!"

"And so you shall, *matushka*, in the morning."

Instantly, wildly, she felt like grabbing at the wheel and forcing him to stop the car, but in that moment a long and laden trailer came towards them out of the night and passed them on the road with a roar that set Chrys's nerves humming like the steel-threads of a violin wound too tightly to take the assault on them.

"Will it make you happy," she said tautly, "to make me hate you?"

"I promise you won't hate me, *petite*. What lies ahead of you will be a revelation . . . an experience so enjoyable that you will thank me for bringing you to Kent instead of taking you home to prosaic Kensington."

"You — you actually expect me to *enjoy* myself?" Chrys was almost stunned by the sheer amorality of the man . . . the astounding confidence in his own powers of seduction. "It might come as a surprise to you, *milor*, but there are some girls around who enjoy being — good."

"Chaste is the word, Miss Devrel. A Victorian, not much used term, these days, and related to the chastity-belt and the blush."

"With men like you around the chastity-belt should be brought into fashion," she said frigidly.

"You give me credit for not a single virtue, eh? I am all darkness and devilry in your eyes, is that so?"

"Yes! I knew it from the first moment I laid eyes on

you. That man, I said to Dove, likes to make fools of women!"

"How flattering! And would you like to know my thoughts of you?"

"No, thank you!"

"Ah, but you would! You clamour to know even as you make your denial. My immediate thoughts upon recognizing you as a dancer I had seen at the Bolshoi were that you had an aura of coolness like that of a fountain in a Moorish patio. That you were white-skinned as the *houri* dreamed of by the Arab in his enclosed garden ... but disdainful of men as the she-tiger who rejects affection as if it were a thorn in her throat. I knew by the candour of your blue eyes that no man had yet made you his mistress ... I knew from the shape of your lips that you were passionate but fastidious."

"Please, don't stop there," she said sarcastically. "I am sure you must have guessed the colour of my lingerie and the location of the tiny mole on my shoulder-blade."

"*Tu es très charmante*," he drawled. "I cannot wait to see this mole on the shoulder-blade."

"You will be lucky, *milor*. It will be over my dead body."

"What a pity! You intend, then, to fight to your last breath for your honour?"

"I – I'd put up a pretty good fight." She flung a look at him, a wing of hair windblown across her face. "You are taunting me, of course? You don't really intend to take me to Kent?"

"We are now in the county of Kent, *matushka*. Can't you smell the apples in the orchards? It reminds me of certain parts of Russia ... that was why ... yes, this is Kent, and we are on our way to an apartment overlooking the Bay of Sandwich."

"Oh – you are being monstrous and taking glory in being so! How dare you do this to me?"

"What am I doing to you when my hands are entirely

occupied with the wheel of the car?"

"You are taking me somewhere in Kent where I don't want to go! And you imagine that when you get me there I shall suddenly be overcome by your masculine charms and swoon in your arms!"

"Ah, what an attractive image. *Ravissante!*" And very deliberately he quickened the pace of the car, as if he couldn't wait to arrive at his retreat by the sea. Chrys felt furious with him, and curiously defenceless. This kind of situation had never arisen in her life before and she didn't know how to deal with the matter. She was utterly at a loss, for each thing she said was outrageously capped by him, and the only resort would be an undignified tussle with him. Could she, if driven to it, claw with her fingernails at those shockingly beautiful eyes, grey and smouldering as the smoke of a desert fire?

"In the old days," he drawled, "they called this kind of thing a Cossack abduction, with the man snatching the girl away on the back of his horse and riding full tilt across the *steppes* with her. After that, of course, she was obliged to marry him, or be labelled a good-time girl to be had by any man who fancied her."

"And is this the modern variation?" Chrys demanded.

"What do you think, *matushka?*"

"I – I think you've got a nerve! I wouldn't marry you if marriage was bliss and every other man already had a wife! I'd sooner be on the shelf until I'm eighty! I'd sooner emigrate!"

"There is something so passionate about a woman's anger that it really excites a man, so beware of such anger, *matushka*. If I dared to look at your eyes as I drive through this dark old village, I should see them blazing like sapphires. It is fine for a woman to hate – the sabre cut is her indifference."

"You would know, of course, Prince Anton, being such an authority on the subject. When did you decide to 'abduct' me? When you found out I had only a sister and not a brother to be put another bullet through that philandering heart of yours?"

"Ah, but don't you care at all that it was very painful for me? I almost died, so you might spare a little sympathy for me. After all, I only went to the silly girl's bedroom in Monaco to give her the necklace she lost at the casino. I suppose, looking back, it was a little absurd of me to go by way of her balcony, but I wished to spare her the embarrassment of telling her strange, wild brother that she had been gambling. She was so delighted to receive her property that she flung her arms around my neck and kissed me ... at which point the brother entered the room and shot me. He must have dragged me on to the balcony, for when the police came, and the ambulance, he said I was a prowler. Later it was established who I was, and people presumed that I was the girl's lover."

"But didn't she tell the truth – explain the real facts?" Strangely enough Chrys didn't doubt the veracity of his story; she had always sensed that a man so worldly would so arrange his *amours* that an irate brother was unlikely to come stalking in on the scene. There was a secretive side to Prince Anton de Casenove; in his veins ran the instincts of men of power who had kept concealed in hunting lodges and tower apartments the *femme chic* of the moment. Swinging a leg over a balcony in search of love was not in tune with the suavity and self-assurance of the prince. He had an aura of sophistication in which boyish escapades played no part ... Chrys felt quite certain that it had never been part of his plan to be caught returning the girl's necklace.

"It suited Mademoiselle to let it be thought that I was in her bedroom in order to be her lover."

"Oh!"

"She thought I would be honour bound to marry her."

"But you aren't all that particular about a girl's honour?"

"Not that of a rather silly blonde with a mad brother."

"I see." Chrys's lips formed an involuntary smile. "It's rather like a stage farce."

"Except that I have a very realistic scar. Would you care to see it?"

"No –" Chrys bit her lip and her smile was gone, wiped away as she remembered her own precarious position, miles from home, with no one at all to know that she was alone like this with a secretive, amorous, self-willed man who was accustomed to having his own way. "Please – can't we go back?"

"It is too late for that – see, there is the Bay and the dark gleam of the ocean against the pale sands."

It was true! She could see the thrust of the cliffs encircling the bay, and she could smell the ocean, and ahead of them, rising against the starlit sky the enormous, almost fearsome bulk of a castle! She stared in sheer amazement at the turrets and round towers as they drew nearer and nearer, and the car swept in through a gateway into the drive of the castle. Gravel crunched beneath the wheels, and lamplight shone in the arched entrances to the towered, grey-walled, romantic residence!

"This is *it*?" she gasped.

"Of course." He brought the car to a smooth halt in front of a massive corner tower, with narrow windows deepset in the stone, with lights burning softly behind them. "Did you imagine I had brought you here on a sightseeing tour?"

"But it's a castle!" She stared around her at the courtyard, and felt the mystery that haunts the environs of an ancient building. Looking upwards, she saw the indented parapets and the thick curtains of ivy mantling the walls. "Why have we stopped here?"

"For the past couple of hours you have been quite certain of my motive in bringing you all this way." He slid from the car as he spoke and came round to open the door beside Chrys. "Come, it is surely traditional for Cinderella to return to the castle after attending the dance."

"I'm staying right here —"

"No, Chrysdova, you are coming into the castle with me." His hands were lean and powerful and utterly determined to overrule her defiance. He almost lifted her from the Rapier, and for a brief and electrical moment she was even closer to him than she had been when they had danced together, the silver silk of her dress shining against the darkness of his topcoat, her slim body pressed to him, wild with the instinct of his strength and his potent male grace.

"Please — be reasonable, Anton! Stop playing the villain!"

"Ah, but villains have a better time of it, *chérie*, than men of virtue." Suddenly he bent his head and kissed her throat, and then, while she still seethed with fury, he marched her into the tower entrance and up a shallow flight of stone steps to an oval-shaped wooden door. He gripped her wrist with one hand, forcibly, actually hurting her, while with the other he inserted a key into the lock of the door and swept it open to a lighted vestibule.

"Well," he drawled, "is it so surprising for someone to have an apartment in a centuries-old castle overlooking a smuggler's bay?"

Chrys could only look at him with blazing blue eyes and hate him for his wicked laughter as he pulled her inside the tower and slammed the door behind them.

CHAPTER V

"I SUPPOSE now you're happy?" she stormed.

"Unimaginably. And now will you enter the *petit salon*?" He opened an interior door of the apartment and stood aside for Chrys to enter. She did so unwillingly, knowing that if she had made a dash for the front door he would have been there ahead of her, to bar the way with mocking ease and the assurance that she was in a strange place and in his hands.

Head held high and with a blaze to her eyes, she walked into the *petit salon*, as he had called it, and found herself in a long, shadowy, sensuous room, with several leopardskins stretched on the floor, oddly wrought lamps hanging from the ceiling, dim mirrors, low tables, and divans heaped with cushions. Lampshades and curtains blended in dark jewel colours, small fine ornaments stood on various shelves, and there were portraits with penetrating eyes – the family de Casenove eyes!

She spun to face him, with a snarling leopard head at her feet, the velvety pelt under her shoes. "And now what?" she demanded.

"Oh, surely your outrageous imagination can supply the answer to that question," he drawled. He came towards her, silent and lithe as the animal beneath her feet would have walked through the jungle, and with a gleam to his eyes that was equally leopard-like. She backed away, into a divan that caught her behind the knees and tipped her among cushions. She lay there for a few breathless seconds, staring at him, then she twisted to her feet out of his reach.

"*Mon coeur!*"

It was a woman's voice, and Chrys swung round to see that a woman had appeared from a curtained doorway, to stand there outlined against the topaz velvet. She wore a kaftan of deep-purple brocade, trimmed with braid around the full sleeves, and she was gazing at Prince Anton with radiant dark eyes set in a high-boned, Slavonic face that was neither old nor young, but had a curious agelessness about it. Her hair was covered by a kind of veil, almost nun-like, and as she stretched her arms towards Anton, they made the graceful speaking movements that a ballet dancer never loses her whole life through.

"*Dushechka!*" He strode past Chrys towards the woman, and with a loving hunger he wrapped her in his arms and kissed her face for several moments.

"You are so unpredictable," laughed the woman. "To come at this hour – and driving, of course, like a hare through the night!"

"Of course, *tu.*"

"Just to see me?"

"Is there another woman whose charm can reach out like yours to a man?"

"Even yet, Anton?" The woman pressed her hand to his heart and studied his downbent, quizzical face. There was something poignant in her gesture, as if she still believed that he might suffer or die of his injury ... and it was in that moment that the truth struck at Chrys.

It struck even as Anton de Casenove turned to her, his left arm still encircling the woman he had greeted so affectionately.

"Miss Devrel, I played a trick on you, but only because you seemed so certain I was abducting you. But all I really wanted was for an English dancer to meet a Russian one. Won't you come and meet Miroslava?"

Chrys had imagined his grandmother miles away in her desert house ... not for one second during that drive had she dreamed that he was really bringing her to see the woman who had fled during a revolution and borne a son to a murdered prince. A son who in his turn had died in uniform.

Seeing her, and the way she touched Anton as if to make sure he lived and breathed and was not lost to her like the other men she had loved, Chrys could understand why she had taught him from a boy to live his life to the full.

To taste the wine of every experience in case the cup was snatched from his lips while he was still a young man!

She approached Miroslava and held out her hand with a smile. "I'm thrilled. *madame*, to meet a ballerina

449

who danced for kings. I can only imagine how exciting it must have been in the days when dashing officers actually drank wine from the slippers of their favourites of the ballet. Prince Anton tells me that you were a great favourite."

"So you are a dancer?" The appraisal of the dark slanting eyes was rapid and expert, taking in the pure modelling of Chrys's face, and the slim suppleness of her body in the silver dress. "And no man has yet enjoyed his wine from your slipper, *hein*?"

Chrys smiled involuntarily, and felt almost at once that fine steely thread of communication which exists between people of the same profession who love it with the same nervous intensity. "The outward trappings of ballet have become very prosaic since your exciting days, *madame*."

"And you wish you could have known them, eh? The stage deep in flowers at the end of a performance, and *troikas* unharnessed from the horses so that handsome, crazy Guardsmen could pull them through the streets, with the ballerinas laughing among Serbian furs like pampered dolls, and often flourishing a whip over the broad shoulders. Yes, crazy, exciting days, never to be known again."

Miroslava glanced up at her grandson. "So when you telephoned this morning, *rouh*, this is what you meant by saying you could bring me a surprise?"

"And do you like your surprise, *dushechka*?" He quirked an eyebrow. "I personally thought it too good an opportunity to miss, to bring you a young ballerina who lives for nothing but her art, but who must give it up for a year to enable her spine to fully heal after a bad accident. I thought that you alone could assure her that once a dancer always a dancer. Miss Devrel fears that her career will suffer if she is forced to discontinue her ballet dancing, but I feel sure you can convince her that to learn other aspects of life during that year will be of immense value to her as an artiste."

"My child, you have my sympathy." The dark eyes

of Miroslava were instantly compassionate. "Yes, now I look at you I see in your face a fine-drawn look of recent suffering, and in your eyes a fear of the future. Anton and I between us must dispel for you the anxiety – but first of all I must know your first name. We Slavs love diminutives and titles, but we dislike formality. I cannot call you *Miss*."

"I am called Chrys."

"Chris – like a boy?" The arching of the dark brow was very reminiscent of the grandson.

"Chrys – golden flower," Anton broke in smoothly. "And now let me take your wrap, *matushka*." He did so, sliding it from her shoulders and making her aware of his tallness behind her, his fingertips brushing her bare arms and leaving, it seemed, a trail of fire in their wake. What was his game? Was he genuinely concerned that she learn from Miroslava that her career could be gripped by both hands and held on to despite this setback? Or was he playing some devious role of his own – his ultimate aim to subdue her resistance to him?

"Perhaps, *Grandmère*, Vera could make us some tea and provide a snack?" he said. "We had dinner at eight, and the drive was a long one."

"*Tout de suite*," she exclaimed. "What am I thinking of not to offer refreshment! But this young dancer, she fascinates me because you bring her to see me!" Miroslava clapped her hands, and like a genie a woman appeared from behind the curtained doorway. She had obviously been listening to the conversation and her face was seamed in smiles as she bobbed a curtsey at Anton and spoke to him in Russian. He replied in the same tongue, and because the woman was about the same age as *Madame*, Chrys realized that she was the maid who had fled from Russia with her mistress all those years ago and had been with her ever since.

"Do come and sit down." Madame drew Chrys to a divan beneath one of the Moorish ceiling lamps, and everything felt so strange and foreign to her as she sat down beside Miroslava and saw the filigreed bracelets

451

piled on to the fragile wrists, and the gleam of henna on the long narrow fingertips. Madame also wore an Eastern perfume, exotic as the slant to her eyes and the tiny mole at the corner of her mouth.

There was power in her, and the magnetism which her grandson had inherited. The drive of a "girl of the people" who had married a prince in secret and lived many years with the memory of his love.

Miroslava was still a woman to reckon with ... to hold spellbound strong and wilful men ... she was exciting, and must have been wonderful as a young woman when her golden-tinted skin was unlined and her eyes filled with the fire of her youth and her passion.

Chrys could understand why Anton de Casenove adored his grandmother; not only had she been his "parent" and his mentor, but she had a rich personality, a wealth of feeling in her heart, and that insidious charm of the woman who had lived fully and without a single regret.

"These two children wish for supper," she called over her shoulder to her maid Vera. "And then prepare the *pussinka* a room for the night. Antonyi can sleep on a divan here in the *petit salon*, and he can cover himself with the fur laprobe which covered me and my coming child when I fled from the revolutionaries."

"You are indomitable, my darling grandmother, and will always be so." He bent over her hand and kissed the hennaed fingers with casual grace. "I wanted Chrysdova to meet a woman who was also forced to give up something which she loved with all her heart. Two things, eh? Your dancing and your husband, with whom you would have stayed but for the child."

"Ivanyi would not leave," she said sadly, "but for the sake of his son – I knew from the first moment of knowing that I should have a son – I left him to be killed by the mob. When his son was born, many miles from Russia but beneath an Eastern sky, I developed some trouble in my left leg and was never able to dance again as a ballerina. These things seem like a punishment at the time, and you search your mind and your heart for the reason."

Miroslava paused and gave Chrys a long, intent look. "It could be, my child, that you must learn other facets of living before going on with your career. Art is wonderful, but not to make of it a bondage. Great dancers have done so and it has killed them before their time. Pavlova lived only to dance and she sacrificed the passionate reality of her own being so that her Dying Swan could be immortal. It was wonderful to see her, with her dark head bound in the pale swan's feathers, and her limbs as graceful as the swan's neck – but there was an element of tragedy in her performance that could break your heart. Day by day, hour by hour, she had given herself to the dance – her very soul."

Miroslava made an eloquent gesture with her speaking hands. "To be a Slav is to have a love of suffering. The Russian soul, *l'âme slave*. But even so I would sooner sacrifice myself for another human being. The perfection of love can be the greatest art of all, but alas too few people take the trouble to perfect the art of love."

"Chrysdova has forsworn love." Anton had made himself comfortable on a divan, stretched full length and relaxed as a dark, sleek cat of the jungle. His eyes dwelt lazily on Chrys, such a fair contrast to his grandmother and himself. "She dreams only of being a ballerina, and is in agony at being parted from the torments of the *barre* and the *pointe*. What strange, complex creatures women are; almost less fond of the creature comforts than the male of the species."

"You see and hear speaking a male creature who very much likes his comforts," said Madame, drily. "That is when he is in Europe, for the real fact of the matter, Chrysdova, is that he has two sides to him. I have known him endure and exult in the most trying desert conditions, just like *l'arabe*. Though to see him at the moment one would think him terribly lazy and luxury loving."

Chrys smiled and gave him a swift look that avoided a meeting with his eyes, which she knew to be glinting in the lamplight, like a kind of gem made up of fascinating shades of grey. It flashed across her mind yet again that no man had the right to possess such wickedly marvellous eyes, with the added deceit of double black lashes. Such eyes could conceal a thousand wicked thoughts.

"Are you on a visit to England, *madame?*" Chrys asked. "I know from what your grandson has told me that you have a house in the East, with the fascinating name of *Belle Tigresse.*"

"So Anton has told you about the house, eh? It used to be my desert abode, but now it belongs to him. I grow old, *pussinka*, and the climate of the East is no longer good for me, or my faithful Vera. Ah, how the years have quickly passed, and yet they were filled with incident! Vera and I have settled here in Kent, with its apple orchards which remind me of the Russia of my girlhood. Did Anton not tell you that he was bringing you to see his grandmother?"

"No, *madame*." Chrys shot him a severe look. "He behaved disgracefully and let me assume that he was – abducting me."

"Like a Cossack, eh?" Miroslava laughed with great enjoyment. "Anton is so like his grandfather – look, there on the mantel! There is a photograph of Ivanyi."

Chrys arose from the divan with her own particular grace, and knew herself watched by the grandson as she took into her hands the silver-framed photograph of the dead prince. He wore a superb white uniform embroidered with an eagle, gauntlets on his hands, a sword in his hilt, leather kneeboots, and a fur-trimmed hat. On a less handsome man the uniform would have been fabulous, but Prince Ivanyi had a distinction, a dashing air of a man who took what he could not beguile from the ladies. The eyes ... Chrys didn't need to turn her head to compare the pictured eyes with those she could feel almost tangibly on her person.

"In the twin frame," said Miroslava, "there is a picture of myself as a girl ... a girl who danced on the very air in those far-off, legendary days of the Maryinsky, of snow-capped towers, and jingling *troikas*. It was all really true, and yet now like a dream."

Chrys gazed with wonderment at the vivid, eloquent face of the young Miroslava, wearing a black off-the-shoulder dress, with full sleeves, a satin bodice, and a flared chiffon skirt.

"That was when I danced the *pas de deux* of Siegfried and Odile." There was nostalgia, and a note of husky longing in the deep voice of the woman who had known great happiness and deep sorrow. "Ivanyi always liked the costume, and that particular role for me. He always said I was too passionate to be a heroine. He knew me well, did my dark huntsman, my Orion, like a star that burned with too much flame for long living. I was his black swan, and always he was my dark huntsman ... not always a kind or forgiving man, but irresistible as honey to the bee, as flame to the moth. I would live again those two years that were my lovetime and not regret a single one of them."

Chrys felt a slight tremor in her hand as she replaced the photograph on the shelf. Never had her own family spoken with such frankness of their personal feelings ... the love between her parents had always seemed a gentle, patient, tolerant emotion, binding them closely like the pattern of a durable carpet. She had never thought of their love as being like a flame, and she knew instinctively that it never had been. Their love was made to wear, to endure ... but now she read in Miroslava's eyes the story of another kind of love.

She was glad that Vera entered the room in that moment, wheeling before her a trolley on which stood a lovely old samovar of silver, tea-glasses in filigreed containers, and plates of sandwiches.

"Food!" exclaimed Anton, as if he had not eaten for hours. In a single supple movement he was on his feet and bending over the trolley. "What have we here,

Vera? Smoked salmon, I hope?"

"Have you not always loved it, *barin*?" smiled Vera, addressing him as the "master" but looking at him as if she still thought of him as the wild boy who had been delivered into the care of his grandmother by the elopement of his mother.

Chrys found it difficult to picture him as a boy, and when Miroslava talked of him as *l'arabe*, yet another side of this worldly, well-dressed, cynical man-about-town came into focus to confuse her still further. She was beginning to wonder which was the real Anton de Casenove. Last night he had appeared wholly as a rake who chased after women ... tonight she learned that his motive in being in that French girl's bedroom had not been an amorous one at all but a recklessly gallant one.

Watching him with Miroslava now convinced Chrys that he cared for no other woman on this earth but Madame. She alone held the key to his sardonic personality. She alone knew what inner devil drove him to the gaming tables of Europe; on bold safaris through the drawing-rooms of the *beau monde*, charming his way into the hearts of women but never offering a single proposal of marriage.

Was it possible that he reaped a sort of revenge on his mother by making women love him, only to laugh at them as he flung himself into the saddle of a swift horse and galloped the aroma of their perfume out of his nostrils?

Seen in this light he was even more dangerous. A rake was forgivable, for he loved women too well. Anton de Casenove didn't love women at all. To him they were all as faithless as his mother had been ... that gay and reckless mother who had run off and left his father to die in the war.

Chrys watched him as his fine teeth flashed in a smile and his dark head almost touched the jade tassels on the Moorish ceiling lamps. The silver samovar purred as the tea-glasses were filled from the little tap at the side of the urn.

The scene was cosy enough, but the feelings that smouldered beneath the surface were those of people strange to Chrys, and with an intense emotionalism bred in their very bones. They hated ... or they loved ... in equal fiery measure. There was little of the gentleness which Chrys had witnessed in the lives of her parents; and in the romance between Dove and Jeremy.

Anton brought her a glass of tea and as he placed the filigreed container in her hand, his eyes looked down into hers. She almost shrank away from him among the cushions of the divan ... she didn't believe for one moment that he cared about her career as a dancer, her future, or her feelings.

"You will have some sandwiches?" he asked, and there was no doubt about the thread of mockery that ran through his words, as if he had noticed her withdrawal from him, her avoidance of his fingers as she took the glass of tea. "You must be feeling a few twinges of hunger after that long drive into the country?"

He knew that whatever twinges she felt were in no way connected with hunger. He knew far too much about women and the workings of their minds and their hearts ... he played on that knowledge and used it to make fools of women.

Well, thought Chrys, the time had come to show him what one female thought of him and his penchant for tearing the pride off women as a naughty boy might tear the wings off pretty moths.

Chrys met his look and quite deliberately she let her blue eyes fill with coldness and dislike. Blue eyes, she had once been told by a ballet teacher, could look as chilling as they could look heavenly, and she knew she conveyed a cold disdain to Anton when he shrugged his wide shoulders and walked away from her.

She turned with a smile to Vera. "Yes, please, I will have a couple of those delicious-looking sandwiches."

"Something," drawled Anton, "has put an edge on

Miss Devrel's tongue."

"Our Kentish air, perhaps," said Miroslava.

But as Chrys drank her tea and ate her sandwiches, she could feel Madame studying her profile with reflective eyes. What was she thinking, that it was unusual for a girl to be so cool towards her grandson.

"So what will you do, *pussinka*, during this year when you must 'rest' from your dancing?" Miroslava asked her.

"I – might travel." It was then that she made up her mind on this issue which Dove had raised. "I don't like the idea of working in an office, nor do I think I'd be much good at it, so I shall loan myself out as a travelling companion. My sister knows someone who is going abroad very soon, and if I am not in the vicinity of theatres and the people I know in ballet, then I might avoid the temptation to return to the stage before it is wise for me to do so."

"So you have decided to spend twelve long months with the 'dotty aunt', eh? Are you not afraid that she will send you dotty?" The words were interposed with such suavity from the occupant of the other divan that Chrys was wildly tempted to aim a cushion at his head.

"Ignore him," smiled Madame, "and tell me to which part of the world you expect to travel."

"Somewhere in the East, I think. Anyway, I must first persuade my sister's fiancé's aunt that I'm capable of making a good companion." Chrys smiled a little, and kept her gaze from that other divan. "I've always been so independent, and I've heard that companions are rather at the beck and call of their employers."

"I am sure you will cope admirably, *pussinka*. Ballet teaches one the art of patience even as it portrays the most emotional aspects of life, such as desire, suffering, and love. A great *maître de ballet*, who was himself a Russian, once said to me long ago that a dancer can be anything that she chooses to be, a sword, a chalice, or a rose. You will be very patient, Chrysdova, and enjoy your travels, and prepare yourself to return to dancing with a fine strong backbone again."

"My fear is that I shall be less of a dancer." Chrys sighed. "I worked so hard to become a soloist, and there are so many young and talented dancers ready to step into your shoes. It was such a bad stroke of luck to have that fall . . ."

"These things, my child, are sent to test our strength of character." Miroslava took her hand, the left one, and gazed into the palm of it. "You have a long life-line, Chrysdova, so there is plenty of time for you to become the ballerina of your dreams. But tell me, have you no other dreams?"

"Of romance?" Chrys spoke a trifle scornfully, and was very much aware that Anton was listening with arrogant laziness to their conversation. "It was something I never allowed to interfere with my career."

"But we must all be madly in love just once in a life-time," said Miroslava whimsically, while her rings pressed into the slenderness of Chrys's hand. "Art has an imperious voice, but love has a seductive one. When you hear it—"

"No," Chrys broke in. "I don't intend to hear it, or to listen to its unreason. So few marriages survive the career of the wife; so many obstacles are put in her way that her career is sacrificed. Perhaps I'm selfish—"

"No." Miroslava spoke firmly. "You have not the lips that express self-love and self-interest alone. There is a fine sensitivity to their outline, which means you are capable of *stradan*. The selfish are incapable of this in its acutest sense."

"*Stradan*." Chrys murmured the Russian word for suffering, even as she recalled with a shudder that crashing fall and the pain like claws in her spine. Yet it wasn't this kind of suffering which the word signified; it went deeper and embodied the soul of a person. *L'âme slave*. It meant that she was complicated, self-tormenting as these people with whom she drank Russian tea.

"Yes, it is all there, the temperament of the artiste."

Miroslava patted her hand and smiled in her worldly way tempered by her warmth of heart. "Rebellion, and innocence, with a dash of cynicism learned on the ladder to solo dancing. The cast-iron fragility. The determination that you need no one – no one but yourself to reach the stars. *Pussinka*, do you think I don't know? But I also know that when love came along with its voice like no other voice I had to listen. You too –"

"No!" Again Chrys shook her head. "I'm not like my sister. She longs for the chains –"

"Chains, you call them?"

"Can you deny that they aren't?" Chrys looked steadily at the Russian woman who had loved, and borne a child, and found herself finished as a dancer because of love's chains.

"Velvet chains, perhaps." Miroslava looked deeply into Chrys's blue eyes. "This coming year will be your testing time, Chrysdova. If you come through it without an entanglement, then you will become the mistress of the dance instead of the wife of a man. I predict this – but I also say to you – beware! We have the choice to begin love, but not always to end it. If we slay it, then we pay with the coin of loneliness."

"It's a chance I'm willing to take," said Chrys, with the bravado of her youth, and the untroubled coolness of the girl who only felt fully alive when she danced. She was confident, sitting there in the firelight of Miroslava's castle room, with the lamplight gleaming softly on her fair hair. She even dared to look at Anton de Casenove, who reclined at his ease, with his dark head against a cushion, and a cheroot between his lips. His eyelids drooped over his grey eyes, so the lashes concealed their expression. He didn't speak, and yet he seemed to challenge her statement with that lazy look.

"I mean it," she said. "It won't bother me to be a bachelor girl."

"But it might bother the bachelors." Miroslava glanced at her grandson. "Do you find Chrysdova a pretty creature, *mon ami*?"

"She is an ice-witch left by the frost when it sculptures its way across the *steppes*," he drawled. "If the *matushka* goes to the East then she might be in danger of melting a little in that ardent sunlight. A rich sheik might see her and snatch her for his *harem* – see, Miroslava, how scornful she looks! She doesn't yet know that the East is the most unchanging place left on earth, where *harems* still exist within secluded courts to which no man is admitted except the sheik himself."

"Nothing is decided," said Chrys, who didn't argue with him about his own knowledge of the ardent side of Eastern life. "I may not suit as a companion, so then it will mean a nine-to-five job in a city office."

"Most unexciting," he rejoined, "and most unlikely for you. I think the desert is on the cards for you ... *le destin*."

"Which is all very well," said Madame, "but we will not get ourselves involved in a discussion about destiny at this time of the night. Look at Chrysdova! She has the look of a child who is trying hard to keep her eyes from closing, and I am an old woman who needs her dreams. No doubt, *mon ami*, you are well used to staying awake all night at the card table, not to mention your night riding in the desert."

"Talk not of things desired and distant as the stars," he jested, rising to his feet, tall in the lamplight, which cast strange shadows across the distinction and the devilry of his lean face. Chrys could imagine him both as a gambler, and a desert rider, a cloak billowing out from those wide shoulders like the wings of a hawk.

He came to Miroslava and assisted her to her feet, and he held her frail but still graceful figure close to him for a moment. "I owe to you, *dushechka*, the good that is in me. But remember also what you taught me when I was a boy. 'Make yourself a lamb and the wolf will eat you.' Come, do you recall that you said it to me?"

She laughed a little and pressed her cheek against his dark jacket. "I remember, and I would have you no dif-

461

ferent, son of my son."

He bent his head and kissed his grandmother's forehead, and as he did so his eyes flicked across the face of Chrys, as if he were curious about her reaction to his affection for Miroslava. She was caught by his eyes, held by his gaze, and she saw deep in his eyes laughter like a tiny flame. She knew he laughed at her because she had believed he meant to seduce her ... it was awful that he should know her thoughts ... mortifying that he should be in a position to be amused by her naïvety.

Chrys jumped to her feet. "I am ready for bed," she said, and instantly the dark eyebrow was peaking above the grey eyes, and her cheeks flamed as she realized how he interpreted her remark. His pleasure in her confusion was diabolical, and she only wished that she might get her own back with him.

But tomorrow they would part ... she to go and see this aunt of Jeremy's ... he to ride, or play cards, or find some other woman to tease.

"Come," said Miroslava, taking her arm. "I will show you to your room."

"*Bon soir*, Miss Devrel," drawled the prince.

"Goodnight, *m'sieur*," she replied, and was glad to escape from his mocking face, his lean elegance, his slightly sadistic treatment of all women but Miroslava.

A little winding staircase led to her bedroom. A secret stairway in days gone by, she was told. "A lover's stairway, perhaps," murmured Miroslava, as she led Chrys into a turret bedroom, with cupboards deep in the walls, bowed glass windows, and an icon affixed to the wall, with a silver lamp lighting it.

"Sleep well, *pussinka moiya*." Miroslava patted Chrys's cheek, pale now the flush had left it. "I am pleased that Anton brought you to see me. On the bed you will find a nightdress and a robe, and the bathroom is at the turn of the corridor. You will be all right?"

"I shall be fine, *madame*. You have been very kind to me."

"Kinder than Anton, eh?" There was a knowing

gleam in the dark eyes that regarded Chrys by the soft light of the lamp. "He is not like other men you have met, I think. He is subtle, and appears to say what is in his mind without really saying it at all, which I know can be very confusing and infuriating for a woman. Ivanyi was the same, and in the way of heredity Anton is so much like him. The same pride and self-will; same daring and defiance of the conventions laid down by others. When I first met Ivanyi I was a little terrified, but I was also a Tartar and so I fought with him every inch of the way into love."

Miroslava smiled a little, and moved her hands in a very foreign way. "Destiny does weave the pattern of one's life, and it will be intriguing, eh, if you should meet Anton again in surroundings a little wilder than the apple orchards of Kent? Had you thought that this might happen, if you go East with this woman as her companion?"

"I don't want to meet him —" Chrys bit her lip. "What I mean to say, *madame*, is that Prince Anton and I have nothing in common, not really, although I found him a marvellous dancer. It would be better if we didn't see each other again —"

"Safer, do you mean?" Miroslava gave a soft laugh and turned to the door. "Be warned, *pussinka*, that if you play for safety you will find the game of life a rather dull one. It may be what you want, to be safe, but it will be such a waste. *Bon soir*, Chrysdova. Sleep and dream."

"Goodnight, *madame*, and thank you again for your kindness to me."

"Your blue eyes invite kindness, my child, but I speak as a woman." Miroslava again laughed softly as she closed the door of the bedroom behind her, and like her grandson left a subtle insinuation in the air that was faintly perfumed by the oil that burned in the *lampada*.

Chrys breathed it, and it seemed redolent of the distant East . . . a strange and beckoning scent, like that of hidden courtyards and jasmine gardens.

Her pulses quickened ... she would go tomorrow and see the woman who desired a companion for her travels in the East. It was a vast place and her path might never cross again the path of Anton de Casenove.

But if it did ...? The question stole into her mind and played there like an imp of the devil. She wondered what she would do, and gazed as if for future protection at the wall icon lit by the silver lamp.

There was, however, one thing she was very sure of ... Dove must be dissuaded from inviting the prince to her wedding. Chrys had made up her mind that when she parted from him the following day, the parting would be as definite as she could make it.

It would be a goodbye, not *do svidania*!

CHAPTER VI

IT was a wonderful old tree, rich with foliage and with a broad trunk which had divided to form almost the shape of a heart, as depicted on playing cards. So ancient was the tree that the names carved upon it dated back to Norman times and the tribulations of lovers at the cruel courts of the old kings.

Chrys had woken early in the bedroom with the cool pale walls and the golden icon, and not hearing a sound from the other rooms she glanced from the window near her bed, and the old tree on the lawn below seemed to beckon to her. She decided at once to take a stroll round the castle grounds, and after taking a shower she slipped into the white shantung dress which Vera had brought to her last night, with the kind suggestion that she might have need of it. It was delightfully reminiscent of the Thirties, and the sleeveless jacket in crochet-work reached to Chrys's hips. She loved the outfit, and could hardly appear in daylight in a silver

464

dance dress. Such an apparition on the lawn might be taken for a ghost in the early morning mist.

Mist in the morning at this time of the year was invariably a sign of a glorious day to come, and as Chrys wandered about the velvet lawns, she breathed the drifting sea air and felt rather like a very young girl on holiday again. She was hungry for a large breakfast, and felt a longing to drive to the edge of the sea and to swim in the joyous water.

She paused where a thick cluster of honeysuckle covered a grey stone wall and she had a certain feeling that Miroslava and her son would expect her to stay for the day. She touched the flowers, and the dew was on her fingertips and she wondered if she would be wise to surrender to this holiday feeling; to stay a while longer in the dangerous company of Anton de Casenove. He had a flair for making life exciting and expectant, and Chrys knew that she ought not to yield to the charming peril of the man.

She wanted above all to remain the well-balanced dancer, admired for her coolness and the way she had of keeping the men at bay. She wanted to dance in the cool halls of career, without the turmoil of desire in her life.

She was old enough, and woman enough, to have felt it tingling in her veins when she had danced in his arms last night. He would have that effect on anyone, and it would be sheer madness to fall in love with him.

She stroked the honeysuckle and the soft salty air stroked the skin of her arms and her neck and moved her hair with its caress. She tilted her chin. Was she such an innocent that she had to run away in order to protect herself from a mere man? If she returned to London today it would be to an empty flat. Dove would be at work, and after cooking her lunch there would be little for Chrys to do, except to go and see a film or sit in the park with a book.

No, she wouldn't run away! If Miroslava asked her

to stay here in Kent for the day she would do so, and take Anton's attentions for what they really were, a mixture of charm and deliberate enticement, with not a bit of heart behind them.

With a smile on her lips she returned across the lawn, which was now fingered by the sun that was breaking golden and bright through the mist that veiled the blue sky. She entered the archway that led to the winding stairs and upwards to Miroslava's apartment. Suddenly she gave a gasp as someone came round the curve of the narrow stairway – long-legged, wearing a white shirt open at the throat, and a sardonic smile about his lips.

"Bonjour," he greeted her. "You are an early riser – though we did wonder if you had taken fright and plunged off in search of the nearest railway depot."

"*Bonjour, milor.*" She gave him a smile that hid a certain turbulence of her nerves. He mustn't know that she had thought of making a bolt for it; he was the type who liked too much to give chase. "I looked from my window and saw that grand old tree on the lawn and just had to go and read the initials. So strange and sad, somehow, that they still linger while the owners of them have long since gone to dust."

"You are a romantic, Chrysdova, though you delight in denying it. I have come to fetch you to the breakfast table, and I hope you have an enormous appetite, because Vera always cooks French-fried potatoes with the ham and eggs when I am staying here with Grand'mère."

"I am ravenous," Chrys admitted. "It must be the sea air, because I never feel all that hungry in London."

"Come!" He held out a hand to her, but she ignored it and raced past him, slim enough not to brush too closely against him. But his soft laughter was even more effective than actual contact would have been this early in the morning; it mocked her, and it knew all about her fear of his fascination. It told her in more

than words that he was delighted that she wasn't unafraid of him. She bit her lip as she entered the morning-room where Vera was laying the table. She wished
to goodness she could be ice-cool with him, and delicately she moved out of the doorway as he entered the
room behind her.

Vera turned to give her a smile. "Ah, I see that the
dress fits you, *mademoiselle*, and it looks much nicer
on you than it ever did on me. How grand to be young
and pretty, eh? On such a day as this will be, and with
the *barin* to show you this Kent which Madame and I
have grown to love."

Vera bustled away to bring in the food, and Chrys
cast a glance at Anton which couldn't help but reflect
her curiosity.

"You are staying." It was a statement, not a question. "You are not basically a city girl, so what has the
city to offer you on a summer's day? Here we have the
orchards and the sea – do you like to bathe?"

"Yes –" The word came to her lips involuntarily.
"But I have no bathing suit, *milor*."

"That is no problem." He lounged on the deep win-
dowseat and with his arms stretched at either side of
him, the collar of his shirt was thus opened against
the smooth brown skin of his throat and chest. Chrys
picked up a goblet from the oak sideboard and studied
that in order to keep her gaze from the man, who in
all conscience was devastatingly good to look at.

"That goblet is a hundred years old," he informed
her. "It is made from real Bohemian glass and it is for
a bride and her groom to drink from on their wedding
day. A romantic notion, eh? First he drinks, and then
the bride follows suit, and the wine is an old Russian
wine which has been blessed. When Miroslava fled
from Russia there were few things she could take with
her, but the goblet she could not leave behind.
She wrapped it in her chemise so it would not get broken – hold it to the light and see it sparkle like a ruby."

Chrys obeyed him and caught her breath at the

beauty of the thing, perfectly oval and balanced on a long jewelled stem. "How gorgeous are really old things! One can see at once that they are fashioned by dedicated craftsmen and not turned out on a conveyor belt in some high-rise factory with plateglass windows."

"So you are admiring my second greatest treasure, eh, child?" Madame came into the morning-room at that moment and Chrys nodded and gave her a warm smile.

"What is your other treasure, *madame*? May I be impulsive and ask to see that as well?"

Miroslava chuckled and gestured with a ringed hand at her grandson. "By all means take a good look, *matushka*. I brought from Russia just two things that meant my very life to me, my marriage goblet and my unborn baby. There stands the son of the child I bore in the desert, who was destined never to know his father. I am grateful to the powers of heaven that Anton knew his own father as a boy. He was a fine man. Anton, of course, is more of a devil, but what woman is proof against a devil who has charm?"

"And what man is proof against Vera and her magical hand with French-fried potatoes?" he smiled, coming to the table as Vera wheeled in the food trolley and pulling out a chair for his grandmother. Chrys replaced the goblet on the sideboard and quickly took her own chair. The sun was now streaming through the lancet windows and making delightful patterns across the lace tablecloth and picking out the silver lights in the cutlery and the toast rack.

"I never partake of a big breakfast," said Miroslava. "Toast and coffee are sufficient for me, but I enjoy watching young people at work on good food."

"We aim to oblige you in every respect, Grand'-mère." Anton broke a roll and helped himself to butter while Chrys was busy helping herself to eggs, slices of gammon with the fat all crinkly, and puffed chips as golden as new pennies.

Vera joined them at the table after she had brought in the coffee, and it was a lighthearted meal, with Madame and her companion full of tales about the old days in Russia. Chrys enjoyed this hour because she felt secure ... it was being alone with Anton that shook her composure and made her feel as unsure of herself as she felt of him.

"You are not returning to London straight away?" Miroslava enquired of Chrys, her dark eyes roving the fair hair of her young guest, lit by the sunlight and softly loose on her shoulders. "It would be such a pity, for you have no rehearsal to dash to. Why not spend the day with us?"

"With you?" Chrys spoke eagerly. "Yes, I should enjoy that. You can tell me all about the Russian Imperial ballet ..."

"Ah, but I did not mean for you to stay cooped up indoors." Miroslava glanced in Anton's direction. "It will be good for my grandson to have the company of a *nice* girl for the day. You can drive into Applegate and take with you a basket lunch to enjoy on the beach. You can forget ballet for once, *matushka*, and relax in the sun. All work and no play is not good for a pretty girl. It is against nature."

"But–"

Anton quirked an eyebrow at Chrys. "But is a word invented by the mule to excuse his obstinacy. You like the seaside, no?"

"Yes," she admitted. "But I don't want to bother you by expecting you to take me sightseeing."

"I assure you it will be no bother." And as he leaned forward to help himself to marmalade, his eyes looked into hers and held a ray of amused awareness. "Even nice girls can be quite distracting, and I have nothing else to do."

A remark which in itself struck her as the height of decadence. *Nice* men worked for a living; they didn't play at cards for money, or gamble on the horses.

"Anton means that he is idle when he is here in Europe," Miroslava said, as if she had noticed the way Chrys had looked at him, a hint of censure in her blue eyes. "There is work enough at El Kadir, so don't pretend, Anton, that you are lazy and improvident. I never brought you up to play all the time, now did I? I taught you that play is the reward for hard work, as it is in ballet. Now confess to this girl that you are not a rake, for I believe she has the idea that you are."

"Confession, this early in the day?" His eyes laughed, and with a swift supple movement he was on his feet, around the table, and on his knees to Chrys — who gazed at him with fascinated blue eyes despite herself. His face seemed to her to be almost frightening in its male beauty, like the golden mask of a tombed prince ... as if indeed there were things buried in his soul which he had kept hidden a long time and would not reveal ... unless like a stroke of lightning love came to him and made him reveal himself.

"Oh, do get up off your knees!" The words broke from her, half-laughingly. "You make a mock of everything."

"Better than making a gloom of it, surely?"

"I — I suppose so." She sat there as tense as a cat confronted by a tiger, aware in all her nerves that he wasn't as playful as he made out to be. "Well, what do I have to do? Stroke you to make you purr?" she demanded.

"Would you like to stroke me?" His eyes were wickedly amused, and yet a soft, beckoning lambency had crept into them, and she felt her clenched fingers uncurling and the oddest, most maddening urge was creeping through them. To offset this she struck at his shoulder and felt the hard muscle and warmth of him. "You haven't the frame of a layabout, *milor*."

"I fence and I ride," he drawled. "The pastimes of a rake."

"True, but if you stay down there on the rug much longer you'll have housemaid's knee, and I understand that it's rather painful."

470

He gave a laugh and in one supple movement was standing over her. Then he glanced at Miroslava. "You see how it is, Grand'mère? The English girl remains elusive and hard to catch because she refuses to surrender her independent right to have a mind and a will of her own. She is the cat that bristles instead of the minx that flatters. She is a challenge, eh?"

"Well?" Miroslava studied Chrys, who sat there with a characteristic tilt to her chin, and the elusive outline of a dimple near her lips. "Are you pleased to be a challenge to a man who has been wooed by two European princesses, a Romanian countess, and the daughter of one of the richest oil sheikhs?"

"My unsophistication is the challenge, *madame*. I amuse him – for a day or two."

"You think so?" Miroslava studied her grandson, and then she changed the subject until breakfast was over and they went into the *salon*, where Madame took a dark Russian cigarette from a box and fitted it into an ivory holder. Anton lit it for her, and then she sat down on a divan and gave a little satisfied sigh. "You are going to the beach, you two?"

"Of course." He didn't wait for Chrys to agree or disagree. "I must bathe in English waters before I make my return to the desert. What a *memoir du coeur*, what coolness to remember under that hot sun – that of the English sea and a girl like Chrysdova. The combination is irresistible."

"I really think that I should be getting back to London," Chrys said, in a cool voice. "My sister will be worried about me –"

"You can telephone to let her know that you are perfectly all right," he said, and there was a sudden note of iron in his voice, a warning that his mind was made up for her and that she would be unwise to argue with him. "Come, the phone is in the hall, and while you give Dove a ring I will go and make sure that Vera packs a perfect lunch for us."

He took her by the wrist and she knew it would be

useless to appeal to Miroslava, who sat smoking dreamily, as if the scent of her cigarette awoke memories which she didn't wish to have disturbed. His fingers were like steel about her wrist, and she cast him a furious little glance as he made her go to the phone. "I suppose," she said, "this is how you treat your desert women?"

"Invariably," he drawled. "I am always dragging one or the other around by the hair."

Chrys glanced at him, and when his lip quirked she had to smile herself. "A harem would bore you, wouldn't it, *milor*? You like to go out and hunt your prey; you don't like tamed birds."

"The *ennui* of anything tame would be impossible to endure." He gestured at the telephone on the little round table. "Go ahead and ring your sister. Tell her you are in perfectly safe hands."

"You must be joking!" Chrys scoffed. "You forget that Dove has seen you."

"You think I am entirely what I appear to be?"

"Aren't you?"

"No more than you, *chérie*." And lightly, as if to soothe her ruffled feelings, he passed a lean hand over her silky hair. "*Soie sauvage*, a golden banner of your spirit and your courage. You are well named, Chrysdova. Now," his tone of inflexibility lay under the velvet, "inform Dove that you will not be home until tonight."

"Tyrant," muttered Chrys, as she dialled London and the number of the office where her sister would be at work. Anton watched her and waited long enough for her to be in speaking contact with Dove, then he sauntered in the direction of the kitchen and left her to explain that she was down in Kent still and would be staying the day as the weather was so good.

"Are you alone with *him*?" Dove's voice echoed along the line with a thrill of curiosity and indignation in it. "Are you being quite wise, Chrys? I mean, you know what he is! His reputation is awful where women are concerned!"

"It isn't quite true." Chrys was surprised by the cool authority of her assertion. "I don't know how it ever got about that he's women-mad — actually he isn't a Casanova at all but much more of a lone wolf."

"Still a wolf, darling, so mind he doesn't eat you up." Dove gave a laugh. "Do you like him, Chrys? Come on, open up to your sister at least. Do you find him good-looking?"

Chrys thought of the lean, wicked distinction of his face, in which were set those mercurial grey eyes, slanting outwardly, and densely lashed "Yes," she said briefly. "The fact of the matter is that I'm here as the guest of his grandmother, so for heaven's sake, don't go jumping to any romantic conclusions, Dove. She's a wonderful woman and has danced in ballet herself, so we have plenty to talk about." Chrys knew she was fibbing a bit, but she really didn't want Dove to get the idea that a romance was about to bloom between herself and a man who was merely using her as a distraction. A man who had been wooed by titled women didn't fall in love with a girl such as herself.

"Oh, so he has a family here in England?" said Dove, surprised and just a little note of disappointment in her voice, as if she had half-hoped that Chrys was in danger of a romantic seduction. She had often asserted that Chrys was too cool about men and needed to have her heart shaken up. "I didn't know about that."

"Well, you know now, sister dear, and you can return to your typewriter and your thoughts of Jeremy without being anxious about me and my honour." Even as Chrys used the word she rather wondered if it would still be intact at the end of the day. Was she quite certain that she could handle a man like Anton? Her nerves quivered, forcibly, as he suddenly appeared in the alcove from the interior of the flat and stood there silently, framed by the arch in his dark narrow pants and his soft white shirt, his eyes narrowed like a pleasured cat.

"Bye, Dove! Yes, I shall be sure to make the most of the sunshine." The receiver sang as Chrys laid it in the cradle, and thrusting her hands into the pockets of the hip-length jacket she stood there daring those grey eyes that glinted behind the double lashes that were black as soot. Her heart beat quickly – had he caught the word she had used a moment ago? She hoped to goodness he had not. It might give him ideas! If he needed any?

"The food basket will be ready in a while," he said blandly. "We can buy you a swimsuit at the beach, and possibly some suntan oil. Your skin is very fair and must be protected. How easy, Chrysdova, to protect the outer covering, but always what is inside us must remain vulnerable, eh?"

"You don't strike me, *milor*, as being at all vulnerable," she rejoined. "You have remarkable assurance, which I believe it would take a lot to shake."

"You think I am hard and arrogant?" His expression didn't change, but she saw the sudden flexing of his forearm muscles, as if he controlled an urge of some sort – perhaps to shake her, a mere slip of a girl who dared to say honestly what she thought of him. Far too many women had flattered him, and so made him contemptuous of them. Did he desire to be contemptuous of her? Was this his reason for making her stay the day with him? Was he out to prove that she was like all the rest – out to get a man.

She tilted her chin and the pure contours of her face revealed the pride she felt in her independence. "*Les extrêmes se touchent*," she said in French. "We are so extreme you and I that we are bound to clash as individuals. I think you have great charm and that you use it deliberately to play games with people. People think of you as a sort of modern-day Casanova, but you don't really love women, do you? You really like to be cruel to them in revenge –" There she broke off and

474

colour stormed into her cheeks. What was she saying? Whatever had led her to speak like this? Was she attempting to *reform* the man?

"Don't stop there," he drawled, "just as you were about to tell me that I am not a great lover at all but really a great fraud."

"Well, you are," she flung at him. "All the time you are secretly laughing at women for falling for you. You judge them all by your mother – except for Miroslava, and she, of course, is an exceptional person. Such people are rare."

"Are they, Chrysdova?" His direct stare was very disconcerting. "So rare, do you think, that I am never likely to find one for my own?"

"Not if you go on looking in all the wrong places," she rejoined. "I think in your heart that you distrust love and so you avoid it be meeting people you know you don't really like. Sophisticated people –"

"Like my mother, eh?"

"I imagine she was like that."

"Lovely and heartless – the mirage and never the real oasis."

"Yes – but it really isn't any of my business." Suddenly she was in desperate retreat from the subject and wished she had never mentioned it. She cast him a quick, almost appealing look, and then hastened in the direction of the *salon*. Miroslava was there to offer a little protection from him for a little while longer.

An hour later Chrys was inevitably alone with Anton for the rest of the day, beside him in his car as they drove through the sunlight in search of the sea and the sandy beach at Applegate.

The warm breeze blew her hair from her brow and played caressingly about her neck. She had to relax from this maddening tension which had built up between herself and Anton, and closing her eyes she willed the relaxation of the ballet dancer just before the curtain rose out there on stage. She coaxed each toe, each finger, each separate muscle to uncoil, and she told herself that the best way to get through this day with Anton was to pretend to herself that it was a piece of theatre and not to be taken seriously for one moment. She must enjoy it as she would a *pas de deux* with a particularly expert dancer, and not allow anything he said or did to impose itself on her inner self. She knew him for what he was. She knew that he came to Europe in search of fun and that his real life lay in the desert.

The old dancing discipline imposed on herself she allowed her eyes to open and met the sun with a smile. "It is an enchanting day," she said. "It really would have been wasted in stuffy London."

"I understood that it had become swinging London," he murmured. "I must say that on this occasion I have noticed some oddly dressed, and rather shaggy young people around the town. They all seem to have diddy bags with them and to look in a perpetual trance, as if they never stop walking."

"I believe a lot of them are tourists from other countries," said Chrys, and her smile deepened. "Tourists of a slightly different calibre from yourself, *milor*. One could never say that you are oddly dressed and ungroomed, and I am sure your worldly possessions would not fit into a diddy bag, as you call it."

"I have fitted them into a desert tent before now," he rejoined. "We have our herds at El Kadir and I have more than once followed them into the hills with the men."

"What is it like," she asked, "to be the lineal head of a desert tribe? I gather that you are."

"I am. My father was accepted as almost a son by the Sheik who befriended Miroslava, and when he died a hero in the war it was almost by mutual consent of the various clansmen that I take his place. The Sheik's workers and servants had been in his family for generations; born and bred to his leadership, and his own sons died as boys. His workers loved my father, and it seemed natural enough that I take his place. The people bring their debts and sins and troubles to me, and I sit in judgement on them. This may sound arrogant to you, but it is a natural way of life in the desert. I take responsibility, and when I am absent the job falls to my deputy who has the impressive name of Haroun bin Raid."

"Tell me about Belle Tigresse." She had relaxed almost unaware, for in the strangest way he seemed much nicer when he took on, in a manner of speaking, his desert cloak.

"It is a large, white-walled house with a central dome, set within a walled garden that shelters it from the desert winds and the summer *khamsin*. It has shutters of blue, and the doors are painted blue — to ward off the evil eye." Anton gave her a quick sideglance. "Did you know that blue is the colour the Devil cannot tolerate? That he hides from it as if it might blind him? It is the colour of heaven, sky and sea. The colour of the Madonna's cloak. And the colour of the Son of God's eyes. Did you know, *mutushka*?"

She shook her head, and tried not to believe that his words had also shaken her heart.

"What are the social events in the desert?" she asked quickly.

"Births and marriages are our main events." Now a thread of amusement ran through his voice. "These are much celebrated, and my *chef* makes a huge *coucous d'honneur* to send to the family in which a marriage or a birth has taken place. The head of the family sends to me in return, as Sidi of the tribe, a huge slice of wedding cake, or a box of sugared almonds from the baptism of the child. This is called *baraka*, the good will between man and master."

"Don't you attend their parties?" she asked, for a sudden picture of him all alone in his white-walled house arose in her mind, stretched on a divan, grey eyes half-closed against the smoke of a narrow strong cheroot.

"Occasionally. Arab weddings are odd, erotic af-

477

fairs, but sometimes in the evening of a christening there will be a fire dance, which is to say that bonfires are lit and couples dance around them, and the old half-Spanish, half-Moorish songs are sung, for most of the musicians that attend these festivities are from the cities such as Fez and Morocco. They are marvellously evocative songs. You should hear them, *matushka*. You would enjoy them."

"I am sure I would." And now in place of that lonely figure she had imagined, she saw him cloaked by firelight, a slumbrous delight agleam in his eyes as he listened to the barbaric music of the East.

"Why do you come to Europe when your heart is in the desert?" she asked him.

"To see Miroslava, my child. And to singe my wings in the way of a bachelor. I am thirty-three, Chrysdova. Would you have me live like a monk?"

"It is none of my business how you live, Prince Anton." She had expected him to be honest, but all the same she didn't like the little sting his honesty left like a welt across her own guarded heart and body.

"Would you sooner hear that I keep a *harem* at *Belle Tigresse*?" he mocked. "I leave alone the daughters of my desert clansmen, not because I don't find them lovely, but because I should soon have a *harem* on my hands if I dared make love to any of those girls. Their fathers would then make me a gift of them – do you see how it is?"

Suddenly she did see and her sense of humour reasserted itself. "Yes, I do see, *milor*. Better to make a fool of a society belle, even if it means getting shot for your trouble."

He laughed softly by her side, with a sort of purring menace. "I was not having an affair with that particular young lady, but no matter. You must understand that I am several men in one. I have Russian blood in which there is also Tartar blood. I was born in a desert house, the son of a Russian and a Frenchwoman from Paris. I was brought up among tribesmen, sent to France to be educated, and to serve for a while in her army. I sometimes wonder myself if my soul has the shape of a triangle."

This time Chrys laughed. "Do you feel strange when you come to Kent, *milor*? It is all so very English, so green with a vista of blue where the sea locks in the land."

"English as yourself, *matushka*. Gold, blue and green." The meaning in his voice was all too plain, and a quick glance at his profile showed her the line of silent laughter beside his mouth. He swung the car with graceful expertise around a bend in the road and there ahead of them lay one of those arrestingly pretty villages only to be seen in England, with cottage-type houses in which hollyhocks stood tall and deep-belled in the small front gardens, and with a small inn about halfway down the road, its black and white timbering catching the sunlight and its mullioned windows like gleaming, friendly eyes.

"Would you like to stop for a drink?" Anton asked her. "We have plenty of time – all day, in fact, to spend at the beach."

"It would be nice," she said. "It does look a quaint old place – and so very English."

He laughed in that purring way of his and turned the car into the driveway fronting the inn, which was named the Plough. The car slid to a smooth halt and Anton leaned over to open the door beside Chrys, and at once she was on the defensive against his physical closeness, and the brush of his darkly lashed eyes over her face.

"Are you to be your sister's bridesmaid?" he asked, unexpectedly.

"Why – yes." She was startled by his question, and this widened her eyes and intensified their blueness as she looked at him, held there in her seat by his extended arm.

"Have you no wish yourself, *matushka*, to be a bride?"

"I told you – marriage would interfere with my career."

"Marriage would become you," he murmured. "You were made for a man, not for an audience to enjoy."

"Anton – please –"

"Please?" He quirked an eyebrow and leaned a little nearer to her, so that she felt the warmth of his brown skin and felt in him all the vital desires of a man in the very prime of life. "What would you like me to do to please you – treat you as if you were my maiden aunt?"

"Be nice and don't flirt," she pleaded. "Tomorrow we both go our separate ways and this – this could be a day to remember without regret."

"Would you regret my lovemaking?" His tone was half-mocking, and yet his eyes were beautifully still and serious. "I should light a candle in a chapel to the memory of it. Beauty and innocence are a rare conquest, these days." So saying he flung open the car door, and she caught the brief ravishment of his eyes as she fled from him into the inn. It was cool in there, with a few people seated on the oak settles, or leaning against the bar. Heads turned to study her, and then the man who followed her into the lounge. The way these Kent farmers looked at Anton made her want to laugh, nervously. He was so very foreign by contrast to them. So tall and dark and illimitably sure of himself. His fingers sought her elbow and she knew instinctively that he was letting the other men know that she was his!

She didn't pull away ... it was safe to surrender to him ... in the company of other people.

"And what will you have, sir?" As always Anton commanded service without raising an eyebrow. He glanced at Chrys and she said she would have a Campari and soda.

"Make that two," he said to the barman, after which he took a long, interested look round the lounge, while Chrys seated herself on one of the bar stools and tried to look as composed as the various glances in their direction would allow.

"I believe," Anton murmured, "these good people think we are a couple of the jet set. Do you mind? That I have this odd effect on the English?"

She smiled a little and knew that his question held a double meaning.

"You have the look of what you are, *milor*," she said.

"And what is that, *matushka*?" He gazed down at her with mocking eyes.

"Prince Lucifer!"

"You dare to say that – here. Would you care to say it when we are alone?"

"Why, don't you care for the truth?" She gave a laugh and lifted her drink to her lips. "You are fond of dishing it out to other people, I have noticed."

"So I am! So you think of me as the dark angel, eh? Fallen from the good graces of heaven?"

"Mmmm." She nodded. "Ever since we met you have been trying to make me fall – now haven't you, Prince – Anton?"

His eyes held hers, glinting like steel, mesmeric, shutting out all other faces so that only his dark face filled her world in that moment. "From the first moment we entered that lift, you and I, we were like two stars bound upon a clash. The impact has been shattering, eh? When we part neither of us will easily forget this meeting – confess that, at least!"

"Of course I confess it," she said. "It isn't every day that a girl meets Lucifer in the flesh."

His eyes slowly narrowed in a smile . . . a dangerous smile. "If you want me to prove that I am no angel, *chérie*, then you are going the right way about it." His fingers touched her bare arm for the briefest moment, and it was as if a flame ran over her. She tautened . . . for there was in his touch a bewitching, enslaving, seducing quality.

481

"I am a person, not a puppet," she retorted. "You can't do just as you please with me. I have more to do with my life than be *your* plaything for the little while it takes you to become bored with your toys."

"Do you really believe that my life is littered with discarded playthings?" He laughed a little and drank his Campari. "Is it part of your defence that you have to believe me entirely cruel? Dare you not believe that I can also be tender?"

"*L'amour tendre,*" she murmured. "And then *l'amour tragique.*"

"My child, I avoid hearts that I might break," he drawled. "Tell me, am I in danger of breaking yours?"

"Mine, *milor,* is given to my career."

"Then if I make love to you I cannot really harm you – not if your heart is not involved."

"My pride would be involved, *milor,* and I don't care to be the caprice of a Russian prince, thank you all the same for the offer."

"If I had to in the desert, you piece of English ice, I would soon have you melting. You have no idea how seducing the desert can be upon the senses, especially at night when all is silent and the stars flood the sky and the jasmine awakes in the enclosed gardens. I see you there, in a lovely silk robe of blue, the border of each hanging sleeve embroidered with *fleurs de lys.*" He lit a cheroot as he spoke and flame and smoke tangled together in the glance he gave her. "There is a place to which I ride when the dawn arises all veined with black and scarlet. I call it the Jade Oasis, and never on this earth was there a place more lovely, or more lonely. Think of riding with me, *dorogaya.* Does your blood not stir in your veins, Chrysdova?"

It did ... uncomfortably so, and she didn't protest when he indicated to the barman that two more drinks be brought to them. She wanted her senses to be dulled, not tingling as he had just set them tingling with his too vivid description of his wonderful oasis.

"Have you taken many of your European conquests to see your Jade Oasis?" she asked in a deliberately cool voice. "I am sure they were enchanted, by the place and by your escort."

"Don't, child," he leaned close to her, and his teeth gleamed white through the smoke of his cheroot, "try me too close to the edge of my Russian temper."

"Why — would you whip me?" She dared his eyes, her own eyes flashing jewel-blue with her defiance of him and her response to what lay in the heart of his desert. Surely only a mirage and nothing that could be firmly grasped as a real and lasting heaven. She would not be coaxed by his mirage only to find herself left thirsting in the desert. He was too attractive, too devilish to be listened to.

"A whipping you could take." His eyes raked over her, taking in the youthful pride and defiance. "I should have to use a thousand kisses to defeat you and bend you to the sand."

"You think I'd let you?" She gave a scornful little laugh, but avoided looking at his lips, in which a touch of cruelty mingled with a certain quirk of tenderness.

"Most women would think it cruel not to be desired," he drawled. "You really are an extraordinary creature, Chrysdova."

"Why, because I resist your wiles, Prince Anton?"

"Are you quite certain they are wiles?"

"The art to charm and the ability to conquer lie in your eyes, *milor*. You are like a falcon, but I am no dove. I have been trained to obey my *maître de ballet*, but beyond that I am my own mistress and I intend to remain so."

"You prefer water when I can give you wine?"

"What — *vin du mal*?" she shot back at him.

"That, Chrysdova, is not nice." Instantly his fingers were about her wrist and he was making her aware of the steel and fire in his touch. "You are a delight to the eyes, but you have a shocking distrust of men. Truly a sand-cat, far readier to scratch than to purr. By heaven, I'll make you purr before I am finished with you!"

Still holding her by the wrist he pulled her from the bar stool and walked her out of the inn. She didn't dare to struggle for her freedom, not in front of those people in the lounge, but when they reached the car she dug her fingernails into him and demanded her release. "I'm not coming with you to the beach," she flared. "I'm going back to London."

"Scared?" he taunted. "Afraid of a mere man?"

"Damn brute!" she flung at him, and then gave a gasp as he swept her up in his arms and dropped her neatly into the front seat of the Rapier.

"And stay there!" he ordered, striding round to the other side and sliding in behind the wheel. "You stay where you are, my girl, and like it!"

"I hate you!" she stormed, nursing her wrist. "I really do hate your arrogance. It's written all over you! You're so used to playing lord of the land that you can't bear it when a mere woman stands up to you. You like women to be horizontal – weak and willing –"

"Stop it!" he ordered. "In a moment you will be in tears."

"Never! I wouldn't cry for you if you were –" Sharply she broke off and turned her head away from him. The car shot away from the inn and sped along the road to the sea. Tears were blinding her eyes and making a haze of the sun, and she hated that as well. Never in her life had she felt so on edge with anyone; never had life felt so complicated, not even when she had lain in a hospital bed and feared for her future as a dancer. There had been doctors to reassure her, nurses to soothe away her fears – but right now there was no one but herself to fight her battle. She was all alone with Anton ... and a broken heart was harder to mend than a broken bone or two.

The beach at Applegate was long and undulating, with fine tan-coloured sands and groups of rocks at the sea's edge to make it picturesque. The waves came in to the beach in long silky swirls, whipping softly back and forth against the rocks. It wasn't a crowded beach, but Chrys was very relieved to see a few family groups, and young people in the water, their laughter flung and caught in the net of the sun and the spindrift.

After parking the car Anton had made Chrys go with him to a shop that sold beach wear, and he had bought her a white suit, a pair of scarlet waders, and a beach ball. With mockery incarnate in his eyes he had tossed the ball into her arms. "Something for you to play with," he had jibed. "Something nice and safe, and if you lose it what will it matter? No one will weep over a lost beach ball, will they, *matushka*."

Down on the beach he had sought out the attendant and hired a beach hut, and now Chrys was inside, the flap closed against intrusion while she took off her clothes and stepped into the one-piece bathing suit. As she pulled the soft white material up over her limbs, up over her hips and her bust and slipped the straps over her shoulders, she felt tiny nerves contracting in her stomach.

With an assumption of nonchalance she was far from feeling Chrys left the beach hut and was glad to find that Anton had quitted the steps and was half-way down the beach talking to a small girl. Chrys heard him laugh, and for the first time that sensuous, purring sound was absent from his laughter and she felt a strange little shock of – of envy. How nice to be young enough to be unafraid of his charm ... and Chrys ran towards the sea, flying into its embrace as if in search of protection.

She was swimming lazily when Anton joined her, and she told herself he was like a lean, brown tiger-shark swimming around her, brushing her legs with his fingertips, teasing and agile, and then suddenly gone from her side as he swam out and out into the dazzle of the hot sun on the water. She told herself she wouldn't follow him, and then she just had to, for the lure of the sea was upon her and she was a good swimmer, having been born on the sea coast and possessed of parents who believed in the health giving properties of the ocean.

"Race you to the beach!" he called out, when she had almost caught up with him.

She turned with all the grace of her dancing body and side by side they swam back to the sands, into the waves that were curling there. Anton gave a hand to her and almost unthinking she took it and was drawn to him as if she were a pin, a feather, a plume of bright water, her hair a long wet mane unloosened from its knot, and each curve of her slender body almost nude in the thin white covering of the bathing suit.

She had no time to catch her breath as a warm wet arm locked itself about her, firm as whipcord, and not to be denied. His mouth came down to hers and with a kind of sea-drugged, sun-drugged compliance she allowed her lips to be taken and roughly, firmly caressed by his. Her hands came up against his chest, half protesting, and then stilled by the shock of pleasure, contracting all the many tiny, sentiently placed nerves in her slim, cloistered body.

He was so close to her, all pewter smooth and firmly muscled, that it was as if for a split moment in time, a forked second of pure lightning, they were fused into a smouldering unit of one. It was he who drew away first, leaving on her mouth, and on her waist, the impress of his lips and his hands. She tossed back her hair and unable to meet his eyes she looked instead at the long, deep scar on the left side of his chest, just about where his heart would be.

"*Ma doue!*" His eyes were shimmering. "What a swim – and what a kiss!"

"You'd have hurt me if I hadn't let you." High on her cheekbones she could feel a flush, and on her lips she could still taste the sea water from his lips ... so intimate, almost like the taste of tears. "It is easy enough for men to be brutes – they know very well that women are sensitive to pain."

"Hush, child!" His arm swept down as if he were a Czarist cutting down a malcontent. "Don't be so sure that men can't feel pain in the very marrow of them. They are equally human, and you have a lot to learn about them."

"Do you plan to be my tutor?" she demanded. "Was that lesson number one? Good heavens, lesson number two must really be something!"

"Indeed it is." His eyes narrowed to a shimmery grey. "Would you like me to demonstrate? We could go straight through the course."

He took a deliberate step towards her and she retreated so hastily that she tripped over a rock and fell to the sands before she could save herself. She lay there breathless while he towered over her and looked down at her with the threat of more of that devastating lovemaking in his gaze. She had to find a weapon against him and she began to laugh. "Oh, Apollo, who caught at love and filled his arms with bays!"

"Chrysdova, lovely and man-scared," he mocked. "With hair such as yours, and that mouth, you should be all passion. On your feet, you little coward, and come give me my lunch."

She knelt and made him a mock salaam. "I live but to obey your commands, O lord of light. What will you have – caviare and wine?"

His hands reached for her and swung her to her feet. He bent his head and his teeth brushed her shoulder before she could pull away. "The goose paté was very good," he jibed. "Just a little salty, but nonetheless tasty."

"You are ridiculous!" Chrys broke free of him and ran in the direction of the beach hut, and all the time she could feel that teasing, nibbling pressure of his teeth against her shoulder. She knew the name for it, she knew that it was called love play, and she told herself she would have to find some excuse to get away from this beach before the sun waned and the sea and the sands began to go dark.

She laid the checked cloth on the sands and took from the lunch basket the savouries and delectable-looking sandwiches Vera had packed for them. There was also a bottle of wine, and carefully wrapped wine glasses, and as she set these out Anton came and sprawled on the sands. "Hand me the corkscrew," he said. "I know there is one because I put it in myself."

Chrys found it and gave it to him and he proceeded to uncork the wine. "Make yourself comfortable," he said, "and don't flit about like a hostess listening for the doorbell. All who are coming to the party are present and correct."

She sat down at the other side of their spread, opened a napkin and took a couple of sandwiches. A glass of wine was held towards her and she took it with a murmur of thanks and was relieved that her hand didn't shake. "How chic," she said, "to be drinking wine at a picnic."

"I have the feeling that you would prefer lemon squash," he drawled. "Much less likely to go to the head. I drink to your pure blue eyes, *matushka,* and the way they remind me of the desert sky when the blue hour approaches. Do you drink to me?"

"Why not?" She raised her glass. "Here's to knowing you, Anton. When I dance in a Russian ballet I shall think of you."

"I am glad to hear that you don't intend to quite forget me." He popped a savoury into his mouth and looked at her over the rim of his wine glass. "What ballet had you in mind – The Snow Princess?"

She smiled and nibbled a pickle. "Do you go back soon to your desert house, *milor*? It must be a wrench for you to leave Miroslava?"

"It is," he agreed, "but I can no longer expect a woman of her years to endure the heat and often the loneliness. She is better at the castle. She has her music and her memories, and kind old Vera."

"You must at times feel lonely yourself, *milor*." Chrys took a quick sip of her wine. "Now that your grandmother is no longer at Belle Tigresse."

"Do you care — really — that I might now and then be lonely in my desert house?" There was a little crack as he broke a hard-boiled egg and peeled the shell.

"I think when you are a little *triste* you saddle up and ride to your Jade Oasis," she said, handing him the salt for his egg.

"Taking with me my *belle amie* of the moment?" He shook salt on to his egg and bit it in half with a snap of his teeth.

"We were talking of loneliness —"

"Ah, so we were, little one, but it is not always a fact that a man is no longer lonely because he has with him a woman — not that I have ever taken a woman to the oasis. There are two sorts of loneliness, that of the body, and that of the soul. We are locked within the prison of ourselves — perhaps only one person alone can enter with the key to our inner mystery and all our secret agonizing. Perhaps only then does the restlessness go away like an ache that has troubled one for a long time. You must, Chrysdova, feel lonely yourself at times — and don't bother to deny it. Don't say again that your career suffices. Your trouble is that you don't trust a man to give you the same joy, the same heady sweetness that your dancing gives you. You trust in your dancing to fill your life — but what if it doesn't? What then will you have, if you let your feelings lie like frozen crocuses under that snow-cool skin of yours?"

"It is my business what I do with my life," she rejoined. "I don't plan to have affairs just to compensate for this year when I must remain inactive as a dancer —"

"I was not talking about affairs," he cut in. "You were not made for those, but you were made lovely, and love will come to you whether you will it or not. If you give it the frozen shoulder, *ma petite*, it may never come again with such passion and power."

"What would you know about love, Prince Anton?" She gave him a cool look, and yet could feel her fingers gripping the hot fine sand with nervous tension.

"To you it is just another game of roulette. Tonight the girl in red, or the one in black, and when the game grows tedious you walk away and you don't even glance back to see if the girl is weeping. If I ever loved it wouldn't be your kind of love!"

"If snow ever burns and flame ever freezes," he mocked, and he reached for the wine bottle and there was a reckless look on his face as he filled his glass. "Will you join me in another glass of this provocative wine that loosens the tongue?"

"No thanks," she said, and in that instant she made up her mind to go home. She ate her sweet, an iced *purée* of fruit, and she listened to the tide coming in, and the gradual quietening of other voices on the beach. She was aware, almost without looking, when Anton turned his face against his arm and closed his eyes. She waited, patiently and quietly, and then when she dared fully to look at him, she saw his dark lashes still on his cheeks, and she saw his chest rising and falling evenly in sleep. She stared for a moment at the scar that was a crescent of white against the tan of his skin. A strange little shudder ran all through her, and then she slipped to her feet and walked silently to the beach hut. Within ten minutes she was dressed and her hair was combed. She checked her purse to make sure she had money enough for the train fare to London ... and she walked away from Anton de Casenove without looking back.

This time she would be the one to walk away ... before he did so, and left her in tears.

CHAPTER VII

"WILT thou have this woman to thy wedded wife? ... Wilt thou love her, comfort her, honour and keep her ..."

At that point in her dreaming, while Dove still seemed to stand beside her bridegroom in pale satin and lace, Chrys awoke to find herself in a cabin aboard a ship, the bedclothes half off her restless figure, while deep in the heart of the vessel the engines beat firmly and regularly.

She sat up and stared at the luminous dial of her travelling clock. It was still early morning, though a faint light was outlining the window facing her bed. She could hear the soft breathing of her cabin companion in the twin bed, and she gave a slight smile. Maud Christie was well travelled and she slept soundly, undisturbed by the motion of the ship, by the strange scents that stole into the cabin, a mixture of ozone and weathered timber and a faint whiff of coffee always on the air.

Chrys, as a dancer, had travelled to various cities by jet plane, but this was the first time she had voyaged in a cargo ship that also carried a few passengers. It was a new, exhilarating experience, and today they would arrive at Port Said, and she would have her first glimpse of a desert city, on the edge of the vast and golden sea of sands.

She took a biscuit from the tin on her bedside table and made herself comfortable against her pillows as she nibbled it. Maud Christie had been doubtful about employing her at first. She had said bluntly that she had in mind a middle-aged woman used to the job of being a companion. A young, pretty toe-dancer who would attract the men like bees to a jampot was not her idea at all of what she required. They'd get halfway to their destination and some young man would steal her away and leave Maud stranded again.

"No, you're hopeless," she had said, waving Chrys to the door. "Go and get yourself a modelling job, young woman. It will pay better than I can, and no doubt amuse you far more."

"It would bore me to distraction," Chrys had laughed, for right away she had taken to Maud, with her

491

forthright air, her solid figure in a tweed suit, and her hair that was cut short but still retained some of the gold of her youth. She had a humorous mouth, and rather fine eyes, and Chrys felt certain that she would be interesting to work for, and not too bossy.

"I thought the youth of today wanted only to enjoy the glamorous side of life, with no respect for the past, and little interest in anything but the thrill of the moment. Are you telling me, young woman, that you're different from the other members of your generation?"

"We aren't all flighty," said Chrys. "Some of us have a serious side, Mrs. Christie."

"Maud, if you don't mind?" The decision was as rapid as that. "If you are going to travel to the desert with me, where the sun will darken that fine white skin of yours, and where the *khamsin* can spring to life within the flickering of an eyelid." Maud had jangled the blue Arabian beads that she wore with her English tweeds. "There are many discomforts in the East, to match its many delights, and there will be hell to pay, I promise you, if you let me down and prove inept, or as hungry for a man as my last fool of a companion."

"Men are my least concern." And Chrys spoke with such decision, and even a hint of scorn, that Maud studied her somewhat critically.

"Been hurt, or let down by one of them?" she asked.

Chrys shook her head and explained that her career came first.

"A bit dangerous, that." Maud pursed her lips. "Love is like the *khamsin*, say the Arabs, always waiting to overwhelm the unwary."

"I'm not unwary," said Chrys. "On the contrary, I'm very wary."

"Well, let us hope so." And after that Maud proceeded to tell Chrys what she would need for the journey, and here she was, with the sea voyage almost over and England left far behind, with its constant reminders that Dove was partly lost to her in the loving arms of Jeremy, that her parents were content with each other and their garden at Westcliff, and another member of the ballet company had stepped into her shoes and would dance the roles which had been planned for her during the forthcoming season.

This trip out East was her only consolation and Chrys was determined to make the most of it.

She was up, bathed and dressed in crisp tailored blue by the time Maud Christie joined her for breakfast at the Captain's table. The sea was looking gloriously blue and unruffled, and Captain Laurent gallantly remarked that the sea was trying to compete with the colour of Mademoiselle's eyes.

Chrys smiled at the compliment, but absently, for in the distance she glimpsed like a mirage the gleaming minarets and domes of an oriental city, floating on the horizon, and making her heart beat so much faster than the admiration of any man.

"Is it real, or am I imagining it?" She pointed towards the scene, etched so clearly by the brilliant sunlight.

"One's distant glimpse of the tropics never fails to stimulate the imagination," said the Captain, and his smile was worldly and indulgent of her excitement as his Gallic eyes dwelt on her face. "I hope you will not be disappointed when you actually breathe its many aromas, mademoiselle, and discover that the sun's gauzy veil hides an ancient and sometimes raddled face."

"Don't disillusion the child before she has had a chance to see Port Said for herself," Maud chided him. "We seasoned travellers grow into cynics, but Chrys is new to the world of Eastern sunlight and mysticism. Don't listen to him, child. Frenchmen are realists about everything, including romance. They only give their hearts to a fine wine and well cooked food."

"How dare you libel the world's best lovers!" Captain Laurent looked mock-injured. "All during this all too short voyage I had hoped that I was winning the heart of this golden English flower, who this morning looks as if the waves just gave birth to her, so fresh and new and untouched by life. You are a lucky woman, Madame Christie, to have such a companion for your travels."

"I am hoping I stay lucky," Maud retorted, wiping the marmalade from her lips. "I don't want any of you men snatching her away from me. I am a garrulous woman and I like someone to talk to in my own tongue while I pursue my own particular devil, which is the travel bug. It seems to have its roots in my feet and I can't stay in one place for long."

A few hours later Maud's feet, and that of her companion, were on shore and their baggage was being passed through the Customs office. Maud had brought cameras and a typewriter, not to mention a casket of Indian tea, a couple of well-upholstered sleeping bags, a pressure cooker and a folding bath. These were all packed in a trunk, which had to be opened for the officer's inspection, and Maud muttered to Chrys that anyone would think she was smuggling arms into the country, the fuss they were making.

"The *sitt* plans to camp in the desert?" exclaimed the official, in passable English. "Will that not be inconvenient for two ladies?"

"It would be," Maud rejoined, "if we didn't have the things you are looking over as if they're machineguns!"

The olive-faced official, in his impeccable white uniform, shook his head in the age-old puzzlement of the male Eastern intellect in conflict with the mind of the European female. He relocked the trunk and chalk marked it. "Welcome to our country, to you and your daughter," he said to Maud. "May you enjoy your visit."

"Thank you, young man." She marched on airily out of the customs office, looking oddly pleased in that way of childless women that Chrys should be taken for her daughter. Porters followed them, carrying the baggage, and quite soon a horse-drawn arabeah was at the kerb and they climbed into it. It was shaded from the hot sun, and Chrys was delighted that Maud hadn't chosen one of the more modern closed-in cabs. Chrys settled herself for the drive to the railway station, the shadows of the awning fringe dancing against her face as Maud settled up with the men who had now loaded their cases and the much-travelled trunk on to the floor of the cab.

Then they were off, clattering gaily through the narrow streets of closely built houses, their wooden balconies forming a sort of broken bridge above the heads of the people and the various vehicles that honked and clanked their way over the uneven paving stones of the roads that ran like a maze through the town.

Chrys breathed the tangy aromas that came from the hooded shops and houses, and gazed with brilliantly alive eyes at the Eastern scene. It was still the middle of the morning, so the town was clamorous. But later on, when the sun reached its zenith, the people would disappear behind closed shutters and silence would fall over Port Said. Every shadow would stand still in the blazing heat, and not a lizard or the tail of a cat would be seen.

The strangest sight of all was outside the railway station, where a band of dancers in robes and turbans were whirling to the wailing music of pipes and drums. Chrys, who was interested in all forms of dancing, was naturally intrigued and could have stayed watching for quite a while, but Maud said they would lose their train and there wouldn't be another to Beni Kezar for hours and she wanted to reach the desert town before nightfall.

"There's a small hotel there and no real need to book in advance for the one or two nights we shall be staying, but if we arrive late the chances are that we shan't find a porter to manage our baggage." Maud smiled and patted Chrys on the arm. "There will be plenty of colourful characters where we shall be going, and plenty of time for you to watch their antics."

"Coming," said Chrys, with a farewell glance at the dancers, and beyond them to the mosque with its great studded doors and a square shaped minaret slotted with glass like a great lantern. She saw a grey Citroen car sweep into the kerb and a heavily robed figure emerged from it, sweeping past the orange-sellers and the peddlers of charms, matches and postcards with an imperious disregard for the charms that his full sleeve swept from the tray of one of the youths.

Instinctively Chrys darted forward to help the youth retrieve his wares, and she felt the fierce glance that stabbed at her from beneath the Arabian headcloth bound with an *agal* of golden thread. She ignored the look, knowing full well that upper class Arabs disapproved of women such as herself, who saw no harm in helping the boy to pick up the cheap little charms out of the dust. Arrogant brute!

"Here you are," she said to the boy. "That seems to be the lot."

He didn't understand her, of course, but with a quick shy smile he thrust one of the charms into her hand and obviously said in Arabic that she was to have it for helping him.

"Take it," said Maud at her elbow. "And for heaven's sake don't offer to pay for it. These people are as proud as Lucifer, and grateful as saints for a kindly helping hand. Just say to him, *naharic saide.*"

Chrys obeyed with a smile, and tucked the charm into the pocket of her blazer.

"What do the words mean?" she asked Maud, as they entered the station, with a pair of porters in tow with their belongings.

"May your day be blessed. Lovely words, aren't they? The Arabic mode of speech really is a graceful one, although the men have such throaty voices that they appear to be growling instead of speaking almost biblical language. The East was always my husband's favourite place to visit. He brought me here as a bride." Maud laughed nostalgically. "Although at that time I thought it rather unfeeling of him to bring me to the desert on a dig when I was dreaming of a country cottage and strolling hand in hand along a flowery lane. But I soon learned to love life *en grande tente*, surrounded by miles of untamed desert. I enjoyed digging up relics of the past alongside Malcolm, and I missed him like the devil when he died. That's the trouble with love. It doesn't die with the people who engender it ... it lives on. You might be wise, young Chrys, if you can avoid love. But on the other hand ..."

The unfinished words were significant, and Chrys said prosaically, "I should like to send off a wire to my parents if possible. Just to let them know I've arrived safely at Port Said. My mother thought I was off to the wilds when I went to Russia, and this time she believes I shall disappear into the desert and be seen no more!"

"The telegraph desk is in this direction." Maud led the way through the clamour of the crowd, and when they reached the counter, she left Chrys to write her wire while she went to the news-stand to buy papers and magazines for the train journey. It wasn't until Chrys had her fair head bent over her task that she suddenly felt a hand feeling its way stealthily into her pocket. She knew that her face blanched as she realized that her pocket was being picked, and she swung round with a cry of protest which immediately caught the attention of a tall, robed figure at an adjoining counter. There was a flash of arrogant eyes within the shadow of the *burnous*; a glimpse of a thin dark moustache across the upper lip of the lean, foreign face. It was the same man who had knocked the charms from the peddler's tray, and Chrys wished to goodness that she had kept a tighter hold on her nerves. The pickpocket had slid away into the crowd, and all that he took with him was the cheap little charm, for obeying Maud's injunction Chrys carried her purse firmly in her hand.

"*Pardon, mademoiselle!*" The Arab spoke in accented French. "You have some further trouble with a youth of the town?"

She flushed vividly, for the sarcastic words implied

that she was a flirt who had been asking to be annoyed. "It is perfectly all right, m'sieur. Someone trod on my foot."

"I thought for a moment that you had been robbed." He made a significant movement with a lean, sun-dark hand. "Women such as yourself are a natural target for the bold, bad element swarming here in Port Said."

"What do you mean – women like myself?" Her eyes blazed in her face, from which the flush had abruptly fled leaving her cheeks pale with annoyance. It seemed to her that the arrogant superiority of this Sheik, as she supposed he was, was far more infuriating than the sidling up to her of a petty thief. The thief had got away with something valueless, but this man seemed to imply that she was a fool . . . or worse.

"You are a tourist, are you not?" he said. "On your first trip to the East, I presume. You should be more on your guard, *mademoiselle*. The next time an attempt might be made to steal your person."

"Really!"

"Yes, really." The eyes that glinted within the folds of the gold-roped headcloth seemed to be infinitely mocking, and yet at the same time diabolically in earnest. Then as Maud approached the counter, the Arab bowed and strolled off with a tall, haughty self-assurance, making no sound as he moved away, like an alert and graceful animal.

"Don't tell me you've been flirting with one of the local Sheiks?" said Maud, half amused, and half serious. "It doesn't do –"

"On the contrary! The darned man was being officious and sarcastic." Chrys gazed after him with fury in her eyes, noticing how the crowd fell back to give passage to his robed figure. "He seemed to imply that I should be on a lead and not allowed to run free. I expect he's one of those who has a harem filled with tame gazelles!"

"Very likely," laughed Maud. "Now have you sent off your wire?"

"No, but I won't be a moment." Chrys quickly scribbled a message of reassurance to her parents and handed the form to the clerk. Then she went with Maud to the train, where they settled themselves in a first-class carriage, and Chrys listened to the excited voices of the passengers and the porters, and remembered amidst the strangeness of it all the accident at a London railway station which had led her to this moment. Her face was reflective, and after several moments she became aware that Maud was gazing at her with a hint of curiosity.

"Still thinking about your brush with the Sheik?" she asked.

Chrys shook her head. "He had the type of arrogance I hoped I'd seen for the last time. There was something in his manner – a sort of mocking superiority – which reminded me of someone else. I suppose men of the East, and those who assume their ways, have an affinity – but it's rather disturbing to suddenly see it again."

"The men who inspire anger and fury, and a sort of fear, are deeply fascinating to some women." Maud opened a magazine with an air of casualness. "Sure you aren't fascinated?"

"Quite sure," said Chrys, and suddenly she laughed. "For someone who threatened me with hell if I should lose my head over a man, you seem, Maud, determined to awake my interest in one of the brutes."

"It isn't that," said Maud. "I merely find it hard to believe that someone as pretty as yourself should have her head so well screwed on. Any other girl would have been in a regular dither of excitement to be spoken to by a Sheik. He was obviously that from the look of him, and the manner. You do realize that some of these personages have a lineage as ancient as that of an English duke? They expect to be treated as if the sun shines out of their eyes."

"Especially by a member of the female sex, eh?" Chrys crossed her long slim legs and admired the blue and white styling of her court shoes. "Well, I don't suppose we shall be seeing that particular desert hawk again, so I'm not about to worry that I spoke up to him instead of swooning."

"I saw him board this train, as a matter of fact." Maud flicked the pages of her magazine. "He entered a reserved compartment, with the curtains drawn, and for all we know he might be travelling to Beni Kezar. Destiny, or *kismet* as the Arabs call it, might throw you into his path again. If so, then you'd better give him a smile or two. He may be the local *kaid*, who has the power to give or withold permission for horses and porters to be supplied for our trip to the ruins."

"He may be no more than an overbearing Arab with an inflated sense of his own importance," said Chrys. "Ah, the train is starting! We're on our way!"

"You sound like an eager kid on her way to a sandy beach instead of the vast and mysterious desert." Maud looked indulgent. "I'm glad you aren't the nervous sort, or haven't you yet realized that the desert is hot and lonely and unpredictable?"

Chrys thought over Maud's words, and for the first time she seemed to realize that she was heading into a world of lonely vistas and hot bright noons filled with the silence of eternity. Her blue eyes dwelt on her employer and for the briefest of moments a little fear and uncertainty stirred in their depths. She had given no heed to her parents' suggestion that she work in Westcliff and live at home with them during her year of enforced retirement from her ballet career. She had rushed headlong into this job, as if she needed desperately to get away from England, and it was only now that she felt a sense of dislocation, the jolt of being miles from the safety and security of the seaside town where she had been born and gone to school, and knew every street.

"Chrys, have I made you feel uncertain?" Maud asked.

At once the hint of fear was veiled by Chrys's lashes.

She shook her head. "The strangeness of it all just swept over me – you know, a feeling of being wafted as if on a magic carpet from the places so well known to the edge of the unknown. I read somewhere that the desert is a sphinx, which accepts some people and rejects others."

"It is a place of moods," Maud agreed. "It can be capricious, and inclined like a jealous lover to expect total surrender to its mixed charms. Look out of the window, Chrys, and see the unveiling of some of those charms."

Chrys looked and caught her breath in delight. The train swept past a huge oasis of towering palms, whose sleek trunks and pendant leaves were reflected in the mirror-like surface of a huge pool. On the edges of the oasis there was a native village, and the inhabitants could be seen going about their tasks in their dark blue robes, while camels stood tethered like sand-coloured idols among the trees.

It was like a tapestry, vividly seen and then swiftly out of focus as the train sped on its way.

It was the first glimpse Chrys had had of the pastoral East, almost a scene from the Old Testament itself, and her quick sense of adventure swiftly banished from her eyes, and her thoughts, that flash of alienation. She sat close to the window and drank in the various scenes of village life, to which Maud was so accustomed that she read a magazine article while Chrys absorbed with growing wonder the sand-gardens of the village dwellers, the children with dark-honey skins, graceful and thin as fawns as they darted among the houses of sun-tried mud, flat-roofed and slotted with narrow dark windows and doors.

Cups of tea were brought to them about noon, and Maud unpacked the sandwiches and tomatoes which the *chef* of the cargo ship had supplied. "I don't care for the lunches served on trains," she said. "The chops are usually tough and everything is smothered in mint sauce."

Chrys was perfectly happy to lunch here in their compartment, picnic fashion. The sandwiches, some of smoked salmon and others of thinly sliced beef, were delicious, and she knew in her secret thoughts that she didn't fancy seeing again that tall, fierce Arab with the black moustache like a whiplash across his upper lip. He had seemed capable of carrying out any threat to a woman, being what he was, an Arab to whom women were mere objects of pleasure, or displeasure.

She ate a beef sandwich and felt certain that like the desert itself the attitudes of its men had not changed for centuries. It was not a country to engender, or invite change. It was ruled by the sands, which encroached upon each mile of cultivation like the greedy seas that gnawed the cliffs of northern lands. Already she had glimpsed one or two veiled women, and the strangeness of those covered faces still lingered in her mind to underline the *purdah* attitudes still deeply ingrained in the Eastern soul.

After lunch it grew terribly warm in the compartment, and though Maud drowsed, Chrys found the heat almost suffocating and all at once she had to escape into the corridor to try and get a breath of air.

She arose from her seat and carefully opened the door of the carriage. She stepped outside and immediately felt a welcoming breeze along the passageway. She had discarded her blazer and it was such a relief to feel the slight coolness against her neck and her bare arms.

Lost in her relief, leaning with eyes half-closed as the train sped through the hot sunlight towards its destination, she was unaware of a figure at the far end of the corridor until the aroma of a cigarette began to steal to her on that whisper of a breeze. But for several moments more her relaxation was undisturbed, until suddenly her nostrils taughtened, her senses grew alert, and every nerve in her body came alive to the fact that the aroma of the smoke was strangely familiar ... and had no place to be so, here on this oriental train!

Her eyes flashed open and she turned her head and saw instantly the tall figure in the flowing robes. He stood yards away from her, silent and still, and yet directly she noticed him he became as intrusive as a bee inside the glass of the windows.

Even as a sense of animosity flickered through her, the familiarity of the cigarette smoke was explained. She must have caught a whiff of it on his robes, when she had stood near to him at the telegraph counter. She resented his presence, even though he seemed unaware of her. He made it seem almost compulsory that she return to the guardianship of Maud, to sit sedately in that stuffy carriage until the afternoon heat waned and gave the relief that she wanted right now.

Well, she wouldn't retreat, unless he had the nerve to approach her.

He didn't stir an inch in her direction, yet all the time Chrys remained in the corridor she was aware of him, and she hated the strength of his silent personality and the unsettling effect he had upon her. In the end she wanted to return to the calm company of Maud, and when she finally did so she felt ridiculously like a female in flight.

She didn't tell Maud that she had seen the Arab again, but was glad when as the sunset flared over the sands the train arrived at Beni Kezar and they were kept too busy checking their baggage as it was loaded on to a trolley to notice if the Arab left the train at the same station as themselves.

"That seems to be everything," said Maud. "Now let's get to the hotel for a cool bath, and a nice hot dinner."

"Amen to that," said Chrys, and as they left the station into the dusk of the evening she glanced up at the sky and saw a shooting star falling through the velvety darkness. "Oh, look! How lovely, Maud!"

"You might think so," said Maud drily. "The arabs believe that a shooting star is an arrow of Allah thrown to pierce an earthly devil."

503

"It could be cupid at work," jested Chrys, and then she caught her breath as a moment before they entered their cab she saw a tall, unmistakable figure enter an adjacent cab and drive off into the night.

Maud gave her an enquiring look as she caught her small gasp. "I hope the 'arrow' hasn't pierced you, Chrys."

Chrys smiled, and once again she kept silent about seeing the Arab, but as their cab swept through the dark streets to the hotel she prayed fervently that they wouldn't see him there, lording it over everyone.

It wasn't a large hotel and they were soon shown to their adjoining rooms, with a bathroom close by. "I'm dying for a bath, so it's age before beauty," said Maud. "I'm told that dinner is at eight, so we have plenty of time to dress for it. See you later!"

Left entirely alone at last, Chrys unpacked what she would need for the night, and then went out on the balcony to take a look at Beni Kezar by the light of the stars. Plumbago plant sprawled all over the ironwork of the balcony, and the air held a tangy freshness which Chrys breathed in to the bottom of her lungs. That air came from the desert, she surmised, and she leaned forward and explored with her eyes the rooftops and minarets of this desert town. Beyond its walls lay the savage, untamed sands. Wild, relentless place of dreams, and demonic sunlight. Scandalous and secretive as a woman, holding, so it was said, heaven and hell for those who dared to travel there.

There were ruins about fifteen miles from Beni Kezar which Maud wanted to see again. She had last visited the place with her husband, and Chrys suspected that her employer wished to renew old memories far more than she wished to search for relics.

Anyway, whatever her reason it would be interesting, and would surely add to Chrys's own experiences of life.

She returned to her bedroom, to find Maud in the adjoining doorway, towelling her short hair. "The bathroom is all yours, Chrys. The hot water system hums like a rocket about to take off, but it actually works. Mmm I feel so refreshed after that stuffy train journey, so now you cut along and have your soak."

Chrys was off at a run, and there in the ornately tiled bathroom she emptied about half a bottle of cologne into the water and sank her slim body into it with a sigh of sheer luxury. She splashed about for as long as she dared, and returned to her room feeling thoroughly refreshed herself. She was almost dressed for dinner and putting on her nylons when Maud entered, clad in beige lace and winding the small gold watch on her wrist. "It's nice to dress up," she said, "and we shan't be able to in the desert. Shirts and shorts will be the order of the day there – my, Chrys, you do have nice hair! Mine was almost that colour when I was a girl, but the years and many hot suns have taken out all the colour and left me quite grey. You are almost Nordic, Chrys. Any of that blood in your family?"

"Not as far as I know. My sister Dove is fairer still." Chrys fixed her floss-combed hair into a tortoiseshell slide, and ran a powder-puff over her face.

"When we get into the desert, Chrys, I'm going to suggest that you wear a hat. I have a floppy-brimmed one which will suit you. The Arabs rather like golden hair – it's such a contrast to the brunette hair of their own wives and girls."

"Now don't you go telling me that I'm likely to be carried off," Chrys protested, half laughing, and half serious. "That darned Arab threatened me with the same fate!"

"The one at the station?" Maud stared at Chrys, the smile wiped from her lips. "You realize that he's here at Beni Kezar?"

"So you noticed as well?"

"Could hardly avoid doing so. He's unusually tall, and those golden head-ropes mean he's an important man. Did he really make such a threat?"

"Well, I felt a hand in my pocket – that little charm

was stolen while I was at the telegraph counter, and he noticed and said I had better be careful or someone might steal *me* next time."

"Very likely he was kidding you," said Maud, "but let's hope we don't run into him again. I don't suppose he's the *kaid* of Beni Kezar, or there would have been a contingent of bodyguards with him. He's probably a local landowner, with a big house somewhere on the edge of the town."

"With high walls and a *harem* somewhere inside them." Chrys tilted her nose in scorn. "If he has ideas about adding me to his collection, then he's in for a shock. I was once told that I'd scratch like a sand cat if I was ever taken advantage of."

"I believe you would, at that." Maud looked her companion over, and a hint of worry showed in her eyes. "You dress so simply and manage to look so eye-catching. I wonder if I did right to take you on as a companion. This place is half off the map, and some of its people are still rather primitive. Chrys, when we make camp in the desert, promise me that you'll never stray too far away. I don't know how I'd face your parents if anything happened to you."

"Maud, I'm twenty-two and perfectly capable of taking care of myself." Suddenly it was Chrys who was offering Maud reassurance. "I'm sure I'm far too thin to attract the roving eye of an Arab. I thought they fed their women on honey and doughnuts in order to make them nice and plump. Look at me! I haven't an ounce of fat on me."

"True," said Maud, breaking into a smile. "Let's go and remedy that right now. I'm ravenous!"

They locked their doors and made their way down to the hotel dining room. There were very few guests, and they were the only Europeans at the present time. A waiter conducted them to an alcove table, where in comparative privacy they ordered their meal from the man, who was clad in spotless white, except for a red cumerbund and turban. Maud ordered for both of them, juicy lamb cutlets, runner beans, and creamed potatoes. And as a starter, savouries wrapped in vine leaves, with a plate of rice and mushrooms. She vetoed wine, murmuring in an aside to Chrys that Arabs looked down on women who imbibed. Instead she asked for Arabian coffee, which was brought to them with their savouries.

It was a rich, hot, satisfying meal, and Chrys was able to eat with appetite because that arrogant Sheik was nowhere in sight to watch her every action. No doubt he was enjoying *kous-kous*, surrounded by his adoring flock of kohl-eyed concubines!

"You'll have a sweet to finish with?" said Maud.

"Please, but nothing too sweet after that very satisfying dinner. Fruit perhaps."

"Fruit it shall be." Maud called the waiter and told him they should like some grapes, washed in ice-water. While they waited for the grapes to be brought to them, Chrys fingered the bowl of apricot-coloured roses which stood on the table. For some reason they made her think of high white walls and rambling cloisters, and sheets of greenery studded with these delicate and highly scented roses.

She gave a start as another of the silent-footed waiters came to her side and with a small bow handed her a small box, waxed and sealed, but unmistakably with her name printed on the label.

"What is it? What does he say, Maud?" She looked at the package as if it contained a small bomb.

"He says a man brought it and requested that it be given to Mademoiselle Devrel. Take it, Chrys," Maud urged, "and stop looking as if it might explode in your face."

"Whatever can it be?" Chrys took the box and murmured her thanks to the waiter. "No one here knows my name, apart from the hotel manager."

"It looks to me suspiciously like a present," said Maud. "Do open it and find out, or I shall bust a stitch with curiosity."

"But I don't know anyone here at Beni Kezar who could be sending me a present. It must be a hoax!" Picking up a knife, Chrys inserted the blade under the seal and broke it. Then she lifted the lid of the box and found inside a small card, and with a frown she read the few words written upon it in perfect French. "A small token to replace what was removed from your pocket." Without speaking Chrys handed the card to Maud, who read it and then looked at Chrys significantly.

"What has he sent you to replace the charm?"

Chrys lifted the cottonwool in the box and disclosed a tiny gold hand, perfectly made, with a blue gem set in the back of it. "Look, Maud!"

"The Hand of Fatma, and a very beautiful example of the charm." Maud looked intently at Chrys. "I know you will want to refuse it, knowing who has sent it to you, but I would advise you against returning it to the Sheik. He will not only be highly insulted, but out here no one takes lightly the significance of Fatma's hand. You will see it impressed into the walls and lintels of the houses, and women hang the charm around the necks of their newborn children. It is said to bring good fortune to those who wear it."

"But, Maud, this charm is made of gold, and the gem in the back of it looks like a small sapphire. How can I accept from such a man a gift like this? He may presume that I wish to encourage him, and that's the last thing I want to do!"

"Not if you accept the charm with a polite little note. You know, 'Dear Sir, It is good of you to send me the Hand of Fatma, and I feel certain it will make my visit to Beni Kezar a pleasant one.' There's nothing coy or inviting about that sort of note."

"You seem to be making it a point of honour that I accept the charm." Chrys fingered its smoothness, with each detail of the hand etched with minute perfection, adorned by that gleaming little sapphire. It was as if he had had her eyes in mind, and she gave a little shiver as she remembered the glint of his eyes within the almost monk-like head-covering which had prevented her from seeing his face clearly. All she knew for certain was that he wore a thin dark moustache, which was somehow significant of the inherent danger of the man.

"I believe he meant to put me in an awkward position," she said to Maud. "He probably thinks that I will return the charm and give him cause to feel insulted, so I'm going to surprise him and keep it. It's really rather pretty, isn't it?"

Maud smiled a little, for Chry spoke with a touch of defiance which revealed her inmost doubts about accepting the golden hand. "Oriental men are darned subtle," she said, popping a black grape into her mouth. "But I certainly think it better for you to accept the gift than refuse it. It doesn't do to offend these people, and if you type your note of thanks on my machine, then it will seem more impersonal than if you wrote it. I notice that he's highly educated. His French is far more perfect than mine. Did you notice if he was good-looking? Some of these men are extremely so, though on the other side of the coin you do find some of them as round as barrels, with enough hair on them to stuff a sofa."

Chrys smiled absently, and wished to goodness the donor of the gift had been rotund and bearded and fatherly. She shook her head when Maud proffered the dish of grapes, and was glad when it was time to go upstairs and sleep.

She felt curiously disturbed on this her first night in the East, and it took her some time to fall asleep beneath the fine muslin swathing her bed.

On the bedside table lay the Hand of Fatma, an appealing little charm, and yet somehow significant of the subtle codes of honour and quicksilver temper of the people of the East.

CHAPTER VIII

DESPITE having lain awake until quite late, Chrys awoke feeling invigorated and ready for the day that lay ahead of her. She lay gazing up at the tent of pale green netting over her bed, and saw the sun as through gauze striking through the long opened windows. Alien sounds drifted up from the streets that lay at either side of the hotel; she heard goat bells, and the clatter of donkey hooves, and then there came the cry of the *muezzin* from the nearby mosque. *Allah ila la Allah.* So it was still quite early, despite the warm gush of sunshine into her room.

The sun was so beckoning that Chrys could not lie idle another second and she pushed aside the yards of mosquito netting and slid out of bed. The polished wooden floor was warm under her feet, and when she glanced at her travelling clock she was surprised to find that it wasn't long after daybreak.

She opened the adjoining door and saw that Màud was still fast asleep. Well, she wasn't going to waste all this wonderful sunlight by lazing in bed herself, so Chrys hastened to the bathroom, had a wash, and returned to dress herself in narrow white trousers and a lemon shirt. She clipped back her hair, dashed lipstick over her mouth, and decided to have a look at the market stalls that were setting up in the streets below.

She felt delightfully cool, and looked it as she made her way downstairs to the foyer. There were only a couple of the staff about, emptying ashtrays and flower vases, and polishing the floor, and they gave her a rather startled look as she left the hotel. It was evident that the other guests were not such early risers, probably taking breakfast in their rooms, until it was time to go sightseeing in a horse-drawn cab.

As Chrys stepped into the street, a dozen mixed aromas sprang at her. That of Arabian coffee and spices, and the stronger smell of the goats and donkeys. She turned into an alleyway, and found herself in a sort of street of coppersmiths, with highly polished bowls and pans displayed on colourful old carpets. She saw a boy glossing the surface of a great meat dish with a handful of sawdust and lemon, and heard the little hammers beating against the pewter.

Some of the traders coaxed her to buy their wares, but she walked on resolutely, knowing full well that if she stopped to admire anything she would find herself involved in a bargain for it. She turned out of the street of coppersmiths into another that sold leather goods, slippers of all colours, some of them for babies and made of the very softest of leather. There were purses and satchels for sale, and beautiful bags on a shoulder strap buckled with silver or brass. Chrys would have loved to buy one, but she hadn't enough cash with her.

She wandered through the street of silks, and came at last to the stalls selling jewellery and trinkets of every hue, some of it worthless, and some of it quite stunning. She saw a tray of charms, and was reminded of yesterday, and the Hand of Fatma which she had left on her bedside table, gleaming like a small living object as the sunlight touched it. She compared it to other similar charms she saw on the stalls, and knew that it was different, and of greater value.

She came upon carpets being sold in an open court-yard, where they were laid out to show their wonderful patterns, with several lovely Persian cats curled among them. It was like wandering into the Arabian Nights, and her nostrils tautened to the drift of perfume from funny little cubbyholes in the very walls of the *souk*. She peered into one of these tiny scent shops and was beckoned in by the perfume-seller, to have her wrist stroked with a little glass rod dipped into carnation and rose perfume, into orange-flower, jasmine and musk. The phials lay in dozens of little drawers, and she couldn't resist the temptation of a scent called Rapture of the Desert, and another for Maud.

The *souk* lay in a maze which brought her directly back to the hotel, and this time there were guests in the foyer, who greeted her with smiles and wished her a good morning in French or German. It seemed that these days British people came less often to the East, and she felt the young foreigner as she glanced into the restaurant to see if Maud had yet come down to breakfast.

Ah, there she was! Seated at the table they had shared at dinner last night, and in conversation with a young man Chrys had not seen before. He wore khaki trousers and a white shirt, tucked into a black leather belt that matched his kneeboots. When Maud spotted Chrys and waved, the man turned round and stared at her. He was about thirty and had a tanned face surmounted by hair so light it looked bleached.

Maud introduced him as Peter Dorn and said that he was already working at the diggings and that he had been a pupil of her husband's. He shook Chrys's hand and she was unsurprised when he spoke to her with a Dutch accent.

"This is very much a delightful surprise, Miss Devrel. When I heard that Maud had arrived at Beni Kezar with a new companion, well I did not expect to find that companion so – young."

Maud grinned and invited him to stay and have breakfast with them. "I don't doubt that you've already had rolls and coffee, but being a Dutchman, Peter, I'm sure you can put away some bacon and eggs."

"I think I can." He sat down beside Chrys, and she saw his nostrils flicker as he caught the aroma of the scents the Arab had applied to her skin. "I will guess that you have been wandering in the *souk*, eh? And were enticed into one of those mysterious little perfumeries?"

"I couldn't resist buying something." Chrys handed Maud a phial of scent across the table. "Yours is called

Garden of Carnations, Maud."

"How nice of you, Chrys, to think of an old woman!" Maud immediately stroked the tiny glass rod against her throat. "Mmmm, I'm now likely to get carried off to the tent of an amorous man of the desert."

Chrys laughed, while she felt Peter Dorn gazing inquisitively at the Arabic lettering on her own phial of scent. "Do you believe that rapture might be found in the desert, Miss Devrel?" His sky-blue eyes met hers and they were teasing and at the same time inquisitive.

"All I really hope to acquire is a sun tan, a good riding horse, and a little knowledge of how to dig for ancient relics," she replied, giving him a very candid look without a hint of flirtation in it. He was a good-looking man, with virile forearms fleeced with blond hair, but Chrys looked as undisturbed as if he had been an elderly professor. When the waiter came to the table she asked Maud to order for her scrambled eggs, kidneys and toast. "I'm ravenous after my explorations. One could spend a fortune in that *souk*. Such carpets! And some of that copper and pewter ware! Not to mention the handbags! All handmade and with something inimitable about them."

"I will judge that you have had your first taste of being fascinated by the East and its oriental witchery," said Peter Dorn. "Beware. It can cast spells over certain people, and they find themselves unable to break the spell. Have you yet seen the sun set over the desert sands?"

She shook her head. "I must admit, mijhneer, that it's an experience to which I am looking forward with a great deal of interest. I have seen pictures of such sunsets, but I have not yet seen the reality. Is it as magical as I have heard?"

"Even more so — and may I call you by your first name? Is it Christine?"

"No, it's Chrys, spelled like the beginning of the flower."

"Very nice. I like it." He spoke with Dutch decision.

513

"You must allow me to find a good horse for you, and then you must allow me to show you your first sunset."

"Thank you." Chrys glanced at Maud. "When shall we be making camp in the desert?"

"If Peter can help arrange matters with the local *kaid*, then I thought we might set up camp tomorrow. Today we could do some sight-seeing, and buy provisions, and have tea in the gardens of the mosque. What do you say, Chrys?"

"Marvellous!" Her eyes glowed, and the sun through the windows stroked the tawny-gold of her hair. She felt young and zestful, and that depression of the past few weeks had lifted suddenly from her spirits. Madame de Casenove had been right to urge her to come to the East. It was a place of forgetfulness, so far from familiar things, and with an underlying sense of mystery of which she had been conscious ever since setting foot on Eastern soil.

She tucked into her breakfast with youthful appetite, and was watched admiringly by the Dutchman. "What a change to see a young woman enjoy her food these days," he said to Maud. "I thought they were all on strict diets to preserve their svelte figures."

"Chrys is the energetic sort who burns off the spare inches. She was up with the lark this morning, and isn't one of your indolent creatures of glamour, Peter. That's why I wanted her for my companion. I can't stand the bored and primping sort, who scream at crawlies, and want men in attendance all the time."

"Well, I shall be in attendance at the camp, but I hope you won't mind too much." Peter Dorn's smile was charming, and not overbearingly sure of itself. "I shall try to blend in with the background."

"An Arab might succeed in that, but not a Dutchman," drawled Maud. "I have an idea Chrys and myself will quite enjoy having you around. I hoped, in fact, that you might be at the diggings, but wasn't sure if you had returned from Peru. How was it there?"

"Cold." He gave an expressive shiver. "I was glad to

get to the desert, and was most pleased when I found your letter awaiting me here at the hotel. To work again with Malcolm's wife is always a pleasure."

"You're gallant, Peter." Maud bowed her head in acknowledgement of his compliment, both to herself and her late husband. "You were always his favoured pupil ... ah, they were good days, and I think I travel so much these days in order to keep myself from being lonely."

Maud and Peter talked about the days gone by, while Chrys drank her coffee and listened to them. He stayed at Beni Kezar all the morning, helping them to arrange about porters to take their baggage to the camp site on the following day, and he also went with them to the *kaid*'s stables, where they hired their mounts and received official permission to use the waterhole at the camp site. Peter then had to get back to the dig and said regretfully that he wished he could spare the time to take tea with them that afternoon.

They watched him ride off, and Maud looked well pleased. "I'm glad we have a European male at the camp," she said. "We shall sleep easier at night."

"I had no idea that you had a few old-fashioned ideas, Maud." Chrys spoke teasingly. "I believed you were fully emancipated from the idea of male protection."

"Oh, I can take care of myself," Maud said at once. "But I have with me on this trip a young and attractive girl who has already caught the eye of one of the local Sheiks."

"Don't remind me!" Chrys tried to sound flippant, but now that Maud mentioned the man, she was glad herself that Peter Dorn would be on hand to look big, blond and masculine. "I suppose I have to accept his blessed charm?"

"Just to be diplomatic, Chrys. Come along, we'll type him a polite note of thanks and arrange for a boy to deliver it to him."

"But we don't know his name or address," Chrys

515

pointed out.

"The waiter will know. The one who brought the package to you."

But it turned out that the waiter didn't know, for he was a new employer at the hotel and had not been resident before at Beni Kezar, so it seemed like fate that Chrys should have to accept the Hand of Fatma without even a word of thanks for it.

"*Mektub, mektub*," said Maud philosophically.

When later on they drove to the mosque gardens for tea, the sky was a clear, unclouded blue and the air was as heady and dazzling as great sips of champagne. Chrys leaned forward in the *arabeah* and filled her eyes with all the passing scenery, crowned by the great palms, which all seemed to take a natural *salaam* above the heads of the people, and the line of camels marching solemnly in the direction of the desert, loads of bedding and pots swaying on their backs, the women and children walking among them while the men rode high on the humps.

"What a typical sign of male superiority!" said Chrys scornfully.

"Not really." Maud looked at her companion with twinkling eyes. "The camel is a truculent beast and they need firm guidance or they'd dash off like hares with all those Bedouin belongings heading for Timbuctoo. They aren't too comfortable to sit, which is another reason why the women much prefer to walk. See how gracefully they walk! Being curled up on the neck of a camel would spoil that posture of theirs, and they know it. Can you hear the bells on their ankles? These women are the most feminine in the world, and they often choose quite deliberately to wear that one-eyed veil."

"So in the East, what one sees is not always the obvious truth." Chrys gazed after the Bedouin women in their long indigo blue robes, with a lilt to their walk and a magical sort of music at their heels. "Maud, it must take years to come to terms with the contradictions of these people!"

"Of course, my dear. You won't learn everything in a mere matter of weeks. Did you like Peter?"

"He's charming, but aren't you afraid, Maud, that I shall lose my head over him?"

"Somehow I don't see it happening. Two fair people rarely click, for nature has a positive love of opposites." And to bear out her statement, when they reached the gardens Maud took Chrys to see all the varied plants and flowers, growing in a profusion that took licence from the sun. The petunias, the gold and red nasturtiums, starry violet jasmine, and peonies like flame in contrast to the huge white geraniums, and sheets of purple bougainvillaea.

The sun picked out glittering motes in the bright tiles of the forecourt of the white mosque. Pigeons strutted on the stone coping of the fountains, and the drowsy perfume of the flowers mingled with that of the water against the hot stone.

Chrys felt again as if she had wandered into the Arabian Nights, and almost hypnotic was the sound of the cicadas hidden like leaves among the juniper and cypress trees.

This was not prayer time, so they were allowed into the lower hall of the mosque, with its painted panels like Persian carpets, and its marble-tiled floor, and cupola-arched doorways. A sigh was like a whisper, a whisper was like a shout, and the air was filled with an essence of musk and sandalwood and crushed jasmine petals.

They were served with tea and cakes beneath a giant fig tree, which stretched its branches and hung its great leaves like a green parasol above them.

"It's all very beautiful," Chrys murmured. "Achingly so."

"Wait until you see the magnificent loneliness of the desert ... that will really set your imagination soaring. It's an added blessing that you can ride."

"I learned when I was younger, but I haven't done

much riding in the past few years. A dancer has to take care of her legs."

"I daresay," said Maud drily. "It wouldn't look exactly artistic to see a bow-legged ballet dancer. Missing your old haunts yet?"

"No, they all seem strangely far away." Chrys caught her breath. "I think the lure of the East has come upon me, Maud. I thought I could be cool and distant towards all this, but suddenly I feel like a moth caught up in the threads of a gaudy web. I'm sunstruck, overwhelmed, and too entranced to struggle for my freedom. The sensation is dreamlike ... shall I wake in a while and find myself alone in the flat I shared with Dove?"

"Do you want to?" Maud studied the face of Chrys beneath the shifting green light of the fig leaves.

Chrys considered the question and then shook her head. "While I had my dancing I had all I needed. But now – now I have become vulnerable like other lonely people. I believe the East calls to the lonely at heart."

"It does, Chrys, and you are sensitive enough to realize it."

"You have no more doubts, Maud, about bringing me here?" Chrys spoke seriously. "I don't want to be a liability. I'll wear that floppy hat, even dress like a boy, if it will make me seem less – alien to the Arabs."

"I don't think," drawled Maud, "that it will be thought quite proper if a young boy is seen in the double tent, especially at night. Arabs have a rather salacious sense of humour. No, things should be quite safe with Peter Dorn at the dig."

They took a final stroll around the lovely gardens before driving home to the hotel. While Maud paid the driver Chrys stood and gazed at the sky, where the sun seemed to be smouldering away in a fountain of colour and flame. She visualised the sands of the desert bathed in that riot of colour, barbarous and yet beautiful, and the image quickened her breath and made her lips part ... almost as if ready to receive a kiss. She was looking like that as a car came to a halt at the corner of the square, in front of one of the old, shuttered-looking Arab houses that faced the hotel. Three men emerged from the limousine and made their way to the huge, nail-studded door of the house. Each man was robed, and walked with that feline grace so apparent in some of the Arabian people. Dignity and aloofness matched that grace, and as Chrys glanced across the road one of the men turned a moment and looked directly at her, standing there in her pale dress in the rich dying light of the sun.

It was no mistake, the height, the stance, and the gleam of a high red boot under the great cloak. He even seemed to incline his covered head slightly, and she pictured a smile curling on the well-cut lips under the black moustache.

Then the great door of the Arabian house was opened and the trio of men disappeared into the courtyard, with its glimpses of a fountain and the tall silhouettes of palm trees. Then the door closed, but Chrys had the disquieting feeling that eyes gazed at her through the narrow iron grille in the door, and she felt them to be mocking and dangerously persistent as the eyes of a tiger stalking its prey.

She was glad to escape into the hotel with Maud, but when she was alone in her room she picked up the little Hand of Fatma as if compelled and felt in that moment a strange sense of fatalism. He had sent her the charm to let her know they would meet again, out there in the desert, and she was faced with the decision to remain at Beni Kezar, or make some excuse to Maud and catch the late train back to civilization, where men in picturesque robes did not make silent and subtle threats which seemed to sway a girl between flight and fury.

She stood there in the darkening room, the charm clenched in her hand, and she knew that a confrontation with him was inevitable if she entered the desert, the great gold garden, where menace and enticement threw their shadows across the sands.

She would throw this charm in his face and tell him to go to the devil . . . she would tell him scornfully that she wasn't remotely interested in becoming an inmate of his *harem*!

Despite this resolve Chrys awoke the following morning with a knot of tension at the base of her stomach, so that she couldn't eat and drank cups of coffee for her breakfast. She and Maud were setting out early so they wouldn't lose the first coolness of the day and arrive at the camp in the heat of the sun. Chrys was presented with the floppy-brimmed hat which was meant to hide the brightness of her hair, and as she put it on and pulled the brim down over her left eye, she reflected that it was a pity she hadn't been wearing the hat at the railway station, along with her plain shirt and pale brown riding trousers.

"Well, will I pass as a member of a desert dig?" She grinned at Maud, and betrayed not a hint of her nervous excitement, which the coffee had stirred up instead of settled.

The older woman studied her and looked quizzical. "I'm afraid you'd look beguiling in a sack, Chrys. That old hat of mine looks dashing and sort of Garbo-ish on you, and those trousers never looked that good on a boy."

So they set out on this clear and beckoning morning, riding the horses which they had hired from the *kaïd*, with their porters and loaded camels following on behind. Chrys glanced behind her and was fascinated by those long-necked animals, with a leather thong fastened into a nose ring so the driver, seated way up on the powerful humped back, could guide his beast and be master of its truculent disposition.

Soon they had left behind them the old, sun-burned walls of the town and outcrops of rock appeared, breaking through the sand like bare white bone, with scrub-mimosa flowering here and there to make a bright splash of colour.

Hills rose against the dazzling blue sky like the

battlements of old ruined castles, and the breeze that blew across the peachy-coloured sand was filled with a tang of wild, unknown places. The jingle and rustle of the harness was pleasant on the morning air, for the hooves of the animals were muffled by the sand, so that they seemed to be gliding across velvet itself.

They passed a few quiet Bedouin encampments, wherever a small stream flowed among a group of palm trees, where the low black tents were pitched, curtained at one end and wide open at the other, where the cooking fires were built, and where the gold-skinned children played among the goats and the small herds of *mouflon*, the little sheep like balls of wool, and often the only means of support for these rambling gipsy-like families. The black sheep among them wore strings of blue glass beads, Chrys noticed. They were obviously "lambs of Satan" and needed extra protection from the evil eye.

The tall women in their homespun dresses, clad like Ruth and Rachel, filled their fat-bellied waterjars at the stream, and Chrys wondered what it was like to be always a tent-dweller, wandering from oasis to oasis, and bearing with a patient smile the extremes of hot and cold weather, the primitive conditions of being a wife and a mother many miles from the civilized comforts of a city woman's life.

As Chrys rode by on her Arab horse, obviously a girl despite her masculine attire, the Bedouin women gazed after her, and they probably wondered what her life was like. She smiled at them, but they considered her with gravity, as if she were even more strange to them than they could ever be to her. And they were right! The desert was their proper background, into which they blended with a rugged, biblical grace. She in her trousers and brimmed hat must seem to them a peculiar species of womanhood.

When the last encampment was left behind, the horses and their riders, and the laden camels, were engulfed in the silence of the rolling sands, turning to white-gold as the sun rose higher and cast its brilliant hot light down over the desert. The heat of the day was beginning, like a cloak of saffron silk, heavy and clinging as it touched the skin. Chrys became aware of the heat like gloves on her hands as she held the reins of her mount, and the back of her shirt clung against her shoulders. She was glad of the brimmed hat, shielding her untried eyes from the ashen blaze of the sand.

How far away was England and all that had happened there to bring her to this desert. She looked about her, and it was real and not a mirage. The heat and the shimmer of the sands were a living reality and she was a part of it all. She sat upon the red saddle of a grey Arab horse, and was surrounded by a sea of molten gold, sculptured sometimes into the shape of waves . . . glowing and relentless, a place to be lost in without a guide, who sat high on his camel, a pattern of heart-shaped hoof marks left in the sand behind them.

They stopped to drink tea and to eat jammy doughnut puffs in the shade of some rocks, and Maud asked her how she was enjoying her first encounter with the desert.

Chrys looked at Maud and the answer lay in her eyes. In the shadow of the hat's brim they were intensely blue; the magic of it all was trapped in her eyes like a little flame. "It's tormenting and it's wonderful," she said. "It's like nothing else I've ever known."

"You don't find it monotonous?" Maud gave her a very direct look over the rim of her mug of tea. "It must all seem very different from the colour and enchantment of your world of ballet. Ballet was more real to you than real life, so you told me, and now you have seen the primitive desert-dwellers, and the black tents they live and die in, living a life in which theatres and gaiety play no part."

"In the difference of it all lies the fascination." Chrys gazed around at the couched camels, and the porters with their lean faces and fierce eyes that were falcon-like in their quickness and their regard, their feet as tensile as their hands and tanned to the shade of leather. Chrys hugged her mug of tea, and felt as if all the secrets of the silent desert were being slowly revealed for her.

"Seduction isn't true love," Maud murmured. "You might look at it all next week and wish yourself on the steamer home."

Chrys smiled and shook her head, for confidence was suddenly spreading through her like a weed, strangling any last-minute doubts she had about venturing into the Garden of Allah. The desert all around them had become a dazzling ocean of gold, but she was no longer afraid of what it held in store for her.

She crumbled the remnants of a doughnut and threw the crumbs into the shade of a rock. Tiny azure birds flew down on them, making a cawing sound ... despite the hawks of the desert the blue birds still came and made it their home. Perky and pretty, they pecked at the crumbs, bright specks of chestnut on their little backs.

"I think, Maud, that in some ways my training in ballet has prepared me for the desert life. The dance demands a spartan règime and loads of stamina and soul. Even applause cannot spoil a ballerina, for she knows that early the next morning she must be at the *barre*, training alongside the novice, and sweating every bit as hard to keep trim and supple and disciplined. Here in the desert I shall ride and dig and keep fit, but if I had taken a desk job for a year I dread to think of the consequences! It is better for the legs to become a little bowed than for the ballet dancer's bottom to spread!"

Maud laughed and climbed to her feet. "Come along, Pavlova. We've only about another hour's ride to the diggings, and I am sure Peter is impatient for our arrival. He'll get no end of a kick out of taking you on as a pupil, and you may even be lucky enough to find a Roman bowl."

"I'd get a thrill out of that myself." As Chrys swung into the saddle of her horse she felt not a twinge of pain from her back injury and was certain today that fortune smiled on her, almost as warmly as the desert sun.

The porters urged their grumbling camels to their feet, and Chrys half-turned in the saddle to watch the men tuck their bare feet around the long necks of the animals. Bells jingled on the harness of the camels, and the *djellabas* of the men were stark white against the shaggy buff coats. The *cheche* of one of the men was draped almost like a mask across his face, and she felt the glitter of his eyes as he caught her looking at him. At once she looked away from him, and cantered her horse to catch up with Maud.

But as she rode along she was distinctly aware of that rider high on his camel saddle behind her. It was instinctive with her to notice grace of movement, and that particular porter had mounted his animal with long-legged movements of peculiar grace, and up there on that high saddle he didn't slouch but sat there as proudly as a prince.

Her heart jarred strangely in her side. Her thoughts flew over the sands, over the water, to a terrace above the Thames, where she had danced with a man whose movements had been as animal and supple as those of the Arab riding in the wake of her horse. He too had been masked, and she wondered if he was still enjoying the night spots of London, or whether he had yet returned to his house called *Belle Tigresse*.

She felt the quick beating of her heart as she rode along, and fought the odd compulsion to glance again at the porter behind her. Surely it was coincidental that a movement of the body, a turn of the head, a flick of the eyes, had reminded her of a man she would far sooner forget? Surely it was a flash of the old anger that made her blood run fast through her veins! They had parted with bare civility. He had clicked his heels and gone out of her life.

"Beware of melting when you reach the desert," he had said, in that taunting way of his. "And if you do melt, be sure you are in the correct pair of arms."

"There is one thing for sure," she had retorted.

"They will never be *your* arms."

"Perhaps not," he agreed. "But on the other hand there is an old Arab saying to the effect that the most unlikely thing to happen is nearly always the thing that does happen."

It was those words, and the tiny mocking smile at the edge of his mouth, which haunted Chrys and made her look twice at every man she saw out here, seeing in the slightest gesture a resemblance which probably never existed at all.

She restrained herself from looking round and prodded her mount to catch up with Maud's. Probably eager to reach the Roman diggings where she had last searched for coins and relics alongside her husband, Maud had given her mount quite a bit of rein and they had forged well ahead of Chrys when all of a sudden she saw the horse shy wildly at something across his path. The long forelegs threshed the air, and the next instant Maud was flung half out of the saddle, with her right foot holding her in the stirrup as the horse bolted in fright across the hot sands.

Chrys gave a cry of alarm and gave rein to her own mount in an attempt to catch up with the bolting horse. She was terrified for Maud, who looked in grave danger of being badly hurt if suddenly flung from the saddle.

Fleet as her mount was, something flashed past on long thundering legs and with loping strides soon shortened the distance between itself and the frightened animal that was dragging Maud as if she were a puppet. The camel and its rider were soon ahead of the horse, and swerving skilfully in front of it they brought it to a standstill, head hanging and flanks heaving, its rider still at a painful angle, caught by her foot in the twisted stirrup.

As Chrys galloped towards the group, she saw the rider of the camel kneel his animal, dismount swiftly and make for the figure of Maud. He gentled the horse, and was lifting Maud from its back as Chrys rode up to them and leapt from her own saddle.

She ran forward, crying Maud's name. The man who had saved her turned his head to look at Chrys, and the *cheche* blew from his face, and eyes of a most unusual grey looked into the wild blue eyes of Chrys, and she was shocked, and at the same time too concerned for Maud to even speak his name as she stepped forward to where he had placed the shaken, perhaps injured woman, holding her so that she rested in the crook of his arm.

Maud winced painfully as Chrys knelt beside her. "Hurts like the devil!" She gestured at her right foot. "'Mustn't blame the horse. I think a *jerboa* darted in front of him and startled him. I didn't grab the reins tightly enough and he was up and away. Lucky my foot caught and held me, but I – I think it's twisted."

"Allow me, *madame*. I shall try not to add to your pain." A lean hand emerged from the full sleeve of the spotless robes and the fingers passed briefly over Maud's ankle, causing her to bite down on her lip even at so gentle a touch. "I fear the stirrup may have crushed a small bone, *madame*." The smoke-grey eyes that did not belong to an Arab porter gazed into Maud's eyes. "It is essential that you see a doctor as soon as possible, and as it would not be possible for you to ride back to Beni Kezar, and there is not a doctor at your camp, I suggest that you allow me to take you to my house. I have a geologist friend in residence there who is also a qualified doctor, and it is not such a long ride as the one back to town."

Maud was staring at him, absorbing his excellent English, and his lean but not Arab face with sheer amazement. Chrys at the other side of her watched the exchange of looks, and knew exactly what was passing through Maud's mind. *Who on earth was this handsome devil who spoke like a gentleman instead of a porter?*

"Maud, I had better introduce you." Chrys looked at him then, and there was a wry little smile on her lips.

"This is the Prince Anton de Casenove, who has a pre-dilection for masks and subtle games, and I can tell you now that he has been following us around since the first moment we arrived at Port Said. The moustache fooled me, because when last we met he was clean-shaven, and I had not yet seen how Arab clothing can be a disguise in itself. In London the Prince wore the smartest tailoring from Savile Row, and I suppose if I expected to see him out here, I expected the same suave apparel, not *un arabe* from his head-ropes to his Moroccan leather boots!"

"This is –" Maud shook her head in bewilderment. "This is really too much for me in my shocked state. A Prince?"

"Quite so, *madame*." He inclined his head and a slight smile flickered on his lips. "Miss Devrel and I knew each other in London. But if she had known that I was coming to this part of the desert she would have gone to Timbuctoo in order to avoid me. My wicked sense of humour could not resist a little masquerade, but as things turned out it was a good thing I was on hand today. The camel and I were useful, eh?"

"Much more than useful, *m'sieur*." Maud gave him a deeply grateful look. "I couldn't have held on to those reins much longer, and if I'd gone under those hooves – well, by now I'd be in paradise, or the other place. Thank you, young man, but all the same I think we ought to press on to camp. Perhaps your doctor could come to me there –?"

"It would be much more comfortable for you at my house, *madame*." He spoke firmly. "Already that ankle is much swollen, and you are still very much shaken by your experience. I definitely think that you and your companion should come with me to *Belle Tigresse*. In fact I am going to insist that you do so."

"Are you indeed?" Maud looked at him with obstinacy, and a touch of the alarm which he automatically inspired. Chrys was still feeling annoyed that he had fooled her, but desperately glad that he had been on

527

hand to divert a really bad accident. She kept silent, for this must be decided between Maud and Anton. The battle of wills was theirs this time, and as she knelt there she felt the sun striking down hot against her head, and she realized that during her race to catch up with Maud's horse the hat had blown from her head. She put up a hand and pushed the tawny hair from her brow, which was beaded with a fine sweat. She felt the flick of Anton's eyes, over her hair, her face, and the boyish shirt and trousers which she wore. She refused to meet his grey and devilish eyes ... but somewhere inside her a little flame was leaping.

She was furious with him, and she wanted to tell him just what she thought of him for that game he had played on the train, pretending to be a mysterious Sheik in pursuit of her! The mortifying part was that he had succeeded so well in making her feel that she was in danger of her virtue!

How she longed to pay him back ... later on ... when he wasn't quite the hero of the hour.

"And why do you think you can give me orders?" Maud demanded of him, speaking the words through lips that were drawn with pain. "Because you probably saved my life, eh?"

"No, *madame*." He gave her his most charmingly sardonic smile. "Because *Belle Tigresse* is a rather lonely house these days, and it would welcome both of you. Also it will be more comfortable for you than a tent in the desert, for you can take it from me that you have more wrong with your foot than a mere twist of the ligaments. You are in bad pain, I can see that."

"It is rather sickening," Maud admitted. She glanced at Chrys. "Well, what do you say, my child? You're kneeling there without saying a word, but I'm sure you're thinking quite a lot. Do we accept the Prince's invitation?"

Chrys wanted to cry out that it was the last thing she wanted them to do, but the pallor of Maud's face and the obvious distress in her eyes made her say quietly:

"I think it would be only sensible, Maud. You will be well cared for there, and made comfortable. I – perhaps I could go on to the camp site. Peter will be there –"

"That is the very reason why you cannot go there, Miss Devrel." The Prince broke in on her words, not harshly but in a voice as smooth as silk. "The *kaid* would be most displeased if he knew that a young man and a young woman were sharing alone a camping site which he has put at the disposal of Mrs. Christie. I am afraid that desert etiquette goes against your obvious desire to be alone with Mr. Dorn. If Mrs. Christie comes to stay at *Belle Tigresse*, then you must accompany her, and you have already agreed that it will be to her best advantage to be my guest while her foot is mending."

In the silence which followed his words, that little flame of fury leapt higher in Chrys, while Maud's head drooped against the robed arm of Anton. Chrys swallowed the angry words that leapt to her lips, the hot denial that she "desired to be all alone with Peter Dorn" and instead she agreed to go with Maud to his desert house.

They went on horseback, the thin and now rather feverish figure of Maud held firmly in the saddle in front of Anton, her head at rest against his robed shoulder. The porter and the two camels followed on behind, and the sun was like a golden blaze in the sky when the white walls of the house rose against the tawny sweep of the sands, the green fronds of gigantic palm trees shading the dome of it, and the courtyard beyond its arched entrance.

CHAPTER IX

IT was such an unexpected house, all alone like this in the midst of the golden sands, and so fascinating with its dome of coloured glass over the central courtyard, so that the sun was filtered down in a myriad jewel colours, and the rampant tropic vegetation took on a mysterious jungle look, and curtained everything of stone or marble with a cloak of flame and purple and rich cream flower. Scents were trapped here, and the kick and scrape of cicades, not to mention the lizards that lay stone still or scuttled dragon-green across the tiles.

Chrys had come out from the cool hall, drawn by the fascination of this jungly courtyard, the colours playing over her white shirt and her pale skin as she drew breath and absorbed the relief of leaving Maud in the capable hands of Doctor Ben Omair.

The master of the house had gone off to acquaint Peter Dorn with details of the mishap, and as Chrys wandered about and explored this amazing patio, she wondered exactly what he would say to the young Dutchman. She hoped that Peter would be allowed to come here. He was so blond and big and solid that he would dilute the exotic atmosphere of this place and dispel some of the heady magic with a hearty breath of common sense.

She mounted some shallow curving steps into another part of the house, and found herself walking beneath dark cedar beams, between ivory-white walls, and upon a massive carpet of mellowed colours. Here in this long cool room were squat coffee tables with mother-of-pearl inlay, low divans covered with wonderful old prayer rugs, and graceful, jewelled, lethal scimitars attached to the walls. There were also lances, and some fine old horse pieces. And there were books, massed on cedarwood shelves, of all sizes, and in a variety of languages, with bindings of deep-toned leather.

A man's room! Redolent of an aromatic smoke that clung to the pages of the well-read books . . . and to the robes in which the Prince had dressed himself in order to fool her into thinking she was being pursued by one of the local Sheiks.

Darn him! She glared at a jewelled scimitar as if she would have liked to do him an injury with it. And then a reluctant smile touched her lips as she sank down on a thick animal pelt and took a delicious sweet from a hammered box on a nearby table. She lay back on the pelt – not knowing it to be that of a Siberian tiger – and her teeth crunched the nut buried in the thick chocolate.

Her gaze roved about this room that was such a mixture of the strongly masculine and the subtly sensuous, and she imagined him here taking coffee, clad in one of those monkish *haiks*, those narrow, adroit feet clasped in thonged sandals.

In London she had thought him the most worldly man she had ever met ... now suddenly she was confronted by a more primitive side to him, all the more disturbing because the man was so educated, and at the same time so unafraid to do the crazy, maddening things that tamer men never even thought of. Chrys tried to picture Dove's husband in any other role but that of the devoted, time-keeping, candid young lover, and she smiled, and realized that in Dove's shoes right now she would have been hopelessly bored.

She listened to the hot, humming silence that lay over *Belle Tigresse* as she lay, too languorous to stir, on the furry pelt that was longer than her own figure. She let her eyelids fall slowly like shutters over her sun-tired eyes, and she wriggled her feet out of her shoes. Mmmm, it felt good to relax after all the tensions of the morning ... she would stay here awhile, in the restfulness of this shadowy room, and then she would go and see how Maud was feeling.

And there on the pelt Chrys fell fast asleep, her tawny hair mixing with the tawny fur, emotionally worn out and secure in the knowledge that Maud was in good hands.

She slept dreamlessly for some time, and awoke quite suddenly to find herself in strange surroundings, and aware that she was being scrutinized. Her eyes flew open, and there in the light of a lamp, booted feet deep in the carpet, wide cloak held back by an arm

crooked on his hip, stood Prince Anton. She swept the
tousled hair back from her eyes, and knew instantly
that she must look childish. She started to scramble to
her feet, and immediately he took her by the shoulders
and brought her to her feet quite close to him.

Still bemused from her nap, she looked at him without knowing quite what to say. Although close to her,
he seemed a stranger in his Arab clothes, and the line
of his moustache made him look so ruthless. It was as
if he had left the civilized part of him back in London,
discarded with his Savile Row suits and his *savoir faire*.

"It did not take you long to find my private sanctum," he said. "I wonder if some strange instinct led
you to it? We are all creatures of instinct, you know,
and here in the desert the primitive senses come close
to the surface of ourselves and that is why for a while
the newcomer feels as if he or she had quaffed a little
too much champagne. Do you feel heady, a little dizzy,
and yet tensely aware of the slightest sound, the smal-
lest movement, the softest flutter of bird wing or
petal?"

He described so exactly how she felt that Chrys
would have lied if she had denied his description. His
very touch on her shoulders was so acute as to resemble
a pain.

"I suppose you're vastly amused that I didn't guess
it was you on the train?" she said, her head thrown back
so she could look at his face. "You have a strange sense
of humour, *milor*. I suppose the Hand of Fatma was
meant to warn me that your hand was reaching out to
me? What is it you want of me . . . the usual melting
heap of womanhood at your feet?"

He quirked an eyebrow, and the edge of his moustache seemed to quirk as well. "If you are going to be
a guest in my house, then there is one thing you must
know from the start. I am not addicted to the usual,
and much prefer the unusual. Secondly although you
are now in the *seraglio* of my house, meaning the part
where women are not normally allowed, there is no

harem at *Belle Tigresse*, and the only woman on the premises apart from Mrs. Christie and yourself is the housekeeper. If you are reassured that I won't suddenly demand your presence in the master bedroom, attended by eunuchs who will force you into my arms, then it might be possible for you to enjoy your stay without too much strain on your valued and closely guarded independence."

"Did you see Peter Dorn?" Her cheeks had flushed at his sardonic summing up of the needling little fears she did feel as a reluctant guest under his roof. It was a large house, a fantastic collection of rooms screened by *meshrebiya* balconies, roofs and flights of steps seen through copings of stone sculpture, walled enclosures, wooden doors draped in pale jasmine and deep violet plumbago.

There might well be a secluded wing to which no one went but this man in his picturesque robes, seeking the pleasures of which she had only a misty awareness. Although in ballet she had danced in the strong arms of warm, lithe partners, she was curiously innocent of what men really thought and desired.

There lay in the eyes of Anton de Casenove a thousand answers to any questions she might have asked, but she felt there would always be a part of him that was secluded and not to be known. The smoky beauty of his eyes, the black and screening lashes, the little stabs of mockery, all were aimed at shaking her youthful poise. He saw right through her with those worldly eyes, but there were depths to him, secrets known to him, which made her head spin.

He was really a thorough wretch, she told herself, as if all the time he inwardly laughed at her and planned her seduction. As the lean, sun-browned fingers pressed the fine bones at the base of her neck, she sought wild refuge in the Dutchman.

"What did Peter say about the accident? Will you allow him to come and visit Maud?"

"I would not dream of depriving either of you of a

visit from him," Anton drawled. "I don't want a frustrated young tigress prowling around my house, ready to fly at me with tooth and claw. He will come tomorrow to lunch. For myself, as I have been riding the hot sands, I feel in need of some tea. You will join me in the courtyard, but I am sure that first you would like to go and change into a dress. It would be cooler, and far more attractive than the riding trousers."

As it happened she felt like a change of clothing, so she didn't argue with him. She also fancied a cup of tea, out there under the cool greenery and the trailing flowers. She glanced at her wristwatch and was amazed to see how the time had fled.

"Come, I will show you to your apartment," he said. "In time you will grow accustomed to the house, but at first it can bewilder the stranger. Arabian houses are built rather like old English castles, so that one can always find a place to hide, but can very easily go astray."

With an imperious sweep of his cloak he led her from his own quarters and along corridors, up sudden flights of steps, and around unexpected corners of this odd and fascinating house until he paused outside an oval shaped vermilion door and opened it for her.

"I shall be in the courtyard when you are ready," he said. "One of Hazra's children will be sent to wait for you here in the corridor, to see that you don't lose your way."

"Thank you, but who is Hazra?" Chrys stood in the frame of the vermilion door and looked up at him; the boots and robes and rope-bound head-covering made him very tall and imposing, and she saw again how easy it had been to mistake him for an Arab. The dense brows, the strongly etched cheekbones, and that devilish black moustache all added to the illusion. She felt quite sure that the years he had spent in the East had almost made him an Arab at heart. He seemed to exude the very breath of the desert through his bronzed skin, and the very light of the sky seemed to glitter in his eyes.

534

"She is my housekeeper." With a mocking inclination of his head he swung on his booted heel and strode off, taking it arrogantly for granted that Chrys would obey his orders without a murmur. What was so annoying was that she could really do nothing else but obey them. She couldn't ask for a pot of tea to be brought to her room because she didn't know the language, and she was simply dying for a cup!

She withdrew into the rooms which were to be hers while she remained a guest at *Belle Tigresse*, and she saw that her suitcases had been placed on an ottoman at the foot of the carved bed, draped in clouds of almond-pale netting. The bleached walls of the room were like rough silk to the hand, and the furniture was darkly ornate, while the windows were set within richly carved wooden cages, through which in days gone by the women of the household would have looked without being seen. A wonderful old lantern, fitted with panes of coloured glass, hung between the windows, and there were painted cupboards, carved brackets on the walls filled with copper ornaments, and over the floor lay one of the fabulous Eastern carpets, teeming with warm colour and a thousand intricate designs.

Beyond the bedroom lay a smaller room, less ornate, with a divan and a little carved table, and a shelf of books. And beyond that was the bathroom, and Chrys stood speechless in the doorway, both amazed and a trifle shocked by the black marble bathtub that was sunk into the floor, with chiselled nymphs decorating the huge mirror, and a leopard skin across the black and white tiles.

After her first breathless moments of adjustment to such luxury, Chrys felt an irresistible urge to wallow in that tub and let her cares go by.

But *he* would be waiting, and he was impetuous and impatient enough to come charging up here in search of her if she did not appear for tea. She had to make do with a cool splash at the pyramid wash-basin, and after spraying herself with cologne she took a pale blue, shake-out dress from her suitcase and zipped herself into it. She brushed her hair until it crackled and shone, dashed lipstick across her mouth, and noticed how large and deep her eyes looked as she took a glance at herself in the wall mirror.

She looked like Alice in Wonderland, she thought, but there just wasn't time to do adult things to her hair, so leaving it to swing free on her shoulders she left her apartment and went out into the corridor. She glanced around for this child who was to take her downstairs to the courtyard, and her gaze fell instead upon a slim creature in a dress of coloured stripes, whose long black hair was pinned back in slides, and whose eyes were the colour of dark honey set round with long black lashes. In her earlobes hung small gold hoops, and her narrow feet were bare below the rather long hem of her dress.

She and Chrys stared at each other, one so fair, the other so dark, with a skin of warm, flawless amber and rather full lips.

"Are you Hazra?" said Chrys, for to her mind this was no child but a young woman, and Prince Anton had said that only his housekeeper, apart from Maud and herself, shared this house with him in the capacity of a woman.

"I am Saffida, and the *sidi* has asked me to conduct Mademoiselle to the courtyard." The girl spoke in French, with a soft and attractive accent, and behind her heavy lashes she was studying Chrys with an unchildlike curiosity.

Chrys looked at Saffida and felt a stab of scorn that Anton should call her a *child*. The girl was a raving little beauty, with centuries of Eastern love lore running in her veins.

"Are you Hazra's daughter?" Chrys broke into a rather dry smile. "I was expecting someone much smaller and younger."

"I have very much grown since the *sidi* was last here." The girl's full lips made a sort of bee-stung

536

movement. "I am now ready for marriage."

"At what age," asked Chrys, "does the marriage of an Arabian girl take place?"

"At fourteen, if she has sufficient dowry."

"You are more than that, surely?"

"I am sixteen, *mademoiselle*, and the *sidi* will provide my dowry."

"That is very generous of him, Saffida."

"Is it not the custom in your own land?"

"Well, not exactly." Chrys glanced at the girl as they stepped out of a sculptured doorway into the coins of sunlight tumbling down through the feathery branches of some pepper trees. "In England the father usually pays for the wedding —" There she broke off as Prince Anton stepped from among the trees, bare-headed now, and clad in a slash-throated tunic of grey silk, with narrow black trousers and sandals with a leather thong holding them to his feet.

"Ah, so there you are! *Merci, mon enfant*," he said to the Arabian girl, slanting a smile that held not a hint of flirtation. In answer to his smile Saffida placed her slim hands together and gave him a graceful, feminine version of the *salaam*. Her lashes fluttered and her golden ear hoops caught the sunlight. Then she turned and walked silently away on her bare narrow feet, showing the heels that were hennaed.

"What a very pretty *child*," said Chrys. "I was expecting a gamine and found myself face to face with a sylph."

"Was it a pleasant surprise?" he drawled, leading her to a wicker table set among the jasmine-draped trees, with deep wicker armchairs at either side of it. He drew out one of the chairs and Chrys had to walk close to him in order to sit down in the chair. She felt tangibly the masculine strength and warmth of him, the casual mockery, and the princely magnetism. As she sat down that magnetism seemed to cause a strand of her hair to cling against him. She felt him take the strand in his fingers and though he did no more than stroke it back against her neck, she felt as if he touched the entire surface of her skin and left it tingling.

She was glad when he sat down in the opposite chair, sprawling his long legs across the tiles, and taking the ease of a tiger in the sun. Even his eyes held a lazy smoulder as they watched her pour the tea from the long spout of the silver pot into the cups of pale china stamped with tiny coronets.

She handed him his cup and saucer, and then sat back with her own, half closing her eyes with the relish of the tea.

"It is good, eh?" he murmured. "Especially when the throat is dry."

As always there seemed a double meaning to his words, but she chose not to take any notice, though she felt the faint quivering of her nerves as she sat there with him, among the angel's trumpet with its flared blossoms, the henna and saffron plants, and the great clumps of roses.

"Did you know that in the days of the Arab lords these courtyards were made for the woman?" He leaned forward to take a coconut cake from the silver dish. He bit into it with his white teeth, and he kept on looking at her with those smoky eyes, and she could smell the scent of the camphor trees, and there was a coloured facet dancing on the leaves . . . like the dancing, dangerous light in his grey eyes.

"It's a beautiful courtyard," she said. "It must evoke for you, *milor*, a pleasant image of all those lovely women of the *harem*."

"Does it not evoke for you an image of their master?" he drawled.

"Perhaps." She shrugged carelessly. "An enormous man, I think, with jewelled fingers and a rumbling laugh, and one of those spade beards with a dash of silver in it."

"And how would you have felt about being his – guest?"

"Quite safe, I'm certain. I'm not opulent enough to

make a very desirable candidate for the *harem*."

"Come, you thought quite the reverse on the train, and I should have relished seeing your face, *chérie*, when you were presented with the Hand of Fatma from a man whom you thought to be one of the local Sheiks."

Chrys glared at him. "It was all very amusing, wasn't it? But not quite such fun for poor Maud. I'm only here for her sake. I'd give anything to be elsewhere."

"With the big Dutchman, no doubt?"

"Yes! He hasn't the *droit du seigneur* attitude towards women that you have! A girl can talk with him in a friendly way, without the constant worry that he will do something unexpected. You, *milor*! Why, it's like taking tea with a tiger!"

He laughed lazily. "So I set you on edge, eh? You don't know from one moment to the next what to expect from me. I wonder what you are expecting right now? I can see how tensed you are, and yet I am doing my best to play the kind and generous host."

"Your generosity is only matched by your despotism!" The words broke from her lips and would not be controlled ... it was almost as if she were driven to provoke him, but when she saw the narrowing of his eyelids over the glitter of his eyes, the rigid tensing of his forearm muscles, and the flare to his nostrils, she knew that she had gone too far. For an electrifying second they stared at each other, and then he had loomed to his feet and thrusting aside his armchair he came to where she sat and without ceremony he yanked her to her feet.

"I have been as patient with you as I intend to be. I have taken from you the final insolence! You little dancing girl!" His fist held her hair so that when she tried to wrench herself away from him the painful tug at the roots of her hair drove her back against him. She felt his hard bare chest under the tunic, and she looked up at him wildly and saw the raw little flames in his eyes a moment before he tipped her over his arm

539

and forcibly kissed her.

She wanted not to feel a thing, but to be like cold stone in his arms, but instead, for an eternity of breathless, riotous, unimaginable seconds, she was lost ... lost to herself and to all the world outside and beyond this desert courtyard. He was brutal, and then he was indescribably warm and wanting. The desire to hurt and crush gave way to the keener pleasure of kissing her eyes, the backs of her ears, the soft curves of her neck, and her shoulders.

Something thudded close to her ribs, and the sensation was so pleasantly puzzling until she realized that it was his heart beating against her. It was then that her legs literally folded beneath her and with a low and throaty laugh he lifted her and carried her into the house, up a shallow flight of curving steps to the place he had called the *seraglio* ... mockingly, of course, but as always with an underlying hint of the truth.

"Call me tyrant again, you sand cat," he growled against her earlobe.

"Let me go –" she pleaded, but the words had no strength, no reality, not the faintest desire to be obeyed.

"Is that really what you want, *dorogaya*?" His eyes were on her lips, studying them as if through smoky fire. "I swear if I let you go those long white legs of yours will melt you at my feet, and that was always an attitude which you swore never to assume."

"You've had too many women at your feet," she said, and there was a tremor to her voice, and to look at him was to feel again the pang of almost intolerable pleasure which his lips on hers had awakened in her body. She had so wanted to be the one woman whom his touch did not disturb. She had wanted to be cool and unruffled, and able to walk out of his arms without a hair out of place.

Instead ... the contrast panicked her and she began to struggle in his arms. "Anton, this has gone on long enough! Put me down!"

"If you say so." He dropped her among the cushions

540

of a divan, and then with that leopard-like grace of movement which she would recognize in a crowd of a thousand men, he knelt beside the divan and leaned towards her and his eyes were smoky-grey and drowsy, and there seemed an incoherent purr in his throat as he took her arm and ran his lips all the way to the crook of her elbow, where they stayed, warm as a flame against the smooth, soft skin.

" 'O, hair of gold! O, crimson lips! O, face made for the luring and the love of man!' " Only he could speak such words and make them alive and meaningful. "Wilde was more the poet of love than Byron or Shelley. Don't you think, my little sand cat?"

She gazed at him in the lamplight and there was a golden, barbaric quality to his looks in that moment. Cossack and prince, and an of the desert. She could feel the fascination of him stirring through her veins and the old desire to resist him awoke in her ... she must stop this before she became just another name on his list of conquests.

"You are very accomplished in the art of seduction, Anton. Have you plans for Saffida as well as for me, the cool English ballet dancer whom you swore would melt with your charm? Saffida is very pretty –"

"Saffida is a child," he cut in, his eyes narrowing again to that steely glitter, striking across her face and her throat like a knife-edge. "Your implication is not worthy of you, Chrysdova. The one thing above all which I admired in you was your integrity – do you think that I have not a scrap of it? Do you think me such a rake?"

His eyes searched hers, demanding an honest answer, and looking at him she was suddenly aware of all the nice things about him. Nice! The word shocked her in association with him, and yet there was an undeniable truth to it. Sometimes when he smiled ... ah, it was crazy to dwell on the attraction of him ... it was asking for a broken heart to let herself be drawn again into those warm, strong arms.

"You make toys of women," she flung at him. "While they please you everything is wonderful, but their very surrender makes it easy for you to say that all women are the same as your mother was. I won't be your toy! I won't be like them! I won't be made a fool of by those wicked and beguiling eyes of yours. I won't!"

She flung her hands over her own eyes, to shut out his face, and to hide the sudden tears that choked her. She heard him say her name in a roughly tender voice, and then she was pulled against him, her wet face was pressed to his chest and his hand was stroking her hair. "No!" She pushed at him, and the bare skin of his chest was under her hand, and the shocking feel of the scar where a bullet had passed through him. Anton, who was so alive and warm and arrogantly maddening, had almost died, never to be known to her. It seemed incredible, astounding, that she might never have known him. It seemed impossible that by a hair's breadth they had almost never met.

"Look at me," he ordered. "I won't force you, *dorogaya*, I will merely ask you to stop staring at my chest and to look at my face instead. Come, I am being serious. I want you to look at the man who is going to tell you this minute that he loves you. That he has done so since the night he was trapped with you in a lift. Adorable *dorogaya*, for heaven's sake lift your face to mine before I go mad as only a Cossack can!"

She looked at him because she had to, because she desired to, but unbelievingly. He quirked an eyebrow in that inimitable way of his. "You have heard of love, I take it?"

"But you don't believe in it," she retorted.

"I thought not, but it seems that the heart has a will of its own. I could no more let you go after that night we were trapped together than I could let go my own life. Miroslava did not have to persuade me to follow you here. It was destined that I do so. You know it, too. It is there in your blue eyes. Rapture of the desert, *chérie*."

"No –" She shook her head. "I won't listen to you. I won't be swayed away from all that I've worked for, for the sake of an affair with a prince! I'm flattered –"

"You will be spanked in a moment, if you go on about affairs and careers, and all those boring things." He pulled her so close to him that she lost her breath, and in his eyes looking down into hers there was such a heart-shaking look of love that she could hardly bear it.

"Don't do this to me," she pleaded. "It isn't fair! You're so accomplished in making a fool of a woman, and I – I don't know how to handle the situation."

"Don't you?" He smiled down at her wickedly. "You marry me, *dorogaya*, and you live with me a year in the desert, and if at the end of that time you still have this craving to dance, then –"

"You mean – you would allow me to dance?" She touched his face, almost shyly. Such a wonderful face ... it ought to be masked against all those women who would always look at him and desire the excitement of him.

"Of course," he drawled. "We will dance together at the Adonis Club. You remember how well your steps matched mine –"

"Oh, you devil!" Her fingers bent against his cheek, as if she would actually claw him, and then a smile slowly etched itself on her lips. "I have a choice, it would seem. I can be your slave, or I can be a dancer. I wonder which I ought to choose. Both are taskmasters."

"But only one will leave you lonely at night, and in the years ahead, Chrysdova, when the tawny hair loses its lustre and the sapphire eyes no longer sparkle – as they are sparkling right now." He bent his head and he slowly and lingeringly kissed her lips. "Will you deny me?"

"May I have time to think about it, Anton?" She pressed her cheek to the dark cross of hair on his chest, and felt at her fingertips the deep heartbeat, and the deep scar.

"Yes," he agreed. "You have exactly a minute."

"Only a minute?" She smiled against him. "How arrogant of you to expect me to give up a career in just one minute. It took me years to achieve it, and now I must sacrifice it for a man."

She heard him laugh very softly. "I promise that you won't regret your sacrifice, *dorogaya*. Think of all we shall share together. Desert rides and desert dawns. The sands whispering a thousand secrets when I hold you in my arms — as my bride. Come, little white-skinned devil, will you deny me?"

Chrys looked into those smoke-grey, wickedly beautiful eyes, and she thought of what Dove had said to her. "For heaven's sake don't fall in love with the man!"

Chrys smiled and let her arms enchain his warm, brown neck. It was too late for warnings, too late for denials . . . already she was giving herself to her desert prince.